Praise

BARBARA DELINSKY
and Her *New York Times* Bestsellers

LAKE NEWS

"Delinsky spins another engrossing story of strength in the face of cataclysmic life changes."

—*Library Journal*

"Delightful. . . . Readers will be sorry to reach the end of LAKE NEWS and yearn for more about its cast and characters."

—*The Pilot* (Southern Pines, NC)

"Delinsky plots this satisfying, gentle romance with the sure hand of an expert, scattering shady pasts and dark secrets among some of her characters while giving others destructive family patterns and difficult family dynamics to contend with."

—*Publishers Weekly*

"An enjoyable novel. . . . Delinsky is one of those writers who knows how to introduce characters to her readers in such a way that they become more like old friends than works of fiction."

—*Flint Journal* (MI)

"Filled with romance, intrigue, revenge, and salvation, LAKE NEWS is a gripping tale sure to please [Delinsky's] legions of loyal fans and earn her quite a few new ones."

—BookPage

"Recommended. . . . Lily Blake [is] a remarkable heroine."

—Abilene Reporter-News (TX)

"A beautiful love story. . . . Delinsky scores big-time . . . her best novel to date. Considering her resume, this is one hell of a tale."

—The Midwest Book Review

"A book as timely as today's headlines. . . . [Delinsky's] style is as natural as the scenery around Lake Henry and her plot is as homey as the villagers she describes."

—Rockdale Citizen

"Delinsky fans won't be disappointed."

—San Antonio Express-News

"A razor-sharp look at the power of the media and how easily it can breach a person's privacy."

—The West Orange Times

COAST ROAD

"A winner. . . . Delinsky delivers an emotion-packed journey . . . firmly cementing her status as a bestselling writer of top-notch books."

—Booklist

Books by Barbara Delinsky

BARBARA DELINSKY

COAST ROAD

POCKET BOOKS

New York   London   Toronto   Sydney

POCKET BOOKS, a division of Simon & Schuster, Inc.
1230 Avenue of the Americas, New York, NY 10020

This book is a work of fiction. Names, characters, places and incidents are products of the author's imagination or are used fictitiously. Any resemblance to actual events or locales or persons, living or dead, is entirely coincidental.

ISBN: 0-684-84576-8
         1-4165-0376-5 (Pbk)

This Pocket Books trade paperback edition August 2004

10 9 8 7 6 5 4 3 2 1

POCKET and colophon are registered trademarks of
Simon & Schuster, Inc.

Manufactured in the United States of America

For information regarding special discounts for bulk purchases,
please contact Simon & Schuster Special Sales at 1-800-456-6798
or business@simonandschuster.com

acknowledgments

Coast Road was born of three things I admire—the Big Sur coast, people with artistic ability, and men who rise to the occasion. My own instinct as a woman, plus an annual trip to Big Sur, helped with research into those things, but there were other elements of the book that required outside expertise.

I wish to thank Nancy Weinberg, nurse-educator of the Critical Care Unit at the Newton Wellesley Hospital, for the generous sharing of her time, knowledge, and imagination. Likewise, and not for the first time, my thanks to Margot Chamberlin for advice on the nuts and bolts of being an architect. For their help framing Rachel's pieces, I thank Renata, Rob, Chris, and Steve, of the Renjeau Gallery. For her assistance, her ear, and great color, I thank Barbie Goldberg.

As with any large project, some things inevitably hit the cutting-room floor. Although none of the 1950s trivia that Elaine Raco Chase sent made it into this book, I am grateful for her tireless efforts. Nor did anything of Pukaskwa make it into *Coast Road*, despite the generous contributions of Margaret Carney, writer, naturalist, and

acknowledgments

friend; and Bob Reside, Park Warden, Pukaskwa National Park. I was deeply impressed with the beauty and isolation of Ontario, north of Lake Superior, and imagine that it will appear in a future book.

My book group. Ah, my book group. How long have I talked about writing its story? The full focus that I had initially intended went the way of 1950s trivia and Ontario, but what remains is true. No, no, guys. Don't look for yourselves in any of my characters. I promised I wouldn't, and I didn't. I do believe, though, that you will identify with the deeper meaning of the group, as do I.

Again and still, I thank my agent, Amy Berkower, who has worked nearly as hard on this book as I have. I am also grateful to her partner, Al Zuckerman, for his gracious input, and her assistant, Jodi Reamer, for being there every single time I call. I thank my editor, Laurie Bernstein, for making me one of the pins she juggles.

As always, for their enthusiasm, support, and patience, I thank my family—my husband, Steve; my son and daughter-in-law, Eric and Jodi; and the twins, Andrew and Jeremy. Those twinges Jack feels when he thinks of family? Autobiographical all the way!

COAST
ROAD

prologue

WHEN THE PHONE rang, Rachel Keats was painting sea otters. She was working in oils and had finally gotten the right mix of black for the eyes. There was no way she was stopping to pick up the phone. She had warned Samantha about that.

"Hi! You've reached Rachel, Samantha, and Hope. We're otherwise occupied. Please leave your name and number, and we'll call you back. Thanks."

Through a series of beeps, she applied a smudge of oil with a round brush. Then came a deep male voice that was too old to be calling for Samantha. Rachel would have pictured a gorgeous guy to go with the voice, but he'd said his name too fast. This man wasn't gorgeous. He was a ticket agent, a friend of a friend, more sleaze than style, but apparently good at his job. "I have in my hand three tickets for tonight's Garth Brooks concert," he said. "San Jose. Goooood seats. I need to hear from you in five minutes or I'm moving down my list—" Rachel made a lunging grab for the phone. "I want them!"

"Heeeey, Rachel. How's my favorite artist?"

"Painting. You need a credit card number, right? Hold on a second." She put the phone down, ran through the house to the kitchen, and snatched up her wallet. She was breathless reading off the number, breathless returning to the studio. She swallowed hard, looked at the canvas on the easel and six others nearby waiting to be finished, thought of everything else she had to do in the next three weeks, and decided that she was crazy. She didn't have time to go to a concert.

But the girls would be absolutely, positively *blown away!*

She threw the window open and leaned out into clear, woodsy air.

"Samantha! Hope!" They were out there somewhere. She yelled again.

Answering yells came from a distance, then closer.

"Hurry!" she yelled back.

Minutes later, they came running through the woods, Samantha looking every bit as young as Hope for once, both with blond hair flying and cheeks pink. Rachel shouted the news to them even before they reached her window. The look on their faces was more than worth the prospect of an all-nighter or two.

"Are you serious?" Hope asked. Her eyes were wide, her freckles vibrant, her smile filled with teeth that were still too large for her face. She was thirteen and entirely prepubescent.

Rachel grinned and nodded.

"Awesome!" breathed Samantha. At fifteen she was a head taller than Hope and gently curved. Blond hair and all, she was Rachel at that age.

"*Tonight?*" Hope asked.

"Tonight."

"*Good* seats?" Samantha asked.

"*Great* seats."

Hope pressed her hands together in excitement. "Are we doing the whole thing—you know, what we talked about?"

Rachel didn't have the time for it. She didn't have the money. But if her paintings were a hit, the money would come, and as for time, life was too short. "The whole thing," she said, because it would be good for Samantha to get away from the phone and Hope to get away from her cat and, yes, maybe even good for Rachel to get away from her oils.

"Omigod, I have to call Lydia!" Samantha cried.

"What you have to do," Rachel corrected her, "is any-thing that needs to be done for school. We leave in an hour." She was *definitely* crazy. Forget *her* work. The girls had tons of their own, but . . . but this was *Garth*.

She returned to her studio for the hour and accomplished as little as she feared her daughters had. Then they piled into her sport utility vehicle and headed north. Having done her research during the someday-we-will stage, she knew just where to go. The store she wanted was on the way to San Jose. It was still open when they got there, and had a perfect selection. Thirty minutes and an obscene amount of money later, they emerged wearing cowboy boots under their jeans, cowboy hats over their hair, and smiles the size of Texas.

Thirty minutes after that, with the smell of McDonald's burgers and fries filling the car, they were flying high toward San Jose.

Nothing they saw when they got there brought them down. There were crowds and crowds of fans, light shows and smoke, sets that rose from nowhere to produce the man himself, who sang hit after hit without a break, longer-than-ever versions of each, and how could Rachel not be into it, with Hope and Samantha dancing beside her? If she was conservative through the first song or two, any self-consciousness was gone by the third. She was on her feet dancing, clapping high, singing. She cheered with Samantha and Hope when familiar chords announced a favorite song, and shouted appreciatively with them at song's end. The three of them sang their hearts out until the very last encore was done, and then left the arena arm in arm, three friends who just happened to be related.

It was a special evening. Rachel didn't regret a minute of it, not even when Samantha said, "Did you see that girl right in front of us? The tall one with the French braid? Did you see the tattoo on her arm? The rose? If I wanted something like that, what would you say?"

"No," Rachel said as she drove south through the dark.

"Even a tiny one? A little star on my ankle?"

"No."

"But it's *way cool.*"

"No."

"Why *not?*"

"Because she was older than you. When you're twenty-five—"

"She wasn't that old."

"Okay, when you're twenty-two, you can think about a tattoo. Not now."

"It has nothing to do with age. It has to do with style."

"Uh-huh," said Rachel, confident on this one, "a style that makes a statement that you may not want to make at twenty-two, if you set your heart on a particular person or thing that doesn't appreciate that kind of statement."

"Since when are you worried about conformity?"

"Since my fifteen-year-old daughter is heading straight for the real world."

"Tattoos are hot. All the kids have them."

"Not Lydia. Not Shelly. Not the ones I see getting off the school bus."

Samantha crossed her arms and sank lower in her seat, glowering for sure under the brim of her hat. Hope was curled up in the back, sound asleep. Her hat had fallen to the side.

Rachel put in a CD and drove through the dark humming along with the songs they had heard that night. She loved her hat, loved her boots, loved her girls. If she had to fall behind in her work, it was for a good cause.

She wasn't as convinced of it the next morning, when the girls woke up late and cranky. They picked at breakfast on the run and even then nearly missed the bus. Rachel was wildly relieved when they made it, and wildly apprehensive when, moments later, she stood in her studio and mentally outlined the next three weeks.

She worked feverishly through the day, breaking only to meet the girls at the bus stop and have a snack with them, her lunch. Samantha was still on her tattoo kick, so they reran the argument, verbatim at times, before the girl went off to her room in a huff. Hope hung around longer, holding her cat. Finally she, too, disappeared.

Rachel spent another hour in the studio. Half convinced that the otters were done, she stopped and put dinner in the oven. When she returned to the studio, it was to fill another sort of need. But the otters caught her eye again. She gave herself another hour.

Now that the hour was gone, things were flowing. It was always the way.

One minute more, she told herself for the umpteenth time. With alternating glances at field sketch and photograph, she used the fine edge of her palette knife to add texture to the oil on her canvas. The sea otters were playing in kelp. Her challenge was capturing the wetness of their fur. She had started with raw umber and cobalt blue, and had found it too dark. Using raw umber with ultramarine blue was perfect.

"The buzzer rang, Mom," Hope called from the door.

"Thanks, honey," Rachel murmured, adding several last strokes. "Will you take the casserole out and turn off the gas?"

"I already did." Hope was at her side now, studying the canvas. "I thought you were done."

"Something wasn't right." She stood back for a longer view and was satisfied. "Better." Still eyeing the canvas, she set her palette aside, reached for a solvent cloth, and wiped her hands. "I'll clean up and be right there." She looked at Hope. "Did Samantha set the table?"

"I did."

"She's on the phone again?"

"Still," Hope said so dryly that Rachel had to chuckle.

She hooked her baby's neck with an elbow and gave a squeeze. "Five minutes," she said and sent her off.

As promised, five minutes later Rachel was in the

6

kitchen doling out lasagna and salad. Twenty minutes after that, digesting her meal along with a blow-by-blow of the late-breaking news that Samantha had received from her friends, Rachel gave out cleanup assignments. Fifteen minutes after that, having showered herself free of paint smells and put on fresh clothes, she ran a brush through her hair. Then she paused and looked wildly around for the book she had read the weekend before.

She searched the chaos of her bedroom without success. Thinking she might have already set it out, she returned to the kitchen and looked around. "Is my book in here?"

The girls were doing the dishes, Samantha washing, Hope drying. "I'd look," Samantha said with little grace, "but you told me not to do anything until these were done."

Rachel shifted a pile of mail, mostly clothing catalogues addressed to the self-same woman-child. "I was referring to the telephone," she said, checking in and around cookbooks. She doubled over to search the seats of the chairs pushed in at the table. "I remember having it in my hand," she murmured to herself when that search, too, proved fruitless.

"You're not organized," Samantha charged. Rachel regularly preached the merits of organization.

"Oh, I am," she mused, but distractedly. She went into the living room and began searching there. "I just have a lot on my plate right now."

That was putting it mildly. With her show three weeks away and closing in fast, she was feeling the crunch. Okay. She had finally hit gold with the sea otters. But there was still the background to do for that one and six others, and eighteen in all to frame—which would have been fine if she had nothing but work to do in the next three weeks. But there was a dress to buy with Samantha for her first prom, an end-of-the-year picnic to run for Hope's seventh-grade class, dentist's and doctor's appointments for both girls, a birthday party to throw for Ben Wolfe, who owned the art gallery and was a some-time date, and a share-your-career day to spend with three fifth-graders she didn't know.

She had splurged last night. She shouldn't be going anywhere tonight.

But last night had been for the girls and their mother. Book club was just for her. She loved the women, loved the books. Even if it added pressure to an already hectic work schedule, she wasn't missing a meeting.

Hope materialized at her shoulder. "I think it's in your studio."

Closing her eyes, Rachel conjured up the studio, which lay at a far end of her rambling house. She had left it for the day, then returned for an unexpected little while. And before returning? Yes, she'd had the book in her hand. She had carried it there and set it down.

"Thanks, sweetheart." She cupped Hope's chin. "Are you okay?"

The child looked forlorn.

"Guinevere will be fine," Rachel said softly. "She ate, didn't she?"

Hope nodded.

"See there? That's a good sign." She kissed Hope's forehead. "I'd better get the book. I'm running late."

"Want me to get it?" Hope asked.

But Rachel remembered what she had been drawing

before the otters had recaptured her eye. She wanted to make sure that that drawing was put safely away.

"Thanks, sweetheart, but I'll do it." When Hope looked reluctant to let her go, she begged, "Help Sam. Please," and set off.

The book was where she had left it, on a corner of the large worktable. Hope had arrived while she was at the easel. The drawing—a charcoal sketch—still lay on the desk by the window.

Rachel lifted it now and carefully slipped it into a slim portfolio. As she did, her mind's eye re-created the image her sliver of charcoal had made, that of a man sprawled in a tangle of sheets. Even handling the heavy paper, she felt his trim hips, the slope of his spine, and widening above it, dorsal muscle, triceps, deltoid. Had it not been for the hair, it might have been an innocent exercise in drawing the human form. The hair, though, was dark and just a little too long on the neck. The identity was unmistakable; this figure had a name. Better the girls shouldn't see.

Taking care to tuck that last portfolio behind the desk, she retrieved the book and hurried back through the house. She gave the girls quick kisses, promised to be home by eleven, and went out to her car.

chapter one

WHEN JACK MCGILL'S phone rang at two in the morning, the sound cut sharply into the muted world of a soupy San Francisco night. He had been lying in bed since twelve, unable to sleep. His mind was too filled, too troubled. The sudden sound jolted already jittery nerves.

In the time that it took him to grab for the phone, a dozen jarring thoughts came and went. "Yes?"

"Is this Jack McGill?" asked a voice he didn't know. It was female and strained.

"Yes."

"I'm Katherine Evans, one of Rachel's friends. There's been an accident. She's at the hospital in Monterey. I think you should come."

Jack sat up. "What kind of accident?"

"Her car was hit and went off the road."

His stomach knotted. "What road? Were the girls with her?"

"Highway One, and, no, she was alone." Relief. The girls were safe, at least. "She was near Rocky Point, on her way to Carmel. A car rammed her from behind. The impact pushed her across the road and over the side."

His feet hit the floor. The knot in his stomach tightened.

"She's alive," the friend went on. "Only a few broken bones, but she hasn't woken up. The doctors are worried about her brain."

"Worried how?"

"Bruising, swelling."

He pushed a hand through his hair. The disquieting thoughts about work that had kept him awake were gone, replaced by a whole different swarm. "The girls—"

"—are still home. Rachel was on her way to book group. When nine o'clock came and she hadn't shown up, I called the house. Samantha said she'd left at seven, so I called the state police. They told me there'd been an accident, and ID'd her car. They were still trying to get her out of it at that point and didn't know how she was, so I called her neighbor, Duncan Bligh. He went down to sit with the girls. I called them a little while ago to say she's okay, but I didn't tell them about the head injury, and I didn't know whether to tell Duncan to drive them up here to the hospital. That's not my decision to make."

No. It was Jack's. Divorce or no divorce, he was the girls' father. Clamping the phone between shoulder and jaw, he reached for his jeans. "I'm on my way. I'll call Samantha and Hope from the car."

"Rachel's in Emergency now. Check in there."

"Right. Thanks." He hung up realizing that he couldn't remember her name, this friend of Rachel's, but it was the least of his worries, the very least. "Unbelievable," he muttered as he zipped his jeans and reached for a shirt. Things were bad at the office and bad in the field. He was living an architect's nightmare, needed in both places come morning, and then there was Jill. Tonight was the charity dinner that she had been working on for so long. He had deliberately planned business trips around this date, knowing how much it meant to her. His tux was pressed and waiting. She was expecting him at five. Five—and he hadn't slept a wink. And he was heading south to God only knew what, for God only knew how long.

But Rachel was hurt. *You're not married to her anymore,* his alter ego said, but he didn't miss a beat stuffing his shirt into his jeans and his feet into loafers. *You don't owe her a thing, man. She was the one who walked out.*

But she was hurt, and he had been called, and depending on what he found in Monterey, there would be arrangements to make for the girls. They would have to be told how she was, for starters. They were too old to be sent to bed with empty reassurances, too young to face this possible nightmare alone. Rachel was their caretaker, companion, confidant. The three were thick as thieves.

The doctors are worried about her brain, the friend had said. Well, of course, they would worry until things checked out.

He tossed cold water on his face and brushed his teeth. Minutes later he entered his studio—and in a moment's dismay wondered why he still called it that. It had become more a place of business than of art. What few drawings he had done were buried under proposals, spec sheets, contracts, and correspondence—the refuse of an insane number of construction projects in various stages. The place reeked of pressure.

Using the slate gray of dawn that filtered through the

skylights, he crammed his briefcase with his laptop and as many vital papers as would fit, and his portfolio with multiple versions of the Montana design. Tucking both under an arm, he strode down the darkened hall to the kitchen. He didn't need a light. The place was streamlined and minimal. Grabbing his keys from the granite island and a blazer from the coat tree by the door, he set the alarm and went down to the garage below. Within minutes, he was backing out the BMW and speeding down Filbert. His headlights cut a pale gray swath in the smoky night, lighting little of Russian Hill. Other than the occasional street corner lump that could as easily be a homeless person sleeping as trash waiting for pickup, San Francisco was one big foggy cocoon.

Pressing numbers by feel on his car phone, he called information. He was heading south on Van Ness by the time he got through to the hospital in Monterey. "This is Jack McGill. My wife, Rachel Keats, was brought in a little while ago. I'm on my way there. Can you give me an update?"

"Hold on, please." Several nerve-wracking minutes later, he connected with a nurse in the emergency room. "Mr. McGill? She's in surgery. That's about all we know at this point."

"Is she conscious?"

"She wasn't when they took her upstairs."

The doctors are worried about her brain. "What's the surgery for?"

"Would you hold on a minute?"

"I'd rather not—" The sudden silence at the other end said he had no choice. He'd had no choice when Rachel had moved out six years ago, either. She had said she was going, had packed up the girls and their belongings while he was away on business. He had come home to an echoing house, feeling as thwarted and helpless then as he felt now. Then, armored in anger, he had sold the house and moved to one that didn't echo. But now, there was no such out. Her face came to him with every shift of the fog, an urban Rorschach in which her features were beautiful one minute, bruised the next. His nervous heart was beating up a storm.

He pushed the car faster.

"Mr. McGill?" came a male voice, choppy over the speaker but audible. "I'm Dr. Couley. I treated your wife when she arrived."

"What's the surgery for?" he shouted, gripping the steering wheel.

"To set her left leg. Compound fractures, both femur and tibia. They'll be inserting pins—"

"I was told there were head injuries," he cut in. A person didn't die from a broken leg. "Has she regained consciousness?"

"No. There's some cranial swelling. We don't yet know what direction it'll take."

"I want a specialist called."

"Our man is on his way. When will you be here?"

"I'm just leaving San Francisco."

"Two hours, then?"

"Less," Jack said and, slowing but barely, sailed through a red light. "Here's my cell number." He rattled it off. "Call me if there's any change, will you?" When the doctor agreed, Jack punched out another set of numbers. He wasn't as quick to press *send* this time, though. He didn't know what to say to the girls. They weren't babies anymore. And teenagers today were a different breed from the ones he had known. Add the fact that he no longer lived with them, and that they were *girls,* and he was at a *triple* disadvantage.

But this time he couldn't pass the buck. There was no one else to take it.

Katherine. That was the friend's name. Katherine.

Rachel had never mentioned her, but then, Rachel never mentioned anything that didn't deal directly with the girls. The girls had spoken of her, though. He thought he remembered that.

They definitely had mentioned Duncan Bligh, and more than once. He was the rancher who shared Rachel's canyon. The sloping meadow where his herd grazed lay above her redwood forest. Both meadow and forest were part of the Santa Lucias, rising east of the Big Sur coast.

Jack had a bad feeling about Duncan. He didn't like the affectionate way the girls described his cabin, his beard, or his sheep. He didn't like the way they grinned when he asked if Rachel was dating him. Oh sure, he knew they were trying to make him jealous. The problem was that he could see Rachel with a man like that. Mountain men had a kind of rugged appeal. Not that Jack was a slouch. He was tall. He was fit. He could hammer a nail with the best of the carpenters who built what he designed, but he didn't chop down the trees from which the two-by-fours came, and he didn't shear sheep or shoot deer.

Did he want to talk to Duncan Bligh in the middle of the night? No. Nor, though, could he let his daughters think that the rancher was the only man around.

He pressed *send.*

The first ring was barely done when there came a fast and furious "Hello?"

He lifted the phone. "Hi, Sam. It's Dad. Are you guys okay?"

"How's Mom?"

"She's okay." He kept his voice light. "I'm on my way to the hospital. I just talked with the doctor. They've taken her into surgery. It sounds like she smashed up her leg pretty good."

"Katherine said it was her ribs, too."

"It may be, but the leg is the thing that needs setting. Refresh my memory, Sam. Who is Katherine?"

"Mom's best friend," Samantha said impatiently. "I gave her your number."

"You could have called me yourself."

She grew defensive. "I didn't know if you were around, and if you weren't, you'd have had to book a flight and wait at the airport, and then if you missed a connection, you'd have taken forever to get here. Besides, Katherine says Mom has good doctors, so what can *you* do?"

"I can *be* there," he said, but the words were no sooner out than he imagined her retort. So he added a fast "Let's not argue, Samantha. This isn't the time."

"Are you telling me the truth? Is Mom really okay?"

"That's the truth as I heard it. Is your sister sleeping?"

"She was until the phone rang. We knew it had to be about Mom. *My* friends wouldn't call in the middle of the night," she said with such vehemence that Jack suspected they had done it more than once. "Dad, we want to go to the hospital, but Duncan won't take us."

"Is he there now?"

"He's asleep on the chair. Asleep at a time like this. Can you *believe* it? Wait, I'll put him on. Tell him to drive us up." She shouted away from the phone, and even then it hurt Jack's ears, "Duncan! Pick up the phone! It's my father!"

"*Samantha!*" Jack called to get her back.

Her reply was muffled. "No, Mom is *not* dead, but that cat will be if you don't let her go. You're holding her too tight, Hope. You'll *hurt* her." She returned to Jack. "Here. Hope wants to talk."

"Daddy?" The voice was a fragile wisp.

Jack's heart shifted. "Hi, Hope. How're you doin', sweetie?"

"Scared."

"I figured that, but your mom's doing fine right now. I'm on my way to the hospital. I'll know more when I get there."

"Come *here,*" begged the small voice.

"I will," he said, melting at the idea that at least one of his girls needed him. "But the hospital's on the way, so I'll stop there first. Then I'll have more to report when I see you."

"Tell Mom—" She stopped.

"What, sweetie?"

Samantha came on. "She's crying again. Here's Duncan."

"Duncan Bligh here." The voice was curt. "What's the word?"

Jack wanted Hope back. But it wasn't his night. "The word is that I don't know much. I'll be at the hospital within the hour. Don't drive them up."

"I wasn't about to."

There was a muted protest in the background, then an aggrieved Samantha returned. "Daddy, it's *sick* sitting around here while she's there."

"It's the middle of the night."

"Like we can *sleep* with her there? She's our *mother.* What if she *asks* for us?"

"She's in surgery, Samantha. Even if you were at the hospital, you wouldn't be able to see her. Look, if you want to do something, help your sister. She sounds upset."

"And I'm not?"

Jack could hear the tight panic that was taking her voice a step beyond brash. But Samantha wasn't Hope. Two years apart in age, they were light-years apart in personality. Samantha was fifteen going on thirty, a little know-it-all who didn't take kindly to being treated like a child. Thirteen-year-old Hope was sensitive and silent. Samantha would ask the questions. Hope would see every nuance of the answers.

"I'm sure you're upset, too," he said, "but you're older than she is. Maybe if you help her, she'll help you. Give each other strength, y'know?"

"I keep thinking about Highway One, Dad. Some of those places, if you go over the side, you fall hundreds of feet straight down, right onto *rocks.* Was that what happened to Mom?"

"I don't know the details of the accident."

"She might have fallen into water, but that'd be nearly as bad. Like, what if she was stuck underwater in the car—"

"Sam, she didn't drown."

"You don't know that. You don't know whether the only thing that's keeping her alive is a bunch of machines."

"Samantha." She was nearly as creative as Rachel, without the maturity to channel it. "Your mother has a broken leg."

"But you don't know what *else,*" she cried. "Call the troopers. They'll tell you what happened."

"Maybe later. The doctor has my cell number. I want to leave the line open in case he tries to call. And I want you to go to bed. It doesn't do anyone any good if you start imagining what *might* have happened. Imagination's always worse. So calm down. I'm in control of things here. And don't sit up waiting for the phone to ring, because I'm not calling you again until after the sun comes up."

"I'm not going to school."

"We'll discuss that later. Right now, the one thing you can do to help your mother most is to reassure your sister. And get some sleep. Both of you."

"Yeah, right," she muttered.

JACK CONCENTRATED on driving. The fog had stayed in the city, leaving the highway dark and straight. He pressed his middle in the hope that the warmth of his hand would ease the knot there, but his palm was cold and the knot stayed tight. Nerves did that to him every time. Lately, it seemed the knot was there more often than not.

He willed the phone to ring with the news that Rachel had awoken from surgery and was just fine. But the phone remained still, the interior of the car silent save the drone of the engine. He tried to distract himself with thoughts of all he had been agonizing over in bed less than two hours before—contract disputes, building delays, personnel losses—but he couldn't connect with those problems. They were distant, back in the city fog.

19

He would have calls to make, come morning. There were meetings to reschedule.

Or if Rachel woke up, he might be back in the office by noon.

That was likely, the more he thought about it. Rachel was the strongest, healthiest woman he knew—strongest, healthiest, most independent and self-sufficient. She didn't need him. Never had. Six years ago, she had reached a fork in the road of her life and gone off in a different direction from him. Her choice. Her life. Fine.

So why was he heading south? Why was he postponing even one meeting to run to her bedside? She had left him. She had taken ten years of marriage and crumpled it up, like a sketch on yellow trace that was so far off the mark it was worthless.

Why *was* he heading south?

He was heading south because her friend had called him. And because it was his job as a father to help out with the girls. And because he was terrified that Rachel might die. His life with her had been better than anything before or since. He was heading south because he felt that he still owed her for that.

THE VERY FIRST time Jack had laid eyes on Rachel, he decided that she wasn't his type. Oh, he liked blond hair, and she had endless waves of that, but he usually went for model types. Rachel Keats didn't fit that bill. She looked too pure. No long eyelashes, no glossy mouth, no flagrant sexuality, just dozens of freckles scattered over a nose and cheeks that were vaguely sunburned, and eyes

coast road

that were focused intently on the most boring professor
Jack had ever heard.

The subject was rococo and neoclassic art. The professor, renowned in his field, was the man whose grant
was paying for Jack's architectural degree. In exchange
for that, Jack graded exams and papers and helped with
research and correspondence to do with the textbook for
which the grant had been given.

Jack was only marginally interested in rococo and
neoclassic art and even less interested in moving from
Manhattan to Tucson, but the slot had been the only one
open that offered a full ride plus a stipend. Being penni-
less, Jack needed both.

The job wasn't taxing. The professor in question had
been delivering the same lectures, from the same printed
lesson plan, for twenty-plus years. Since Jack read the
lectures beforehand, his presence in the lecture hall was
more for the sake of fetching water or a forgotten book or
paper for the professor than anything educational for himself. He sat far off to the professor's side, where he could
be easily accessed. It was a perfect spot from which to
view the fifty-some-odd students who attended a given
class, out of three times that many enrolled in the course.

Rachel Keats attended every class, listened raptly,
took notes. Jack told himself that his eye sought her out
for the simple constancy of her presence. It didn't
explain, though, why he noted that she went from class
to lunch at the smallest campus café, where she sat
alone, or that she drove an old red VW bug and put a sun-
shade on the dash that was surely hand-painted, since he
had never in his life seen as large or vividly colored a *bug*
sitting behind the wheel of a car as her sunscreen hilari-
ously depicted.

21

She was an art major. She lived in an apartment complex not far from his. She was a loner by all accounts and, if the easygoing expression she wore meant anything, was content.

Not only wasn't she his type, but he was dating someone who was. Celeste was tall and leggy, loaded up top and sweet down below, asked precious few questions and made precious few demands, liked the sex enough that he could do what he wanted when he wanted in between. She cooked and cleaned his bathroom, but he hadn't been able to con her into doing his laundry. That was why he found himself in the laundromat on a Tuesday night when Rachel came through the door.

Those waves of blond hair were gathered up in a turquoise ribbon that clashed with her purple tank top, but her shorts and sandals were white and as fresh as the blush that stained those sun-stained cheeks when she saw him there.

In the extra-long heartbeat that she spent at the door, he could have sworn she was debating turning and leaving. Not wanting her to do that, he said, "Hey! How're you doing?"

She smiled. "Great." The blush remained. She sucked in her lips, raised her brows, and seeming self-conscious, hugged an overstuffed laundry bag as she looked down the row of washers for raised lids. "Ah," she said, spotting two side by side. She smiled at him again and headed toward them.

Jack's heart was pounding. He didn't know why. All she'd done was smile. There hadn't been anything remotely sexual in it. She wasn't his type *at all*. But he slid off the dryer he'd been sitting on, and following her, he leaned

22

up against the machine that backed on one of those she had chosen.

"Rococo and neoclassic art?" he prompted. He didn't want her to think this was a blind pickup, because it wasn't a pickup at all. She *wasn't* his type. He assumed that was why she intrigued him. It was safe. No risk. Just an innocuous hello.

She acknowledged the connection with a simple "Uh-huh." She was blushing still, pushing dirty laundry from the mouth of her laundry bag into the mouth of the washer.

He watched her for a minute, then said, "Mine's in the dryer."

It was probably the dumbest line he'd ever handed a woman. But he couldn't tell her that she was pushing reds and whites together into her machine. He couldn't ask if the reds were shirts, bras, or briefs. He couldn't even look directly at those things, because she would have been mortified. Besides, he couldn't take his eyes from hers. They were hazel with gold flecks, and more gentle than any he had seen.

"You're Obermeyer's TA," she said as she filled the second machine with things that went way beyond red. Her current outfit was conservative by comparison. "Are you training to teach?"

"No. I'm in architecture."

She smiled. "Really?"

"Really," he said, smiling back. She really was a sweet thing, smiling like that. The sweetness remained even when she suddenly opened her mouth and looked around—left, right, down, back.

Jack returned to his own possessions and offered her his box of soap powder.

He was rewarded with another blush and a soft-murmured "Thanks." When she had both machines filled with soap, fed with quarters, and started, she asked, "What kind of things do you want to build?"

The question usually came from his parents and was filled with scorn. But Rachel Keats seemed genuinely interested.

"Homes, for starters," he said. "I come from a two-bit town, one little box after another. I used to pass those little boxes on the way to school and spend my class time doodling them into something finer. Those doodles didn't help my math grade much."

"No. I wouldn't think it." She shot a glance at the text that lay open on his dryer. "Is the book on home designs?"

"Not yet. Right now we're into arches. Do you know how many different kinds of arches there are? There are flat arches, round arches, triangular arches, pointed arches. There are hand arches, back arches, groin arches. There are depressed arches. There are diminished arches. There are horseshoe arches."

She was laughing, the sound as gentle as her eyes. "I don't think I want to know what some of those are." She paused for the briefest time, said almost shyly, "I was a doodler, too."

He liked the shyness. It made him feel safe. "Where?"

"Chicago, then Atlanta, then New York. My childhood was mobile. My dad takes old businesses and turns them around. We move when he sells. How about you?"

"Oregon. You won't have heard of the town. It doesn't make it onto maps. What did you doodle?"

"Oh, people, birds, animals, fish, anything that moves.

I like doing what a camera does, capturing an instant."

"Are you still doodling?" he asked in response to her use of the present tense.

She lifted a shoulder, shy, maybe modest. "I like to think it's more. I'm hoping to paint for a living."

"With or without a day job?" Jack asked. The average artist barely earned enough to eat. Unless Rachel was significantly better than average, she would have a tough time paying the bills.

She wrapped her arms around her middle. Quietly, almost sadly, she said, "I'm lucky. Those businesses keep selling. My mom heads one of them now. They think I'm crazy to be here doing this. Art isn't business. They want me back in the city wearing designer dresses with a designer handbag and imported boots." She took a fresh breath. "Do you have siblings?"

"Five brothers and a sister," he said, though it had nothing to do with anything. He rarely talked about family. The people he was with rarely asked.

Not only had Rachel asked, but those wonderful eyes of hers lit up with his answer. "Six? That's great. I don't have *any.*"

"That's why you think it's great. There were seven of us born in ten years, living with two parents in a three-bedroom house. I was the lucky one. Summers, I got the porch."

"What are the others doing now? Are they all over the country? Are any of them out here?"

"They're back home. I'm the only one who made it out."

Her eyes grew. "Really? Why you? *How?*"

"Scholarship. Work-study. Desperation. I had to leave. I don't get along with my family."

25

"Why not?" she asked in such an innocent way that he actually answered.

"They're negative. Always criticizing to cover up for what they lack, but the only thing they really lack is ambition. My dad coulda done anything he wanted—he's a bright guy—only, he got stuck in a potato processing plant and never got out. My brothers are going to be just like him, different jobs, same wasted potential. I went to college, which makes what they're doing seem smaller. They'll never forgive me for that."

"I'm so sorry."

He smiled. "Not your fault."

"Then you don't go home much?"

"No. And you? Back to New York?"

She crinkled her nose. "I'm not a city person. When I'm there, I'm stuck doing all the things I hate."

"Don't you have friends there?"

"A few. We talk. I've never had to go around with a crowd. How about you? Got a roommate?"

"Not on your life. I had enough of those growing up to never want another one, at least not of the same sex. What's your favorite thing in Tucson?"

"The desert. What's yours?"

"The Santa Catalinas."

Again those eyes lit, gold more than hazel. "Do you hike?" When he nodded, she said, "Me, too. When do you have time? Are you taking a full course load? How many hours a week do you have to give to Obermeyer?"

Jack answered her questions and asked more of his own. When she answered those without seeming to mind, he asked more again, and she asked her share right back. She wasn't judgmental, just curious. She seemed as interested in where he'd been, what he'd done, what

26

he liked and didn't like as he was in her answers. They talked nonstop until Rachel's clothes were clean, dry, and folded. When, arms loaded, they finally left the laundromat, he knew three times as much about her as he knew about Celeste.

Taking that as a message of some sort, he broke up with Celeste the next day, called Rachel, and met her for pizza. They picked right up where they had left off at the laundromat.

Jack was fascinated. He had never been a talker. He didn't like baring his thoughts and ideas, held them close to the vest, but there was something about Rachel that felt . . . safe, there it was again. She was gentle. She was interested. She was smart. Being as much of a loner as he was, she seemed just as startled as he to be opening up to a virtual stranger, but they gave each other permission. He trusted her instinctively. She seemed to trust him the same way right back.

As simply as that, they became inseparable. They ate together, studied together, sketched together. They went to movies. They hiked. They huddled before class and staked out their favorite campus benches, but it was a full week before they made love.

In theory, a week was no time at all. In practice, in an age of free sex with two people deeply attracted to each other, it was an eternity, and they were definitely attracted to each other. No doubt about that. Jack was hit pretty fast by the lure of an artist's slender fingers and graceful arms. He didn't miss the way her shorts curved around her butt or the enticing flash of midriff when she leaned a certain way. The breasts under her tank tops were small but exquisitely formed. At least, that was the picture he pieced together from the shadow of shapes and the occasional nob of a nipple. The fact that he didn't know for sure kept him looking.

Was she attracted to him? Well, there was that nipple, tightest when he was closest. There was the way she leaned into him, so subtle, when they went to a campus concert, and the way her breath caught when he came close to whisper something in her ear. All that, even without her eyes, which turned warm to hot at all the appropriate times. Oh, yes, she wanted him. He could have taken her two days after the laundromat.

He didn't because he was afraid. He had never had a relationship like this with a woman before. Physical, yes. But not emotional, not psychological, not heart-to-heart. Rachel made him feel comfortable enough to say what he thought and felt. Not knowing how sex would mix with that, he avoided taking her to his apartment or going to her apartment, avoided even kissing her.

A week of that was *more* than an eternity. He'd had it with avoidance by the time she invited him over for dinner, and apparently she had, too. He was barely inside the door when that first kiss came. It was a scorcher, purity in flames, hotter and hotter as they slid along the wall to her room and fell on the bed. There was a mad scramble to get clothes off and be close and inside—and it was heaven for Jack, the deepest, most overwhelming lovemaking he had ever in his life dreamed could take place.

When it was done, she sat on the bed with pencil and paper and drew him, and what emerged said it all. With her hands, her mind, her heart she made him into something finer than he had ever been before. She was his angel, and he was in love.

chapter two

THE SURGICAL WAITING ROOM was on the second floor at the end of a very long hall. Dropping into a seat there, Jack folded his arms on his chest and focused on the door. His eyes were tired. Fear alone kept them open.

It was a full five minutes before he realized that he wasn't alone. A woman was watching him from the end of a nearby sofa. She looked wary, but she didn't blink when he stared.

"Are *you* Katherine?" he finally asked, and saw the ghost of a crooked smile.

"Why the surprise?"

He would have liked to be diplomatic, but he was too tired, too tense. "Because you don't look like my wife's type," he said, staring still. Rachel was all natural—hair, face, nails. This woman was groomed, from dark lashes to painted nails to hair that was a dozen different shades of beige and moussed into fashionably long curls.

"It's *ex-wife,*" Katherine said, "and looks can deceive. So, you're Jack?"

He barely had time to nod when the door opened and

a doctor emerged. His scrubs were wrinkled. Short, brownish gray hair stuck up in damp spikes.

Jack was on his feet and approaching before the door had swung shut. "Jack McGill," he said, extending a hand. "How is she?"

The doctor met his grip. "Steve Bauer, and she's in the Recovery Room. The surgery went well. Her vital signs are good. She's breathing on her own. But she still hasn't regained consciousness."

"Coma," Jack said. The word had been hovering in the periphery of the night, riding shotgun with him down from San Francisco. He needed the doctor to deny it.

To his dismay, Steve Bauer nodded. "She doesn't respond to stimuli—light, pain, noise." He touched the left side of his face, temple to jaw. "She was badly bruised here. There's external swelling. Her lack of response suggests that there's internal swelling, too. We're monitoring for intracranial pressure. A mild increase can be treated medically. There's nothing at this point to suggest that we'll need to relieve it surgically."

Jack pushed his hands through his hair. His head was buzzing. He tried to clear out the noise by clearing his throat. "Coma. Okay. How bad is that?"

"Well, I'd rather she be awake."

That wasn't what Jack meant. "Will she die?"

"I hope not."

"How do we prevent it?"

"We don't. She does. When tissues are injured, they swell. The more they swell, the more oxygen they need to heal. Unfortunately, the brain is different from other organs, because it's encased in the skull. When brain tissues swell, the skull prevents the expansion they need, and pressure builds. That causes a slowing of the blood flow, and since blood carries oxygen, a slowing of the blood flow means less oxygen to the brain. Less oxygen means slower healing. Her body determines how slow."

Jack understood. But he needed to know more. "Worst-case scenario?"

"Pressure builds high enough to completely cut the flow of blood, and hence oxygen to the brain, and the person dies. That's why we'll be monitoring your wife. If we see the pressure when it first starts to build, we stand a better chance of relieving it."

"When? What's the time frame here?"

"We've done a head scan, but nothing shows positive. We'll watch her closely. The next forty-eight hours will be telling. The good news is that what swelling there is now is minimal."

"But you said she doesn't respond. Assuming the swelling doesn't get worse, when will she?"

The doctor caught the dampness on his brow with a forearm. "That's what I can't tell you. I wish I could, but it's different with every case."

"Will there be permanent damage?" Jack asked. He needed it all on the table.

"I don't know."

"Does the chance of permanent damage increase the longer she's comatose?"

"Not if the swelling doesn't worsen."

"Is there anything you can do to get the swelling down?"

"She's on a drip to reduce it. But overmedicating has its problems, too."

"Then we just let her *lie* there?"

"No," the doctor replied patiently. "We let her lie

there and heal. The body is a miraculous thing, Mr. McGill. It works on its own while we wait."

"What can we do to help?" Katherine asked from close behind Jack. Startled by her voice, Jack turned, but her eyes didn't leave the doctor's.

"Not a whole lot," Bauer replied, but he looked torn. "Ask nurses specializing in coma, and they'll say you should talk to her. They say comatose patients hear things and can sometimes repeat those things with frightening accuracy when they wake up."

"Do you believe that?" Jack asked.

"It doesn't jibe with medical science." He lowered his voice a notch. "My colleagues pooh-pooh it. Me, I don't see that talking to her does any harm."

"What do we say?"

"Anything positive. If she does hear, you want her to hear good stuff. The more optimistic you are, the more optimistic she'll be. Tell her she's doing well. Be upbeat."

"What about the girls?" Jack asked. "We have two daughters. They're thirteen and fifteen. They're already asking questions. Maybe I should keep them away. There's no point in frightening them if there's a chance she'll be waking up later or even tomorrow. Should I say she's still out of it from the anesthesia, and keep them home?"

"No. Bring them. Their voices may help her focus."

"How does she look?" he asked. "Will they be frightened?"

"The side of her face is swollen and scraped. It's starting to turn colors. One of her hands was cut up by the glass—"

"Badly?" Jack cut in, because that introduced a whole *new* worry.

Apparently agreeing, Katherine added, "She's an artist. Left-handed."

"Well, this was her left hand," Bauer said, "but nothing crucial was cut. There won't be any lasting damage there. Her leg is casted and elevated, and we've taped her ribs to prevent damage if she becomes agitated, but that's it."

"Agitated," Jack repeated, wondering just how much more there *was*. "As in seizures?"

"Sometimes. Sometimes just agitated. We call it 'posturing.' Odd physical movements. Then again, she may be perfectly quiet right through waking up. That's what'll scare your daughters most. They'll be as upset by her silence as by anything physical they see."

Jack tried to ingest it all, but it was hard. The picture the doctor had painted was the antithesis of the active woman Rachel had always been. "When can I see her?"

"Once we make sure she's stable, we'll transfer her to Intensive Care—no," he explained when Jack's eyes widened, "that doesn't mean she's critical, just that we want her closely watched." He glanced at the clock on the wall. It was four-ten. "Give us an hour."

JACK and Katherine weren't alone in the cafeteria. A handful of medical personnel were scattered at tables, some eating an early breakfast, others nursing coffee. Voices were muted. The occasional clink of flatwear on china rose above them.

Jack had paid for one coffee, one tea, and one thickly coated sticky bun. The coffee was his. The rest was Katherine's. Her polished fingernails glittered under the overhead fluorescents as she pulled the warm bun apart.

Jack watched her for a distracted minute, then studied his coffee. He needed the caffeine. He was feeling tired all over. But he couldn't eat, not waiting this way. Rachel dead was unthinkable; Rachel brain-damaged came in a close second.

Taking a healthy drink of coffee, he set the cup down and checked his watch. Then he stretched up and back in an attempt to unkink his stomach. He checked his watch again, but the time hadn't changed.

"I can't picture her here," he said, absently looking at the others in the cafeteria. "She hates hospitals. When the girls were born, she was in and out. If she'd been a farmhand, she'd have given birth in the fields."

Katherine nodded. "I believe it. Rachel's one of the free spirits of the group."

The group. Jack had trouble seeing Rachel in any group. During the years of their marriage, she had been a rabid nonjoiner—and that in a city where the slightest cause spawned a gathering. She had rejected it all, had rejected *him,* had packed up her bags and moved three hours south to Big Sur, apparently to do some of the very things she had refused to do under his roof.

Stung by that thought, he muttered a snide "Must be some group."

Katherine stopped chewing for an instant, then swallowed. "What do you mean, 'some group'?"

"For you to be here, what, all night?"

She returned a piece of the sticky bun to her plate and carefully wiped her hands on a napkin. "Rachel's my friend. It didn't seem right that she should be in the operating room with no one waiting to learn if she lived or died."

"They were only setting her leg. Besides, I'm here now. You can leave."

She looked at him for a minute. With a small, quick head shake, she gathered her cup and plate and picked herself up. In a voice just confident enough to drive home her point without announcing it to the world, she said, "You're an insensitive shit, Jack. No wonder she divorced you."

By the time she had relocated to the far side of the room, Jack knew she was only partly right. He was insensitive *and* ungrateful. Topping that off with rude, he could begin to see why the two women were friends. If he had used that tone on Rachel, she would have walked away from him, too.

Taking his coffee, he went after her. "You're right," he said quietly. "I was being insensitive. You're her friend, and you've been here for hours, and I thank you for that. I'm feeling tired, helpless, and scared. I guess I took it out on you."

She stared at him a minute longer, then turned back to her roll.

"May I sit?" he asked, suddenly wanting it badly. "Misery-loves-company kind of thing? Any friend of Rachel's is a friend of mine?"

It seemed an eternity of pending refusal before she gestured toward the table's free chair. She sipped her tea while he settled, then put the cup down. Staring at it, she said a quiet "For the record, you are not my friend. Rachel is. She's earned that right. I don't take people to heart readily, and you're starting at a deficit. You're not the only one around here who's tired and helpless and scared."

He could see it then, threads of fatigue behind the neat facade. He hadn't meant to make things worse. He was glad for Rachel, having a close friend like this. No doubt Katherine knew more about who Rachel was today than he did.

He looked at his watch. It was only four-thirty. They had time to kill. He was curious. "Rachel never told me she was in a book group."

"Maybe that's because you're divorced," Katherine reminded him, then relented and said more gently, "She helped form the group. We organized five years ago."

"How often do you meet?"

"Once a month. There are seven of us."

"Who are the others?"

"Local women. One is a travel agent, one sculpts, one owns a bakery, two golf. They were all here earlier. Needless to say, we weren't talking books."

No, Jack realized. They weren't talking books. They were talking about an accident that shouldn't have happened. Turning to that for lack of anything else to attack, he said, "Who hit her? Was the guy *drunk?* Did the cops get him, at least?"

"It wasn't a guy. It was a gal, and she wasn't drunk. She was senile. Eighty-some years old, with no business being on any road, least of all that one. The cops got her, all right. She's in the morgue."

Jack's breath caught. *In the morgue.* The fact of death changed things. It made reality suddenly more real, made Rachel's situation feel more grave.

He let out a long, low groan. His anger went with it.

"She was someone's mother, someone's grandmother," Katherine said.

"I'm sure." He sank back in his seat. "Christ."

"I do agree with you there."

~ ~ ~

THEY actually agreed on another thing—that Jack should be the one to see Rachel first—and he was grateful. Entering a predawn, dim, starkly sterile room whose railed bed held the pale shadow of the woman whose personality had always been brightly colored felt bad enough in private. Having his own uncertainties on public display would have made it worse. Not that there was total privacy. The fourth wall of the room was a sliding glass door. A curtain that might have covered the glass was pushed back so that medical personnel could see Rachel.

Quietly, he approached the bed. His mind registered one machine against the wall and multiple IV poles beside the bed, plus Rachel's elevated leg, which, casted, was three times the size of her normally slim one. But his eyes found her face fast, and held it. The doctor had warned him well. Even in the low light coming from behind her, he could see that around a raw scrape, the left side was swollen and starting to purple. The color was jarring against the rest of her. Her eyes were closed, her lips pale, her skin ashen, her freckles out of place. Even her hair, which was shoulder length, naturally blond and thick, looked uncharacteristically meek.

He reached for the hand nearest him, the right one, free of sutures and tubes. Her fingers were limp, her skin cool. Carefully, he folded his own around it.

"Rachel?" he called softly. "It's me. Jack."

She slept on.

"Rachel? Can you hear me?" He swallowed. "Rachel?"

His knees were shaking. He leaned against the bed

rail. "Come on, angel. Time to wake up. It isn't any fun talking if you don't talk back." He squeezed her hand. "Your friend Katherine said I was a shit. You used to say it, too. Say it now, and I won't even mind."

She didn't move.

"Not even a blink?" He opened his hand. "How about moving a finger to let me know you can hear? Want to try? Or are you going to keep us all guessing about what you hear and what you don't?"

She showed no sign of having heard him.

Nothing new there, he thought. She had gone right ahead and done her own thing for years, certainly for the six they had been apart. So, did she hear him? Or was she deliberately ignoring him? He didn't know what to say next.

Lifting her hand to his mouth, he kissed it and held it to his chest. With the slightest shift, it covered his heart, flesh on cotton, but close.

"Feel that?" The beat was heavy and fast. "It's been that way since I got the call. Samantha and Hope are scared, too. I talked with them, though. They'll be fine." When that sounded dismissive, he said, "I'll call them again in a little while." That didn't sound right, either, so he said, "I'll drive down once I leave here. They'll believe me better if I tell them you're okay in person. Duncan's there now. So, what's the scoop? Is he just the baby-sitter, or what?"

He wondered if she was laughing inside. "I'm serious. I don't know the guy. Do you two date?"

She said nothing.

"Sam informed me that she wasn't going to school. She'll go." He thought aloud: "Or maybe I'll just drive them back up here to visit. It won't kill them to miss one day of school." But they were approaching June fast. "When do finals start?" Rachel didn't answer. "No sweat. I'll ask."

He rapped her hand against his chest. "Wake up, Rachel." She slept on.

He brought her hand to his mouth again. Her skin was as soft as ever, but it lacked a distinct scent, which wasn't like Rachel at all. If she didn't smell of whatever medium she was working with, she smelled of lilies. He had started her on that, way back when he hadn't had enough money and had resorted to stealing lilies of the valley from the shady side of his landlord's house. For their second wedding anniversary, he had found perfume like it. No, not perfume. Toilet water. Perfume would have been too strong for Rachel. Even when he started earning money, he avoided perfume. Light and floral. That fit Rachel.

Light and floral was worlds away from her antiseptic smell now.

Not that she would still be wearing the same toilet water. She would have switched. Wouldn't have wanted the memories, though more than a few were good.

"Wake up, Rachel," he begged, suddenly frightened. He had lived without her for six years, but all that time he had known where she was. Now he didn't. Not really. It was as unsettling a thought as he'd had of late. "I need to know how you're feeling," he warned in a slightly frantic singsong. "I need to know what to tell the girls. I need you to talk to me."

When she remained silent, he grew angry. "Damn it, what *happened?* You're the safest driver I know. You used to save me from accidents all the time—'Maniac on the left,' you'd say, or, 'Jerk on your tail.' Didn't you *see* a car behind you?"

But she might not have. She had been driving north on a road that wound in and around, from the lip of one canyon to the lip of another. She would have been squeezed on the east by cliffs, and on the west by a single lane of oncoming traffic, then a guardrail and a harrowing drop. Once she rounded a sharp curve, she wouldn't see the car behind her until it, too, rounded the curve. If it did that at high speed, she wouldn't see it until seconds before the collision. And then, where could she go?

Feeling the panic she may well have felt, he whispered an urgent "Okay, okay. Not your fault. I know that. I'm sorry I suggested it. It's just . . . frustrating." Frustrating that he couldn't rouse her. Frustrating that the doctors couldn't, either. Frustrating, too, that the offending party was dead and beyond punishment, but he *sure* couldn't say that to Rachel, not if there was a chance she could hear. She was a softhearted woman—hardheaded but softhearted. She would be crushed to learn that someone had died. If she needed to hear upbeat things, that wasn't the news to tell.

And what was? *You'll be pleased to know that my firm's falling apart.* But Rachel wasn't vindictive. So, that wouldn't do it. Nor would *I've lost the touch; nothing I design is right anymore.* Rachel had no taste for self-pity. Nor was she one for jealousy, which meant that he couldn't tell her about Jill. Besides, what would he say? Jill was nearly as softhearted as Rachel. She was nearly as pretty and nearly as bright. She was nowhere near as spirited, or as talented, or as unique. She would always pale by comparison.

What was the point of telling Rachel that? She had left him. They were divorced.

Feeling useless and suddenly more tired than he would

have thought possible, he said, "Your friend Katherine is here. She was the one who called me. She's been here since they brought you in. She wants to see you, too. I'm going to talk to the doctor. Then I'll go get the girls. We'll be back in a couple of hours, okay?" He watched her eyelids for even the slightest movement. "Okay?" Nothing.

Discouraged, he returned her hand to the stiff hospital sheet. Leaning down, he kissed her forehead. "I'll be back."

DAWN was breaking to the east of Monterey when he left the hospital. Once he was past Carmel, the hills rose to stave it off. Inevitably, though, the sky began to lighten. By the time he reached the Santa Lucias and Highway 1 began to wind, a morning fog had risen from the water and was bathing the pavement with a shifting mist.

Jack kept his headlights on and his eyes peeled, but neither was necessary. He couldn't have missed the accident site. Traffic was alternating along one lane while a pair of wreckers worked in the other. One mangled car had already been raised, but it wasn't Rachel's sturdy four-by-four. A mauled section of guardrail lay nearby.

Feeling sick to his stomach but needing answers, he pulled up behind the wreckers and climbed out. The air was cool, moist, and thick in ways that should have muted the brutality of the scene, but what little the shifting fog hid, Jack's imagination supplied.

Rachel's car lay against boulders a distance below. Its top and sides were dented and scraped. Water shot up from the rocks not ten feet away, but the car itself looked dry.

"Better move on, sir. If one stops, others do. Before we know it, we have a jam."

Jack pushed shaky hands into his pockets. "My wife was in that car. Looks like it went head over tail. It's a miracle she's alive."

"She's all right, then?" the trooper asked in a more giving tone. "We never know, once they leave the scene."

"She's alive."

"For what it's worth, she was driving within the speed limit."

Jack looked back at the road he had just climbed. It wound up from a basin lined left and right with cypress, dark and spectral in the fog. "Too bad. If she'd been going faster, she might have been down there when she was hit. Then she'd have gone off onto evener ground."

"She might have gone head-on into trees or traffic. There were a number of cars traveling south. Be grateful for small favors."

Jack tried, but Rachel hadn't asked to be hit. She hadn't done anything to deserve it. He didn't need to be told that she was driving safely—or that she had been wearing a seat belt. If not, she'd have been dead down there on the rocks.

The workers were struggling to hitch cables to her car and haul it up.

"When'll those guys be done?" he asked the trooper. "I'll be bringing our daughters back this way, and I'd rather they not see this."

"Couple of hours, I guess. Can you wait that long?"

He hadn't planned to, but he could. If he found the girls asleep, it might actually work out fine. He could use the time to figure out the most sensitive way to break the news.

chapter three

JACK DIDIN'T SEE MUCH of the rest of the drive. Fog continued to float across the road, lifting and lowering across the rugged terrain, allowing now and again for a glimpse of sea stacks in gray water on his right or the ghost of chaparral against rocks on his left, but an ashen pall lay as thick in his mind as in his eye. The world around him seemed dense, a heavy weight on shoulders that were tired and tense. It was twenty-four hours since he had last slept. Life had been a nightmare. And now he had to face the girls.

Part of him still pictured his daughters as the towheaded little monkeys who had adored him before things fell apart. They were more blond now than towheaded, more adolescent than little, more female than monkey. Yet the same old something twisted deep in his chest whenever their names came up.

They weren't babies. Hugs alone wouldn't be enough. But hugs hadn't done it for a while. They were more cautious than adoring with him now, strangers in many respects.

Thinking about that as he drove through the fog, he had a sudden, brutal sense of the limits of his relationship with his daughters. Taking them to a movie, or to watch a wedding in Chinatown, or to breakfast in Sausalito at Fred's was one thing. Filling in for Rachel, dealing with heavy-duty stuff, was quite another. He faced a trial by fire.

Thirty minutes south of the accident scene, Rachel's canyon rose from the sea. Its road was marked by an oak grove and a bank of mailboxes nine deep. Only one of the nine was painted, the fourth from the left. This year it was fire-engine red, Hope's choice. Last year it had been Rachel's butter yellow; the year before that, Samantha's purple.

He turned off the highway, downshifted, and began the climb. The road was unpaved, narrow, and steep. It hugged the hillside and wound steadily upward, broken only by driveways that careened down and around into private homes. The higher he drove, the thinner the fog. Oak yielded to sycamore and madrone, which mixed farther on up with cedar. Redwood had replaced that by the time he reached Rachel's.

Her home was a cabin of weathered cedar shingles. It meandered over a small space of the hillside, up a bit here, down a bit there. Pulling in on a rough gravel drive, he climbed from the car, and for a minute he stood there unable to move, breathing in something different, drawn to it. Fresh air, he decided, snapping to with an effort. He stretched and rubbed his face with his hands. He needed a shave, a shower, and some sleep. What he got when depended on what he found inside.

Wide wood planks that the elements had blanched led to the front door. His loafers echoed in the silence, but he didn't need to rap on the door. It opened before he reached it. The man filling its frame was far older than Jack had expected—mid-sixties, he guessed, from the pure white of his hair and beard and his weathered skin—but neither detracted from his presence. He was a large man, taller than Jack's own six-two by several inches, but that wasn't what kept Jack from putting out a hand. It was the forbidding look that met his.

"The girls are asleep," Duncan Bligh said in the same hard voice he had used on the phone. That it was lower now did nothing to soften it. "How is she?"

"Comatose," Jack replied, low also. He didn't want the girls waking up and hearing him. "Her condition isn't critical. Her body is working okay. The bang on the head is the problem."

"Prognosis?"

He shrugged and hitched his chin toward the inside of the cabin. "They calmed down, I take it?"

"No." Duncan pushed beefy arms into a flannel vest. "They just wore themselves out." He strode past Jack, muttering, "I got work to do."

Jack raised a hand in thanks and good-bye, but Duncan had already rounded the house and was striding up the forested hillside. "Nice meeting you, too, pal," he muttered. Going inside, he quietly shut the door and leaned against it to get his bearings.

It was the first time that he had been this far. Most often, when he picked up the girls for a visit, they met at a McDonald's just north of San Jose. In the instances when he drove all the way down, the three of them were usually waiting for him at the bank of mailboxes. He could count on one hand the number of times he had been to the cabin, and then, only to the door.

From there he'd had glimpses of color. Now the glimpse became a blur of natural wood, furniture that was green and lilac, purple planters, wild colors framed on the wall. The living room opened into a kitchen, but the back wall of both rooms was a window on the forest. The view here was simpler, more gentle to his eye. Pale shafts of sun broke through the redwoods, a bar code of rays slanting toward the forest floor.

Soundlessly mounting several steps to the left of the living room, he went down a hall and peered into the first room. Between the guy posters on the wall and a general sense of chaos, it had Samantha's name written all over it. The bed was mussed but empty.

Up several more steps and on down the hall, another door was ajar. This room had watercolors on the wall and a softer feel entirely. Both girls were asleep in Hope's double bed, two heads of blond hair as wild as their mother's. Hope was in a ball, Samantha was sprawled. In a gulley between them was a puff of orange fur that had to be the cat.

When none of the three showed signs of waking, Jack returned to the main room and sank into the sofa. Slipping lower, he rested his head against its back. His eyes closed, his body begging for sleep, but his mind kept going. Within minutes he was back on his feet and lifting the kitchen phone.

He called the hospital first and, speaking quietly with the ICU nurse, learned that Rachel's condition hadn't changed.

Next he called his partner at home. In response to a breathless greeting, he said, "Working out?"

"Treadmill," David Sung gasped, and Jack pictured him in the dining room that had been filled with exercise equipment after David's last wife had taken off with the Chippendale table and chairs.

"Sorry to interrupt," he said, "but I have a problem. Rachel was in a car crash last night. I'm down here with the girls."

"Down where? In Big Sur?" The beat on the treadmill slowed. "Not Big Sur. Ess *Eff*. We have a big meeting here in two hours. What kinda car crash?"

"A bad one." Jack kept his voice low and an eye on the far end of the living room so that he would know if one of the girls appeared. "She's in a coma."

"Jesus."

"I stopped at the hospital on my way down, but I need to bring the girls back there. We'll have to cancel the meeting."

"A coma," David repeated, still breathless. "Bad?"

"Any coma's bad."

"You know what I mean. Is she on life support?"

"No. But I can't get to that meeting."

There was a pause, then the blowing out of air and an exasperated "We can't cancel. We've already rescheduled twice." Another pause, another exhalation. "You're not ready for the presentation, are you?"

"Oh, I'm ready," Jack said, and it all rushed back, what had kept him tossing and turning before Katherine had called, "but they won't like what I have this time any more than they did last time."

He had been hired to design a luxury resort in Montana. The client wanted something with reflective surfaces that would disappear under that big open sky, but Jack had been to Montana. Glass and steel were all wrong. Even stone was pushing it. He wanted wood.

When his first design was rejected, he incorporated

granite with the wood. When that was rejected also, he had tried fieldstone and torn it up, glass and torn it up, steel and torn it up. He had gone back to wood and made the design more dramatic, but even *he* wasn't wild about it. The best rendition was the very first.

Only, that was beside the point. "Look," he told David. "I need your backup here. That's what this partnership is about. I can't be there. This is a family emergency."

"There's one hitch. You're divorced."

"Not from my kids."

"Okay. I get that. I do get it, Jack, but these guys have been waiting, and there's many millions at stake. If I tell them you can't be there because you have to be with your kids, they won't buy it."

"My wife's life hangs in the balance, and they won't buy it? Fuck *them*."

"Do that, and they'll take their business elsewhere."

Jack ran a hand around the back of his neck. The muscles there were wire tight. "Let them."

"Y'know, pal, I'd have said the same thing a little while back, but right now I'm worried about Sung and McGill. This is a major project for the firm. Two others went with our associates who went out on their own last month."

"We still have more than we can handle."

"But this is a good one," David coaxed. "We've been doing educational institutions for years, but resorts are hot and lucrative. We're talking jumping to a new level. We can't let a project like this go by default."

"Then *you* take it over."

"Hell, I'd have done that weeks ago, only they want you. They want you, and you've lost your edge."

Jack was suddenly so weary that his bones ached. "I can't handle this now. Tell them . . . whatever, but I can't be at that meeting. I'll call in when I know more." He hung up the phone, knowing that his partner would be swearing and not wanting to hear it. Dealing with Rachel's accident, dealing with his daughters—trying *not* to think about the future—was all he could handle just then.

But Rachel and the girls were all sleeping. Stretching out on the sofa, with one arm over his eyes and one on his stomach, he followed suit.

HOPE came awake as she always did, slowly growing aware, getting a feel for morning before she opened her eyes, listening and thinking before she moved a muscle. She felt bits of sun, weak but warm. She listened to the soft sound of Guinevere's breathing close behind her neck. She began to think—and her eyes flew open.

Swinging her head around, cheek into cat fur, she saw her sister sleeping beside her, and it was suddenly real, what had happened last night. Samantha hadn't slept with her in years. She would have thought it beneath her, if things had been less scary.

Guinevere tipped back her head and gave her a nudge.

She nuzzled the cat for a minute, gathering courage. Moving the mattress as little as possible, she sat up and carefully drew the tabby into her arms. Silently, she backed off the bed and started for the door. Stopping suddenly, she returned, pushed her feet into her cowboy boots, and tiptoed from the room.

The sight of her father in the living room brought

instant relief. She had wanted him there so badly. Samantha had said he wouldn't come—that he hadn't *been* there when they needed him for *ages;* that he was too busy with *work.* But Hope had sensed he would come. She did that sometimes—sensed things—and it wasn't necessarily wanting that brought it. She had sensed that something was wrong long before Katherine had called looking for Rachel, had felt an unease when her mother left. She had thought it was about Guinevere. The vet had warned that the end would be silent and swift, and Hope was prepared. She had been the one to insist that Guinevere die at home, with her. But she wanted her mother to be there when it happened.

It wasn't until Samantha had said into the phone, "Hi, Katherine," that Hope connected the eerie feeling inside with her mom's well-being, and then it was like the bottom had dropped out of her world. She had felt the same thing when they moved to Big Sur without her father—shaky, like she was suddenly standing on only one leg.

Lowering herself to the rug not far from her father, she folded her legs and gently settled Guinevere in her T-shirted lap. The tabby looked up at her, purring softly. Hope imagined that Guinevere felt the same reassurance seeing her as she felt seeing her father.

Only, he didn't look very well, she decided. His hair was messy and his beard prickly. The shadows under his eyes said that he hadn't slept much, which made her nervous.

But he was sleeping now. That said something. If Rachel was dead, he would have woken them right up—wouldn't he have? If she was dead, he would have come sooner—wouldn't he have?

But Hope didn't know how long he *had* been there. She had tried to stay awake, had tried to do what her mother did when she was feeling lonely or down, which was work. But she could only recheck her homework so many times, and the book she was reading hadn't held her thoughts. So she had fallen asleep.

She hated the thought that her mother might have died while she slept. If that had happened, she would feel guilty for the rest of her life.

She was debating waking her father when his eyeballs began darting around behind his lids. Seconds later, his whole body tensed and he jerked awake. He stared at the ceiling, sat quickly up, pressed the heels of his hands to his eyes. He was in the process of pushing them into his hair when he spotted her.

He sounded shaky. "You should have woken me up."

"I figured that if you could sleep, Mom's okay," she said, holding her breath, watching him for the slightest sign of denial.

"She's okay," he said. "She needs to do a lot of mending, but she's okay."

"Did you talk with her?"

"No. She was sleeping. But I think she knew I was there."

"She isn't dead?"

"She isn't dead."

"You're sure?"

He seemed about to speak, then stopped, and her heart stopped right along with it. She drew herself straighter and didn't look away. She was thirteen. If her mother was dead, she wanted to know. She could handle the truth.

Something crossed his face then, and she knew she

had made her point. His voice was different, more reassuring. "No, Hope, she isn't dead. I would never lie to you about that. Deal?"

She nodded, breathing again. "When can we go?"

"Later this morning." He looked at the cat. "So this is the thing that showed up at the front door one day all bitten and bruised?"

Hope fingered the tabby's ear. "The bites healed."

"Gwendolyn, is it?"

"Guinevere. Did you learn anything about Mom's accident? Sam said she didn't know how anyone could survive driving off a cliff."

"Your mother didn't drive off the cliff. She was hit by someone else, and she did survive, so Sam was wrong."

"Is her leg in a cast?"

"Uh-huh."

"Will it heal?"

"Sure. Broken legs always heal."

Hope hated to contradict him, but she knew better than he did on this. "Not always. Things can go wrong. There can be permanent damage. That'd be awful for Mom. She'd have trouble with the hills."

Those hills meant the world to Rachel. She loved hiking them with Hope and Samantha. Hope had one favorite spot. Samantha had another. But Rachel? Rachel had *dozens*. Like the eucalyptus grove. Rachel said that a person didn't have to be sick to be healed by the smell of eucalyptus. Hope couldn't count the number of hours she had sat in that grove with her mother, smelling that smell, listening to the distant bleat of Duncan's sheep, thinking about things that needed healing. Hope usually thought about Guinevere. And about Jack. She wondered if Rachel did.

"Your mom's leg will heal," Jack said now. "Trust me on that."

Hope wanted to but wasn't sure she could. He had missed every one of her birthdays for the last eight years, and only six of those had come after the divorce. He had promised he would be there those first two times, then had been out of town, away, somewhere else. It didn't matter that he called and apologized and celebrated with her later. He had broken a promise.

Samantha said he cared more about buildings than kids. Samantha said that Rachel was *ten* times more trustworthy than Jack.

Only, Rachel wasn't there.

"This comes from the doctor," Jack insisted. "Her leg will heal."

Hope lowered her head, smoothed Guinevere's ruff, and was starting to silently repeat the words in a precious mantra when Samantha's voice came from the door.

"WHEN DID YOU get here?" she asked Jack.

He looked up and, for a minute, muddled by fatigue and nerves, thought he saw Rachel. It was partly the hair—blond but no longer as fine as Hope's, now as wavy and textured as Rachel's when they had met. It was partly the figure, more defined even in the six weeks since he had seen her last. Beneath a T-shirt similar to the one that swam on Hope, Samantha stood confident and as subtly curved as her mother. But it was the voice that clinched it, the echo of caution, even hurt, that he had heard in Rachel on their last night together—and suddenly he was back in their bedroom that night, sorting

53

through the closet for ties to pack while Rachel spoke from the door.

He could see her clear as day, with her tousled blond hair and gentle curves. She had just left the studio they shared on the top floor of their pink Mediterranean-style home in the Marina, and was wearing an old pair of slim jeans and one of his shirts. The once-white shirt was spattered with a dozen different colors, not the least of which was the aquamarine she had repainted their bedroom walls with several months before. Her face was pale and held the kind of disappointment that put him on the defensive in a flash.

"I thought you weren't going," she said.

"So did I, but I had to change plans." He pushed ties around on the rack, looking for ones to go with the suits he had laid out.

"We've had so little time. I was hoping you'd be here for a while."

He didn't turn, didn't want to see her pallor. "So was I."

"Couldn't you just . . . just . . . say no?"

"That's not the way it works," he answered, more sharply than necessary, but she sounded so reasonable and he felt so guilty, and he was tired; it had been that kind of week. "I've been hired to design a convention center. A big convention center. The basic design may be done, but that's the easy part. The hard part is fleshing it out for function and fit, and to do that, I have to feel the city more." He tossed down a tie and turned to her, pleading. "Think of your own work. You make preliminary sketches, but so does every other artist. Okay. Your skill sets you apart. But so do the choices you make on depth, attitude, medium, and you can't make those choices without spending time in the field. Well, neither can I."

She kept her voice low, but she didn't back down. "I limit my travel to one week twice a year, because I have responsibilities here. You're gone twice a month—three times, if you go to Providence tomorrow."

"This is my *work,* Rachel."

She looked close to tears. "It doesn't have to be."

"It does, if I want to succeed."

She folded her arms on her chest—he remembered that, remembered feeling annoyed, because she was such a slim thing, shutting him out with that gesture, and still barely raising her voice, which made what she said even stronger. "That leaves me alone here."

Only in a manner of speaking, he knew. "You have the girls. You could have friends if you wanted to do things besides paint. You could be out every night, if you wanted."

"But I don't. I never have, never once, not when we met, not now. I hate dressing up, I hate small talk, I hate standing around on spikey heels munching on pretty little caviar snacks."

"Not even for a good cause?" Charity fund-raisers were an integral part of social life in the Bay Area, particularly for someone like Jack. He needed to see and be seen. It was good for business.

Sadly, she said, "I can't paint here."

And painting was her world, which made him even *more* defensive and annoyed. "Every artist gets blocks."

"It's more than that." Those folded arms hugged her middle. "I'm dried up, creatively dead. I can't see color here. I can't feel subjects the way I used to. I don't need a shrink to tell me the problem. Art imitates life. I'm not happy here. I'm not satisfied. I don't feel complete. You and I are apart more than we're together."

barbara delinsky

"Then travel with me," he urged, shifting the responsibility to her.

She rolled her eyes. "We've been through this."

"Right. You won't leave the girls. You do it for your work, but not for mine. How do you think that makes me feel? Like a second banana, is how it makes me feel."

"Jack, they're *babies.*"

"They're seven and nine. They can live without you for a handful of days here and there."

"Handfuls of days add up. And maybe it's me. Maybe I can't live without them. It's different for mothers. Very different."

They had been through that before, too. He tossed more ties on the bed.

"Look at those," Rachel cried. "*Look* at those. They're so *conservative.* We were going to be different. We were going to do our *own* thing, not get caught up in the rat race."

"We've done our own thing. You freelance, I have my own firm."

She pressed her lips together. After a minute, she bowed her head.

"What?" he asked.

The eyes she raised were hollow, her voice low. "I won't be here when you get back."

"You said that last time."

"This time's for real."

He sighed. "Come on, Rachel. Try to understand."

"*You* try to understand," she cried, then quieted again. "If I have to be alone, there are other places I'd rather be. I'm moving to Big Sur." Softly, she asked, "Come with me?"

"Are you serious?"

56

"Very."

He was frightened. More, he was *furious*. She *knew* he couldn't move to Big Sur. Big Sur was *three hours* from San Francisco.

"I've done fifteen years here for you," she said, softly still. "Now it's your turn to live somewhere else for me."

"Rachel." Didn't she *get* it? "My firm is *here*."

"You travel all the time. You don't do much more than visit the city anyway. You can commute from Big Sur."

"That makes no sense."

She was hugging her middle again, seeming in pain. "I'm going. I need you to come with me."

Frustrated that she didn't understand the pressure he felt, exasperated that she couldn't give a little, angry that everything about her should suggest that . . . *pain,* he cried, "How can I do that, if I'm on my way to Providence?"

"Dad!" Samantha's shout brought him back to the present. "How *is* she?"

He ran a hand over his face and took a steadying breath. When he was firmly back in the present, he told her about the leg, the ribs, and the hand. Then he reached out and touched Hope's hair, wanting desperately to ease the blow but not knowing how. "The thing is that her head took a bad hit. She's still unconscious."

Hope's eyes flew to his. "Sleeping?" she asked on an indrawn breath.

"In a manner. Only, nothing we do wakes her up. The doctors call it a coma."

"Coma!" Samantha cried.

"No," Jack hurried to say, "it's not as bad as it sounds." He gave them a shortened version of the doctor's explanation, then improvised on a hopeful note.

"Coma is what the brain does when it needs to focus all its energy on healing. Once enough of the healing's done, the person wakes up."

"Not always," Samantha challenged. "Sometimes people are comatose for years. Sometimes *coma* is just another word for *vegetable*."

"Not the case here," Jack insisted. "Your mother will wake up."

"How do you know?"

He didn't, but the alternative was unthinkable. "The doctor had no reason to think she won't. Listen," he began, looking down to include Hope, but she was bent over her cat, shoulders hunched and quivering. He slid to the floor and put an arm around her. "We have to be optimistic. That's the most important thing. We have to go in there and *tell* your mom that she's going to get better. If we tell her enough, she will."

Samantha made a sound. He looked up in time to see her roll her eyes, but those eyes were tear-lidded when they met his.

"Do you have a better suggestion?" he asked.

Mutely, she shook her head.

"Okay. Then this is what I think we should do. I think we should have breakfast and drive up to Monterey."

Hope said something he didn't hear. He put his ear down. "Hmm?"

"Maybe I sh-should stay h-here." She hugged the cat to her chest.

"Don't you want to see your mom?"

"Yes, b-but—"

"She's scared," Samantha said with disgust. "Well, so am I, Hope, but if we sit home, we'll never know whether she really *is* alive."

"She's alive," Jack said.

Hope raised a tear-streaked face to her sister. "What if Guinevere dies while I'm gone?"

"She won't. The vet said she had time."

"Not much."

"Hope, she's not dying today."

"Am I missing something here?" Jack asked, looking from one to the other.

"Guinevere has a tumor," Samantha explained. "The vet wanted to put her to sleep, but Hope wouldn't let him."

So the cat was terminally ill. Jack was wondering what else could go wrong when Hope looked up through her tears and said, "She's not in pain. If she was, I'd let the vet do it. But I love Guinevere, and she knows it. I want her to keep knowing it a little longer. What's wrong with that?"

"Nothing," Jack said.

Samantha disagreed. "Priorities," she told her sister. "Mom's always talking about them. The thing is that Guinevere isn't dying today. If the accident hadn't happened, you'd have left her home and gone to school. So if you leave her home now, she won't know whether you're going to school or to visit Mom. But Mom will."

Jack was thinking that she had put it well, and that maybe there was hope for his elder daughter yet, when she turned to him in distaste and said, "You're gonna shave and stuff before we go, aren't you, Dad? You look gross."

"Thank you," he said. Patting Hope's shoulder, he pushed up from the floor and, needing fortification after—what?—an hour of sleep, went to put on a pot of coffee.

IT WAS EASIER said than done. He had explored the entire contents of both the fridge and the freezer in search of coffee beans before Samantha said, "In the canister."

He looked up. Both sisters were at the kitchen door, Hope a bit behind but watching as closely as Samantha. He tried to sound authoritative. "She always kept the beans in the fridge."

"Not anymore," Samantha replied, not loudly but with even greater authority. Rachel always did the same thing.

Knowing better than to question that tone, he pushed the fridge door shut. Rachel's canisters were brightly painted ceramic vegetables, all in a line on the counter. He opened a tomato and found sugar, opened a cabbage and found macaroni, opened an eggplant and found little nibbles of something he couldn't identify.

"Cat treats," Hope coached. "Try the cuke."

"The cuke has to hold spaghetti," he said and opened a fat yellow pepper to reveal flour. The cuke was the only thing left. "This isn't Rachel," he argued, feeling a little dumb as he measured spoonfuls of beans into a coffee mill. "A cuke is made for spaghetti. It's common sense. That's its shape."

"Mom says you have to break out of the mold sometimes," Samantha said. "When are we leaving?"

"As soon as I have coffee and a shower."

"How long is that?"

The kitchen clock—another ceramic thing that was no doubt also cast by Rachel's hand—was a beaver with whiskers that said it was seven-forty. "Twenty minutes." He arched a brow at Samantha. "Can you handle that?"

"You don't have to be snide. I was just asking. *We*

have to shower and dress, too, y'know, and if I'm not going to school, I need someone to take notes and get papers and give messages for me, so I have calls to make." She left, pulling her sister along with her.

Jack had calls to make, too, but they would have to wait. He had a feeling it was going to be a long day.

chapter four

HAD JACK KNOWN of any other road to take back to Monterey, he would have, but there wasn't a one. Samantha sat in the passenger's seat, hair wet from the shower, mouth clamped shut, eyes riveted to the road. Hope was stuffed in what passed for the BMW's backseat, staring out between the front buckets, her knuckles white on butter-soft black leather by her sister's shoulder, her cowboy boots planted on either side of the hump.

Jack knew what they were thinking. He was thinking it, too, hoping—*praying*—that Caltrans had finished its cleanup and left. Not knowing what else to do, he turned on the radio to create a distraction, and it did, for a minute.

"Just what we want to hear," Samantha remarked in response to an NPR report on starvation and death in another little African state. Between nervous glances at the road, she pressed another button, then another, then another. "Do you ever listen to *music?*"

"What was that a second ago?" Jack asked.

Samantha was working the manual controls. "Geek

chords, and we won't be able to get anything good here, the reception stinks." She flicked off the radio, clutched the hand loop above her door, and fixed alert eyes on the road.

Jack slowed the car to take the first of a series of turns. "What do you normally listen to?"

"CDs," Samantha snapped.

Hope shot her a timid glance. "Mom listens to news."

"Not when one of us is lying half dead in a hospital room."

"Your mother isn't half dead," Jack told Samantha.

"She's in a coma. What would you call that? People in comas die just as easily as not. Lydia had an uncle who was in a coma for months until they finally took him off the machines, and then he was dead in five minutes."

"Your mother's situation is entirely different. She isn't even on life support. The only machines in the room are ones to monitor her vital signs so they'll know if anything changes. She's—"

"*Look!*" Samantha pointed. "That's where it happened. See where the guardrail's gone, and all the mess of the dirt on the road where there isn't supposed to be dirt? That *is* where it happened, isn't it?" she charged, swiveling to watch as they passed the spot. "Slow down. I want to see."

Jack kept driving. "There's nothing to see. The car's been towed. It's probably already in the shop."

Both girls were looking out the back window. "Katherine said she was hit," Samantha said. "What happened to the other driver?"

"I don't know," Jack lied.

She flopped forward again. "You do, but you're not saying. I can tell by your voice. *Mom* would want us to know."

Jack doubted that very strongly, but it was beside the point. Annoyed at being pitted against Rachel, he said, "Right now, your mother would want you to say good things or nothing at all."

"That's what *you*'d say, not what she'd say. She'd want us to say what we think, and what I think is that this accident was more serious than you're saying, which means we're all in big trouble. What if she doesn't wake up?"

"She'll wake up."

"I'm not going to live in San Francisco. My friends are all here. I'm not moving."

"Good *God,* you have your mother dead and buried," Jack charged.

"Daddy?" came a frightened cry from behind.

He found Hope's face in the rearview mirror. "She's not dying, Hope. She'll be okay. I told you that, and I mean it. She was in an accident barely twelve hours ago. This is the worst of it. From here on it's about getting better. Let's take it one step at a time. For all we know, by the time we get to the hospital, your mother will be awake and asking for breakfast."

RACHEL wasn't asking for anything. She was as unresponsive when they arrived as she had been when Jack had seen her earlier. The tightness in his middle was back, the shock of seeing her this way, the fear that in the next breath she would be gone.

"She's sleeping," Hope whispered, and for a minute he thought she might be right. Aside from the bruise, Rachel looked almost normal. She might well have emerged from the coma and fallen into an innocent sleep.

64

The doctor might have tried to call him in the car and been unable to get through. Car phones were iffy that way.

He approached the bed, hoping, hoping. He rubbed her cheek. When she didn't respond, he gave her hand a squeeze. "Rachel?"

"Don't *bother* her," Hope cried in a fearful tone.

Samantha said nothing. Her eyes were wide, her face pale.

Backing to the open half of the sliding glass door, Jack stood with the girls while they adjusted to the scene, and he readjusted to Rachel's not having changed. When he had his disappointment in check, he said a quiet "See? No respirators, no life supports. She broke her leg. There's the cast. She cut her hand, so that's bandaged, and the bruises on her face are where she banged it against the car. Remember when you got a tennis ball in the eye, Sam? Black, blue, and purple for a week, then green, then yellow, then back to normal. But it took a while."

Samantha nodded. Her eyes didn't leave Rachel.

"The IV poles have medicine and food," he went on for lack of anything better to say. "The TV screen behind her registers things like heart, pulse, and oxygen. There's a person at the nurses' station who sees all that and knows if there's any change. They can also watch your mom through the glass. That's why she's here, instead of in a regular room."

Hope moved closer to his side.

"See the top readout?" he tried. "The heartbeat, that little green up-and-down line? See how regular it is?" He felt Hope nod against his arm. "Want to go let her know you're here?" The nod became a quick head shake. "Samantha?"

Without defenses, Samantha looked as young and frightened as Hope. "Can she hear us?"

"The doctor says so. It seems to me that if she can, she'd like to know you guys are here."

"What do we say?"

"Whatever you want."

"Are *you* going to talk to her?"

He knew a challenge when he heard it. Leaving them again, he approached the bed. Taking Rachel's hand, he leaned over and kissed her forehead. He stayed close, with an elbow braced on the bed rail. "Hi, angel. How're you doing? See, I said I'd be back, and here I am. Got the girls with me. They're over by the door. They're feeling a little intimidated by the machines and all."

"I am not intimidated," Samantha said and was suddenly beside him. "Hi, Mom." He heard her swallow, saw her fingers close around the bed rail. "It's me. Sam. God, look at your face. What did you *do?*" From the corner of her mouth closest to Jack, she whispered, "This is dumb. She *can't* hear."

"Do you know that for sure?"

"No."

"Then don't assume it." He looked around for Hope, who was still at the door. When he invited her over with the hitch of his head, she shrank back.

"What are they doing to wake her up?" Samantha asked.

"See that drip?" He pointed to one of the bags that may or may not have been the one the doctor meant. "That keeps the swelling in her head down, so that blood and oxygen can flow and heal the injured tissues."

"Why can't they just give her a shot or something to wake her up?"

"It doesn't work that way."

"Did you ask?"

"No."

"Did you ask for a *specialist?*"

He gave her a stare. "That was the first thing I did. Give me a little credit, huh?" To Rachel, lightly, he said, "Where did this one get her mouth?"

"Like you were perfect?" Samantha asked, not lightly at all.

Jack preferred his daughter when she was too frightened to be a smartmouth. He didn't know whether it was her age, or whether he just brought out the worst in her. In any case, he didn't want things going further downhill, not within earshot of Rachel.

"Tell you what," he said. "I'm going to leave you here to talk with your mother. Don't be bashful. Tell her how awful I am. Tell her that she'd better wake up, because you're *not* moving to the city. Tell her that I don't know *anything*. Get it all off your chest. I have some calls to make." He turned to find that Katherine had arrived and was standing with an arm around Hope. "Hey. Katherine. I'll be down the hall." As he passed, he told Hope, "Right down the hall. I won't be long."

He felt like a deserter leaving the room, but what was the point of staying? Samantha had nothing good to say with him there, Hope wouldn't budge from the door, and Rachel wasn't helping, not one bit.

"Is Dr. Bauer around?" he asked at the nurses' station.

"Tuesday mornings, he teaches in the city," said the nurse monitoring the screens.

"Are you Mr. McGill?" asked a woman who was doing paperwork nearby. She wore a silk blouse under her lab coat, and pearl earrings. They were large. Power

67

pearls. Jack suspected they were supposed to make her look older than the barely thirty that he guessed she was.

"Yes. I'm Jack McGill."

She put down her pen, extended a hand, and said, "I'm Kara. Dr. Kara Bates. I'm in neurology, second under Dr. Bauer. He checked your wife before he left. She's holding her own."

"But not awake yet. He mentioned cranial pressure. What's happening there?"

"It's the same."

"Then the drip isn't helping?"

"It may be, since she isn't getting worse. We'll have to wait a little longer to see improvement."

"And there's *nothing* else we can do in the meantime?" he asked, hearing Samantha in the words; but hell, he was scared, too.

"Not yet. Are those your girls?" Kara Bates asked with a glance toward the room.

On the other side of the glass, Katherine had coaxed Hope to Rachel's bedside. Though Samantha was nearly as tall as Katherine and a head taller than Hope, both girls looked very blond, very young, very frightened.

"I'm not sure I should have brought them. They might have been better off at home. I keep telling them this is temporary, but it's hard for them to see. I don't know what to say to make it better."

"Let me give it a try," Kara said.

Willing to forgive her the pretense of power pearls if she succeeded, Jack walked her back to the room, but he waited at the door while she went inside. Gently, she told the girls much of what Steve Bauer had told him earlier. They listened. Their eyes went from Rachel's face to Kara's and back. They nodded when Kara asked if they understood, and didn't balk when she told them what they could and should do. By the time she was done, Hope was standing at Rachel's side under her own power and Samantha was holding her mother's hand—and suddenly Jack felt angry that two strangers, two women who were no relation at all to his daughters, had been able to reach them when he couldn't.

His family wasn't supposed to be like that. *His* family was supposed to be cohesive and communicative. It was supposed to be everything his childhood family hadn't been.

Turning against a sense of failure, he strode down the hall to the phone.

FIGHTING mental static, he made two calls. Both were to San Francisco.

"Sung and McGill," said Christina Cianni. She had been with Jack since the firm's inception, back then as receptionist, general assistant, overall gofer. The ten years she had on Jack didn't show. Her hair was a rich mahogany, her olive skin smooth as ever, her smile ready, her manner calming. Sitting at the front desk in those early years, she had conveyed an aura of success long before they had any. Now she manned the front phone only when the regular receptionist was on break. She divided the rest of her time between keeping the books and doing PR. The most precious of her traits was her undying loyalty to Jack.

"Hi," he said in relief when her voice cut through the static in his head. She was an anchor in his suddenly topsy-turvy world.

"Jack! I'm so sorry to hear about Rachel! How is she?"

"Comatose. Her injuries wouldn't be all that serious if it weren't for the one to the head. But that's a tough one. I don't know what's going to happen."

"I can't begin to picture it. I'm so, so sorry. How are the girls?"

"Scared."

"Do you think she'd be better off at a hospital up here?"

"Not yet. This team seems on top of things, and if they are, there's no point moving her. But I want an expert to tell me for sure. Can you get me the name of the best neurologist in the city?"

"Done," she said with blessed confidence.

"What's happening there?"

There was a pause, then a pregnant "You don't want to know."

"We lost Montana?"

"Worse. We didn't. They rescheduled for next Tuesday."

He was tired enough to laugh. Only Tina understood him enough to put it that way. She had seen him through years of increasing success when the adrenaline was rushing and wild dreams were coming true. But something had happened to the joy. Lately, it was harder to come by. Lately, there was less actual designing, less creative satisfaction, and more business meetings, one after another after another after another.

"I should be flattered," he said. "What about Napa?" He had designed a restaurant there and was scheduled to meet with the owner, an electrician, a plumber, and a kitchen consultant.

"Next Wednesday."

"Good. I want shop drawings before then. And San Jose?" He was supposed to have a preliminary meeting with the owners of a computer company that had out-grown its space and wanted to build.

"Wednesday, also. David was pushing for this Friday. He wants to get them hooked. Lucky they couldn't make it. You're supposed to be in Austin on Friday." After the space of a breath, she asked, "Think you'll make it?"

Jack closed his eyes and massaged tired lids. Standing there at the phone, he felt shrouded in fog. "God knows. She could wake up later today. Or tomorrow. Or Thurs-day. Or next week. This is bizarre."

"Are you staying down there with the girls?"

"Well, I don't have clothes. But, yeah, I guess I am. Just for a night or two, until we know more of what's going on. Rachel will wake up. She's too healthy not to, but even then, her leg is smashed up, so she won't be doing much driving, which means I'll have to do some-thing about the girls." He pushed a hand through his hair. "Austin on Friday may be tight, but leave it for now. Clear my appointment book for tomorrow. I'll take it a day at a time."

"David won't be happy."

"No. I don't suppose he will." But Jack couldn't worry about David. There were now more urgent players in his life.

The second call he made was to one of those. His "Hey" was gentler, but the sense of wallowing in fog remained.

"Jack!" It came through with the delighted smile that he thrived on. Jill always liked hearing from him, liked being with him, and it showed. What man wouldn't value that?

"It's early," she said, still smiling audibly. "I didn't think you'd be calling so soon. Is your meeting done?"

"Never took place. I have a problem, Jill. Rachel's been in a car accident. She's in Intensive Care. I'm here with the girls."

There was a pause, then, minus the smile, a cautious "In Big Sur?"

"In Monterey. She's in a coma." He passed on the basics of the case. "She could wake up in five minutes, five days, five weeks—or never. The doctors have no way of knowing, and the girls are terrified. I can't leave them alone right now."

The pause that followed was long enough for him to hear the static in his mind loud and clear. Finally, Jill said, "You won't make it to the ball." Her disappointment was as obvious as her delight had been. She wore her feelings on her sleeve. Usually that was a plus. He preferred it when her feelings were positive.

"Not unless she wakes up within the next few hours. I'm sorry, Jill. I really am. I know what you've put into tonight, but you're not the only one I'm doing this to. I canceled three meetings today and just told Tina to do the same for tomorrow. I stand there looking at Rachel, thinking there has to be something that someone can do to bring her out of this, but no one has any answers. So it's a stinking, lousy waiting game."

"You can't be there all the time. Isn't there someone who can stay with the girls tonight?"

Duncan Bligh could, he supposed. Maybe even Katherine Evans. But Jack remembered the scene he had just witnessed and felt again the same annoyance—annoyance, defensiveness, pride. It had become a matter of principle.

72

"The girls are my responsibility. They're still young. They don't understand why this has happened. Not that I do. But I can't leave them, Jill. Not today. The situation is too shaky. I mean, I don't know what in the hell to say to them, how to make things better, but I can't just drive off. Trust me. This is not what I want to be doing right now."

"I'm the cochair of this," Jill said. What she didn't say, because she wasn't a shrew, but what Jack heard, was that she didn't want to be without a date.

"You told me you'd be running around most of the time."

"But I wanted you there." It wasn't whiney—mere statement of fact, which only increased his sense of guilt.

"I know." He pushed a hand through his hair, torn between what he knew Jill wanted and what he wanted to give her but couldn't. "I know. But I've slept a total of one hour in the last twenty-four. I drove down here with my laptop and scads of papers—no change of clothes, no comb, no razor. If I try driving back to the city, I'll either nod off at the wheel or in the middle of your lovely black-tie dinner. Either way, it wouldn't be pretty. I feel really bad, Jill. If I could be in two places at once, I would."

"She isn't your wife anymore."

This, too, was softly spoken, another simple statement of fact. What Jack heard was something entirely different. What he heard was, *I've dated you for two years, Jack. I've met your business partner, been at your business dinners, spent weekends with you here and in Tahoe—I've even met your daughters. Doesn't that say something? Haven't I finally come to mean more to you than your ex-wife?*

David had said something similar. Jack answered her

now in kind. "She may be my ex-wife, but there's nothing ex about the girls. They're still my daughters." No fog in his mind when it came to that. "They're only thirteen and fifteen. Their mother is in a coma from which she could either wake up or die, and the next day or two are crucial. How can I leave them alone here, so that I can go back to the city to party?" He caught sight of Katherine heading his way. "Hey, I gotta go. I'm really sorry, Jill. I'll call you later, okay?" He hung up the phone and drew himself up. Katherine looked like she might have gotten a little sleep, certainly had freshened up. Her pantsuit was linen and stylishly creased, her makeup immaculate, her long curls just so. Her expression was all business.

"Are the girls still with Rachel?" he asked.

"They are." She tucked a hand in her pants pocket. "Are you heading back to the city?"

"No. I just cancelled everything so that I can be here."

She looked startled by that. Then someone called her name. She swung her head around and paused for a second before breaking into a grin. "How goes it, Darlene?"

Darlene didn't miss a step. All big white teeth in a dark, dark face, she gave Katherine a thumbs-up in passing and was gone.

Jack pushed off from the phone booth. When Katherine fell into step beside him, he said, "You didn't think I'd stay?"

"I didn't know what to think. All I know about you is what I've heard from Rachel. And it sounded like you were better at leaving than staying put. She felt abandoned."

That quickly, he stopped. Katherine did the same. "Abandoned?" he echoed. "I didn't walk away from this marriage. Rachel did. She was the one who packed up and left the city."

Katherine looked about to say something, then pressed her lips together and simply nodded.

"Go ahead," he invited. "Say what you want." He was just tired enough, just frustrated enough, just worried enough to pick a fight.

She thought for a minute. When she spoke, her tone was innocuous, but there was challenge in her eyes. "I was going to say, the way Rachel sees it, you'd already left. Her moving on was just in response. San Francisco stifled her. She couldn't paint there. She was frustrated, and bored."

"If she was bored, it was her own fault. There were dozens of things she could have done and didn't." He told himself to walk on. This wasn't the time or place. But Katherine Evans had scratched a festering scab. He stood his ground. "She blamed *me* because she was bored?"

Katherine gave a small shrug. "The only person she wanted to do things with in the city was you, but you weren't around."

"No, I wasn't." *Definitely* not the time or place, but hell, this friend of Rachel's had accused him of abandonment, and beyond keeping his voice low, he couldn't let the charge go unanswered. "I was working my tail off to build a successful practice, so that I could keep us housed and fed and, P.S., let her paint without worrying about earning money. She wouldn't take money from her parents. I wanted to give her everything I thought she deserved." *Enough!* a voice inside him said, but the rest of him didn't listen. "What in the hell did I ask of her? To dress up and go out once or twice a week? Was that so much? God only knew she did it enough as a kid. She was *raised* dressing up. She could do the party thing with her eyes closed. Besides, she knew it was business. If you're trying to build a name, you have to be seen."

"She knew that," Katherine conceded. "The traveling bothered her more. To hear her tell, you were on the road more often than not."

Jack turned away, swearing under his breath, then turned back in the very next beat. "Rachel told you all that? Funny, she didn't tell me about you. Who the hell are you, to be coming between my wife and me?"

"It's *ex-wife*," Katherine said, seeming bewildered, "and you asked. Who I am is Rachel's *friend*. I love her and the girls. They're like family. I don't want them hurt."

"And I do? Wrrrrrong." This time when he set off, he kept going.

IF SIMPLY to spite Katherine Evans, Jack stuck to his daughters like glue. He stayed with them at Rachel's bedside for a time, took them to breakfast in the cafeteria, returned with them to sit with Rachel again, took them to lunch. In between, he spoke with a neurologist from the city, who agreed to see Rachel the next day.

Of the medical personnel who came and went from Rachel's room, the nurse heading the case was the most encouraging. Her name was Cindy Winston. She wore white leggings, a long blouse to hide plumpness, and thick glasses, but there was a quiet to her, an endearing shyness. She spoke slowly and softly and seemed kind as could be. If Kara Bates was a teacher, Cindy Winston was a friend. The girls hung on her every word.

"Keep talking," she told them. "Tell her what you've been doing." She looked at Rachel. "Tell her jokes. Tell her you're sad. Or angry. Or scared." She looked at the girls again. "You can laugh, or cry. Those are all normal things. She'll understand them."

"What if we run out of things to say?" Samantha asked.

Cindy studied her own hand. "Then touch her. That's important. See me?" Though she was addressing the girls, Jack looked. She was massaging Rachel's shoulder, had been doing it the whole time she was talking. "Your mother feels. Touching is a way to connect." She demonstrated with measured movements. "Don't be afraid to lift her hand. Or bend her knee. Or brush her hair. Or move her fingers or toes." She let that sink in, then asked, "Does she have a favorite scent?"

Hope's eyes lit. "Lily of the valley."

"You could bring some in."

"And it'll help?"

"It can't hurt."

UNFORTUNATELY, Cindy Winston's comfort was short-term and specific. More generally, more *urgently,* Jack wanted to know when Rachel was going to wake up, but no one was saying.

He drank so much coffee to stay awake that by late afternoon he was starting to shake. When Katherine arrived with several friends, he barely heard the introductions. As soon as they were done, he ushered the girls to the car.

They had barely hit the road when, in a big, bold voice, Samantha said, "So what do we do?"

"Do?" It was too general, and he was too tired. How to answer?

"If Mom dies."

"She's not going to die."

"Then if she lies there for a while. Who's taking care of us?"

"Me."

"Where?" The word was thick with distrust. He remembered what she had said earlier about not living in San Francisco. This wasn't the time to challenge her, not about a quandary so far down the road, not to mention an improbable one. Rachel would wake up. There might even be a message on the machine saying that she already had, by the time they got home.

"Big Sur." The logical short-run choice. He wasn't thinking about work, couldn't think about work. "If there's no change by tomorrow, I'll drive up for clothes while you guys are in school."

Sam was horrified. "We can't go to school."

"You can't not go. It's the end of the year. Aren't exams coming up?"

"Yes, but—"

"I'll pick you up at school." Since the school in Big Sur went only to sixth grade, the girls were bused to Carmel. From Carmel to the hospital in Monterey was a ten-minute drive. "You can spend the rest of the day at the hospital."

"Like I can *really* concentrate on classes?"

"I really think you should try. I really think your mother would want you to. I really think we have to try to maintain a sense of normalcy."

"*Nothing* is normal."

It was a truth so bluntly stated that he wanted to strangle her. "Look, your mom's apt to wake up anytime now. This won't go on forever."

"How do you know?" came Hope's small voice from behind.

He caught her eye in the rearview mirror. "Because it *won't*. Your mother is young and healthy. She'll heal. She'll wake up."

"You don't know it for sure," Samantha argued.

"No. But what's the alternative? Would you rather assume she's going to die?"

"No! I just don't know what's happening! There's a mess of things we're supposed to be doing, doctor and dentist—"

"My picnic—"

"My prom, for which I have *no dress*. Mom was taking me shopping this week, but if she's in the hospital, who'll do it?"

"Me," Jack said.

She sagged into the seat and looked out the window. "Yeah. Right. You don't have time. You never have time."

"I'll make time."

"Like you made time for my gymnastics meets?"

Her gymnastics meets. She hadn't done gymnastics in years, not since well before the divorce. There had been a time when he attended every meet. Then work had come in the way and he had missed more and more. She had been young. He wouldn't have thought she remembered. He was shaken that she did, and with such venom.

"This is different," was all he could say. Then, angered at being put on the defensive when there were two sides to every story, he held up a hand. "Y'know, what's happened to your mother is kind of hard on me, too. I'm past the point of being tired right now. What I'd like is a little silence."

"Did you call Grandma?"

He let out a defeated breath. Incredibly, he hadn't thought about Victoria Keats. But then, not incredibly at all. Victoria sent lavish gifts but rarely visited in the flesh. Since the gifts were largely unwanted and went unused, her presence in their lives was minimal. There were phone calls, but they were often more trying than not.

"Nope," he said as gently as he could. "Haven't called Grandma. Think I'll wait. If your mom wakes up soon, there won't be much need." He was taking the coward's way out, but what the hell, he had enough else to deal with without that.

He felt Hope even before she spoke, a tiny, timid warmth by his shoulder. "What'll we do for dinner?" she asked.

Jack thought of black tie and tails, beef Wellington, elegant dancing at the Fairmont with Jill, who adored him—and the same static he had heard earlier rang in his ears again. Dinner, shopping, doctor, dentist, picnic— with a glint of panic, he wondered if he was up for the task Rachel had set him.

What were they doing for dinner? "Something," he answered gruffly. "Now, shh. Let me rest."

"Are you going to fall asleep at the wheel?" Samantha asked, but the question was more frightened than snide.

"Tell you what," he said, "it's your job to make sure I don't. Watch my face. If my eyes close, hit me. Okay?"

THE REST of the ride was accomplished in silence. Jack was aware that the sky was clear, that a low western sun skipped over the ocean to gild the hills, that it was spring and not winter. But he was too tired to absorb details, too numb to see color.

The spot where the accident had happened came and went without comment. They reached the oak grove and the bank of mailboxes, left the highway, and were quickly immersed in the canyon's growth, trees thickening as they climbed. The instant they pulled up at the cabin, Hope said something about seeing Guinevere and raced from the car. Samantha followed, squawking about urgent phone calls.

Jack straightened and closed the car door, then stood rooted to the spot much as he had been earlier that day. Something about the air held him captive, something about the late afternoon shade, the grandeur of the redwoods, the silence, the smell.

The smell. That was it. It was clean, strangely sweet, unique. He inhaled, exhaled.

And the silence. Listening to it, he realized that the static in his head had cleared. He stood a bit longer, savoring the novelty.

Then, having gotten a second wind, he went in to see about dinner.

chapter five

HOPE WOKÉ UP with a stomachache. Curling into a ball, she had barely pulled the comforter over her head and begun to wish that Rachel was there when she heard a plaintive meow. She threw the comforter back and was up in an instant. Guinevere was crouched on the wood floor, eyeing her beseechingly. Not far from her was a middle-of-the-night accident.

"Ooooh, baby, it's okay, it's okay," Hope cooed, gently lifting the cat and cuddling her. "That's no problem, no problem at all. I can clean it up right away. You're such a good girl." With exquisite care, she placed the cat in her bed and ran to clean up the mess before Samantha or, worse, her father could see.

SAMANTHA woke up with a crick in her neck. It wasn't until she clamped the phone to her ear with a shoulder and winced that she knew its cause. *Repetitive tongue disorder,* her mother called it. But what could she do?

She'd had to call Shelly about math, John about science, Amanda about Spanish, and by the time that was done, Brendan was calling to talk about nothing in the annoying way he had of thinking she was interested in just the sound of his voice. And then there was Lydia. What time had they hung up? Twelve-thirty? One?

"ICU, please," she told the receptionist. When a nurse came on, Samantha identified herself with the confidence her mother said would get her answers. It was an act. She felt no confidence at all deep inside, in the place that feared Rachel might have died during the night. "How's my mom?"

"She's doing just fine."

Samantha's hopes soared. "She woke up?"

"No. Not yet."

So what is "just fine" supposed to mean? Samantha thought. "Thank you," she said with more disappointment than grace, and hung up the phone. Gnawing on her cheek, she wrapped tight arms around her knees and rocked on her bottom. So this was her punishment, this being left alone with her father. It was Rachel proving the point she had been trying to make the afternoon before, that though Samantha might complain that her mother wouldn't let her get a tattoo, she had no idea how lucky she was.

Samantha thought about that argument. If it hadn't taken place, Rachel wouldn't have been distracted. She would have put her book-group book down in the kitchen, instead of carrying it to the studio. If she hadn't gone back there for it, she would have been on the road two minutes sooner, and if she had done that, she wouldn't have been hit. So was the accident Samantha's fault?

It wasn't fair. She studied as hard as she could and still got B's instead of A's. She couldn't play the flute like Lydia or sing like Shelly. She had been best at gymnastics, then she had *grown*. So now her looks were her strength—and what good did it do? Rachel fought her at every turn. The coolest kids were piercing third holes in their ears and getting ankle tattoos. The *coolest* kids were wearing mascara and tight tops to school. Lydia wasn't, but she wasn't *cool*. Poor, sweet, dorky Lydia—who was getting cold feet; Samantha knew it.

She also knew that if *Rachel* hadn't liked her prom plans, Jack was going to like them even less.

JACK woke up with a hard-on. He didn't bother to think back on what he'd been dreaming. No need. Rachel was everywhere—in the rowdy billow of fabric topping the windows, the velour robe hooked on the door, the nubby shawl draped on the rocking chair, the dried flowers in a vase that was plump, green, and—so help him—fertile. She was in the overflowing basket of clothes waiting to be washed, the haphazard pile of books and magazines that sat on the floor beside a huge hand-sculpted piece of clay with multiple arms holding baseball hats and a cowboy hat that went with the boots below. The chaos was vintage Rachel, but hell, he could keep his eyes *closed* and see her. The scent of lilies permeated the sheets.

Throwing grogginess aside, he grabbed the phone. When he heard a click and no dial tone, he pressed the button several times, wondering what else could possibly go wrong. Mercifully, the dial tone came.

It was only a minute before he learned, with relief, that Rachel was still alive; with fear, that she was still comatose; and with unexpected pride, that Samantha had had the wherewithal to call the hospital on her own.

He wasn't used to feeling emotions so early in the day, much less three such hefty ones. At least his erection was gone. He didn't want to have to analyze that.

Pushing the covers aside, he went to the window, hooked an elbow on the frame, and peered out. Morning fog filled the canyon, but it was different from the fog that filled his courtyard in the city. This one was softer, gentler. It was flannel gray and fuzzy green, and for a minute, not understanding what lured him, he just stood there and watched. Nothing moved. Nothing changed. He saw trees, moss, and fog. His eyes lapsed into a sleepy stare.

"Daddy?"

He looked over his shoulder at the door. Hope's face was all that showed through a narrow wedge of space.

"I don't feel good, Daddy. My stomach hurts."

Just that quickly, so did Jack's. He straightened. "Hurts, as in pain?" If it was appendicitis, he would pull his hair out.

"No. Not pain."

"Ache?"

"I guess."

He went to the door and touched her cheek. "You don't feel feverish. Think it was something you ate?"

"I don't know. But if I go to school and start feeling sick, they'll have to call *you,* and if you're in the city, you can't come, so maybe I should just stay in bed."

She didn't look sick to him. She didn't feel sick to him. The freckles she had inherited from Rachel lay soft on creamy skin. "Don't you want to see your mother?"

Her eyes widened. "If I sleep this morning, I can go when Sam goes, can't I?"

She seemed genuine enough about that. So it had to be the cat. "Where's Guinevere?"

Bingo. He saw instant worry. "In bed. I don't think she feels good, either. If I stay here with her, the *two* of us will feel better."

Jack rubbed the back of his neck. What to say? "Well, that sounds fine. Except what if one of you isn't feeling great tomorrow, either? Or the day after that?" The cat was dying. Dying didn't get better in a day or two. "Between your mother and Guinevere, you could miss the rest of the school year. I don't think either of them would want you doing that."

"But if I go to school and then go see Mom, Guinevere will be here alone for a whole, long day."

"Didn't Sam say she'd sleep most of the time?"

A meek nod.

"Well?"

A hard swallow. "She's my cat. I can't leave her all alone. Not . . . not now. I love her."

He pushed a hand through his hair, but the gesture seemed inadequate even to him. So he put an arm around her shoulders. They felt small and frail under a T-shirt that reached her knees and was nearly as wide. Bare bits of skinny leg showed between where the T-shirt ended and her cowboy boots began. "I know you love her, Hope." He tried to think of a solution. If children were buildings, he could redraw the background. He was creative when it came to architecture, not parenting. "You'll be with her all weekend."

She didn't say anything, just looked up at him with fear on her face and the beginning of tears in her eyes, neither of which made him feel great.

He had a thought. "What would your mom say?"

Hope gave a one-shouldered shrug.

"Would she let you stay home from school?"

"No. But she'd be here to check on Guinevere."

And he wouldn't. It went without saying. He was dropping the girls at school in Carmel, heading north to Monterey and the hospital, driving north again to San Francisco, back down to get the girls at school, up to the hospital again. Big Sur was forty-five minutes south of Carmel. It didn't make sense to add ninety minutes, round trip, to all that other driving, just for the sake of the cat.

"I can't leave her alone, Daddy," Hope begged. "Not all day. Not when she's so sick. Would you leave Mommy lying there all alone, all day long?"

"Mommy's different. There are doctors and nurses—" He realized he had fallen into a trap when she began nodding.

Sighing, he gave in. But he really didn't want Hope missing school—okay, largely because he *really* didn't want to have to drive down to get her midday. There had to be another way. "What about Duncan?" If the man was so all-fired devoted, he could do this. "Think he'd check on her?"

Hope looked skeptical. "He's gone a lot, too. But he comes home for lunch." She brightened marginally. "I could ask."

DUNCAN had a counteroffer that Hope liked even better, though Jack had no idea why. He didn't understand why Guinevere would be better off spending the day at Duncan's than at her own house.

"He has faith," was all Hope said when Jack asked,

and he didn't push. He had been hearing about Duncan's faith for years. The girls mentioned it in the same breath with the man's name, so often that Jack had actually asked Rachel whether Duncan belonged to a cult. Big Sur had its share of free spirits, aging hippies, sun worshipers, he was told. Rachel had laughed roundly.

So Duncan was religious. Fine. What mattered more to Jack was that in the rush to get dressed and carry the cat, litter, and food to the small ranch three minutes up the road, Hope forgot about her stomachache.

Jack waited by the car while she got the cat settled. When Duncan came out, he said, "Thanks. This means a lot to her."

"How's her mother?"

"The same. I'm heading there now."

"Better call Ben."

"Who's Ben?" he asked, but before Duncan could answer, Hope had taken the big man's hand and was looking up at him with reverence.

It was some picture—beautiful Hope, with sunny blond hair, hazel-gold eyes, and now, finally, just a touch of color under her freckles, and Duncan, who approached homely with his big white beard, long ears, and leathery hands.

"I'll come for her later," Hope was saying.

The big man nodded, gave her hand a squeeze, and nudged her toward Jack.

WHEN JACK arrived at the hospital, Rachel was freshly bathed, lying on crisp white sheets, smelling as antiseptic as she had the day before. He had brought a tube of cream from her bathroom and began rubbing it onto those stretches of her skin that were bare.

"Better," he said when the scent of lilies rose. "More you. I'm flattered. I'd have thought you would switch." He touched lotion to her cheeks, working carefully around the bruise. "Black-and-blue here," he told her. "If they didn't know better, they'd be wondering who hit you. Good thing I was in San Francisco." Not that he had ever raised a hand to Rachel—*or* to either of the kids. For, whatever other faults he had, that wasn't one. As the son of an avid disciplinarian, he had seen enough raised hands to last him a lifetime. "I'll bet you have a headache."

She didn't respond. Her hand lay limp, her arm dead weight. He studied her eyes for a sign of movement behind the lids. When there was none, he checked the monitor screen. Her heartbeat was undulating evenly. She was definitely alive. He wondered if she found his worry amusing.

He told her about getting the cat to Duncan's, about waiting ten minutes for Samantha to finish blowing her hair stick straight, about dropping the girls at school with minutes to spare. He told her his plans for the day. He told her that she was messing up his life in a major way, and when she didn't respond even to that, he left the room in a fit of frustration.

He found Kara Bates in the hall. The pearl earrings had been replaced by onyx squares, powerful in their own right on ivory lobes, a foil for black hair knotted stylishly in back. So, she wanted to be taken seriously? He could give her that chance.

"Shouldn't Rachel be reacting to something by now?" he demanded. "It's been a day and a half."

Kara stuck a thumb over her shoulder. "It's been a

month and a half for the family in there. These things take time, Mr. McGill. Your wife isn't getting worse. Her stats are stable. There's been no drop in oxygen saturation, no rise in arterial pressure. We have to assume that something's working the right way in there."

"Easy for you to say."

"No," she said crisply. "Not easy at all. I want to *do,* not to wait. This isn't easy for any of us."

"I have a neurologist coming from the city. He said he'd be by today."

She reached behind the desk and produced a business card. "He was already here. He suggests that you call him midafternoon."

"Did he see her file?"

"Her file, her, everything. He says he agrees with our diagnosis. He doesn't feel that anything else should be done right now."

Jack ran a hand through his hair. Another hope thwarted. "If you were to make a guess as to when she'll wake up—"

"I can't do that."

If she wanted to play in the majors, she had to do better. "Try."

She simply shook her head. "I'd like to give you hope, but I just—don't—know. Head injuries are like that. The best I can do is to say that Rachel is a good candidate for recovery."

That was only part of what Jack wanted to hear.

HE SHOULD have felt better driving north toward San Francisco. This was his city, his turf. It was where his home was, where his business was. He had seen remarkable success here, had felt the headiness of landing plum jobs and the satisfaction of seeing his designs built. He was known here, respected here. He had a potential significant other here.

But his middle grew tighter the closer he got and was joined by an odd grogginess. It was like his mind was a leg that had fallen asleep. Tingly. Dense.

He stopped at his house first, hoping to get his bearings there, but the place felt cold. Frequent traveler that he was, he tossed a duffel on the bed, quickly filled it with clothes, packed up razor, shaving cream, hairbrush—seeing little of it, barely thinking. In the studio, he stuffed a briefcase with papers from the fax, a portfolio with plans in varying stages of completion. He didn't bother to look out at the courtyard. Nothing to see—it was foggy again. He spent a total of ten seconds flipping through yesterday's mail before tossing it aside, then started out the door, stopped short, and returned. Standing in the front hall, whose walls had been rag-painted a charcoal gray that he had thought handsome at the time, he called Jill.

"How'd it go?" he asked as soon as she said hello.

"Jack! Where are you?" The enthusiasm in the simple question invited more.

"My place, but not for long. A quick stop at the office, then I'm headed back. I told the girls I'd pick them up at school. Rachel is still comatose. How was last night?"

"It was fine. Successful."

"I knew it would be. You do things like that so well." She was a warm, generous hostess, whether entertaining at home, at a restaurant, or in a ballroom. They had met as fellow guests at someone else's party two years before, and he had been immediately impressed. She was poised and intelligent, knew how to ask questions, could discuss politics with the best of them, but—important, here—knew when not to. "How much did you raise?"

"We're still tallying the last of the raffle receipts, but it looks like we topped a quarter of a million."

"That's great, Jill. Good for you. You must be thrilled." He *was* pleased for her, even if his voice didn't show the inflection. She had worked hard. She deserved good results.

"I missed you," she said.

I missed you, too, he should have been able to say. But he was too preoccupied with Rachel's condition to have thought much about Jill. "You deserve better than a guy who ducks out at the last minute, even though his reasons are good. Was it very awkward?" He was inviting her to yell at him, all the while knowing she wouldn't.

"No. You were right. I was running around. You'd have been stranded. Will I see you, Jack?"

"Not enough time, Jill."

"Not even for a *minute?* Just a quick run in on the way to the office?"

"I can't."

"When will you be back again?"

She had asked that question often during the past two years. Jack traveled constantly. Any woman he dated knew that. Jill was the first who had accepted it graciously. And why not? She had her own life, her own causes, her own friends, and was a mature, giving individual. He loved those things about her. He especially loved the fact that she made him feel wanted. He would always need that. But she didn't nag—and she wasn't nagging now, though the question sounded different this time. He could have sworn he sensed fear. It was the same fear that he had sensed a time or two before, when she alluded to a future together.

Usually he skirted the issue by blaming his work. "You don't want to be tied to a man married to work," he would tease. Or he would say, "Let me get through this patch, and we'll talk again," or even, "My life isn't my own, Jill, not with so many big projects going on."

This time he simply said, "I'll be back as soon as I can. Pray for Rachel?"

Knowing that, bless her, she would probably do just that, he drove to the office, but the minute he pulled into the space that he paid dearly for each month, he had the urge to back right out and leave. There were problems here, too many to label or count—none to do with economic survival, though that was what he had spent a lifetime fearing. More to do with *him*. He felt confused. The grogginess in his head became a buzz. He wanted to run, escape, *flee*.

But this was his firm. As a name partner, he had a responsibility to the twenty-some-odd people that he and David employed.

Taking the stairs two at a time, he crossed through the brick-walled foyer with only a passing nod at the receptionist. He strode down the hall, looking at none of the open cubicles lest his eye be caught, and didn't stop until he reached Tina Cianni's glass-enclosed office.

She was on the phone. Eyes widening, she hung up within seconds. "What are you doing here, Jack? You're supposed to be in Monterey." More cautiously, she said, "How is she?"

"Alive. But still comatose."

Tina released a breath. "Well, the alive part is good. How are the girls?"

"Hanging in there. What's doing?"

She paused, gave him a warning look. "You don't want to know."

Again? "Is it worse than a coma?"

"David would say it is," she said dryly. "Michael Flynn was supposed to have revised plans done for Buffalo last night. Calls are coming in fast and furious. Every day those windows don't go in is costing John Perry a pretty penny."

Jack knew that all too well. The last time he had worked with this particular developer—on a series of housing clusters—heavy snows had brought work to a standstill at three crucial points. Each day of delay meant another day carrying the construction mortgage with interest. This time the project was an art gallery with adjoining studios, a project closer to Jack's heart than most, and the windows had come in wrong. The contractor swore he had ordered the right ones. Whether he had or not was moot. Reordering and waiting for delivery could set them back two months.

As designing partner, Jack had done the original work. He had revised the plan to incorporate the windows as delivered. Michael Flynn, as his project manager, was supposed to see that what Jack designed was built, which meant making blueprints of Jack's revisions, getting them to Buffalo, and following them there posthaste.

"Where is Michael?"

"Home. He ran out of here at three yesterday to take his two-year-old to the doctor. She was having a massive poison ivy attack, and his wife panicked. He was rear-ended on the way home, then tripped and fell down a flight of stairs with the child in his arms. It's a miracle neither of them was killed. The little girl is fine. Michael thinks he broke his ankle. It's swollen. He's going for X rays."

The buzz in Jack's head grew louder. "Where's everyone else?"

"They're working, but it's slow. When Michael ran out, he implied that he was nearly done, but he wasn't. Alex and Brynna are on it."

Jack took a tired breath. He should have been irate. His name would be the one tarnished if Buffalo was upset. His reputation was the one at stake.

But he felt numb. "What else?"

"Boca. Regulations and committees. Back to the drawing board."

The project in Boca was a combined office building and shopping mall. He had already revised the design not once, not twice, but *three* times to satisfy the quirks of one vocal member of one crucial committee. With preliminary approval of that revised design, he had put two draftsmen to the task of producing working drawings. He had already compromised to the limit, not to mention swallowed wasted hours for which he had to pay his draftsmen without reimbursement. Was the money worth it?

Tina was right. He didn't want to be there.

"Shall I cancel you out for tomorrow?" she asked.

"Yeah."

"You look done in. Did you sleep?"

"Some." Dropping his head back, he eyed the ceiling. He couldn't focus on Buffalo, couldn't focus on Boca. But he was the leader of the firm, and morale was low.

So he walked down the hall and stopped at one cubicle after another, making his presence felt in the barest way—a question here, a suggestion there—wading through the static in his head for relevance. He was singly responsible for three-quarters of the design work the firm did. It was good work, increasingly important work. *Metropolitan Home* had photographed his museum in Omaha; *Architectural Digest* was doing a piece on his library in Memphis. He was getting invitations to bid on some of the most exciting projects—that, and repeat clients. Every architect dreamed of tying himself to a conglomerate with ongoing projects, and the dream was coming true for Sung and McGill. Still, Jack felt detached, felt angry to be in the office.

Mercifully, David was on-site in Seattle. Jack wasn't up for explaining himself. How could he explain what he didn't understand?

His own office was in a far corner of the suite. Like his studio at home, it harbored more business than art. Oh, there were pictures on the wall, lots of black-and-white under glass, elegant renderings of his favorite projects, reprints of magazine pieces—and for a minute, looking at them, he felt that old glory and the glow. There had been nothing, absolutely nothing, like the high of seeing his first design turned into a home. And there were other highs—the high of designing something bigger, more complex, more expensive; the high of winning an award or being solicited for work by a client so powerful that Jack was stunned. He felt pride. Yes, he did. But it was distant.

He needed a break. Maybe that was it. He had been working nonstop for too long. He and Rachel used to take vacations, trekking through remote areas of Canada or South America, always with pads and pencils, often with the girls. Since the divorce, he hadn't taken more than an occasional long weekend to himself, and then always for something more lazy and posh. Jill wasn't a trekker. She was a skier, so they did that together. But it didn't clear his head the way vacations with Rachel had.

Maybe he was burning out. There had to be an explanation for the revulsion he felt.

Then again, the revulsion could be from fatigue. Or worry. Any normal person would feel shell-shocked given the recent turn of events. Any normal person would feel the need to decide what was most urgent and focus solely on that.

Rachel called it prioritizing. This time, at least, she was right.

Pocketing a pile of telephone messages, he returned to the front desk and told Tina to cancel Austin.

Then he headed south to Monterey.

FOR A PETITE woman, Rachel had incredibly elegant arms and legs. Jack had always attributed that elegance to a grace of movement, but he saw it now even as she lay inert. He rubbed lotion over her hand—flexing it from fingertip to knuckle to wrist as he had seen the nurses do—then smoothed it along her forearm to her elbow. Her upper arms had no fat, just the gentle muscle of an active woman. He had always admired that in her. She wasn't one to play the weaker sex, was as quick to lift what needed to be carried as to ask for help.

Admirable. Humbling. Hard to be the stronger sex when she just took it upon herself to do things. He remembered being furious with her, way back in Tucson, when they had moved in together. They had been dating for three months, had decided that paying two rents was

barbara delinsky

foolish, and had chosen his place over hers for its size
and its sun. On the appointed day, he had raced to her
apartment straight from school to start moving, only to
find nine-tenths of the furniture already gone. And there
she was in his place, sweaty, dirty, grinning from ear to
ear as she pointed out where everything was and how
well it fit. His fury didn't last long. She was too excited,
too proud, to eager to make life easier for him. Lord, he
had loved her for that strength.

Strength. Independence. Self-reliance. Stubbornness.

"Hi." Katherine's voice brought him back. She was
another strong one, here to see her friend even when her
friend's husband—*ex*-husband—kept taking his frustra-
tions out on her.

"Hi," he said, determined to be kind. "How's it going?"

"It'd be better if Rachel woke up. Still sleeping?"

"Still sleeping. I bore her."

Katherine actually smiled. "She said you weren't
always boring. She said you were fun at the beginning."
The smile faded. "She looks the same. Isn't there *any*
change medically?"

"None. I was hoping she'd be awake by now." That
was one major source of worry. He sought Katherine's
thoughts on another. "Think I should call her mother?"

The sudden caution on Katherine's face said she knew
something about Victoria Keats.

"What do you say, Rachel?" Jack asked dryly. "Should
I call your mom?"

He half expected Rachel to jump up and cry, *No! no!
no!* The fact that she didn't do so much as blink said a lot
about the depth of her sleep. She and her mother didn't
get along. As far as Rachel was concerned, Victoria combined the worst of new wealth and of corporate America.

She was more materially than personally involved with life, even when it came to her only child. He doubted Rachel would want the woman near her—unless, perhaps, she was dying.

"I'll wait a little longer," he told Katherine. "She's bound to wake up soon. My man from San Francisco examined her and agreed with Bauer's plan. So we all wait." He grunted. "This isn't how I like to operate."

Katherine took a hairbrush from the bed stand. "No, I don't guess that it is. Men like action. This brush is hers. Did you bring it?"

"Yes, and you're only part right. Men like *progress*. They don't care how it's achieved, as long as it is. So maybe it's happening." He studied Rachel's face, studied the pale lashes lying in a perfect crescent beneath her eyes, a whisper of freckles, scrapes and an ugly bruise, a slack mouth.

Katherine began brushing Rachel's hair. Her fingernails flashed as she worked. "Are the girls in school?"

Jack could have sworn those fingernails had been brown the day before. Today they were red.

"Yup. In school." Moving the sheet aside, he warmed lotion in his hands and began rubbing it onto Rachel's uncasted leg. "I didn't think Rachel would want them missing another day. Besides, I had to drive to the city and didn't want them here alone the whole time. I'll pick them up in an hour. They'll see her then." He eyed the monitor. "This is hard for them."

Katherine slipped an arm under Rachel's head, gently raised it, and began brushing the hair in back. "I have a hunch this is only part of it."

He paused. Carefully, he flexed Rachel's knee. "What do you mean?"

"I have a hunch that your being here raises other issues."

"The divorce? Uh, I don't think so. They're worried about their mother. They're worried about a school picnic and a prom. They're worried about who's cooking dinner tonight. They're not thinking about the divorce. The divorce is old news."

"They're thinking about it," Katherine insisted, all pretense of hunches gone. "I'd wager Samantha's *obsessed* with it. She's resenting authority anyway. Most teenagers do. It's the age. She's been pushing her limits with Rachel, and now suddenly you're in the picture, taking over after being out of her daily life for so long. She's probably thinking that you don't have the right to tell her what to do."

"Did she say that?"

"No. But I'd guess she's wondering why you're here." She raised her brows and said in a mild singsong, "I've wondered it myself." She gently returned Rachel's head to the pillow and began brushing the hair in front.

Jack stared at her for an astounded minute, looked down at Rachel, then back. "My wife is in a coma. Where else would I be?"

"She's your ex-wife. You keep forgetting that. Is it an unconscious slip?"

"Rachel and I share more than a decade together and two children. It's only natural that I'm here. Don't make more of it than it is."

"It *is* more, if you still love her."

He did not. "We've been divorced for six years. I barely know who she is now and what she's done all that time. How can I love a woman I don't know?"

"Men cling to memories, sometimes. You wouldn't be the first."

"You're amazing." He didn't mean it as a compliment.

She stopped her brushing and smiled. "Is this another fight? I love fighting my friends' battles when they can't do it for themselves, and Rachel can't, that's for sure." The smile waned as she looked at Rachel. "At least if she's listening, she'll like knowing we discuss the girls. They've always been her first priority."

"Yup, and right now they're mine."

"Do you know about the cat?"

"How not to? We had to cart the damn thing up to Duncan's this morning. Hope wouldn't hear of leaving it alone all day long."

"She loves that cat," Katherine said, sad now as she studied Rachel. "The thought of it dying before was bad enough. Now it's even worse. She's apt to be feeling abandoned by everyone and everything she loves." Her eyes met his. "So there's another way in which the divorce comes into play. She felt abandoned by you. She won't abandon that cat. That's one of the reasons she absolutely refused to let the vet put the poor thing to sleep."

"Because of the divorce?" He thought that was pushing it a little.

"Know what I think?"

He couldn't wait to hear.

"I think you're here to make up for all you didn't do back then."

"I'm here because the girls need me."

"And Rachel?"

"Old times' sake."

Katherine smiled. "It's guilt."

"Guilt? Fear of abandonment? Christ, you have us all figured out. What are you? A shrink?"

"Close." She set the brush on the bed stand. "I'm a hairdresser."

Of all the things he thought she might have said, that wasn't one. "You're kidding."

"Why would I kid you?"

"You don't look like a hairdresser."

She laughed. "Like I didn't look like a friend of Rachel's?"

"A *hairdresser.*" He couldn't believe it. "The last time my wife stepped foot in a hair salon was on the day of our wedding. She swore she'd never do it again."

Katherine gave him a tiny shrug. "Apparently, she saw the error of her ways."

chapter six

JACK MCGILL reminded Katherine of her ex-husband. Roy had the same arrogance, the same myopia. To this day he thought the divorce was about her being unable to fill his needs, which was a joke. The guy's needs had been basic—food, clothes, sex. Any fool would have sufficed.

Unable to fill his needs? Not quite. *Unwilling* was more like it. He had refused to acknowledge *her* needs, which had been just fine for years. She had a career. She had friends. She found loyalty, sensitivity, intellectual stimulation elsewhere. But the one time she had needed him, he hadn't been there for her. After that, being his personal maid had grown old fast.

She had been his first wife. He was currently divorcing his third in five years. She found a certain validation in that. He was a slick one, Roy was. Slick, shallow, self-centered.

Don't judge a book by its cover. She had learned that the hard way, with Roy. She had been snowed by the package, hadn't seen the mettle—or lack thereof—

beneath. Roy. Then Byron. Different men, same pain.

Arms folded, eyes down, she tried to put it aside as she took the elevator to the coffee shop, but the setting didn't help. She didn't like hospitals in general and this one in particular. But she did know her way around. Heading straight for the tea bags, she grabbed an Earl Grey, filled a Styrofoam cup with hot water and paid, took a seat at one of the small tables, and wondered how long Jack McGill would hang around if Rachel's coma went on.

She was dunking the tea bag with more vehemence than was truly necessary when a voice said, "Excuse me? Haven't we met before?"

She looked up. The man regarding her with curiosity wore a blazer, shirt and tie, and jeans. His hair looked damp. It was more pepper than salt, thick, and well cut. Katherine noticed things like that. It went with her line of work. She also noticed that he was good looking. But then, so was she. And he'd just handed her the oldest line in the book.

Her expression said as much.

He was unfazed. "I think it was yesterday morning. Early, early morning." He extended a hand. "Steve Bauer."

Ah. Now she saw it. Rachel's neurologist. On her own, she never would have recognized him out of scrubs and cleaned up.

It was still the oldest line in the book, but she offered her hand. "Katherine Evans. I'm Rachel Keats's friend. Have you seen her today?"

"Early. I've been in surgery ever since." He glanced at the coffee machine. "I need caffeine." Holding up a finger, he left.

Katherine didn't like being told to stay put. Roy used

to do that—to point out his instructions, like she couldn't understand without a diagram—and while Steve Bauer hadn't exactly *pointed,* his finger had spoken.

Her first instinct was to get up and leave. For Rachel's sake, she didn't.

"Better," he said between sips from a steaming cup when he returned and slid into a seat. "Have you been with Rachel?"

"Yes. She seems the same. Isn't there anything more that can be done?"

"Not yet. The fact is she's not getting worse. That's good."

Katherine felt a stab of annoyance. She was growing impatient, worrying about Rachel. "You people all say that, but I have to tell you, it doesn't do anything for me. A coma seems one step removed from death. I don't want her taking that final step."

"I know." He sat back in the chair.

She waited for him to reassure her, but he didn't. So she waited for him to tell her how frustrating his job was, how difficult, how heart-wrenching. When he didn't do that either, she said, "How do you stand it?"

"Stand what? The waiting? It's standard protocol for head injuries. Do you live nearby?"

"Not terribly," she said, realizing where *his* mind was.

"You look familiar."

"You saw me yesterday."

"You looked familiar then, too." He seemed genuinely puzzled. "Maybe I'm wrong. Sometimes when you see a face that sticks in your mind, you start thinking you remember it from further back. You've never worked here?"

"No." To show him how far off he was—maybe even

shock him, the way she had shocked Jack McGill—she said, "I'm a hairdresser."

The ploy backfired. He looked intrigued. "Are you now? In Monterey?"

She shook her head.

"You have spectacular hair."

She shot a beseeching glance skyward.

"I'm serious," he said.

"That's what worries me. I'm sitting here upset because my best friend is in your hospital in a coma and there's nothing you or your staff can do to help her, and you're noticing my *hair?*"

Smile fading, he backed off. "It was an innocent comment."

"It was inappropriate."

"No. What would be inappropriate is if I discussed the medical details of your friend's case with you or, worse, made empty promises about her recovery. In lieu of that, I made an observation. You do have spectacular hair. Nice nails, too. How do you keep them like that if you're washing people's hair all day long?"

She stared at him. "Rubber gloves."

"Is it your own shop?"

It was, but she wasn't saying so. She didn't know why doctors felt they could ask all the questions. It was one step removed from their wanting to be called "Doctor," while calling their patients by first name. "Where do *you* live?" she asked, doubting he would answer.

But he did. "Pacific Grove."

Oh my. Pacific Grove was posh. Another doctor feeling the brunt of managed care? Not quite.

"I bought a little house there seven years ago," he said. "It's right down the street from the water."

"Do you have family?"

"One ex-wife. Plus two sons and a daughter, all grown and moved out."

That surprised her. Despite the graying hair, his skin was smooth. She would have put him in his mid-forties. "How old are you?"

"Fifty-three."

And genetically sound, apparently. Lucky him.

"How old are you?" he asked back.

Feeling suddenly off balance, she sighed and rose with her tea. "Old enough to know I'd better be getting back to my friend. I don't have long. Bye."

THERE WERE ten teenagers waiting for Jack when he pulled up at the school. Hope opened the door first and scrambled into the tiny backseat. "How's Mom?"

It was a gut-wrenching question. He kept his answer as light as he could. "Pretty good. Still asleep."

Samantha slipped into the passenger's seat, pointing at the others crowding on the curb at the open door. "These are my friends—Joshua, Adam, Shelly, Heather, Brendan, Amanda, Seth, and you know Lydia. They want to know how Mom is. Did she wake up?"

He had raised a hand in general greeting. "Not yet. But she's okay."

"Is she getting better?" asked the girl leaning in closest to Samantha. He guessed it was Lydia, whom he did know, but only by name. Not that it would have mattered if he had met her before. She was a carbon copy of the other girls—snug T-shirt, slim jeans, long hair swishing with every move. Actually, Lydia wasn't exactly like the others. She still wore braces, still looked more sweet than sophisticated. Her hair wasn't as straight, shiny, and neat. She had natural waves. So did the other girls. Now that he looked, Samantha's was the straightest. She was the most sophisticated-looking of the bunch.

He wasn't sure if that was good or bad.

"The doctors say she's healing," he answered.

"Can we visit?" asked another girl. He had *no* idea which name from the list was hers.

"Maybe in another day or two."

A boy face materialized among the girls, looking even younger. "I'm Brendan. My mom says to tell you she's totally on top of plans for the prom, so you shouldn't worry about a thing. She talked with Samantha's mom on Monday, and everything's set."

Samantha pushed her friends back. "We have to go." She slammed the door.

"What's set?" Jack asked.

"Prom plans. Let's leave. I want to see Mom."

He put the car in gear and pulled away from the school. "What prom is this?"

"The one I need a dress for. I told you about it."

She might have, but he'd had a lot on his mind. "What prom? You're only fifteen."

From behind him came a pleading explanation, clearly meant to ward off a fight, "Ninth and tenth have a prom."

"When?"

"A week from Saturday," Samantha said. "I need to buy a dress this weekend. You said you'd take me if Mom isn't better. She should have woken up by now. This isn't good."

"It isn't?" asked Hope, no longer making peace, simply scared.

"It's fine," Jack said. "The doctors are pleased with her progress."

"What progress?" Samantha asked.

"Vital signs. All good." He didn't know what else to say. Rachel was only supposed to be in a coma for a day or two. He had thought she would have woken up by now. The wait was unsettling.

"Daddy?" from the backseat.

"What, Hope?"

"What're we going to do about my picnic? Mommy was supposed to run it, but if she has a broken leg, she won't be able to drive, and it means going back and forth to school and calling other moms and picking stuff up and all that."

Jack felt a little like he was holding an armload of bricks, staggering with the addition of one, then another and another. He could handle buying a dress for the prom. All that meant was standing in a store, saying yes or no, and producing a credit card. Running a picnic was something else. It sounded pretty time-consuming to him—not to mention out of his realm—and he still had his own work to do. He could ignore that all he wanted for a day or two or three. But it was there, hanging heavy and hard in the back of his mind. It, too, was longing for Rachel to wake up.

He figured he could fill the car with two-liter bottles of soda and get them to a designated spot, maybe even buy a couple of dozen subs. But run the whole thing? There had to be another parent who could do it.

"I'll call your teacher tonight. Do you have the number?"

"Mommy does. And tell her about Career Day. Mommy can't do that."

"What about her show?" Samantha asked.

"What show?"

"Mom's supposed to have a show at P. Emmet's. It's a gallery here in Carmel."

"I know where P. Emmet's is." He wasn't *that* far removed from the art scene. The charming little side streets of Carmel had gallery after gallery. P. Emmet's was one of the best. He was impressed.

"The opening is two weeks from Sunday. What if she isn't awake by then?"

"She'll be awake," he decided. The list of things Rachel was missing was getting too long. He was just a stand-in, muddling along.

"But what if she *isn't?* Or what if she doesn't wake up until a week before? The paintings aren't done. She was kind of freaking out about that. I think you need to talk with Ben."

"Ben?"

"Ben Wolfe. He manages the gallery. He's the one who set up the show for Mom. They've been dating," she added—smugly, he thought. "Well, you are divorced. You didn't expect that she'd sit around doing nothing, did you? You date. What does Jill say about your being down here?"

"Jill understands that I have responsibilities," he said. At least, he assumed that she understood. He owed her another call. He owed her lots of other calls.

"Ben sells more of Mom's work than any of the other galleries do. He's giving her a solo show."

He whistled, doubly impressed.

"What if her paintings aren't done?" Samantha asked. "This is the only solo slot he has for months. She really wanted it. What do we do?" He felt another weight hit the load he held. His shoulders ached. The bricks in his arms were starting to teeter. "I'll talk with Ben," he said and tucked the thought away, back behind a growing need for Rachel to wake up, and fast.

THE THOUGHT didn't stay tucked away for long. Ben Wolfe was at the hospital when Jack and the girls arrived. He had auburn hair and wire-rimmed glasses, an average-looking man with regard to height, weight, and presence, certainly not one to catch the eye when he entered a room—certainly not the offbeat personality Jack would have guessed Rachel would go for. And she had thought *Jack* was conservative? Ben Wolfe was the epitome of it, but it worked for him. Between his crisp white shirt, neatly tucked into tailored gray slacks, and the reputation of the gallery, Jack guessed he had to be capable enough.

The woman with him was something else. Everything about her screamed rebel, from the pink streaks in her hair to the half dozen earrings she wore in one lobe to her layered tank tops and skinny skirt. She was clearly an artist. Jack guessed she hadn't hit thirty yet. He had her pegged as the sculptress in Rachel's book group even before they were introduced.

Ben Wolfe. Charlene Avalon. Jack nodded his way through the introductions but quickly focused on Rachel. Her face was peaceful, pale, and still. The tiny kick in his belly told him she hadn't moved since he had seen her last.

He touched her cheek. Then he took her hand. Holding it made him feel better, as though he had every right in the world to be there.

The girls were beside him, staring at Rachel, unsure.

To Hope, at his elbow, he said, "Want to tell her what you did in school today?"

"I flunked a math test," Samantha announced before Hope could speak.

"*Did* you?" Jack asked in alarm, because her performance in school was suddenly his concern.

Hope was shaking her head, saying in her timid little voice, "She just said that to see if Mommy hears. Hi, Mommy. It's me, Hope. I'm still wearing my lucky boots."

"That is so dumb," Samantha said.

"It is not. They make me think about Sunday night. I'm wearing them until she wakes up." To Rachel, she said, "Guinevere is at Duncan's. I hope she's okay." She raised frightened eyes to Jack. "Did you call to check?"

He should have thought of it, but hadn't. "I figured Duncan would be out with his sheep." He checked his watch. "We'll try him in a bit."

"Charlie knows Duncan. She visits him a lot."

"He has a shed filled with rusty old stuff," Charlene said. She was at the foot of the bed, her eyes not leaving Rachel for long. "He lets me take what I want for my work."

"You work in metal?"

"Clay until I met Duncan. Rachel introduced us."

Duncan and Charlie? If Duncan was too old for Rachel, he was *definitely* too old for Charlie. "How did you meet Rachel?"

"Through Eliza."

"Eliza?"

"You met her yesterday," Samantha told him, and while he didn't remember meeting any Eliza, he knew better than to argue. There had been friends in and out.

112

He hadn't paid them much heed. "She owns a bakery in town," Samantha added. "It's French."

"How did your mother meet her?"

"At the *bakery*," Hope said with innocent delight. "It's the kind of place that makes sandwiches, too. When we first moved here, we tried eating at lots of different places, but we kept going back there because Eliza made special stuff for Sam and me, and then she and Mommy used to sit talking while we helped in the kitchen."

"You'd hate it," Samantha said, flipping her hair back. "There's always a line. You'd have to wait right along with everyone else."

So Jack hated waiting in restaurants. Was that so bad? He hated waiting, period. *You know that, Rachel, don't you? Some tiny part of you must be enjoying this.* "You didn't really help in the kitchen, did you?" he asked. He was sure it would have been against state regulations.

"Well, we didn't *cook*," Samantha conceded, "but we did other stuff, like fold napkins and decorate the chalkboard. Eliza's cool."

Jack asked Charlie, "How did you meet Eliza?"

"I used to work for her. I still do sometimes. Mostly I just stop in to visit. We're friends."

"And she's in this book group?"

Charlie nodded, returning worried eyes to Rachel. "We never expected this on Monday night." She clutched the earring that dangled lowest, a feathery thing. "She won't like that cast. It'll slow her down." She looked at Jack. "Ben and I were wondering what to do about the show. You do know there's one planned?"

"Of course," Jack said as though he had known about it all along. "The opening's in two weeks. I'm guessing she'll be awake long before then."

"Still, the cast's a problem."

The cast wasn't the only problem. There was also the bandaged hand. Granted, the better part of artistic talent was in the mind, but the body was the mind's major tool.

Jack caught Ben Wolfe's eye. "Can we talk a minute?" Drawing Samantha into his place beside Rachel, he went into the hall. When Ben joined him there, he asked, "Any chance of delaying the show?"

Ben shook his head. "I've been trying, but nothing's working. I've called everyone else who's scheduled to show, and none of them can be ready this fast. Since summer's a busy tourist season, our inventory is at a high, which means we don't have space to do more than one show at a time. They're scheduled back-to-back from now through September."

"How many of Rachel's pieces are ready?"

Ben nudged his glasses higher. "I'm not sure. She promised me eighteen. Only five or six may be done, and none are framed yet."

Jack wondered how that had happened. In all the years of Rachel picking him up at the airport, she had never been late. Granted, there had been close calls. More than once, she had come straight from work, disheveled and reeking of paint thinner, or covered with paste from some project she had been doing with the girls, but grinning, always grinning, and definitely on time. She prided herself on being where she was supposed to be when she was supposed to be there.

"It's not her fault," Ben rushed on. "She was doing us a favor, actually. Another artist was supposed to have this slot and chose London instead. Rachel's been selling so well that it seemed the logical choice. She likes to do the framing herself, but if push comes to shove, we can do it in the shop." He slipped a hand in his pocket, glanced back at the room, and lowered his voice. "What's the story? Is this long-term?"

"Beats me. Can you do a smaller show?"

"Yes. I'd hate to, if enough of the work is there. Maybe if I drive down and take a look at what she has, I'd get a better feel for where we stand."

Jack was surprised the man hadn't already done that. If Ben and Rachel were seriously dating, he would have spent time in her studio. Jack always had. Rachel's art was an intimate part of her, foreplay of a sort. Making love among oils had always been way up there among his list of turn-ons. That had started back in Tucson, in sweltering heat, when the smell of the oil would have been overpowering had it not been diluted by sweat and sex. At least, that was what they had told themselves. Granted, they had ceiling fans to dissipate the heat, but it didn't hurt the desire. Nor had the arrival of children. The studio door had a lock. They used it often and well.

"No need for you to do that," Jack said now. Ben Wolfe was too tepid for Rachel. He would never challenge her spirit, would never want to wallow in sweat and sex and oils. He was too neat, too pale. Nothing he did in bed would match what Jack had done.

Feeling dominant, he said, "I'll take a look. Got a business card?" Minutes later, he had one in his hand. "I'll let you know what I find."

WHAT JACK found were photographs. He came across them that evening—after cleaning up the remnants of pizza, calling Hope's teacher to beg for help with the picnic, spending two hours at his laptop and another grappling with design problems faxed to him from Boca—when, too tired to face Rachel's studio, he settled for searching her drawers. Cindy Winston had suggested that she might be more comfortable in familiar clothes; certainly the girls would be more comfortable seeing her in them. Given the obstacle of the cast, a nightgown made sense.

Propriety wasn't an issue. Rachel's nightgowns were prim affairs. She had always been into warm flannel things, claiming that San Francisco nights were too damp to go without when she was alone in a too-big bed. Her double bed in Big Sur was small compared to the king they had shared, and it was covered by the kind of thick goose-down comforter that he had never allowed her to buy lest he roast, and even then, her drawer was filled with neck-to-ankle gowns.

He had to hand it to her, though. They were vivid. He chose a purple one, a turquoise one, and a chartreuse one, and was debating about one that was poppy red, pushing it aside to see what was left, when he found the frames. They were facedown, seven frames covering the entire bottom of the drawer, familiar to him even after all this time, even from behind.

He turned over the largest first. It was in the kind of elaborate gold frame that only Rachel's mother would buy and that Rachel had always kept to remind her of that. Inside, extravagantly double-matted, was the formal picture taken at their wedding, of bride and groom standing dead center, flanked by two sets of happy parents. Jack and Rachel had both hated this picture. They had seen it as the perpetuation of a myth—bride and groom looking all done up and unlike themselves, with smiling parents who rarely smiled in real life.

Their engagement picture was better, but what a fight they'd had over that. It was totally casual, totally them—and totally unlike what Rachel's mother had wanted for the newspapers, but they had held out. He touched it now, the simple wood frame onto which Rachel had shellacked bright foils and decorative paper. Seventeen years younger, their faces were vibrant, defiant, happy as only the innocent could be. Rachel hadn't changed much, he decided. When he had seen her six weeks before, she had looked every bit as vibrant, defiant, and freckled. And he? Not much change in height, weight. His hair—*pecan, as in the nut,* Rachel used to say—had gone from tan to weathered, and he had crow's-feet at the corners of his eyes. The face he saw in the mirror each morning was broader, more mature, with a distinct worry line between the brows, an occupational hazard.

And the other pictures? Saving the smallest for last, he turned over four of him, taken by Rachel at various times, in various places. He had been happy. That showed in each print. He assumed she had kept these four for the sole purpose of leaving them lying facedown, buried deep.

But there was one more. It was his favorite. Feeling a catch deep inside, he turned it up. He hadn't missed it at first, had been so consumed by anger after Rachel's departure that he had only wanted things around him that were new. In time he went searching through the cartons in his attic. So. She'd had it all along.

Framed in a rustic stone frame, the photo was one that Rachel had snapped a year before the divorce. It showed the girls and him tumbling together in the tiny yard behind their Pacific Heights home, with Rachel behind the lens but so clearly involved in the scene that she might have been its subject. A tangle of arms and legs there might be, but three pairs of eyes, three smiles, three laughing faces were looking straight at Rachel with varying amounts of daring and love.

Jack had always treasured that picture. In the days that followed Rachel's taking it, when he felt increasingly distanced from her, it had said that—bottom line—things were all right.

Then Rachel had left, and the whole thing had seemed even more a myth than the pomp and circumstance of their wedding.

Setting the little stone frame carefully back in the drawer, he followed it with the four pictures of him and the engagement picture, but when it came to putting the wedding picture in place, he couldn't. That one didn't fit. It was the bad apple in the bunch. He couldn't help but think it contaminated the others.

Bent on burying it alone and as far from the others as possible, he opened the very bottom drawer—and felt a hard knocking in his chest. After a long minute, he moved his hand over a collage of fine lace, silk, cotton damask, even gingham, and was suddenly back in time to early evening in a warm Tucson apartment more than sixteen years before.

The apartment was larger than his old place. Since he had his degree and a new job, they could afford it. They had moved in the week before.

Jack returned from work to find Rachel in the spare bedroom that was supposed to have been a studio. With the wedding barely a week off, it had become a repository for daily deliveries. The latest gifts, still boxed, were nearly lost in a sea of empty cartons, torn paper, and discarded ribbon.

Rachel was a golden figure sitting at a long table in the midst of the mess. Her hair was in a thick ponytail; her freckles were bright; her face, arms, and throat were tanned amber above a lemon yellow tank top. She was working at a sewing machine, so intent with the whirring start and stop, the shift of levers and turn of fabric, that she didn't see him at first. The surface of the table was covered with pieces of fabric, predominantly whites and ivories, a few pale green or blue.

He couldn't imagine what she was doing. Victoria had refused to let her make her wedding gown, and she had already made curtains for the rest of the apartment. Curious, he came closer.

She looked up and broke into a smile, then held up her arms and tipped her head back for a kiss when he came over her from behind.

"What are you making?" he asked, thinking that she was adorable upside down.

"A shower quilt."

"For rainy days?"

"Not rain showers. Wedding showers."

He took a better look at the fabrics then, from what was in the machine to what was already sewn to the pieces in line. "Oh my God. Isn't that lace from the tablecloth your mom's Irish connection sent?"

"Not sent," Rachel said, clearly delighted. "Brought. To my shower."

The shower had been in New York the month before. Knowing how lavish it would be, Rachel had attended only under duress. Her greatest joy was in returning home empty-handed after instructing her mother to keep the gifts for herself. Not only had Victoria sent every last one to Tucson, but, to add insult to injury, Jack and

Rachel had then had to move the whole lot of them from their old apartment to this one.

A shower quilt. Jack's eye returned to the pieces of fabric with greater insight. Among them, he saw now, were bits from peignoir sets, satin sheets, table linen, aprons.

"She insisted I needed them," Rachel said, still looking up at him backward. "Do I ever wear silk nighties? No! Do I use fancy tablecloths? *No!* Do I want to sleep on sheets that have to be *ironed?* No, no, no. A quilt is far more practical."

"Do you know how expensive these things are?" Jack asked, but distractedly. Even all these years later, what he remembered first about that moment was the view into Rachel's tank top.

"I know exactly how expensive they are. Mom told me. That's why I'm so pleased to have put them to good use rather than let it all sit in boxes and drawers unused."

When Jack tore his eyes from her breasts long enough to look again at what she'd done, he had to agree. There was skilled hand stitching as well as machine stitching, in the kind of creative arrangement of fabric that only someone with Rachel's eye could achieve—and several different levels of poetic justice. Not only was there the sheer cost of the materials, and the fact that Rachel wouldn't be using these things as Victoria wanted, but there was the fact that Victoria *hated* it when Rachel sewed. She had taught Rachel to sew, herself, but she believed that they had outgrown the need to make their own clothes when Rachel's father came into his first money, a decade before.

"She'll die when she sees this," he warned.

Rachel shook her head, more serious now. "She won't

ever see it. She's not coming out here, Jack. This isn't where she wants me to be living, so she'll ignore the fact that I live here."

"And that hurts."

"Not as much as it used to." The smile returned. "Not since I found you."

She often said things like that, little things that made him feel loved, and she was right. It did help ease the hurt. He kissed her long and deep, and might have gone on forever if he hadn't worried about her neck, bent back this way. Ending the kiss, he framed her head for support. "For that, I'll help with shower thank-you notes."

"No need. They're all done." Her smile grew wry. "My conscience drew the line. I couldn't take a scissors to these things until I'd done that." She raised both brows. "But you can do some of the notes from *my* wedding list."

"I already am," he protested. Their initial deal had been for each to write notes for gifts coming from his or her own side. Then Keats gifts began outnumbering McGill gifts twelve to one, and he had taken pity on her. Spotting several unopened cartons, stacked and rising from the maelstrom, he sighed. "More today. Are you sure you know what's where?"

She lowered her arms and looked around. "Exactly. These are in piles."

"I don't see any piles."

"You're not looking at them the right way. Everything here"—her hand slashed the center of the room and swung left—"is duly acknowledged. Everything here"—her hand went the other way—"needs notes. *And* among these on the right"—she started pointing clockwise—"we have silver, gold, glass, fabric, and unclassified, as in *disgusting.*"

Jack saw something emerging from the disgusting pile and agreed. It was either an ornate lamp, a humongous candlestick, or something he had yet to make acquaintance with.

Rachel's arms came up again. She tipped his head forward to meet hers tipping back. Her throat was delicate and sleek, he thought. Stroking it, he felt her voice.

"Invite half the world," she said, "half the world sends gifts. Does half the world care what we want? No. We registered for plenty of stuff that we wanted, but half the world knows better. Do we want these things, Jack? No. Are they *us?* No! So not only do we write gracious thank-you notes to half the world, but we have to find a place to *put* this stuff."

Jack wasn't putting it anywhere. "Make that, find a place to *dump* this stuff."

"I wanted it all done before we left. I wanted this to be *our* place when we got back. So, why am I sewing a quilt instead of attacking this mess?" He knew precisely why she was doing it.

"The answer," she said, grinning, "is that since we're leaving for New York the day after tomorrow and I don't have a chance in *hell* of getting everything acknowledged and cleaned up and put away or dumped, I might as well have some fun."

At the slightest urging of her fingers, he lowered his head and kissed her again.

Her voice was more mellow when he let her up for air. "Whose wedding is this, Jack?"

"Ours. Ours. We agreed on that. What happens on the outside isn't what we'll be thinking and feeling on the inside. You love me, don't you?"

"I do, I do."

"Madly and passionately."

"Quite."

"Then look at it this way. We're doing our own thing about where and how we live, so we can cut your mother some slack here. But this does it. Evens the score. Our good deed is done. No more compromise. No more guilt."

"No more guilt."

"No more guilt."

"Okay."

HAD IT BEEN up to Rachel, they would have eloped. Looking back now, Jack wondered if it would have made a difference, perhaps gotten them off on a better foot.

But Victoria Keats had had her heart set on giving her only child the dream wedding she had never had herself, and Eunice McGill, of a no-name town a forlorn hour's drive from Eugene, Oregon, in her delight to be able to throw one son's success in her stern husband's face with impunity, had gone right along.

Both women were widows now. Eunice never called Jack. She waited for Jack to call her, then criticized him for not calling sooner. Victoria did call from time to time under the guise of being worried about Rachel, but if she was, it was one small, back-burner worry in a corporate executive's life. What she wanted was a reconciliation. Marriages didn't fall apart in her family. Her friends could be on their second or third, but her daughter's marriage was sound. Jack had a feeling she hadn't told any of those friends about the divorce.

Corporate headquarters were in Manhattan. Victoria

wouldn't have them anywhere else. Nor would she think of living anywhere but on the Upper East Side. She loved the ambiance, the glitz, the cost. Jack didn't know her number offhand, but he knew it would be in Rachel's book.

Jack closed the drawer on the shower quilt. One by one, he put nightgowns over the facedown pictures in the upper drawer and closed it. Opening the one directly beneath it, he slid the wedding picture in under a pile of sweaters. When that drawer, too, was closed, he stretched kinked muscles in his lower back and ran a hand through his hair. He needed a haircut. He had always worn it on the long side, but this was pushing it.

It would have to wait.

He glanced at the time. It would be late in New York. But Rachel had been comatose for forty-eight hours, and faults and all, Victoria was her mother. In good conscience, he couldn't wait any longer.

Sinking down on Rachel's bed, he lifted the phone. "Two minutes," he told Sam, "then I need the line." He hung up before she could tell him to use the cell phone, and started timing off the face of his watch.

chapter seven

WHEN JACK ARRIVED at the hospital the next morning, Rachel was lying on her side with her back to the door. His heart began to pound. *Awake!* He crept forward, cautiously rounding the bed, wondering what those curious hazel eyes of hers would be focused on and what the rest of her face would do when those eyes saw him there. After all, she was the one who had moved out and initiated the divorce. She might not be at all happy that he had come.

But her eyes were closed.

He stole closer. "Rachel?" he whispered, watching her lids for a flicker.

Kara Bates turned into the room. "We've started rotating her. Two straight days on her back is enough. We've also put a pressure mattress under her sheet. It adds a measure of mobility."

Jack swallowed down a throatful of emotion. Disappointment was there, along with fear—because what the doctor was saying suggested that with Rachel still comatose after forty-eight hours, they were looking farther down the road.

"Is there any change at all?" he asked, studying the monitor.

"Not up there. I think her face looks better, though. Not as purple."

Jack agreed. "But if the swelling is going down out here, why isn't it going down inside?"

"The swelling inside is encased," Kara said, cupping her hands a skull's width apart, "so the healing is slower. I was trying to explain that to Rachel's mother, but she wasn't buying."

"Victoria called here?"

"Several times."

Jack should have known. He had left a message on her machine asking that she call him at Rachel's, which she did at five in the morning, all excited, thinking they had reconciled. She was nearly as disappointed to hear that they hadn't as she was upset about the accident. She was in Paris on business, hence the early call. She grilled him for twenty minutes. When she asked if she should come, he discouraged it. He was hoping Rachel would wake up that day.

"She's an insistent woman," the doctor said.

"She's an *insufferable* woman," Jack muttered, then added a cautious "You didn't tell her to fly over, did you?"

"I told her she was stable. The rest is up to you," she said, peering into the small overnight bag on the bed. "What did you bring?"

"Nightgowns. Rachel likes color."

"I was starting to guess that," Kara remarked, arching a brow at the windowsill. It was crammed with flowers. "Those made it past the ICU police *only* because Rachel's problem isn't infectious or pulmonary."

A vague part of Jack had known the arrangements were there. For the first time now, he really looked. There were five arrangements, vases and baskets filled with flowers whose names he didn't know but whose colors he did. They were Rachel's colors—deep blue, vivid reds, rich greens, brilliant yellows. She liked basic and bright. Each arrangement had a card.

We need you, Rachel, heal fast, wrote Dinah and Jan. *To our favorite room parent, with wishes for a speedy recovery,* wrote Hope's seventh-grade class. There was a bouquet of hot-red flowers from Nellie, Tom, and Bev, a tall blue arrangement from the Liebermans, and a vase of yellow roses whose card read, *With love, Ben.*

"She has lots of friends," Kara observed.

"Apparently," said Jack, vaguely miffed. There was actually a sixth arrangement. It was from David. Stuck to the side and behind, it was much larger and less personal than the others.

Kara went on. "We've been getting calls at the desk asking if visiting is permitted. I wanted to talk with you about that. Medically, there's no reason why she can't have visitors."

"In Intensive Care?"

"We're a small hospital. Flowers—visitors—we can be flexible. Hearing familiar voices can help, and Rachel isn't in danger of infection. If she was a heart or a stroke patient, we might worry about someone doing something to upset her. Since that worry doesn't apply with coma patients, we restrict guests only when the family requests it."

Jack could do without Ben Wolfe and his love bouquet. But, okay. He and Rachel were divorced. He dated other women. He had slept with other women. Rachel was free to do the same. To live her own life. If friends had come to be a part of it, he had to give those friends a chance to help wake her up.

It was in his own best interest. He had to get back to San Francisco. Clients needed attention, his associates needed direction, design revisions were overdue. Jill had been a good sport, but she was growing impatient. The whole of the life that waited in the city was starting to make him nervous. If friends visited Rachel, he would at least be free to return to the office. He had been hoping to get a few hours there again today while the girls were in school, but he didn't want to leave Rachel alone.

"Let them come," he told the doctor.

KATHERINE swept in moments later. Her eyes widened, her mouth formed a hopeful *O* when she saw Rachel on her side. Jack shook his head.

She swore softly and came to the bed. "I was hoping . . ."

"So was I."

She leaned down and talked softly to Rachel for a minute, then straightened and sighed. It was another minute before she looked at him. "I wasn't sure you'd still be here."

"Oh, I'm here," he said, but he wasn't in the mood for sparring. He was wondering about those flowers, wondering about the friends Rachel appeared to have made since she had left him. In San Francisco, she had been a loner—independent in that regard, focused solely on her art, the kids, and him. "Who are Dinah and Jan?"

"Dinah Monroe and Jan O'Neal. They're in our book group. You met them yesterday."

He had met lots of people yesterday. One face blended into the next. "Who are Nellie, Tom, and Bev?"

"Bridge friends."

He had to have heard wrong. "Bridge? As in the *game?*"

"Cards. That's right."

He tried to picture it but couldn't. "That's a kicker."

"Why?"

"The *last* thing Rachel would have done in the city was play bridge. It stood for everything her mother used to do while she was waiting to get rich and busy. So what's Rachel doing playing it here?"

Katherine scrubbed the back of Rachel's hand. "Should I tell him?" she asked, looking amused. "The poor guy is mystified, absolutely mystified. Where's his imagination?"

"It's there," Jack assured her. "I'd never be where I am today if I didn't have it. There are people who say I have too *much.*"

"What people?"

"Clients who want a house exactly like one that their neighbor's brother has in Grosse Point, or a library to match a charming little one in upstate New York. I argue with them. I mean, hell, why are they hiring me? Any draftsperson can copy someone else's work. I don't want to give them what's already done."

"But you do," she said with a little too much certainty for his comfort.

"Is that what Rachel said?"

"Not exactly. What she said was that you'd gotten so far into big money that you'd lost your artistic integrity."

He felt offended—by Rachel for thinking it and speaking it, by Katherine for repeating it. "That's not true. And how would she know, anyway? She doesn't know what I'm doing now."

Quietly, smoothly, Katherine listed the six largest projects he had designed since the divorce.

Jack had mixed feelings about several of those. His initial designs, the ones landing him each job, had been exciting. Not so after developers, contractors and consultants, financiers, regulatory boards, and politicians had chipped away at the plans. That was what happened, the bigger the money. You weren't your own boss anymore. So maybe Rachel was right. Maybe he had lost his artistic integrity.

If so, he wasn't discussing it with Rachel's friend. "What does my artistic integrity have to do with playing bridge?"

Katherine smiled. "Spoken that way, not much. The subject was actually imagination. I've often wondered why men have so much trouble understanding how women's minds work. You're right. Rachel hated what bridge stood for in her mother's life, but she had been taught to play, and soon after she moved down here, she met Bev, a bridge player who does the most incredible stuff with acrylics on rattlesnake skin, and somehow playing with her didn't sound so bad."

Acrylics on snakeskin. It was a novel use of a medium. Rachel would have appreciated that. "Did she meet Nellie and Tom through Bev?"

"No. She and Bev advertised in the local paper to complete the foursome. Tom owns the paper. Nellie answered the ad."

"Is Nellie an artist?" It would make sense. Charlie. Bev. Nellie.

"Nope. She's a Carmelite."

"A *nun?*"

"A secular member of the order, but devout."

"Okay." Rachel had never been terribly religious. But, hey. His parents had been devout. "And the Liebermans?"

Katherine smiled with genuine warmth. "Faye and Bill. Faye's in our book group. She's one of the golfers. Jan is the other, and a young mother, to boot. She'll be by later."

Jack was trying to picture Rachel in a group with golfers, but all he could see was the adamant way she had always shaken her head when Victoria suggested they take up the game. "You're not going to tell me that Rachel plays golf now."

Katherine laughed. "No. I doubt either of us would go that far."

"Then how do you come to have golfers in your group?"

"Golfers read," she said, giving Rachel's hand a conspiratorial squeeze.

"Obviously. But what's the connection? If you don't golf, how do you know golfers?"

"They come to my shop. I've been doing Faye's hair for years, and we like talking books. Jan has her nails done every Thursday. She heard us talking once and joined in. When Rachel and I decided to form the group, they were both logical choices."

"What about Dinah?"

"A travel agent in town. We've all used her one time or another."

There was one connection left to make. "And you and Rachel? How did you meet?"

"In the gynecologist's waiting room," Katherine said. With a glance at her watch and a look of concern, she leaned over Rachel's shoulder. "I have a nine o'clock, so I can't stay long. I want to talk to you, Rachel. I miss that." She made a little scrubbing motion on Rachel's back, a casual movement, but the concern remained. "It's Thursday. You've been sleeping since Monday. How about cracking an eye open for me?"

Jack watched Rachel's eyes. The lids were inert.

"Looks like Jack's brought in some of your nightgowns," Katherine said. "I've cleared an hour midafternoon to come by and do your hair." She asked Jack, "Shall I get the girls at school and bring them here?"

Jack was feeling possessive again. "I'll do it."

The corner of her mouth twitched. "I don't think he trusts me," she told Rachel.

"The girls are my responsibility."

She straightened, suddenly sober. "Then can I make a suggestion? Buy a new car. Rachel's is totaled, so she's going to need another anyway, and you can't keep driving around with Hope stuck in that itty-bitty thing you call a backseat. If you want to risk your own life in a car that size, that's your choice, but I don't think you should take chances with the girls."

Jack was startled by the intrusion. "Is this your business?"

"You bet. Rachel can't say it, so I'll say it for her."

"Good morning!" Steve Bauer said, crossing the threshold and approaching the bed.

Katherine pushed off. "Bye," she said in a lighter voice, with an open-hand wave to no one in particular.

The doctor watched her exit. "Don't leave on my account."

But she was already out the door before Jack could wonder why the sudden rush.

JACK needed to work. His laptop was full of messages each time he booted it up. There were more on Rachel's answering machine, and papers piling up by her fax. He had driven north from Big Sur that morning intending, in logical geographical order, to drop the girls at school in Carmel, visit Rachel in Monterey, and continue up to San Francisco. Now that he was with Rachel, the urgency had left.

Bracing his elbows on the bed rail, he studied her face. Even with the vision of fading purple on the left side, he thought it a beautiful face. Always had. He used to tell her so all the time. They were art students then, sitting hip to hip in life drawing class, which he had taken solely to be with Rachel, since it had little to do with architecture. He had used whatever clout he had as a graduate student to wangle credit for it, but it was far from a gut course for him. He had to struggle far more than Rachel to reproduce, in the most minute detail, the face of the model.

"She's the beauty," Rachel used to whisper, pink-cheeked and pleased, if adamant. "Widespread eyes, strong cheekbones, clear skin, no freckles."

But Jack had always loved Rachel's freckles. His father, who had a negative take on almost everything, condemned them as the excess of spirit in a highly spirited person. Rachel had always been highly spirited, all right. Jack took pride in that. When he first met her, freckles had danced unchecked over the bridge of her nose to her cheeks. She was twenty-one then. After the children were born, the freckles faded, then faded more when she entered her thirties.

They were more noticeable now than they had been in

years. His father, God rest his soul, would have declared with disdain that a highly spirited person could be restrained for only so long. So, had marriage restrained Rachel?

The sun might be bringing them out. She was spending more time outdoors, said her work. He had seen several recent pieces in a SOMA gallery. She painted wildlife in its natural habitat.

Or did the freckles show more because her face was so pale?

He ran his thumb over the smooth, unbruised cheek. "Something's agreeing with you here. You're painting again. And you have friends." Suddenly that annoyed him. "What was the problem, Rachel? You could have had a *slew* of friends in the city. If you wanted them, why didn't you? You went off and did what you wanted in just about everything else. Why not that?" He felt the full weight of a confusion that had been hovering just out of reach. "And those pictures in your drawer—why are they there? I'd have thought you'd have cut them up and made them into a papier-mâché statement. That would have been poetic. Kind of like the shower quilt. Are the pictures facedown because you can't bear to see them? Or because you're angry? What do *you* have to be angry about? Looks to me like you're doing better without me than with me."

Sadness lurked under his anger. "What happened to us, Rachel? I never did understand. Never did figure it out." He paused. "Can you hear me? Do you know I'm here?"

Her skin smelled of lilies from the lotion he had spread. It taunted him with memories of a love that was supposed to have lasted forever. "I think you hear. I think you know. I think you're lying in there waiting and watching and wondering what's going to happen. Is this payback time for the traveling I did? You want me to spend more time with the girls? Well, I gotta tell you, I'm spending time with them, and we're doing just fine, so if you thought we'd fall apart, you were wrong. I love my daughters. I always did. Believe you me, when you packed them up and took them away from me, it was *hard.*" Pushing up, he stared at her, then paced to the window, muttering under his breath, "Damn hard. Empty house. No noise. No smiles." He paced back to the bed. "You knew how I felt growing up, and how much I needed what we had. I *relied* on having family waiting when I got home from work. You took that away."

He put his face in close and spoke softly, under his breath. "Fine. It's over. We're divorced. You got that done nice and fast and clean, thank you. But this coma is something else. One day or two, okay. But three days? Wake up, Rachel. I'm doing the best I can, but the girls need *you.* I'm just filling in. You're the main attraction in their lives; always were." After a minute, he said, "And I have to *work.* People are depending on me for their livelihood. I'm being *paid* to make certain things happen, and I can't do it from down here. How long are you planning to let this go on?"

She didn't blink, didn't flinch, didn't answer.

Okay, he wanted to say—because if she wasn't cooperating, why the hell should he?—*that's it. I'm going back to the city. At least there I can accomplish something. At least there I'm appreciated. Ciao. Sayonara. See ya later.*

He didn't know how long he stood scowling at her. But the scowl slowly faded, and in time, he pulled up a chair and sat down.

KATHERINE'S one o'clock arrived twenty minutes late. She would have told the woman she had time only for a quick wash and blow dry, but the woman was a regular customer, flying out that night for a weekend wedding in Denver. So Katherine gave her the cut she needed and was late taking her one-forty-five, then had to deal with a minor uproar when a woman whose highlights had been done by Katherine's newest colorist stormed in with hair that even Katherine had to admit was alarmingly red. In the process of mixing the correct color, she splattered dye on her blouse, so she had to take a fresh one from the small collection she deliberately kept there, and with the bathroom door closed and her back to the mirror, she quickly changed.

She didn't reach the hospital until four. Looking nowhere but straight ahead, she made a beeline for Rachel's room. She felt a letdown the instant she reached it and saw that Rachel was still comatose.

Hope was reading a book on the bed, inside the rail, legs folded, boots on the floor. Jack stood facing the window with one hand on his hip and the other tossing a cell phone in his hand. The tray table beside him was covered with papers.

She gave Hope a hug. "How's your Mom?"

The child turned a longing look on Rachel. "Okay."

Katherine held her tighter. "What're you reading?"

Keeping her finger in her place, she closed the cover so that Katherine could see the title. It was an aged hardcover, John Hersey's *A Bell for Adano*.

"Is this from a school list, or a Mom list?"

Hope lifted a shoulder. "A Mom list."

"Do you like it?"

"Uh-huh. Mom said she did. Look." She opened to the inside cover, where Rachel's name was written in the precise hand of a schoolgirl who hadn't yet found her individualism. The date was below it.

"Wow," Katherine said. "Twenty-seven years ago."

"She was my age then. I think that's kinda neat."

"Me, too."

Jack turned around. "How're you doing?" he asked, but headed off before she could answer. "I'll be back."

Katherine watched him go, then turned questioning eyes on Hope.

"They wouldn't let him use the cell phone in here," Hope explained. "It messes up the monitors."

"Ah. He seems distracted."

"It's work. Look." She pointed at a flower arrangement on the sill. It was the newest, tallest, most lavish one there. "From Grandma."

Katherine might have guessed it. She also guessed it wouldn't be the last of Victoria's gifts. "That was sweet of her."

"Uh-huh." Hope refocused on Rachel, looking so sad this time that Katherine ached for her. "Do you think she knows I'm here?"

"Definitely."

"Really?"

"Really."

Hope considered that, then said, "Sam's down the hall."

"I know. I passed her on my way in." She had been tucked up in a phone booth with an algebra book in her lap, a pencil in her hand, and a huge wad of gum in her mouth. The sudden cessation of talk and the too-wide grin she gave Katherine suggested that she wasn't doing math.

"She was in here with Mom for a long time," Hope said in quick defense of her sister, "but she wanted to use Dad's phone, and he had to make his own calls. She'll be back. I called Duncan's. Guinevere's sleeping. She's been doing that a lot."

"What is it they say—that cats sleep eighteen hours a day?"

"She's been doing it more. Sometimes I think she isn't really sleeping, just doesn't have the energy to move. Like she's in a coma. Like Mom's."

"Uh-uh-uh," Katherine scolded gently. "Not like Mom's. Guinevere has a tumor. Your mom does not."

"Then why doesn't she wake up? How can she hear me and know that I'm here, without waking up to let me know? Doesn't she want to?"

"More than anything, I'd bet," Katherine said. "She's probably trying her best and annoyed that she can't . . . can't break out of whatever it is that's holding her there. We have to be patient. We have to let her know we'll be here until she does wake up."

Hope glanced cautiously back toward the hall, then whispered an urgent "Sam is scaring me."

Katherine leaned closer and whispered back, "Scaring you how?" She imagined Sam was talking gloom and doom about Rachel, trying to act old and wise, trying to get a rise out of Jack. But it wasn't that.

"The prom," Hope whispered. "I think they're planning something. I can't say anything to Daddy, because he'll get angry at her and then she'll get angry at me. And it's not like I *know* anything. I just *feel* it." She hunched her shoulders, which made the rest of her look even smaller. "She'll kill me if she knows I told you this. But I don't want anything *else* to happen."

"Tell you what," Katherine suggested. "How about I drop a few hints to your dad? No one needs to know you said anything. I'd only be doing what your mom would be doing."

"Mom would be talking to the other mothers. But Sam knows Daddy won't do that. *That's* what scares me most."

Katherine figured it would scare Rachel, too. "I can handle this," she said for the benefit of mother and daughter both. "Trust me?" she asked Hope, just as Jack returned. When Hope gave her a wide-eyed nod, she smiled and pulled a $5 bill from her pocket. "I'm desperate for tea. Would you run down and get me an Earl Grey? Maybe your dad would like coffee?"

Jack asked Hope for anything strong and black. Katherine waited until she had left before eyeing the work on the table. "Rachel said you were a workaholic."

"Not always. What you see here is my conscience. I'm holding people up because I'm not doing what I've committed to do. Except for picking up the girls, I've been here all day."

Katherine hadn't expected that. "I thought you were driving up to the city."

He tossed the phone on the table. "So did I. I changed my mind."

"Why?"

"Beats me." He pushed his hands through his hair. It looked like he'd done it more than once. Katherine had to admit that he seemed tired, and felt a trace of sympathy. He had a lot more on his mind this week than last week. She hated to add to it but had no choice. "Hope

139

seems worried, but I think she'll be okay. How's Sam?"

"Actually," he said, sounding surprised, "she was pretty sweet this afternoon."

"That could mean trouble."

"Yeah, well, I'm not looking a gift horse in the mouth."

"Maybe you should," she said, only half teasing. "Teenaged girls are wily. I know. I've been there. Is she all set for the prom?"

"We're shopping for a dress this weekend."

"Want me to take her?"

"No. I'll do it. It should be an interesting experience."

Katherine would have gladly gone along. She had shopped with the girls before. Apparently, though, Jack was taking that responsibility he had mentioned earlier very seriously. Fine. Then she felt less guilty worrying him. "Is she still going to the prom with Brendan?"

"In a manner of speaking," Jack said, but he looked puzzled. "I can't get a feel for how paired up this is. In my day, you had a specific date, but Sam's pretty vague about who's with who. There are ten of them going in the limo from Lydia's house. The girls are spending the night there after the prom." He hmphed. "I think that's what did it."

"Did what?"

"Changed her mood. She tossed the spending-the-night thing at me when she was leaving the car this morning, fully expecting I'd refuse, but I don't see anything wrong with it. It sounds to me like a big sleepover. They've been doing sleepovers for years."

"Are you sure it's only girls?"

That gave him pause, but it passed. "She says it is. She says Lydia's parents will be there."

"I think," Katherine tried, making a show of debating it herself, "that Rachel might want you to give them a call."

Jack's jaw went harder. "If I did that, it would suggest I didn't trust my daughter."

"This isn't about trust. It's about checking in and being involved."

"I take it you've been through this. How old did you say your kids were?"

Katherine didn't have kids, and it hit home. There had been a time when having a child had meant the world to her. Then she had been advised to wait a bit. Then Roy had left. And Byron had come and gone. And suddenly she was forty-two.

"Low blow," Jack surprised her by saying. "Sorry, but I'm going through a tough time here. I've never parented a teenager before, not for more than a weekend, and *not* for things like this, but I'm trying my best to do what's right, and it isn't easy. Samantha and I don't exactly have a love fest going on down there in Big Sur. She doesn't like what I bring in for dinner, doesn't like the coffee I brew. She doesn't like my talking on 'her' phone, or sleeping in Rachel's bed or using Rachel's shower, or driving her to school. As far as she's concerned, I'm a major inconvenience in her life—like I was the one who caused the accident, like I'm enjoying all this, like I should sleep on the sofa night after night. She's given me lip about almost everything I've done— but maybe, just maybe we've turned a corner. She actually smiled at me when I picked her up at school." Pleading, he paused for a breath. "Let me enjoy it for a little bit, huh?"

JACK thought about enjoying it a bit as he drove down the coast. It wasn't the first time he had used those words in response to the antics of Samantha McGill. The first time was fifteen years before, when she was five months old and vehemently opposed to sleeping through the night. They had been living in San Francisco a full month, Samantha in a room that Rachel had painted the same hot pink and navy as her room in Tucson, so she didn't have the excuse of a strange place. She had been fed cereal at six, along with Rachel's milk then and again at eleven. It was now two in the morning, and she wanted more.

The battle had been going on for two weeks, and they were exhausted. Jack was working a new job, pulling sweatshop hours as junior architect in a San Francisco firm. Rachel was pulling similar ones caring for the baby, doing the last of the unpacking, sewing drapes, and painting furniture and walls. They had both been dead to the world when Samantha's wails blasted in from the next room.

Rachel moaned and took cover under Jack's arm.

Jack pressed the pillow to his ear. "She can't be hungry," he mumbled.

Rachel mumbled back, "She isn't. Go back to sleep."

But the wailing went on.

Rachel slipped out of bed and, wrapped in his largest red flannel shirt, went off to the baby's room. The crying stopped. She returned to bed and curled up against him again. They had barely settled, spooned together, when the crying resumed.

Jack pulled the blanket over their heads. That muted the sound, but it went on. Still under the covers, he turned to face Rachel. "She's not hungry," he whispered into the warm, sleepy dark that would have been purple had a light been on. "Think she's sick?"

"Not sick," Rachel mumbled. "Angry. Pediatrician said to let her cry."

They let her cry. After five minutes, the wailing was more persistent. Jack threw the blanket back and started to get up.

"Don't you dare bring her here," Rachel cried.

Jack wasn't about to. He wasn't touching that baby. He had changed a diaper earlier. One per evening was his limit. "I want to make sure she isn't stuck between the slats and the bumper."

"She wasn't before," Rachel murmured, but she was right behind him, tiptoeing from their room to Samantha's with her fingers hooked on the waist of his shorts. When he stopped at the baby's door, Rachel settled against his back with her cheek to his skin.

In the fragmental glow of a tiny night-light, he saw a pale crib, polka-dot bumpers, a mobile with Rachel's felt creatures cut and pasted in every color imaginable, and beneath it, his angry daughter.

The wails were higher pitched now, but he backed away. "She's kicking her arms and legs, the little pest."

They returned to bed and lay entwined for a minute, listening to a fury of cries, before Rachel snaked free. "She's working herself into a frenzy," she said and disappeared into the night.

Seconds later, the crying stopped. Two minutes later, Rachel climbed back into bed. They held their breaths, listening, holding each other, on edge. "That did it, that did it," Jack whispered hopefully.

Samantha screamed.

Rachel laughed. "Whoa."

"Whose idea was it to have this baby?"

"Not mine," she said, laughing again.

"Not *mine.*"

The crying escalated.

"Let her cry," Jack whispered.

Rachel snuggled closer. "She'll wear herself out."

"Just a matter of time."

But they were wide awake. When wails became screams, Rachel announced full-voice, "I can't sleep with that noise."

"*You.*"

Rolling away, she pushed out of bed and closed all but inches of their door. Back in bed, she pulled him under the covers again to dull the sound coming through the walls. "Kiss me," she said. "Drown it out."

"This is a sexy moment? With that *racket* going on?"

"Kissing's what started it, isn't it? So fight fire with fire."

Jack had to admit it made sense. If the first kiss he gave her lacked passion, he put more into the second. By the third, he was hearing less beyond the bed. His mind was filling with the sweet sounds of Rachel, the warmth of her mouth, the swell of her breasts, the gentle curve of her belly. He had dispensed with her shirt and was fully erect when she said with an audible smile, "It's working."

"Oh, boy," his voice was hoarse, "is it ever."

She laughed brightly. "Samantha, not you."

Sure enough, the noise from the other room was slowing to the sounds of a tired baby on the verge of sleep. But was Jack tired? Not on your life! "That's nice," he practically purred. "Might as well enjoy it a bit." Lacing his fingers with Rachel's on the pillow, he came over her, found just the right spot between her open thighs, and thrust in.

AN AMBER SUN hung low on the horizon when they arrived back in Big Sur. Samantha headed for the house. Hope headed for Duncan's. Not knowing quite where he should head, Jack remained standing by the car. He took several deep breaths. Curious about what it was in the air that he found so appealing, he wandered off the gravel drive, through alternating patches of redwood sorrel and dark, packed earth, to a fallen tree. Purple flowers were budding around the lowest of the dead branches. He sat down midway along the trunk.

Looking straight up, he found the tops of the redwoods, where the foliage was the fullest, and watched for movement. It was a cool, dry, quiet May night. The air smelled of thick textured bark, of patches of moss, of sweet cedar from the lower canyon. At a sound on the forest floor, he spotted a ragged bird hopping among the brush. It was a Steller's jay, its feathers a motley slate blue and gray.

"You won't find much here, bud," he murmured. The forest floor was too heavily shaded to allow for food. Berries and bugs would be more plentiful beneath the live oaks and madrones.

Still the jay foraged, hopping downhill, then up. Jack watched for a bit. It was a mindless interlude that ended before he was quite ready. At the sound of footsteps in the undergrowth, he turned. Hope was coming toward him cradling the tabby. Her face was so serious that for a minute he feared the cat had died. But its eyes opened and its paws and tail shifted the smallest bit when Hope sat down on his tree.

"She didn't eat today. Nothing."

Jack didn't know how to console her. Rather than say something dumb and meaningless, he slid along the branch until they were arm to arm. She was petting the cat, running her small hand over its fur, from nose to ears, over neck, back, and rump, all the way to its tail. She repeated the motion again and again, a hypnotic stroking. In the silence of the forest, Jack heard the cat's purr.

"She likes that," he murmured.

Hope nodded. She kept up the petting. The purring went on.

After a bit, curious, Jack stuck in one stroke between Hope's. The cat's fur was surprisingly soft, surprisingly warm. He tried it again, half expecting that the cat would raise her head and express her objection to a stranger's touch. But Guinevere didn't. Without moving her chin from the crook of Hope's elbow, she simply looked up at him with total trust.

It nearly did him in.

chapter eight

BY FRIDAY MORNING, when there was still no change in Rachel's condition, Jack requested a consultation with his man in the city, William Breen. Jack had every confidence that the man was the best. Not only had Tina come up with his name, but Victoria Keats had faxed him the very same one.

The conference took place by phone in Steve Bauer's office. Besides Bauer, there were Kara Bates, Cindy Winston, and Jack.

The latest stats were sent to Breen's computer. Bauer orally reviewed them. Kara gave interpretations based on her observation of the patient. Cindy described Rachel's lack of response during bathing, turning, and range-of-motion exercises.

Jack kept thinking that the millions poured into research each year would surely have produced some procedure, some medication to help Rachel, but in the end, Breen said, "I wish I could say there's something else to try, but we wouldn't be doing anything different if she were in San Francisco. Her case is typical. She continues to hold her own. This is only the fourth day."

Jack hadn't expected the coma to last *two* days, and said as much.

"Mm, that would have been nice," the doctor responded, "but head injuries don't always do what's nice. Her GCS score is holding steady."

"Yeah," Jack remarked. "At rock bottom." He had learned about the Glasgow coma scale. Since Rachel showed no eye opening, no verbal response, and no motor response, she had the lowest possible score.

"But the data says she's not getting worse."

"Will she?" Jack asked. "Is there a chance she'll take a sudden turn?" He still felt a clinch in his stomach every time the phone rang, every time he arrived at the hospital after being out of contact for even a brief time.

"She could," said the doctor. "But if that were to happen, your team will know immediately and be able to act. With comas, it's a waiting game. I'm sorry, Mr. McGill. I know that isn't what you want to hear, but it's a little like defusing a bomb. Hurry the process, and it's apt to explode."

ON HIS way back to Rachel's room, Jack placed a call to Victoria. She had wanted an expert involved in the case; he wanted her to know it had been done. He also wanted to thank her for the flowers and to give her an update on Rachel's condition, discouraging as it was.

He had to settle for leaving a message in New York. Victoria was still abroad.

WHEN BEN WOLFE arrived, Jack was sitting by Rachel's hip, feeling useless. After trading bland observations about her hair, which spilled nicely from the topknot Katherine had made, the swelling of her face, which was down a little, and the perkiness of her turquoise nightgown, Jack stood and said, "Talk to Rachel. I'll be back." Ben was no threat, and he had something to do.

From the bank of phones down the hall, he called Jill. At the sound of her voice, he felt a guilty tug. "Hey."

"Hey, yourself," she said with pleasure. "I was wondering when you'd remember I was here."

His guilt increased. "It's been a rough couple of days. The girls are pretty upset. I'm still at the hospital. Rachel hasn't woken up."

"I know."

"Ah. You called my office."

"No." She sighed. "I didn't want Tina to know that you hadn't called me, so I called the hospital."

He felt even worse. "I'm sorry, Jill. I've had a lot on my mind."

"You could have called," she chided. "Didn't you think I'd want to know how Rachel was doing?"

She would. She was that kind of person. And he couldn't say why he hadn't called. That was one of many things that were muddled up in his mind.

But she expected an answer. So he said, "I've been trying to juggle everything here—work, the girls, Rachel. It's a nightmare."

"One phone call, Jack. It would have taken ten seconds."

Ten seconds, max. But damn it, she wasn't as harried as he was. "You could have called me in Big Sur," he countered. "Rachel's number is listed."

There was a silence. Then a sad "I think you forgot."

He pushed a hand through his hair. "I didn't forget."

"I think it didn't matter enough to you to talk with me."

"No," he sighed, "there's just nothing to tell. Not so long ago I was in conference with some of the best medical minds around, and *they* had nothing to say. There's nothing, Jill. We can't do a damn thing but sit here and wait."

"You're missing my point. If I meant anything to you, you'd want to hear my voice. It would be a comfort."

How could her voice be a comfort when it reminded him of the dozens of loose ends he had left hanging in the city? He put his elbow on the top of the phone and his head on his fist. "This isn't a good time, Jill. It just isn't."

"Is that my answer?"

He sighed. "No. It isn't. But I'm grappling with something difficult. I need a little time."

"You always need time."

"You knew that when we met. You knew I had a demanding life."

"I didn't count on the demands coming from your ex-wife," she said, then caught herself. "God, I'm sorry, Jack. That was selfish of me. She's in a coma. She may die."

"She's not dying. My guess is she'll wake up by the first of the week."

He heard a cautious "I won't see you until then? Not even on Saturday night?"

Over the past few months, Jack had spent every Saturday night with Jill that he hadn't either been with the girls or out of town—and he looked forward to those nights. He relaxed with Jill. He could count on her to be stimulating, physically and intellectually. He did love her—until she got that tomorrow look in her eye. Then he felt boxed in, which was what he felt now.

"Can't do it this Saturday," he said, annoyed. What did she think he would do with the girls while he drove three hours north on a Saturday night? Okay, Samantha was fifteen and would probably have plans of her own, but she was too young to drive, they lived in the middle of nowhere, and their mother was critically ill. "I have to be there for the girls. They have lists of things for me to do for them this weekend, and between all that, I'll be taking them to visit their mother. The doctors want them to talk with her. They say the girls will keep her focused, maybe help bring her back. Time'll be tight this weekend."

Jill said, "I see."

But she didn't. He heard hurt between those two little words. "Maybe Monday, when they're at school," he said, because he was going to have to drive up to the office again whether Rachel woke up or not. "Want to plan on lunch?"

She was that easily pleased. The smile returned to her voice. "I'd like that."

"Say, one o'clock, at Stars?"

"Not Stars. Here. I'll make lunch."

Lunch at her house would be a longer affair. It would be harder to eat and run, and he didn't know how much time he would have. But Jill was special. Of the women he had dated since the divorce, she came closest to being right for him. She didn't mind his travels. She was wonderful at business dinners. One on one, she was a charming companion and a devoted lover. During the few times she had seen the girls, they had gotten along well. How not to get along with Jill? She deserved better than days without a call.

So he said, "Sounds good. I'll look forward to it.

Thanks for being understanding, Jill. That's the biggest help to me right now."

He hung up the phone feeling like a total heel.

THE FEELING followed him right back into Rachel's room.

Ben was saying something to her and looked up, red-faced. "We were talking about the show."

Jack couldn't resist. "What was Rachel saying?"

"Not—a whole lot. I was telling her that you've been looking through her work. What do you think? Do we have a shot at going ahead?"

Jack hadn't looked through her work. He hadn't been in her studio other than to check the fax machine, and then he had walked in and out without seeing a thing. It was deliberate. He knew that. The why of it, like the why of not calling Jill at least once a day, wasn't clear.

So he stated the obvious. "We have a shot at having a show if she wakes up. If she doesn't . . ." He waggled his hand.

"How many pieces are done?"

"I'm not sure. I didn't count."

"Maybe I should take a look."

"Nah. There's no need for you to drive all the way down." There was the possessiveness again. The man might be benign enough, but Jack didn't want him in Rachel's house. "I'll do the counting tomorrow, when I'm not worried about getting the girls to school. Will you be at the gallery this weekend?"

"Sunday, from twelve to five."

"I'll stop in." He put out his hand. "Thanks for stopping by. We really appreciate it."

Ben shook his hand. He looked back at Rachel as though wanting to say something, thought twice, and quietly left.

JACK actually dozed off sitting in the chair by Rachel's bed. One minute he put his head down beside her hand, the next he woke up with a jolt.

"I'm sorry. I didn't mean to wake you."

He looked groggily at the woman who had arrived. She wasn't a natural beauty. Her nose was too long, her face too narrow, her silver hair too thin. But she was put together nicely, wearing a silk tunic and slim pants, and there was a gentleness to her. There was also a wonderful smell. It appeared to come from the large, zippered container she held.

She felt familiar, soothing.

He stood. "I've met you, haven't I?"

Her eyes smiled. "I'm Faye Lieberman. I've been by before. Rachel and I are in book group together."

"Ah. Faye of the beautiful blue flowers," he said. "You're one of the golfers."

She blushed. "Well, I'm not very good at it, but my husband wanted to retire here to play, so I figured that if I didn't learn, I'd be bored silly." She set the zippered container on the tray table. "This is dinner. There should be leftovers for the weekend. I figured you could use a little something homemade by now. Heating instructions are inside."

"Bless you," he said. They could indeed use a little something homemade. He was touched. "That's very sweet of you."

153

"It's nothing. How's Rachel?"

"Lying here listening, but not saying a word."

Faye went to the bed rail and touched Rachel's arm. "I'm here, Rachel. I brought food for your family. Not exactly chicken soup. Jack, here, needs something more solid. At least, that's what my Bill always says. Chicken soup is for children and invalids. We know better, though, don't we?" She glanced at Jack. "Rachel made my chicken soup recipe once a week through much of the winter. Not that it gets very cold here. I kind of miss that, the change of seasons."

"Where are you from?"

"Originally New England. Then D.C. My husband was with the State Department." To Rachel, she said, "He signed up for your investment course."

"Rachel's investment course?"

Faye smiled and moved a hand to erase the misconception. "Rachel took it and liked it. We figured it would give Bill something to do. We'd like to invest a little money for our grandchildren. Right now, college seems a long way off, but it isn't getting cheaper. How are the girls?"

The girls! Jack shot a look at his watch. "Waiting to be picked up at school as we speak." He squeezed Faye's shoulder and eyed the zippered bag. "They'll be thrilled. It's been take-in all week. You're a good soul to remember us."

She waved off his praise. "It's in the genes. This is what Jewish mothers do best. Enjoy."

THEY did that—all five of them. Samantha had invited Lydia and Shelly to stay overnight in Big Sur, a fact that

Jack didn't learn until the two additional girls were jammed into the BMW, at which point it seemed more of an effort to say no and pry them out.

Maybe Katherine was right. A bigger car would help. Still, it seemed premature.

The insulated bag held chicken in a wine-and-tomato sauce, with carrots and potatoes. To a person, they ate well and with good humor. Samantha and her friends alternately tossed their hair behind one shoulder or another and chatted about everyone and everything that came to mind. Hope, with her own hair in a scrunchy at her nape and Guinevere on her lap, listened to them with something like awe, and Jack wasn't much different. Samantha and company moved from topic to topic in stream-of-consciousness style and had an opinion on just about everything. Jack was intrigued by the sheer stamina of their mouths.

It wasn't until the next morning, though, that he understood the deeper implication of the sleepover. "Of *course,* they're coming shopping with me," Samantha said when Jack had the temerity to suggest that he drop the two girls at their homes on the way. "That's the whole point! I can't pick out a dress myself, and you're not a woman. If Mom can't be here, I want my friends."

He wanted to say, *No way! I have my hands full with my own two kids. I don't need two extras. Besides, I can't bring an army to the ICU—not to mention that they can hardly all fit in my car!*

He also wanted to say, *What is that under your eyes? Since when do you wear eyeliner? Does your mother know about that?*

But he didn't want Samantha growing grumpy again, not when they were beginning to get along. So he bit down both thoughts.

They hit Saks. They hit Benetton. By the time they hit the three other specialty stores, he was regretting his decision. Had it been just Samantha and he, she would have found something at the first store, and they would have been long since done. Hope was getting antsy. *He* was getting antsy.

"One more stop," he informed them when they were standing on the street corner, debating which way to go. "The next place is it. So think hard. There was a perfectly good dress back at Saks."

The girls held a prolonged three-way summit. When they finally agreed to return there, Jack exchanged a smug look with Hope. The smugness disappeared when the dress Samantha carried to the cash register wasn't the baby blue one he had meant. This one was short, slim, and black.

"Uh, Sam, isn't that one a little too . . . much?"

"Too much how?"

"Sophisticated?"

"I'm fifteen."

"You look about twenty-two in that dress."

"That's the point," she said with a sudden broad smile.

That smile did something to Jack. It gave him a glimpse of the beautiful young woman she was quickly becoming. He felt a jolt inside, a startling burst of pleasure and pride, followed closely by fear. Fifteen was nearing the age of consent. Was he ready for that? No. Could he prevent it? No.

"Would your mother like this dress?" he asked, suspecting that the Rachel who loved color and flow would have her qualms.

"She would *love* it," Sam said and, with another of those killer smiles, held out a hand for his credit card.

JACK gave serious thought to getting that new car during the ride from Carmel to Monterey. Lydia and Shelly insisted that they wanted to see Rachel, so five of them piled in again, but the dress was the final straw. For an itty-bitty thing, it caused a huge stir. Samantha wanted it hung. When there was no room for that, she decided that it should lie flat, but there was even less room for that. Jack, who knew something about fabrics, finally informed her that she could ball the thing up and it would bounce right back into shape without a wrinkle, especially once she had it on, it was that tight. That set her off. She finally agreed to drape it over the seat, but she wasn't happy with him, which meant that all his efforts to please had gone for naught. He would have given his right arm just then for a Cherokee.

Buying a car was something big, though. It was a major expense—and, yes, Rachel would need something new, but even if she was awake when they got to the hospital, she wouldn't be driving for a while, and then she would want to pick out her own car. He had done it for her once before, and wasn't making the same mistake twice.

They had been married for seven years. Her red VW was far older than that and had died and been revived more than once. It was still chugging along, but it badly needed a new radiator. Thinking to surprise her, now that he was finally making good money, Jack drove it off one morning under the guise of doing repairs and returned home with a Volvo. She had been heartsick. It was one of the first all-out, top-of-the-lungs arguments they'd had—or one of the last? He couldn't recall. Arguing

157

wasn't their style. And she had calmed down. Rachel wasn't one to beat a dead horse. The VW was gone. The Volvo was theirs. The dignity of her surrender had made him feel worse.

He hadn't thought about that argument in years, had always chalked it up to a case of principle and pride on Rachel's part, the feminist in her wanting to make her own decisions. At the time, his star was rising fast. Hers was on hold while she raised the kids. She had a right to be feeling defensive.

Only, she hadn't said that she wanted to make her own decisions. She had said that she wanted them to make decisions together. She had said that that was what couples did, and didn't he *want* her input?

Well, he did. She should have known that. But before long she was starting to make more of *her* own decisions, all without consulting him. She claimed he was out of town. He suspected it was tit for tat on an ongoing scale.

All of which had nothing to do with the present. He asked her about a new car. She didn't answer. So the decision was his. And he wasn't rushing out to buy.

He could lease one, he supposed. But even that was a lengthy commitment. After all, he was only filling in until Rachel woke up.

Better to wait.

JACK lingered with Rachel. He moved her hands around his, lacing their fingers, spooning their fists. He brushed her hair. He studied her face.

The girls knew their way around the hospital well

enough to take themselves to the cafeteria for cold drinks, a while later for lunch, a while after that for frozen yogurt. Lydia's mother came to visit and left with Lydia and Shelly. A refreshingly docile Katherine came and went, as did Charlie with the pink streak in her hair, Jan with the no-nonsense manicure, the mommy's beeper, and a golfer's tan, and a nondescript Nellie and Tom.

When others were in the room, Jack backed off. He didn't know these people. They were part of the life that Rachel had made without him. Oh, they were cordial. They introduced themselves and said kind things about the girls. But the situation was as awkward for them as it was for him. He was the bad guy in a room full of good guys.

Still, he outstayed them all. He helped the weekend nurse bathe Rachel and exercise her limbs. When her lips looked dry, he got Vaseline from the nurses' station. When her head looked uncomfortably angled, he propped it with pillows.

"When are we leaving, Daddy?" Hope asked every hour or so. Her cat was with Duncan. She wanted to get her.

Jack understood that; still, he put it off. He told himself that since the weekend staff didn't know Rachel, he could help out, but there was more to it. He felt better when he was with her, felt that his being there was a good thing in a bad time. He felt *decent* being with her, felt calmer. There wasn't any static here. There were no choices to make. All that was asked of him was to be, to talk, to assist. It was life at its primal best.

But Samantha was due at another friend's for a birthday overnight, and Hope, who kept trying to bury herself in a book, was giving him the most beseeching little looks, so he finally trundled them off.

RACHEL'S studio waited.

After dropping Hope at Duncan's, Jack drove back to the little local market for groceries. He put the leftovers of Faye's chicken into the oven. He put a load of laundry in the washing machine. He sat out under the redwoods, breathing woodsy air. The midday warmth had ebbed. It was a clear, cool, sweetly fragrant late afternoon.

Hope joined him, and they sat together for a while. He ran his hand along Guinevere's back, feeling warmth and weakness. He prayed that Hope was right, that the cat wasn't suffering. He knew Hope was.

Rachel's studio waited.

Jack put dinner on the table and took his time eating. Between bites, he asked Hope about school, about her friends, about the book she was reading. He told her he was proud of the way she was taking care of Guinevere, and when she burst into tears, he leaned over her chair and wrapped his arms around her. She still smelled of little girl, all warm and sweaty. He knew it wouldn't be long before she would be wanting short, skinny black dresses, too. For now, though, she was all innocence.

He wanted to say something about the cat, but he couldn't think of anything to make her feel better. So he just held her. It seemed fine.

When her tears slowed, he said, "Hey. Want to give me a hand?"

"W-with what?" she asked against his arm.

"Mom's paintings. We have to see what's what, so we can tell ole Ben what to do about a show. I've been putting off going in there."

"Why?"

"I don't know. I guess because I've always liked her work."

"So why don't you want to look at it?"

"I do." He realized that didn't jibe with what he had said before. "But her work always gets to me."

"Makes you sad?"

"Not sad."

"Happy?"

"It makes me . . . *feel.*"

Hope looked up at him, her eyes wet but wide. "She was doing sea otters on Monday. They are—*so*—*neat.* They're still on the easel. Want to see?"

She was beautiful from the inside out, his youngest daughter. Sweet, sensitive. Too often dominated by her older sister, but not tonight. Tonight she was the little girl who used to crawl into his lap and make him feel like a million bucks.

He smiled. "If you take me."

THEY spent an hour in the studio. Then Hope went to her room to read, and Jack spread the contents of his portfolio on the kitchen table to work. He had barely taken a look at what was there when he turned around and went back to the studio.

Rachel had made things easy. Tacked to her board was a list of the paintings that she had planned to include in the show. The pieces she had been working on just prior to the accident stood closest to the easel. Other pieces stood in clearly marked stacks. He had gone through them with Hope as a buffer. She saw subject matter and felt mood, but was most concerned about telling Jack little stories that went with each. He let her talk, pleased to see her focused on something other than the cat.

Now he went through the pieces, studying each one, moving on, then back. Rachel painted wildlife. In addition to the sea otters so graphically depicted, there were gray whales and Arctic wolves, egrets, quail, and loon. There were deer in snow and deer in high grass. There was a meadow of butterflies, and a rattlesnake so well camouflaged that a casual viewer would miss it. There was a coyote, looking Jack in the eye with such a vivid mix of fear and warning that he nearly backed off.

This was why he had put off seeing Rachel's work. He had always found it strong to the point of being intimidating. Whether she used oils, watercolors, acrylics, or pastels, she caught something so real and direct that he felt it—a look, a mood, a need. There was no mystery to why her following was growing. In a state and age where environmental concerns were rising, she captured the vulnerability of the wild.

Take the rattlesnake. There might well have been a caption below it that said the damned thing wanted nothing more than to fade into the woodwork and that it wouldn't harm a thing unless it feared harm to itself.

Powerful stuff to create with just the stroke of a brush or palette knife. He could never do anything like that, didn't have the vision or the skill. She was far more talented than he.

He suspected that that was why he had pursued architecture. True, he had been on that track before meeting Rachel. But they'd had such fun with each other that for a short time he had toyed with the idea of spending a lifetime painting with her. He hadn't, ostensibly because one of them needed to earn money. Deep down inside, though, he knew that his work would always be inferior to hers.

Still, they *had* had fun.

He went through her pieces again. Eleven paintings were done and ready to frame. Seven, including the otters, were finished except for the background, which held sketchy forms but no more. Field sketches and photographs were affixed to the back of each piece.

His best guess? She would need a week and a half to finish the seven. And the framing? The moldings were stacked in long strips by the baseboard. She had picked a wide wood frame, so simple and natural that it would enhance rather than compete. Pushing it, she could do the framing in several days.

Two weeks of work for a show two weeks away. It would have been a cinch, if the artist weren't in a coma.

HE had planned to tell Ben Wolfe exactly that at the gallery Sunday afternoon, but before he could say a word, Ben led him into an adjoining room. Three paintings, framed much as Rachel planned to frame the rest, hung in an alcove. Ceiling spots hit each canvas in such a way that the subject was perfectly lit and riveting. Ben knew his stuff.

"We had four," he explained, seeming taller and stronger on his own turf. "One of them sold last week. Another of the four isn't for sale at all. Rachel won't let it go. Not that I blame her. I'd hold on to it, too, if it were mine. It's my all-time favorite." He was looking at the one he meant, but Jack had already picked it out. A layman might not have caught the difference between the three. Not only wasn't he a layman, but he was personally involved.

The painting that Ben loved, that Rachel refused to sell, was one that she and Jack had done together. The subject was a pair of bobcat pups on a fallen log, the background a meadow surrounded by trees. They had come on the scene during a busman's weekend hiking through—yes—the same Santa Lucias that Rachel now called home. She had done the pups, he the background.

The pups were more vivid now than he remembered them being. She might have touched them up, but the background was exactly as it had been—all his.

"What do you love about it?" Jack asked Ben. So maybe he, too, needed stroking.

Ben, in his innocence, didn't hesitate to tell him. "The background is complimentary to the rest, but different, very subtly different. It makes the bobcats more striking."

"Have you told Rachel that?"

"Many times."

"What does she say?"

"Just that it was done a long time ago. So where do we stand? How many more paintings are in her studio?"

Eleven, Jack thought, but he was still looking at the picture he and Rachel had done together. She hadn't told Ben about his participation. Dishonest, perhaps, but interesting. The piece wasn't for sale. That was good.

"Do we have a shot at the show?" Ben asked.

"I, uh, I think . . . yeah, actually, I think we do," Jack said, because they definitely had a shot at it. That wasn't the real question. The *real* question was how Rachel would feel if Jack picked up a brush and collaborated with her again.

chapter nine

JACK WAS FEELING stronger. He didn't know why, since Rachel's condition hadn't changed. He figured it had to do with being more rested. Life in Big Sur didn't make evening demands. He had slept more in the last few days than he had in months.

It surprised him. By rights, he should have been lying awake worrying about Rachel and the girls and what might be if Rachel didn't recover. He should have been losing sleep over work and the firm, should have been staring at the ceiling wondering what to do about Jill. And he did think about all those things—but during the day. Rachel's bed was firm, and even if the scent of her on the sheets roused the devil of his id, he had always slept well when he was with her.

He thought about that now, driving south along the coast with the girls in the car. Rachel was a cuddler. For him, that had meant having a breath of warmth against back, front, arm, or hip, depending on how she was burrowed. She snuggled in as though his body were a magnet. During the night, at least, he had always felt competent and strong.

So sleeping better was one possible reason for his current mood.

Another might be the drive itself. He used to find driving relaxing, way back, before they moved to the city. What he felt now reminded him of that. Traffic always thinned after Carmel, allowing him to catch more of the passing scenery—the beach, artichoke fields, the touch of purple where wildflowers were starting to bloom on the low hills swelling beyond. He could feel himself mellowing once he reached this stretch, could feel himself breathing more deeply. Not even the spot where the accident had occurred changed that.

Or maybe it was Rachel's work. He kept thinking about the gallery, about Ben's favorite painting, about the ones in her studio waiting to be finished. He kept thinking that it would be fun to paint again.

It was like there was something new and different in his life. Something exciting. Challenging. *Meaningful* was the word that came to mind, which was odd, since his life was *plenty* meaningful. But there it was.

THE PHONE was ringing when they walked in the door. Samantha ran for it. Jack followed her into the kitchen and waited nervously. If something had happened at the hospital—good *or* bad—he would turn right around and return to Monterey.

Samantha passed him the phone with a look of frustration. "It's David."

Jack felt his own frustration as he took the phone. David had been sending messages all week. He wanted work done, but Jack's mind was elsewhere. "How're you doing, David?"

"Jack? Jack? Is it really you?"

Jack looked out the window. The early evening sun snagging the tops of the redwoods spilled a glow through airy needles and on down densely scaled bark. There was something settling about it. His voice was more forgiving than it might otherwise have been. "It's been a long day, pal."

"No change, then?"

"No change. What's up?"

"I just got a call. Flynn's gone."

"To Buffalo? It's about time."

"To Walker, Jansen, and McCree."

Walker, Jansen, and McCree. The competition. Michael Flynn had defected. He was the third one in six weeks. At least he wouldn't have taken any accounts with him. Clients weren't drawn to Michael. He was a follower, not a leader.

"Will you be long?" an aggrieved Samantha asked.

Jack held up a hand to silence her and said to David, "Okay. We can live with this. It makes sense. WJM's work is more local than ours. Michael has young kids and doesn't want to travel."

"I agree with you there, but what about you? You're the one who'll have to fly to Buffalo in his place."

Habit kicked in. For a split-second, Jack looked ahead to the workweek and debated what he could shift around or cancel to allow for several days in New York. Then he realized that he had already canceled and shifted to the limit to clear the next patch for Rachel.

She had to wake up. It would be a week tomorrow. It was time.

In the meanwhile, there was a solution. There was always a solution. He made a quick mental assessment of the office situation vis-à-vis the Buffalo project. "Brynna Johnson can do it."

David made a disapproving sound. "Brynna's only a draftsperson."

"She's more experienced than the others, and she knows Buffalo. Besides, I think she's great."

"She's pregnant."

Jack hadn't known that. "No kidding? But that's okay. We can still move her up."

"What's the point of doing that if she'll be leaving?"

"Will she?"

"You know how women are these days. What'll happen—trust me, this happens *all* the time—is that she'll say she's taking a standard maternity leave, then at the end of it she'll tell us she's not coming back. Why should we make a woman like that a project manager?"

"Because she's talented," Jack said, thinking of his daughters being in the same boat one day, "and because maybe if we put out for her, she'll put out for us. It's a matter of instilling loyalty."

David snorted. "Loyalty? Good God, I haven't heard that word in a while. Has anyone else?"

Fine. So loyalty wasn't something they had talked much about. But it was time. Instability in the lower echelons of the firm made things harder for the people on top. Jack had to be able to rely on his associates. He hadn't realized how much, until now.

"Maybe if she feels she's moving up with us," he said, "she'll come back after the baby. How far along is she?"

"I don't know. Three months? Four months?"

Jack remembered Rachel at four months. She had barely looked pregnant with Samantha, had looked it a little more with Hope. The early change had been in her breasts and her belly, both gently swollen, creamy, soft.

That was what Jack had seen. The rest of the world had seen that by the fourth month, Rachel had outgrown morning sickness and was feeling good. She hadn't wanted coddling, hadn't wanted extra attention, hadn't wanted anyone telling her not to do what she normally did. All she asked for was the occasional hot fudge sundae with mocha almond ice cream. That was her favorite, her very favorite. The ecstatic look on her face—the way she sucked off each spoonful, scraping the very last of the fudge from the rim of the dish—was a sight to behold.

Rachel in her fourth month of pregnancy had been confident and strong. Brynna Johnson struck Jack as the same type.

"Brynna can go to Buffalo," he decided. "Unless she doesn't want to. In which case we'll send Alex Tobin. But Brynna's my first choice."

"Dad, I need the phone," Samantha whined.

David said, "Why not go yourself? If Rachel is stable—"

"She's in a coma. I can't leave now."

"Okay. Forget traveling. I'll settle for getting you back in the office. Hell, I'll settle for four hours a day. Do it while the girls are in school. If Rachel is unconscious, she won't know you're gone, and if she wakes up, hell, if she wakes up she won't *want* you there. We have work to do, Jack. It'll only wait so long."

Jack and David went back a long way. They had met as draftsmen sharing the bottom rung of the ladder and, commiserating, had started the climb together. Jack was the stronger designer, David the better businessman, but they shared identical dreams of success, recognition, and monetary reward. Early on in those bottom-rung days, when such dreams were a mainstay of survival, they decided to form a firm together someday. It made good business sense. Between their different strengths, their shared goals, and the diversity of their cultural backgrounds, they covered a good many bases.

For two years, the dream remained a dream. They slowly climbed the ladder, becoming junior architects, then project architects. Then, in the blink of an eye, everything changed. On the day when David charmed a large company into hiring them independently of the firm where they worked, they resigned and formed Sung and McGill. In the thirteen years since, they had been of one mind as to what was needed to make the firm a success—and they might still be. Jack just wished his partner was more sensitive.

"I need understanding here, Dave. I need help."

"I gotcha. But for how long? She's your past; we're your present and future."

"Da-ad?" Samantha made two impatient syllables of his name.

He put a finger in his ear and turned his back. "Do you want to call Brynna, or should I? No. Forget that question." David could be abrasive. He feared what the man might say to Brynna. "I'll call her. I'm driving up tomorrow morning. I'll meet with her and make sure she understands what has to be done."

"Have you talked with Boca?"

"Oh, yeah. I've talked with Boca. The problem is with the footprint, which means altering the whole fuckin' design." Why did he fear it wouldn't be for the last time?

His stomach churned just thinking about it. "Listen, David, I have to get off the phone—"

"To do *what?* Jack, I'm the front guy here. I'm the one running around drumming up work. I need to know you're making progress on something. You are working down there, aren't you? The girls are in school all fuckin' day, and there isn't a hell of a lot you can do for Rachel."

For a minute, Jack was angry enough to hold his tongue. When he was in control again, he said, "Actually, there is. I can paint. Hey, my daughter needs the phone. I have to go, Dave. Later." He hung up the phone.

"Paint what?" Samantha asked, tossing her hair back in a gesture that was at the same time negligent and powerful.

"Your mom's stuff," he answered.

She screwed up her face in horror. "You can't do that. Mom's stuff is hers. You can't mess with it."

The phone rang again. He beat her to it. "Yes?"

"It's Victoria. How's my daughter?"

"You *can't,*" Samantha insisted.

"She's the same," he told his mother-in-law, returning the finger to his ear. "The doctors think that's good news."

"I don't. There must be something they can do. I've been asking people here, and they all agree. You don't just sit around and wait. I can't tell you the number of horror stories, *horror* stories, I've heard about times when action wasn't taken that should have been taken. If I were you, I wouldn't want to find myself six months from now looking back and regretting that I didn't push. Didn't my man have *any* suggestions?"

"None that were different from the doctors here."

"The doctors there. Huh. The one I talked with the other day sounded too young to know much. I'd like to consult with someone in New York. I'll be back there later tomorrow. My board was sending flowers. Did they arrive?"

"A few minutes ago, but she's in the ICU, Victoria. It'd be best if you asked people not to send things. We'll only have to give them away." It wasn't the whole truth, but he envisioned Victoria spreading the word and an entire flower shop materializing in Rachel's room.

"You told me not to come, Jack. Has that changed? Is there anything I can do there?"

Samantha tugged at his arm. *Wait,* he mouthed, then said to Victoria, "We're marking time."

"Has your mother been down?"

"I haven't talked with her."

"She doesn't know? That's *terrible,* Jack. Give her a call. She should be told. I'll call you again tomorrow. In the meantime, you know how to reach me."

"It isn't right," Samantha said as he hung up the phone.

"Tell me about it," he muttered, thinking about motherly devotion. If Victoria came to see Rachel, she would drive them all up a tree. And his own mother? A phone call would be bad enough. Somehow, some way she would blame him for the accident.

"So you won't?" Samantha asked.

"Won't what?"

"Mess with mom's work?"

He shifted gears. "I wasn't planning to 'mess' with it. I was planning—I was *toying* with the idea of finishing a few of those pieces so that Ben can go ahead with the show."

"She wouldn't want you doing that."

"Oh? Did you ask?"

Samantha made a face. "That was a mean thing to say."

172

"Well, did you? No, because your mother is in a coma, which means that none of us can ask, so we don't know *what* she wants. She did want this show. Do you doubt that?"

Samantha grunted what he took to be a no.

"And Ben says the show can't be postponed, so what are we supposed to do?"

"Some of her pictures are finished. They can be in the show."

And if your mother doesn't ever wake up or, worse, dies? It may be now or never, toots, he wanted to say, but he held his temper in check. "Know the picture at the gallery of the bobcat pups in the meadow?"

"Of course I know it," she said in disgust. "Anyone who's been in this house knows it. It was in the living room for years. It's Mom's favorite."

"Right," he said, gaining strength. "Do you know that I helped paint it?" Her withering look said that not only didn't she know it, but that she didn't believe it for a minute. "You were six years old. Your mother and I went hiking in the mountains not far from here. When we came back, that was one of the pictures we painted."

"Like, what part did *you* do?" Samantha mocked. "A *tree?*"

There hadn't been many times when one of his children had angered him to the point of losing control, and this wasn't one, but he wasn't taking any chances. Very deliberately, he tucked his hands in his pockets. Had he been his father, he would have used one of them to take the scornful look off Samantha's face. There had to be a better way.

"Have you ever drawn a tree?" he asked.

"Everyone's drawn trees."

"Yeah?" Catching her wrist in a way that was loose but locked, he strode toward the front door.

"Where are you *taking* me?" she cried. "I have things to *do!*"

He didn't talk, didn't look back, didn't stop until they were in the woods and standing face-to-face with the trunk of one of the largest of the redwoods. It wasn't one of the giant sequoias that grew farther north and inland, just a coast redwood, but it would do fine.

Drawing Samantha in front of him, he held her rigid shoulders and said over the crown of that straight blond hair, "What do you see?"

"Bark," she snapped.

"What else?"

"*Bark.*"

"Okay, what color is it?"

"Red," she said, then slowly, pedantically, "This is a redwood."

"Bright red? Brick red? Mahogany? Maroon?"

"I don't know. Whatever."

"If you were to paint it, what color would you make it? Bright red? Brick?"

When she didn't answer, he squeezed a shoulder.

"Darker than that," she muttered.

"Mahogany?"

"Maybe."

"All of it?"

"What do you mean?"

"Would you paint all of it mahogany?"

"Yes," she bit out.

He released one shoulder, reached over it, and touched a piece of the bark. "But what about this part? The way the light hits, it's darker by a shade or two." He moved his finger. "This part's a shade or two darker than that." And again. "This part's almost black. Can you see that?"

"*Yes,* I can see it."

"If you paint the whole thing mahogany, you'll lose the texture." He swept the pads of his fingers over the bark. "Look at the shape of this piece, wider on top, tapering down. And the way this one waves back and forth. And this sickle-shaped piece? You'd lose these shapes if you did the whole thing one color." He looked higher. "And up there? Where the sunset slants in? It makes the bark more orange than red. So you'd miss that, too, if you did the whole thing mahogany." He looked way up. "Now look at the needles."

"You've made your point."

"Look at them anyway," he said, framing her head with his hands and using only enough pressure as was necessary to tip it up. "The needles are feathery. Rich green. No—more blue-green in this light, I think. Warmer, almost lime, where the sun hits." He paused. "Is it the needles that smell so good, or the bark?"

"I don't know. Is it *my* fault that I'm the only one in this family who can't draw?"

Jack was so surprised by the question that he let her go when she twisted away.

"And just because you know about colors," she blurted out, turning from ten feet away, "doesn't mean you painted part of Mom's picture. If you did, why would she have it hanging in the living room? She divorced you. She wanted you out of her life!"

She stomped off, leaving Jack feeling empty again.

～ ➤ ～

175

"MY FATHER is a jerk," Samantha told Lydia. She was breathing hard. "Who does he think he is, barging in here and taking over? He doesn't know what my mother wants. He hasn't lived with her in six years. No, *longer.* He wasn't *there* for at *least* another six years. Probably even *more.*"

"Aw, Sam, he's not that bad."

"You don't have to live with him. You're not the one he's watching all the time. You don't see him trying to take over everything. *You're* not the one who can't borrow your mother's clothes because *he*'s in there all the time. He said he used to help my mother paint, and I'm like, 'Why didn't she ever tell *us* that?' and he doesn't have an answer. I'm *sick* of having him around. I can't do *anything* right when he's here. Know what he wants? He wants me to shut up. He wants me to be sweet and silent and obedient like Hope. But I'm not like Hope. I don't *want* to be like Hope."

"I don't think he wants that. Did he ever say it?"

"He wouldn't say it. But I know. I can see the way he looks at her and the way he looks at me. It's different."

"I thought he was pretty nice."

"That was what he wanted you to think. It was an act."

"He seems really worried about your mother."

"Yeah. Because if she doesn't get better, he'll be stuck with us. That'd cramp his style. Why are you sticking up for him? You don't know the half of it. You should meet the woman he dates. Jill. Jack and Jill. Can you believe it? She's nice enough to make you sick."

"Is he gonna marry her?"

"Poor her, if he does. He's fickle. Before long, he's out looking for better."

"Is that what he did to your mom?"

"Why *else* would they get divorced?" Call waiting clicked. "Why *are* you taking his side? You're supposed to be *my* friend, Lydia. Hold on." She pressed the button. It was Brendan. Normally, talking with Brendan wouldn't hold a candle to talking with Lydia, but Samantha was furious with Lydia just then, so she took the call. "Lydia's being a dweeb," she told Brendan straight out.

"So you know about the party?"

"Know what?"

"Didn't she tell you? She was supposed to."

"Tell me *what?*"

There was a pause, then a meek "Maybe you should call her."

"Brendan. *Tell* me."

"Her parents are staying home," he blurted out.

"What?"

"Lydia let it slip that the guys were coming back afterward, too, so they changed their plans. They're gonna be there all night."

"Lydia let it slip?" Samantha sighed in disgust. "How could she *do* that?"

"Some of the other parents started calling her parents, so they started asking her questions, and it slipped out."

"I should have known." Lydia had been her best friend since third grade, but lately she was too soft. All along she had been nervous about the party. She was scared that someone would throw up, her parents would find out why, and she'd be the one punished. So now everyone would miss out. "She *is* a dweeb. This ruins the whole thing."

"Why?"

"Forget the beer, if her parents are there."

"Yeah, but my mother thought her parents were going

to be there all along, so now I won't get in trouble. Besides, they'll stay in the other room. It won't be so bad."

"Oh, yuk! You're as pathetic as Lydia is." When he had nothing to say about that, she made a guttural sound. "This prom is going to be totally boring. I'm not sure I want to go."

He was silent for a long minute. "What do you mean?"

"I may not go."

He should have protested. If it had been her, she would have. But that was asking too much of Brendan. Instead, after *another* silence, he said, "What about me?"

"I think you should take Jana," she decided.

"You do?"

"Yes." She wasn't going with a wimp.

"You really don't want to go?"

"I really don't. Call Jana."

He couldn't think of a thing to say to that but a weak "Oh. Okay. See you tomorrow."

Samantha hung up the phone and fumed. She had been waiting *forever* for a prom, for limos and all-night parties and beer. She had been to a zillion dances. If she'd thought this was going to be another one, she'd have bought the dorky blue dress her father liked. But this was a *prom.* It was supposed to be different.

Thank you, Lydia. Thank you, Brendan. Neither of them had any guts. Neither of them had a sense of adventure. They were big babies. Was *she* the only one who wasn't?

She knew of another person who wasn't. Picking up the phone, she pressed in his number. She knew it by heart, had called it many times. Before, she hadn't done anything but listen to his voice.

Her pulse raced when it came to her now, a deep, cool, seventeen-year-old " 'Lo?"

"Hi, Teague. It's Samantha. You know, from the school bus?"

The voice turned smooth around a smile. "I think I know Samantha from the school bus, only she hasn't been there all week."

"My mom's been sick, so my dad's been driving me up. How's things?"

"Better now. I was beginning to think you were avoiding me."

She grinned. "I wouldn't do that. I mean, I go to my dad, 'I really want to take the bus,' and he goes, 'But I want to drive your sister, and she won't go without you.' So I'm stuck in the car."

"Hey. Was it *your* mom who had an accident?"

"It was," Samantha said, feeling important. "She was driving up to Carmel when someone hit her. The car went off the road and over the cliff. She was underwater for ages. They got her breathing again, but she's in a coma, and they don't know if she's going to wake up. We've been spending every minute we can in her hospital room."

"Is it gross?"

Samantha straightened her shoulders. "It's actually fine. After a while, you forget about the machines and tubes. They want us to talk with her, so that's what we do. They say she hears us and that if anything can bring her back, it's our voices."

"Cool."

"The thing is that I've been so *obsessed* with my mom and the hospital that I haven't been thinking about anything else, but my dad said that my mom would want me to go to my prom—it's Saturday night—only I haven't

asked anyone yet. So. What do you think? Want to go
with me?"

"Where is it?"

Her heart fell. Teague was a junior. *His* prom would
be held in a hotel. "It's at school," she murmured and
raced on, "but the thing is that we don't have to stay there
long. I mean, it's going to be a dumb little prom, but if
my mom would want me there, I think I should go. I have
a gorgeous black dress that my dad says is too sexy for
someone my age, which shows how much *he* knows. So,
do you want to go?"

"Sure." His voice was smiling again. "I'll go."

She smiled back. "Awesome!"

HOPE sat on her bedroom floor. A book lay open beside
her, but she was studying her calendar, the one Rachel
had made her, with a different watercolor for each
month. Guinevere was on her lap, curled in a limp little
ball, making precious few sounds.

Carefully cradling the cat, she rose and went out in
her stocking feet to find her father. He wasn't in the living room or the kitchen, wasn't in the den, wasn't in her
mother's bedroom. She found him in the studio. He was
leaning against a wall, ankles crossed, arms folded. He
was deep in concentration, studying canvases that he had
lined up on the opposite side of the room.

She stood quietly by the door, telling herself that
maybe she should leave and come back later. But she
needed to talk with him.

"Hi, sweetie," he said and looked at her feet. "Where
are the boots?"

"In my room. What are you doing?" she asked.

"Looking at your mother's stuff. She's good."

"Are you really going to finish her pictures?"

"I don't know. It was just a thought. What do you think? Would your mother be angry with me if I did?"

Hope didn't think so. She hadn't ever heard Rachel say anything bad about Jack. Sam told her she just wasn't listening, but she was. "Daddy?"

"What, sweetie?"

"It'll be a week tomorrow. Do you think Mommy's going to wake up?"

"I do. It's just taking longer than I had hoped it would."

"What do the doctors say?"

"Not much. They're waiting, too. They're pleased that she's not getting worse."

Hope guessed that if Rachel wasn't getting worse, then the bad stuff she was feeling had to do with her cat. She raised her arms so that she could rub her face in Guinevere's fur. It was as soft as ever. But something wasn't right.

"Guinevere's getting worse," she said. "I don't think she hears me anymore. I clap, and she doesn't even turn her head. She's going to die soon, Daddy."

He pushed away from the wall, crossed the room, and rubbed Guinevere between the ears. "Is she in pain?"

"No. She'd meow if she was." She swallowed. Her throat hurt. She had to force the words out. "Daddy, what'll I do when she dies?"

He thought for a minute. "You'll be sad. You'll grieve for her."

That wasn't what Hope meant. "What will I do with *her?* I mean, I can't just . . . throw her out like she was chicken bones."

He looked cross. "You shouldn't be worrying about this now, Hope. It doesn't accomplish anything. This cat doesn't look to me like she's ready to die."

But Hope felt the urgency of it. "She is. I know it, Daddy. I can *feel* it."

"You're just scared."

"No," she insisted. "It's happening. So what am I going to *do?*"

He frowned, not so much cross now as unsure. "What do you want to do?"

"I want to bury her."

He scratched his head and left his hand up there for a minute. She could see that he didn't know what to do. Samantha was right. He didn't think the way they did.

"Okay," he said, surprising her. "You can bury her. There must be a pet cemetery somewhere around here."

But Hope didn't want a pet cemetery. She didn't want to have to go driving to see Guinevere. She wanted the cat nearby, wanted Guinevere to know that *she* was nearby.

"Or we can bury her in the forest," Jack said, glancing out the window. "Somewhere close. Would you feel better if we did that?"

Much, Hope thought, nodding.

"Done," he said and pulled her close.

She didn't say anything for a minute because her throat hurt again. This time it was in relief, because Sam was wrong. He did understand. That meant he cared.

"Daddy?" she whispered so Sam wouldn't hear. "You won't leave us alone, will you?"

"How could I do that?"

She knew that if Sam annoyed him enough, he could and would. "If Mommy doesn't wake up and you have to go back to the city to work, you could hire someone to stay here."

"I won't."

"Do you promise?"

"I promise."

She sighed. Even more softly, with the smallest bit of breath, she said, "I love you."

He didn't answer, but she felt his cheek against the top of her head, and in that instant, the clock turned back and she believed.

WHEN SHE woke up the next morning, Guinevere hadn't moved from the spot where Hope had put her the night before. Frightened, she leaned close, close enough so that the cat would feel her breath. "Guin?" she whispered, rubbing the cat's cheek with a fingertip. When she felt the smallest movement against her finger, she let out a breath.

She draped an arm lightly around the cat and lay close, thinking, *I love you, Guinevere, I love you,* and heard the whisper of an answering purr. Then it stopped. For several minutes, Hope didn't move. "Guin?" she whispered. She stroked the cat's head and waited for a purr, stroked again, waited again. When there was nothing, she buried her head in Guinevere's cooling fur and began to cry.

"Hope?" Jack called, coming to the door. "Are you up?"

Gulping sobs bubbled up from inside. When she tried to stop them, they only grew louder. She pulled Guinevere closer, hoping she was wrong, hoping she was wrong. Only, she knew better. She could *feel* it, a giant emptiness, a big hole, a huge aloneness.

"Sweetie?" He touched her head. "Hope, what is it?" He touched the cat, left his hand there a minute, and just when she was thinking that she didn't know what she was going to do because everything she loved always left her, he slipped his arms around her and Guinevere both, and leaned over close.

He didn't say anything, just sat there sheltering them, and when Samantha came in asking when they were leaving, he said, "Hope's not going today. Guinevere just died."

"I'm sorry, Hope," Samantha said, softly now, close by.

"We're burying her here," Jack told her. "Want to take the bus today?"

Hope didn't hear an answer. She had started crying again, because the words were too real. *Guinevere just died.* Besides, Samantha wasn't the one she wanted just then. The one she wanted was holding her tight.

IF ANYONE had told Jack that while his wife was in a coma and his firm was floundering, he would be splitting firewood into planks to build a tiny coffin for a cat, he would have had them committed. But it seemed like the best thing to do.

Hope sat on the ground nearby. Guinevere was wrapped in the wash-worn baby afghan that Rachel had crocheted and that Hope had slept with for the first eight years of her life. Tatters and all, it was her prized possession. Once she wrapped Guinevere in it, she stopped crying. She held her bundle as though it were gold.

Jack found satisfaction splitting the logs and putting hammer to nail. When the small coffin was finished, he dug a grave, dug deeper than was probably necessary, but he didn't want other animals digging it up. Besides, it felt good to work, felt good to build up a sweat and breathe hard.

The exertion also tired him out enough so that when Hope placed her little bundle in the coffin and he nailed it shut, put it in the hole, and began covering it with dirt, he didn't feel quite so raw.

Hope cried. It was inevitable. Jack held her against his side and let her get it all out. Then they sat, just sat for a bit—and again it was absurd. The last thing Jack had time for was lingering in the forest on a Monday morning. He had to shower and visit Rachel, then drive on into the city to work. But Hope seemed to want him to do this. And he had to admit there was a peace to it.

They sat side by side facing Guinevere's grave. After a time, in a voice that held the remnants of tears, and reverence, Hope said, "Know why I picked right here?"

"No. Why?"

"The view." She pointed. "See through the trees? That drop-off? That's the canyon opening up."

Jack followed the line of her finger and, yes, saw the drop-off. Beyond, given depth and distance by a whisper of mist, was a palette of forest greens. He turned to Hope to remark on its beauty, but she had shifted her head and narrowed her eyes.

"If you look past it," she said, "way past it—what looks like clouds is really ocean."

"How can you tell?"

"If those were clouds, they would be whitish gray or blackish gray. Those are bluish gray. Can you see?"

Actually, he could.

"Mom taught me that. And to listen." She cocked her head. "Do you hear it?"

"The silence? You bet."

"No," she scolded with a small smile. "The *stream*."

He listened. "That's silence."

She shook her head.

He might have argued. But if Rachel had heard a stream, there was a stream. He knew not to question it. Rachel *felt* the outdoors. That was one of the things that had first intrigued him about her. In Tucson once, she had made him sit with her for hours in the desert with his eyes closed, listening. He had heard the scampering of a pack rat, the slither of a snake. He had heard wind whispering down the fluted trunk of a saguaro.

Remembering that as he sat here in this breathtakingly lovely place, he had a sense of what Rachel might have given up when she had moved to San Francisco with him. She lived and breathed the fresh outdoors. She connected with flora and fauna as many people didn't. She knew her terrain.

So he listened for the sound of a stream. He swallowed to clear his ears and listened again, sorting the outside world from the flow of blood in his head. And he heard it, a faint, distant *shhhhh* far to the left.

"Over there?" He pointed.

Hope grinned and nodded.

"How far a walk?"

"Five minutes. It runs down the mountains into the ocean. I've walked it all the way down with Mom."

"How does it cross the road?"

"It goes under a bridge. I'll show you sometime," she said, but her voice was less sure, and she didn't look at him.

He knew she was thinking that once Rachel woke up, he would be gone. But even if Rachel woke up that very day, she would still need help. Okay, so she might not want him around all the time. But spring was full and summer approaching. There were new shades of green here. The idea of a streamside walk held appeal.

He smiled, feeling the same sense of anticipation that he had felt driving back to Big Sur the night before.

chapter ten

THE DRIVE from Big Sur to the hospital on a Monday midmorning took an easy forty-five minutes. Jack arrived feeling mellow—only to find another patient in Rachel's room. He hurried to the next room, thinking he had made an innocent mistake, but an entire family of grim-faced strangers there told him he had been right the first time. His heart stopped for the fraction of a second it took for him to reason that he would have been called if Rachel had died. Then, surgery? Nearly as bad.

Holding Hope's hand, he strode to the nurses' station. "Where's my wife?" he asked, and spotted Cindy emerging from a room at the far end of the corridor. He headed there with Hope in tow. "Where's Rachel?"

Cindy waved them along and into the room from which she had just come. It was a regular hospital room, with a TV, a bathroom, and several easy chairs. Katherine was in one of those chairs. Rachel was lying on her side facing her, and for a split-second, unable to see her eyes, Jack thought the change meant she had woken up.

Katherine had a fast smile for Hope, but her expression before and after told him that it wasn't so.

"It's been a week," Cindy said in her slow, gentle way. "Rachel's condition has been steady the whole time. The doctors thought she could be moved."

Jack had a bad feeling. Even after separating it from Guinevere's death, it still felt bad. "You needed her space for someone else."

"Yes, but that's not why we moved her. She's stable. Her stats aren't changing."

"But what if they do? The whole point was for you to know the minute something happened."

"We're monitoring her from here," Cindy said and, yes, he saw the same monitors, the same wires.

"But those aren't connected to the central desk."

"We'll be checking her regularly."

Kara Bates's voice came from the door. "This is what we call an observation room," she said, entering. "It's one step down from the ICU. Rachel will have the kind of attention here that most patients get immediately after surgery."

"It's only been a week," Jack argued, frightened. "What about that guy you pointed out who's been in Intensive Care for a month and a half?"

"He has heart and lung problems. He's not stable. Believe me, Rachel is far better off. She's functioning on her own, perfectly steady. She isn't going anywhere."

Jack fought a sinking feeling without quite knowing its cause. The bruise on the side of Rachel's face was healing—scabbing a reddish brown where it had been scraped, turning green where it had been hit—and the stitches had been removed from the cut on her hand. She looked paler than ever, though, and thin. He worried about that. She had never had pounds to spare.

Hope climbed onto the bed, tucked in her cowboy boots, and sat by her mother's hip. She didn't say any-thing. After a minute, she gingerly lifted Rachel's hand and put it in her lap. Her head was down. She slowly curled into herself. When she started to sniffle, she lifted Rachel's hand to cover her tears.

Jack caught Katherine's look of alarm. *Guinevere,* he mouthed.

She winced and nodded.

He touched Hope's bowed head, lightly stroking her hair as he had the cat's fur. He wanted to say something, but didn't know what. He imagined that letting Hope know he was with her was what she needed most.

But the sinking feeling inside him was starting to take form. He gestured Kara into the hall. "You're giv-ing up on her," he accused. "You're taking her off the front line because you don't think she's waking up for a while."

"That's not it. We're simply saying that since the acci-dent was nearly a week ago and there haven't been any complications, the chances of one occurring now are low. Cindy will still be her nurse. She'll watch the monitors and do side-side-back rotations every two hours. She'll be in here just as often as she was before. Same with Steve and me. This is standard protocol. In a larger hos-pital, she might have left Intensive Care even sooner. The fact is, she isn't critical."

"The fact is, she isn't *conscious,*" Jack muttered, but more to himself than to Kara. She patted his elbow and set off down the hall. Cindy and Katherine replaced her.

Since he hadn't gotten anywhere with Kara, he turned

on Cindy. "Rachel is losing weight. Isn't that dangerous?"

Cindy pushed up her glasses and looked back into the room. "No," she said slowly, quietly, "she's getting the nutrients she needs through a drip. We're still hoping that she'll wake up soon."

"I'm glad *someone* is," he said, but his sarcasm faded fast. "It'll be a week tonight. How long can she survive on an IV?"

"Ohhh, another few weeks."

"What then?"

"We'll consider a feeding tube. It goes directly into the stomach."

He wished he hadn't asked. A feeding tube was long-range, big-time stuff, right up there with putting Rachel in a regular room, which smacked of settling in for the long haul. He had done his homework. Next they'd be talking about a nursing home.

He pushed his hands through his hair and tried to wade through a rising panic. "This is not working for me. I can't accept that this is going to go on forever. There has to be more we can do."

"I've been talking to people," Katherine said. "There are other things we might try."

That cleared his thoughts some. Jack wasn't sure he liked the idea of Katherine talking to people about *his* wife's coma, but he was desperate enough to listen.

"We could read to her," Katherine said, "play her favorite music, bring in her favorite food. The smell might reach her. We could burn incense."

"Maybe get the maharishi in here, too," he muttered.

Katherine nearly smiled. "I was thinking of incense that smells like the woods near her house. A little of that might snap her out of it."

Jack wanted to argue but couldn't. Even now, miles away, he could smell those woods. There was a power to that smell.

"Would it work?" he asked the nurse.

"It can't hurt," Cindy said as she had so often before. Looking past them, speaking just a hair above a whisper, she added, "There's nothing scientific about it—for or against." She put on a smile. "Here's Dr. Bauer."

"I'll go visit with Hope," Katherine said, but before she could leave, someone called her name. She looked past Steve Bauer, broke into a grin, and set off to greet a young, good-looking guy wearing purple scrubs.

Watching her, Jack couldn't help but think that there was something to be said for living and working in a smaller place than San Francisco. People saw one another around town. Familiar faces were everywhere. It was kind of nice, when life was shaky.

He hadn't always felt that way. Growing up in a small town where everyone knew every last thing he did, he had choked on intimacy. So he went to college in Manhattan, where the anonymity was a welcome relief. He would have done his graduate work there, too, if he had been accepted. But Tuscon was where the grant money was, and then he met Rachel.

Rachel loved Arizona. She loved the air, the sun, the open space. She loved the desert landscape, claimed that there was a romanticism to it, that she could feel the ghost of Geronimo riding through the brush. She loved the heat, loved wearing skimpy tank tops and shorts and piling her hair on top of her head, even loved sweating.

She had blossomed as a painter in Tucson. With instruction and practice, she became technically proficient. As her personal confidence grew, her work gained strength. Wearing a large, broad-brimmed hat, she spent hour upon hour in the desert, nearly immobile at her easel, brush and palette in hand. She had the patience to wait for desert creatures to appear, and the stillness not to scare them off once they did. When the desert was in bloom, she was in heaven, but her pleasure extended far beyond that. She saw beauty where others saw hard sand and drab growth. Give her a glimpse of the sun angled low, and she turned bland into breathless.

Jack and Rachel were together in Tucson for three years, married for the last, and in all that time they hadn't disagreed on a thing. Then Jack was offered a job in San Francisco, and still they didn't disagree. It made sense for an architect to be in the city, and the firm was a good one in terms of projects, opportunity for advancement, and pay. Rachel voiced her qualms; Jack had answers for each. In the end, it boiled down to the fact that she could work anywhere, and he couldn't. So they moved.

He wondered now if he had been shortsighted. He had taken her from her element without realizing the effect it would have. She might have found cause for new inspiration in Big Sur, but there had been a long stretch of barren years before that. Her work had suffered. He should have seen it.

And then there was the twist of fate that had him driving to the hospital to be with her for the seventh day in a row. If they hadn't moved to San Francisco, she wouldn't have ended up in Big Sur, wouldn't have been driving the coast road at the same time as an elderly woman who had no business driving at all, wouldn't be in a coma right now.

Coming up on one week. Scary.

KATHERINE offered to keep an eye on Hope while Jack drove to San Francisco. "It's Monday," she explained. "The shop is closed."

But Jack wanted Hope with him. He saw the sad expression on her face and the tears that remained in a state of perpetual threat. He didn't know whether she was thinking of Guinevere or Rachel, but a drive to the city would be a diversion. He felt closer to her after Guinevere. He imagined they had established a bond, and wanted to keep it going.

He was also feeling low himself, brooding about people giving up on Rachel. Given his druthers, he wouldn't be driving to San Francisco at all, but sitting with her, talking to her, badgering her, challenging her—anything to wake her up. Having Hope with him gave him another purpose.

Besides, she was a shield. She was visible evidence of his responsibilities, proof for all to see of the reasons why he couldn't stay in San Francisco for long.

HE CALLED Jill from the phone down the hall and explained about Guinevere's death, about getting a late start from Big Sur, about Michael Flynn's defection. As gently as he could, he said, "I can't do lunch, Jill. Hope's with me, and we don't have much time. I'm sorry. I'll bet you made something incredible." On top of everything else, Jill was a gourmet cook.

"Not yet. I was going to do risotto primavera right before you came. The ingredients will hold. Will you come tomorrow?"

He closed his eyes and rubbed his brow. "I won't be in the city. Not until later in the week."

There was a pause, then a quiet "Does Rachel know you're there?"

"I don't know. But I can't *not* be there."

After another pause, she asked softly, "Why?"

He felt it coming. The deep stuff. And he didn't want it, didn't want it. So he said, "Because it could make a difference, Jill. The girls' talking to her could help her out of the coma. *My* talking to her could help her out of it. She's the mother of my children. I want her well."

She relented with a sigh. "I know."

"Thursday," he suggested, because he was hurting her and he didn't want that. "How about Thursday. Will the veggies hold until then?"

"It's not about the veggies."

"I know." It was about commitments. "Lunch Thursday. I promise."

THEY stopped at Jack's house before heading for Sung and McGill. While he filled a large sports duffel with clothes, he had Hope pile mail into a shopping bag. They worked quickly. The place felt cold and damp. The sun was out, and still the backyard looked gray.

In the midst of putting everything in the car, Jack had a thought. Returning to his bedroom closet, he pushed sweaters aside on the top shelf and pulled down two framed photographs. One was of Rachel and the girls, one of Rachel alone. Slipping them into a bag, he rejoined Hope.

They stopped at a nearby pastry shop for lunch. The

place was small enough and Jack had been there often enough for someone to show a sign of recognition. His order was filled promptly and efficiently, but no one said a word.

Still, they lingered there. He got Hope a refill of Coke, which she drank, and offered her dessert, which she refused. He ordered a piece of marble cheesecake anyway, handed her a spoon, and made her take a bite. He drank his third cup of coffee.

When he couldn't put it off any longer, they headed for the office, where he spent the bulk of the next three hours arguing with contractors, apologizing to clients, assigning tasks to associates, and avoiding David. He succeeded in everything but the last. David found him wherever he was, asking questions about work, time, and Rachel, adding to the pressure he already felt.

In the sudden silence after one tense bout, Hope asked, "Do you like David?" She had her legs tucked under her on the sofa in his office and was alternately reading a book, doodling, and watching Jack work. David had just stalked out clutching the latest design revision for the Montana resort, which Jack had asked him to present at Tuesday's meeting.

"Sure, I do," Jack said. "David and I go back fifteen years. We've shared some exciting jobs, pretty heady stuff. He does the things I can't, and vice versa. I wouldn't be the architect I am today if it weren't for him. This is our firm. We made it ourselves. We're partners."

Hope thought about that for a minute. "But do you like him?"

Jack used to. He used to admire David's dedication and direction. Lately, he had found the man a little too intense. Still, how to argue when the firm thrived?

"We're a good team. He keeps the fire going under me when I might be tempted to relax."

"Mom doesn't like him," Hope said quietly.

"Really?" It was news to Jack. Rachel had never said a word. "Why not?"

"She says he's hard."

Hard—as in *insensitive, cutthroat,* and *driven?* "Some would say I am, too."

"Mom never said that," Hope said quickly.

"She didn't ever yell and scream and curse me out?" he teased.

A sheepish grin. "Well, maybe. But she always apologized after."

"What did she say?"

"When she apologized?"

"When she was cursing me out."

"Oh, you know"—she lifted a shoulder—"stubborn, selfish. But she said it took two to make a marriage work and two to make it fail, so she was as much at fault as you were."

That was interesting. To hear Samantha talk, Jack had always assumed that his "desertion" was the only thing discussed. He was the bad guy, Rachel the good guy. He couldn't imagine Hope saying something different, if it wasn't so.

He covered his surprise by flipping her doodle pad around. Her pen had recreated Guinevere, capturing vulnerability with a minimum of strokes.

He turned back a page and forward a page. Each one offered a similarly evocative beauty. He had known Hope could draw but had never made much of it—largely, ironically, to protect Samantha, though it appeared that Samantha was well aware of her inability.

But Samantha wasn't there just then. On a note of genuine awe, he told Hope, "You are your mother's daughter."

"What do you mean?"

"You see the same things she does—small, subtle things, feelings—and you can put them on paper. That's more than I can do. It's a real talent."

Hope gave a modest little shrug, but her cheeks were pink. "I loved Guinevere. Drawing her makes me feel like she's still here." Her voice caught. Her eyes fell. "I keep thinking of her back there."

"I know you do."

"I'll miss her."

"You were good to her. I'm proud of you."

Tears gathered on her lower lids. "She's still dead."

"But you made her last days good ones. You were a loyal friend to her." He wanted her happy. "We could get you another cat if you want."

Without a minute's thought, she shook her head. "I want to remember Guinevere for a while. She was always a little scared of new people, and she didn't like playing with toys, but she slept with me from the night we found her, and she always purred when I whispered to her. So if I was loyal, it was because she was loyal. I don't want another cat taking her place so soon."

"BRENDAN says you're not coming with us. Why *not?*" Lydia asked. They were at their lockers at the end of the day. Samantha had avoided Lydia that long.

She scooped her hair off her face. "I'm going with

Teague Runyan. He has a car. It'll be better this way."

"Better for *who?* Teague is trouble. He has a *police* record."

"He was accused of shoplifting. It was a case of mistaken identity. The charges were dropped, so he does *not* have a police record."

"He was suspended from school for cheating."

"For one day. That's how serious it was."

"There's no way my parents will let him into the house."

"If your parents weren't home," Samantha said archly, "they'd never know. Why did you *tell* them there would be guys there?"

"They started asking. I couldn't lie to their faces."

"Well, they're not my parents, so I don't have that worry."

"Does your father know you're going with Teague?"

"Sure. He trusts me."

When Lydia didn't have an answer to that, Samantha felt a small measure of satisfaction. The satisfaction waned, though, when Lydia gathered her books and, shoulders hunching as she hugged them close, walked away alone.

⌒ ⌒ ⌒

IT WAS LATE afternoon by the time Jack returned to the hospital. Katherine had picked up Samantha at school and returned with a CD player, which was now running softly on the bed stand not twelve inches from Rachel's head.

"Garth," Samantha told him, seeming unperturbed by the change in rooms.

"*She's* a fan, too?" He knew that the girls were and

had assumed that the concert had been for them. His Rachel had been partial to the likes of James Taylor, Van Morrison, and the Eagles.

"A *big* fan," Samantha said.

Hope confirmed it with a nod, which didn't leave much for him to do but to set up the pictures he had brought.

Samantha was immediately drawn to them. "Where'd you get those?"

"I've had them," he said casually. "I want the doctors and nurses who walk in and out to see your mother with her eyes open. I want them to view her as a living, breathing, feeling individual."

"Grandma sure does. Look what she sent."

Three large boxes were stacked by the wall behind the bed. Each one brimmed with hot pink tissue and the kind of frothy white stuff that Rachel hadn't touched since she had cut it up and sewn it into a quilt.

"Nightgowns," Samantha said unnecessarily.

Hope sat on her heels and began looking inside the boxes. "Mom won't wear these. Why did she send them?"

Jack was saved from answering by the arrival of the travel agent, Dinah Monroe. She wore a smart suit and her dark hair in a shiny bob. After fingering the lingerie with genuine admiration, she kissed Rachel's cheek and, in an upbeat tone that warred with the concern in her eyes, told her about the client from hell for whom she had spent most of the day booking an Aegean cruise. More easily, she kidded Samantha about a mutual friend and shared sympathetic memories of Guinevere with Hope. She didn't stay for more than ten minutes and was followed soon after by Eliza, of the dark eyes and dark curls, arriving with warm pecan rolls packed in layers of bags. The minute she opened the innermost one, the sweet scent wafted out. Jack began to salivate. After ten minutes of gentle chatter with Rachel, Katherine, and the girls, she was gone.

The rolls remained in the tray table. Jack was eyeing them and wondering what to do about dinner when a new face appeared. This latest visitor was male but effeminate, Harlan by name, one of Katherine's operators. He hugged the girls and kissed Rachel, chatted with each for a short time, then left. Jack had barely begun to get over the feeling that he was the outsider here when Faye arrived with another zippered bag.

"Brisket," she told him. "Noodles and veggies included. Just heat and serve." She didn't stay much longer than it took to tell Rachel about the abysmal game of golf she had played that day, her surprise enjoyment of the book group's next book, and her three-year-old granddaughter's preschool play. Then she, too, was gone.

Half an hour later, when Charlie Avalon arrived with an earful of beaded hoops and a cedar-scented candle, Jack waved Katherine into the hall. "Tell me the truth," he said when she joined him. "These visitors dovetail too neatly. Someone orchestrated this. Was it you?"

"Definitely. They wanted to come, but it won't do Rachel any good to have them all here at once."

"Did you tell each one what to bring?"

"I didn't have to. They knew what to bring." She frowned. "Do you have a problem with this?"

He did. But he wasn't sure what it was.

Yes, he did. It was the outsider thing. He was feeling usurped.

"The girls have CD players," he said. "I gave them each one last Christmas. They might have wanted to bring Rachel their own."

"If they want to, that's great. They can also bring CDs from home. And books." She studied him. "Are you jealous?"

"Jealous of what?"

"Of my bringing a CD? Of Rachel's friends bringing other things? Of Rachel's friends, period?"

"No. *No.* I'm just surprised. She used to be more of a loner. I had no idea she had so many friends, and *good* friends. They've gone out of their way to help out."

"Don't you have friends who would do the same if the situation was reversed?"

Jack had many, many friends. But *good* friends? Jill would come, for sure. David? He . . . couldn't quite picture it.

"Do Rachel's friends make you feel left out?" Katherine asked.

"Of course not. Why do you say that?"

"It's just how you look, standing over by the window. It's like you're realizing that you don't know who Rachel is now and what she's doing with her life, and even though you're divorced, that bothers you. Is it a control thing?"

He was astounded by her gall. "Are you serious?"

"Uh-huh. From what Rachel says, you had the upper hand in the marriage. Your job, your needs came first. I'd call that controlling. Old habits die hard."

"Thank you, Dr. Freud," he said, then added an annoyed "Is there some reason you're telling me this?"

"Uh-huh. Rachel would do it if she could, but she can't."

"Rachel would *not.*" Not *his* Rachel. "She was never one to bicker and carp."

"But she thinks. She feels. She's thought a lot about her marriage since it ended. She's learned to express herself more than she did when she was married."

"She expressed herself plenty then."

Katherine just shrugged.

"Okay, what didn't she say?" Jack asked. When she shrugged again, he said, "I can take it. What didn't she say?"

"Important things. She felt that she let them go by the board. It goes back to control. If Rachel could see you in there with her friends, she'd probably say you were jealous. *And* insecure."

"I'm controlling. I'm jealous. I'm insecure." Jack sputtered out a breath. "You're tough."

As insults went, it was weak. Many women would have taken it as a compliment. Apparently not Katherine. It fired her up.

"I've *had* to be tough, because I've depended on men like you and they've always let me down. That's the first thing Rachel and I had in common."

"Ahhh. Fellow man-haters."

"Not man-haters. We have plenty of male friends."

He couldn't resist. "Like Harlan?"

She stared. "Harlan supports a significant other who has AIDS. He cooks, cleans, buys food, clothes, and medical care. He rushes home to make lunch and has passed up training seminars in New York that might have advanced his career, all to care for his partner. You could take a lesson from Harlan."

Forget Harlan. Forget even that young guy in the purple scrubs. Something else had stuck in his brain. "Rachel has plenty of male friends? Where are they? Is Ben the supposed significant other? Or is she dating lots of guys and playing the field—once-burned, twice-shy kind of thing?"

"You're a fine one to talk," Katherine said. "There you are, holding on to favorite pictures of your ex-wife while you string Jill on for, what, two years now?"

"Hah. Pot calling the kettle black. What's with you and Bauer? He's a good-looking guy, but whenever he shows up, you get all high-voiced and nervous, then turn tail and run." He paused, frowned. "How do you know about Jill?"

"Rachel told me."

"That's interesting. Is *she* jealous?"

"Not on your life. She's been thriving since the divorce. You've seen her work. She couldn't paint in the city. Now she can. Something stifled her back there. I wonder what it was."

Jack knew she was about to tell him—and he had suddenly had enough. He held up a hand. "Your clients may sit in your chair and talk their hearts out, but that's *their* need, not mine. My life is not your business. I don't have to discuss it with you."

"Wasn't that one of the problems with your marriage? Lack of communication?"

Both hands raised now, he stepped back. He was about to return to the room when Katherine said a more gentle "Run if you want, but it won't go away."

"Rachel and I are *divorced*. That's about as far away as it gets."

"Is that why you've been here every day for the past week? Is that why you kept those pictures? You care, Jack."

"Of course, I care. I was with Rachel for two years; we were married for ten. That doesn't mean I need to analyze every little thing that's happened since—including those pictures. She has pictures of me; why the hell shouldn't I have pictures of her? You don't negate twelve good years. You don't just wipe them off the screen like they never happened, and that goes for the feelings involved. Rachel is seriously ill. I'm here for old times' sake, because someone I was intimate with for years could *die. And* because she is the mother of my daughters, who happen to need tending."

"The girls could be staying with me, or with Eliza or Faye. We all know them well, and we have the room. We also live closer to the hospital than the house in Big Sur, but you're driving them back and forth, back and forth, when you really want to be in the city."

"It's what I think is best, and since I'm the next of kin, it's my say."

"Isn't it always?"

"Actually," he let out an exasperated breath, "no. I didn't ask for the divorce. I didn't move out. Rachel did." He pushed a hand through his hair. "Why am I telling you this? My life is none of your business. *Butt out,* will you?"

JACK was still feeling testy when he started the drive back to Big Sur, but the coast did its thing. By the time they passed Big Sur, a mist had risen to buffer him from the world, and he was more pensive than irate.

He spent thirty minutes with his laptop hooked up to Rachel's fax line, and another thirty with Faye's brisket and the girls. There wasn't much talking. Hope was teary eyed. Samantha kept looking at her. All Jack could do was to say the occasional "It'll get better. Things like this take time."

Then the girls went to their rooms, leaving him to his own devices. He told himself to work. Or to paint. Instead, he dumped the bag of mail from his house on the kitchen table, and with barely a glance, threw out all but the bills. That done, he looked around the kitchen. Idly, he opened drawers, thumbed through takeout menus from restaurants in Carmel—Italian, Mexican, Thai. Some had items circled. Others had food stains. All had clearly been used, which was a change. In San Francisco, Rachel had always cooked. She had said it was easy enough, since she worked at home. She still worked at home. Had *he* been the one who kept them in? He had always preferred home cooking after being away, so Rachel had cooked. He supposed that could be called controlling.

He flipped through Rachel's mail, tossing junk in the basket, putting bills next to his. Samantha had already taken a handful of catalogues. And the ones that were left, the ones addressed to Rachel? Most were for outdoor clothing. Several were for artists' goods. The rest were for garden supplies. No surprise there. Nor in the CD collection in the living room. Oh, yes, she had a supply of James Taylor, Van Morrison, and the Eagles, but she had half again as many country discs. He supposed it went with outdoor clothing and garden supplies. He supposed it went with a country life. But he hadn't even thought of Rachel as a romantic. Sweet, sentimental, and sensitive—but romantic?

Actually, now that he thought of it, she was. He recalled returning from a business trip once to something *very* romantic. Rachel had picked him up at the airport, typically breathless but on time. It was dark out. The girls were in the backseat, in their pajamas, giggling behind their hands. Looking back, he guessed they had been six and four, or seven and five, which put the time at two to three years before the divorce. There had been tension at home surrounding this trip. Rachel had been quiet driving him *to* the airport. He was missing a school play in which both of the girls had parts.

"If it was just me, I wouldn't mind," she had said the night before he left; but it was an important trip for him, and it had been productive.

The girls giggled most of the way home from the airport. "What are you guys up to?" he asked more than once, to which they had only giggled more.

What they were up to was a rerun of the play in the living room, with scenery taken right from the school— easily done, since Rachel was the chief set designer— and Rachel playing every part except the girls' parts. Jack applauded roundly, then read good-night stories to each girl in turn. He had thought that the ongoing grins and giggles were simply because he was home.

Then he reached his and Rachel's room and found the place ablaze with daffodils in candlelight. Rachel had unpacked his bag and filled the bathtub with hot water and bubbles. There were daffodils and candles there, too. And fresh raspberries. And wine. Without eating a thing, he felt totally full.

All the more empty by contrast now and needing more of Rachel, he went to her studio. His laptop was still plugged in, resting on a mound of Boca paperwork. The canvases he had placed against the wall the day before hadn't moved. He sat down on the floor and studied them.

After a bit, he began rummaging through her supplies. She had oils and acrylics in tubes, neatly arranged on a work desk. Watercolors were in tin boxes. Brushes of varying widths lay on a cloth with several palette knives. There were more tubes and tins in the storage closet, plus her traveling gear—a heavy-duty manual camera and film, a portable easel, a large canvas bag, a folding seat—plus a supply of sketch pads, pencils, and pens.

There was also a metal file cabinet. He opened it to find her professional records—sales receipts, lists of what painting was at what gallery, expense receipts, tax forms, memos from her accountant. He closed it just shy of seeing how much money she made. He didn't want to know that, didn't want to know that.

Instead, snooping idly, he pulled out a portfolio that was stashed between the file cabinet and the wall. It wasn't a large portfolio, either in size or thickness. Squatting down, he set it against the front of the file cabinet, opened it, and found a sheaf of rag paper bound with a thin piece of blue yarn. He pulled it out, untied the yarn, and sat back, resting the sheaf against his thighs.

The first page was blank, a title page without a title. He turned to the next page and saw something that looked like a baby in the very first stages of development. An embryo. He turned to the next and the next, watching the embryo develop into a fetus with features that grew more distinct and increasingly human. Then, in a moment of silent violence, the sac holding the fetus burst. Jack was shaken. He looked at it for the longest time, unable to turn forward or back. When the shock passed, he went on, and then it was as if the explosion hadn't occurred. The fetus grew page by page into a baby, confined in its sac but in different positions.

It was a little boy. As fingers and toes were delineated, so was a tiny penis.

Again, Jack was shaken. He studied the infant, feeling the utter reality of the child, though it was drawn with nothing more than a blue pen. A blue pen, on high-quality, heavy ivory rag.

Only three pages remained. On the first, the baby was simply larger and more detailed, tiny eyelashes, perfectly shaped ears, thumb in mouth. On the second, his little body was turned in preparation for birth, with only elbows and heels, head and bottom making bumps in the smooth egg shape. On the last, the child had his eyes open and was looking directly at Jack.

So real. Jack felt a chill on the back of his neck. So real. So *familiar.*

Turning back to the first page, he went through the sheaf again. He felt the familiarity begin soon after that silent violence. By the time he turned the last page, he had an eerie thought. He pushed it aside, gathered the pages together, retied the yarn, and returned the sheaf to the portfolio. Closing it tightly, he stashed it back between the file cabinet and the wall.

Still, he saw that last picture. It haunted him through the night and woke him at dawn. He phoned Brynna in Buffalo and his client in Boca, but as soon as he hung up, that baby was back.

Watching the girls in the car, he wondered if they knew anything about a baby, but he couldn't ask. Whether he was wrong or right, mentioning it would open a can of worms.

Rachel knew. But Rachel wasn't saying. That left Katherine.

chapter eleven

NATURALLY, KATHERINE wasn't at the hospital when he arrived, but that was fine. Jack had taken her phone number from Rachel's address book—both numbers, work and home. Standing just outside Rachel's room, he called the work number on his cell phone.

"Color and Cut," came a bubbly young voice.

"Katherine Evans, please."

"I'm sorry. She's with a client. Would you like to make an appointment?"

"Not for my hair," Jack remarked.

"Oh. Uh. Then, can she return your call?"

He gave the sweet young thing his number, pushed the phone in his pocket, and returned to Rachel. Drawing up a chair, he put his elbows on the bed rail.

"So," he said, feeling resentful. "She's your unofficial spokeswoman. Make that *spokesperson*. Might as well be politically correct, here. It looks like I have to go through her to get to you." He half expected a gloating smile. Of course, there was none, which, irrationally, annoyed him more. He rubbed his thumb over those immobile lips, found them dry, applied Vaseline. What excess there was, he rubbed into the back of his hand.

"Remember when we used to ski?" They had done Aspen and Vail. They had done Snowmass and Telluride. The trips were gifts from Victoria, the only gifts from her that they had truly enjoyed. While the girls took lessons, Rachel and Jack skied together. One Chap Stick was all they ever brought, and they shared. "That was fun. This isn't. Rachel? Are you there? Can you hear me? It's been a week, Rachel, a whole week. You may be having a ball in there, but it's getting harder on us out here. Hope needs you to help her with Guinevere's death. She disappeared this morning—didn't show up for breakfast and wasn't in the house at all. I ran to Guinevere's grave. No Hope. I was getting ready to panic when she came down from Duncan's. That's starting to make me nervous. I mean, he's a big guy living alone. Could be he's a pervert." Rachel didn't look upset. Neither had Hope when she returned from Duncan's. Jack had watched her closely for signs of distress, but there were none. "She says she needs his faith. If that's the extent of it, I still feel inadequate. We never talked about religion, you and me. Maybe we should have. Maybe the kids need a faith of their own for times like these."

He stood, bringing her arm up with him, and began to gently put it through its paces. "And Sam. She's a trip. I have no idea what's going on in her head. She vacillates between being an angel and a shrew. I'm never quite sure whether she's listening to what I say or whether she's only nodding while her mind is off somewhere else. Do *you* get through to her?"

The ring of the phone was muffled by his jeans. Gently, he set her arm down. Less gently, he flipped the phone open as he walked to the door. "Yeah?"

"It's Katherine," said a frightened voice. "What's up?"

"I need to talk with you."

There was a silent beat, then, "Rachel's the same?"

"Yeah. Sorry. She's the same."

Katherine swore softly. "Can I ask a favor? Next time you call, please tell them it isn't an emergency."

"But it is," he said, looking back at his wife. "I found a pack of drawings in Rachel's studio. Of a baby. A baby boy."

The silence this time was for more than one beat.

"I need to know what those drawings meant, Katherine. That baby had my eyes."

There was more silence. Finally, she murmured something to someone on her end, then said, "I'll be over in forty-five minutes."

BY THE TIME she arrived, Jack had exercised every appropriate part of Rachel's body. He had talked to Kara Bates. He had talked to Cindy Winston. He had rearranged the framed pictures of Rachel to accommodate several more that the girls had produced, showing Rachel running, painting, laughing, further evidence of the vibrant woman inside the shell on the bed. He had listened to Garth Brooks from start to finish, and had asked himself a dozen questions about the baby whose existence Rachel's best friend hadn't denied.

Katherine entered the room looking wary. Pocketing her keys, she kissed Rachel's cheek. "Mmm. You smell good. So he's been rubbing in cream? Isn't that typical. They'll do anything to get their hands on our bodies."

"Sex was never a problem for us," Jack said, out of

the gate at the crack of the gun. "It was good from start to finish. So, were those drawings wishful thinking on Rachel's part? Or was she really pregnant?"

Katherine looked torn.

"Come on, Katherine," he warned. "You've told me other things about Rachel. Besides, you're not denying it, which means she was. Unless I misinterpreted those drawings, she lost the baby." When Katherine's eyes fell to Rachel, he said a gentler "Look. We don't know what's going to happen here. It's been a whole week. I'm sleeping in her bed, using her shower, digging coffee beans out of a canister shaped like a cuke. I'm using her towels. I'm eating her frozen zucchini bread. I'm putting my shorts in her underwear drawer because I'm getting fuckin' tired of living out of a suitcase, I'm—"

"Yes, she was pregnant."

Suddenly real, it took his breath. He looked at Rachel, trying to imagine it. The pain he felt was gnawing. "How could she pick up and leave me, if she was pregnant?"

Katherine's eyes rounded. "Oh no. She wasn't pregnant when she left. It was *before*."

"Before." That made even less sense. "No. I would have known."

"From what she told me, she barely knew it herself. Things weren't going well between you. There was less talk, more silence. When she missed a period, she figured it was because of the strain. She didn't have an inkling until she missed a second one, and even then she let it go. Like I said, things weren't good at home. She didn't know what to do."

He shook his head. "I knew her body. Even two months along—"

"She was three months along."

"I'd have seen it."

"Not if she was thinner to start with. The bloat of early pregnancy would have brought her up to normal."

Jack forced himself to think back. Yes, Rachel had lost weight before the split. And despite what he had said, there hadn't been much intimacy at the end. Either he was traveling or one of them was tired. There was a chance he hadn't seen her undressed in anything but the darkest of night.

"But she would have *told* me," he argued. That was what hurt most. A baby affected him directly. A baby was part *his*.

Katherine sighed. "She tried. You were on a trip when she started feeling sick. She called and asked you to come home. You wouldn't."

Swallowing, he focused on Rachel's still face and struggled again to think back. There had been a trip to Toronto two weeks before the split. Yes, she had called, not feeling well, wanting him home. But the trip had been an important one. A large contract had hung in the balance. Turning to Rachel, he said, "I kept asking you what was wrong. You said, nothing terrible. That was what you said, *nothing terrible*. You had stomach pains. Maybe the flu, you said." He looked at Katherine. "She was *miscarrying?*"

Katherine nodded.

He made himself remember more. "She was pale as death when I came home, but she said she was getting better. I was home for four days. Not *once* did she mention a baby." He felt shaky inside, even close to tears. "Then there was a bunch of trips in close sequence." And an ultimatum before the last one. He recalled being annoyed that she seemed to be in . . . in *pain*. Good Lord. She had cause. "When I came back from the last, she was gone," he murmured, before anger killed the tears. "Why didn't she *tell* me?"

"She couldn't."

"She lost a baby I didn't know about, then left because *I* hadn't somehow figured it *out?*"

When Katherine looked reluctant to speak, he wiggled his fingers. "Come on, Katherine. Talk to me. Tell me what she said."

"She said it wasn't just the miscarriage. It was everything about your relationship. The miscarriage was only the clincher. She saw it as a sign that the marriage wouldn't work."

"Christ," he said and pushed his hands through his hair. "Why didn't she tell me *after?*"

"When, after? When you called, it was to arrange to see the girls, not to ask about her. Nothing that happened *after* suggested she was wrong. She was convinced you'd lost your interest in her."

"Well, I hadn't." He felt an overwhelming sadness. "Ahhh, Rachel," he breathed, lifting her hand to his chest, "you should have told me."

"Would it have made a difference?" Katherine asked.

He felt too hollow to be annoyed. "I don't know," he murmured. "Maybe." He would have liked a son. Hell, he would have liked another daughter. They had talked about having more children, but their finances were stretched with two, and then, once Hope was out of diapers, they enjoyed the freedom.

If he had known she was pregnant, they might have talked. She wasn't the only one who thought her partner didn't care anymore. If he had known she was pregnant, he would have come home from that trip.

At least, right now, that sounded like the right thing to

do. Back then, he was in a different place. He was riding high on success, so involved with it and with his work.

"For what it's worth," Katherine said, "she would have lost the baby whether you were there or not. She didn't blame you for the miscarriage, only for not being with her to lend comfort and support when it happened."

"Yeah." He sighed. "Well, I can see that she did." So now he knew what had actually caused that final break. Not that it helped. He still felt abandoned. Rejected. Alone. Baby or no baby, she had gone off and begun a new life.

Thinking about that new life made him think about her friendship with Katherine. "You said you met her at the gynecologist's office. In Carmel?"

"Yes."

"Did she have more trouble after she left the city?"

"No. She was just having a follow-up exam, getting to know a local doctor. We got to talking. There was instant rapport. One thing led to another. We went for coffee, then lunch, then coffee. She was very supportive."

He would have thought it was the other way around. "*She* was supportive?"

Katherine paled. She gave a quick little tip of her head, a dismissal that dismissed nothing.

"Why were you seeing the doctor?" he asked.

He could see her mind working as she stared at him. Then she glanced back at the door. No one was there. She looked down at Rachel. After another minute, she returned to Jack. "I had just been diagnosed with breast cancer."

His eyes widened. It was all he could do not to look at her chest. "Bad?"

She sputtered out a laugh. "That's like being a little pregnant versus a lot pregnant."

"You know what I mean."

"I do. And no, it wasn't bad in that way. Nothing had spread. The lymph nodes were clear. What they found in me was microscopic, tiny *in situ* ductal carcinomas. I'm living proof of the miracle of early detection. If I hadn't had a mammogram, I'd either be dealing with a lump right now or dead." She took a tiny breath. "That was the good news. The bad news was that I had tiny little grains of it in *both* breasts." She made a gesture that would have suggested beheading had it been eight inches higher.

Jack did look this time, because not once—and he had seen Katherine numerous times in the last week, wearing different outfits, *including* sweaters that clung—not *once* had he thought her body was anything but that of an attractive, shapely forty-something female.

She chuckled. "Your mouth is open."

"I know—it's just—I don't see—"

"Reconstruction."

"Ah." He was embarrassed. "Good as new."

"From the outside," she said, and with those three words, her defensiveness was back. Jack hadn't realized it was gone until then. But yes, she had been softer, very human.

"In what ways was Rachel supportive of you?" he asked.

Katherine studied Rachel for a minute before nodding slowly. "She was there for me, the proverbial phone call away. She talked me through many a rough spot."

"Like?"

"Like deciding between lumpectomy and mastectomy. Like choosing a surgeon and a plastic surgeon, and trying to decide which method of reconstruction was best. Like dealing with the knowledge that until the surgery was done and the lymph nodes were tested in the path lab, I didn't *know* whether the cancer had spread. Like wondering if I would survive the *surgery,* much less the disease." The corner of her mouth twitched. "Aren't you glad you asked?"

He was. Otherwise, he wouldn't have had a clue.

"Rachel was there the entire time—before, during, and after," she said.

"You have no family nearby?"

She folded her arms over those perfectly natural-looking breasts. "Have? No. Had? Yes. I was married at the time. My husband had a squeamish stomach."

Ahhhh. She'd had a husband. The missing piece—and apparently a huge one. "He wasn't there *at all?*"

"Well, he was. In a way." Her tone was wry, bitter. "Roy was a golf pro. We moved here from Miami when he got a job offer he couldn't refuse. He ran tournaments at a club in Pebble Beach. That's big stuff. He didn't have the time to sit in doctors' offices holding his wife's hand." She tipped her head, still wry, still bitter. "I could've lived with that. I mean, it *was* boring . . . tense . . . time-consuming. You'd sit in a cold cubicle in a thin paper gown waiting ninety minutes for one of the team of doctors to appear, and for what, a five-minute meeting? And the whole time you're thinking that this is the beginning of the end and you don't want to die. I'm a pretty composed person, but there were times, waiting, when I broke into a sweat and started shaking and thought that if I didn't get out of that damned cubicle in the next minute I'd go stark raving mad!"

Jack would have guessed that Katherine Evans had come out of the *womb* composed. She was composed even then—but only on the outside. He saw that now. Her eyes and her voice conveyed anxiety aplenty.

She drew herself up. "So Roy couldn't take it, and I didn't push. It would have been worse for me having to deal with his nerves on top of my own. I did everything with only a minimal involvement on his part—the doctors, the preop tests, the surgery, the drains, the follow-up appointments. Rachel drove me to some. Other friends drove me to others. I was fine until they dropped me off at my house."

"And then?"

"Then Roy treated me like I was a leper."

Jack swallowed.

"He was giving me space, he said. He didn't want to risk rolling over and hitting me in bed, so he slept in the spare room. He wouldn't sit too close or stand too close lest he inadvertently bump me. We had a huge bathroom—two sinks, separate Jacuzzi and shower, dressing table, and room to spare—but I had it all to myself. He said he didn't want me feeling self-conscious. He was giving me time to get used to the new me." Her tone was straightforward, her mockery all the more powerful for understatement.

"I recovered from the surgery. It was slower than I had expected—they don't tell you the half. But I gradually gained strength and felt better. I told myself I'd been given a gift of life. I went back to work even before I regained full use of my arms."

He didn't follow. "What was wrong with your arms?"

"The lymph nodes come from the armpit, so there's cutting and internal scarring. That was one of the hardest parts of the recovery, another thing no one warned me about. But I was working for someone else at the time, my clients were loyal, and I was tired of being disabled, so I pushed myself. It was the best thing I could have done. Those first few weeks I faded by noon and wound up at home with a heating pad on my back and cold packs on my arms where the muscles ached from fighting the scarring, but before long, I had full range of motion."

She stopped. Looking at Jack, she was wryness personified.

Treating her with care now, he said a cautious "What then?"

"Roy couldn't get it up."

"Excuse me?"

"Sex. He couldn't handle it. He couldn't look at my breasts. I bought sexy black camisoles so that he wouldn't have to see them. It didn't matter."

"Did you kick him out?" He assumed it was a given.

She surprised him by saying, "Not at first. I figured he needed time to adjust. I did, too. The truth was that I wasn't gung ho about sex then, either. Breasts are important sexual conduits. Suddenly I had none." When he glanced at her shapely chest, she said, "Not the same. Even aside from the emotional element—which is major—the physical response just isn't there. The raw matter is gone. I was grappling with that. So Roy was off the hook for a time."

"Until?"

"Until I learned he was screwing a little redhead from Santa Cruz." She rubbed Rachel's shoulder with her fingernails. "So we had that in common, too."

"Hey, I never cheated on Rachel."

"No, but you left her alone."

"I sure as hell didn't when I was home. So maybe I underestimated what she was feeling when I was gone."

"That's putting it mildly."

Jack was feeling too raw to be criticized. He was still trying to deal with the fact of that baby. "You're taking your anger toward Roy out on me. That's unfair. I'm not Roy."

"Would you be attracted to a woman with no breasts?"

"I'm attracted to a woman in a coma," he said before he could censor the thought. Quickly he added, "Forget Roy. There are other men in the world."

She gave a dramatic sigh. "Yes, well, I told myself that, too, and along came Byron. I met him at a hair show in New York. By then I had my own shop, thanks to my divorce settlement. When you have your own shop, you have to be up on the latest styles and techniques. So I met Byron in New York. What a charmer. Flowers, cards, little gifts. When he flew out here to see me, I put him in the guest room. I said I wasn't ready to sleep with him, and I really wasn't. But he was gorgeous, and there was a definite spark, and he was persistent."

"Didn't he—didn't you—"

"We kissed. I touched him."

"But didn't he—" *Touch your breasts?* Jack couldn't imagine not touching Rachel's. He loved their softness and sway, loved the way they changed when he tasted and touched.

Those were the very things that Katherine missed and would never have again. He began to understand her loss.

"Men can forget everything but their own needs if you push the right buttons," she said, "but it was okay. He was good in other respects. We were taking our time getting to know each other. I thought of him as a friend, as well as a possible lover. Then I told him." Jack waited.

She remained composed. Only her eyes showed the pain. "Oh, it was gradual, his withdrawal. The phone calls came fewer and further between. He had a show in

Paris, so he couldn't fly out for Christmas. When I had to be in New York, he had a show in Milan. After a while, it was me making the calls. When I stopped, that was it. After three months of silence, he called to see how I was. I hung up on him." She took a shuddering breath. "Rachel helped me through that, too. So maybe we did feed into each other's anger and hurt." She gave an evil grin. "But boy, did it feel good."

Jack smiled back. How to be offended, when the woman had just opened herself that way? He doubted many people knew that she'd been sick. She was a survivor on many levels.

He had a sudden thought. "That young guy the other day in the purple scrubs?"

"My anesthesiologist. He had a crush on me. Stopped in at my room every day to see how I was. And the woman in the hall, Darlene? My plastic surgeon's nurse. She's back to working the floor."

"And Steve Bauer?"

Too casually, she said, "What about him?"

"Did you know him before?"

"Nope."

"Was I imagining your reaction to him?"

He could see her start to nod. Then her chin came up in defiance. "No."

"There's a spark."

"Uh-huh. But it isn't going anywhere. In the first place, he's a doctor, and I've had enough of those to last a lifetime. In the second place, he's a man. I'll be very happy to keep those at arm's length for a while."

"You don't miss it?"

"Miss what?" she asked, staring at him, daring him to say it.

"Okay." He couldn't imagine it, attractive woman that she was, but, hey, different strokes for different folks. "So you don't miss it."

"I didn't say I didn't," she relented. "I used to love sex. There are times when I miss it a whole lot. Right now, as Rachel would say, it just isn't high on my list."

"What is?"

"Making a go of the shop. Spending time with my friends. Being there for people who were there for me."

Jack knew she meant Rachel. He also knew that her priorities were noble. That made him feel all the worse—not to mention that by virtue of being male, he felt guilty by association with Roy.

"We're not all bad," he said. "I'm here, aren't I?"

She thought about that for a minute, seemingly without rancor. "Have you thought about the possibility that Rachel may only partially recover? What if she wakes up diminished? What if she can't talk right, or walk right? What if she can't paint? What will you do then?"

He hadn't thought that far. He didn't want to do it now. "Let's get her woken up first. Then we'll worry about the rest. It's been a week."

Katherine nodded and glanced at her watch. "I have to get back to work."

"Thank you," Jack said.

"For what?"

He had to think for a minute. The thanks had startled him, too. "For coming today. For telling me what you did. About Rachel, and about you."

"I haven't told many people. I'd appreciate it if you wouldn't—"

"I won't." He hitched his head toward the door and began walking that way. When she joined him, he said,

"Thank you for being there for Rachel. She's lucky to have a friend like you who can receive *and* give."

"That's a nice thing to say."

"I have my moments." On impulse, he gave her a quick hug.

"What was that for?" she asked when he held her back.

"I don't know. It just seemed right."

"I think you just wanted to feel my boobs."

"With my wife watching?" He looked back at Rachel, wondering if she understood the hug. He went still. "Whoa." He strode back to the bed.

Katherine was right beside him. "What?"

"Rachel?" He leaned over her, his heart pounding. "I saw that, Rachel."

"What did she do?"

"Blinked. Flinched. Something." He took her hand. "Rachel? If you hear me, give a squeeze." He waited, felt nothing. "Come on, angel." He held his breath. But there was nothing. "Try a blink." Again he waited. "I saw something. I know you can do it."

"Rachel?" Katherine tried. "Fight it, Rachel. Push your way up. We want to know you're here. Give us a sign. Anything."

They stood side by side, leaning in over Rachel.

"Maybe I was wrong," Jack said. "Jesus. I could have *sworn* . . ."

"Rachel? Talk to us, Rachel. Move for us."

From behind them came Cindy's voice. "What's happening?" When Jack told her, she leaned in on the opposite side and chafed Rachel's jaw. "Rachel! Rachel!"

Jack was watching Rachel closely enough to pick up the slightest movement, but he didn't see a thing. They waited and watched. Cindy called her name again. With a defeated sigh, he straightened. "I don't know. Maybe it was a twitch in my own eye. I wasn't looking for it and suddenly it happened."

"It might have been involuntary," Cindy said. That the words came faster than usual said something about her excitement.

Jack recalled a term Bauer had used. "Posturing?"

"Posturing is larger—odd arm or leg movements. I was thinking more along the lines of what we call 'lightening.' It's a gradual waking that starts with the fingers or toes."

"This wasn't finger or toes," he said, but his hopes were up again. If Rachel wasn't going to just open her eyes and smile in one fell swoop, he could live with a gradual waking. "It was her face. Could that still be the start of something?"

The eyes behind Cindy's thick glasses said maybe or maybe not. And his letdown returned.

"What do we do now?" he asked. "Anything different?"

The nurse squeezed Rachel's arm from elbow to shoulder. She was back to being calm and slow. "We keep talking. When you saw this movement, were you saying anything she might have reacted to?"

Jack looked at Katherine. "We had been talking about personal stuff, but we were done. We walked to the door. I hugged you." He arched a brow. "Maybe she was jealous."

From Cindy came a quiet "Lesser emotions than that have pulled people from comas."

Still to Katherine, Jack said, "She and I are divorced. She wouldn't be jealous."

It was Katherine's turn to arch a brow. But she didn't elaborate and he didn't ask. She had appointments waiting, and he needed time to think.

chapter twelve

FOR A LONG WHILE after Katherine left, Jack sat on Rachel's bed. He traced each of her fingers, and traced the new scar. He put their hands palm to palm, then fitted her palm to his jaw. He thought about the miscarriage, about the little boy they might have had, and what might have been. He thought about country music and about jealousy. And he thought about what he had never imagined Katherine had lived through.

"We think we know so much," he told Rachel, and realized that Katherine had said the same thing, in different words, more than once. So there was a lesson to be learned. He might be slow on the uptake, but he wasn't hopeless.

FAYE LIEBERMAN came at noon. Her smile was as warm as her silver hair. Her pantsuit was silk and soothing. This time she brought a huge tin of home-baked *rugelach,* plus a bag containing two sandwiches. "You haven't eaten yet, have you?" she asked, stopping with her arms suspended halfway through unloading the bag.

"Not yet."

She held out two sandwiches wrapped in opaque white paper. "They're from Eliza's shop. One is turkey with Swiss cheese, lettuce and tomato, and mustard. The other is roast beef with *boursin*. Choose."

"Which do you want?"

She smiled, pressed her lips together, shook her head. "I'm the least liberated of Rachel's friends. If I were you, I'd pick my favorite. You may not be given a choice again."

He had felt comfortable with Faye from the start, and felt even more so now. Smiling, he reached for the one with *R/B* on the wrapper. "Thanks. This is a treat."

Faye produced two Diet Cokes and handed him one. "See? No choice." Eyes smiling, she said to Rachel, "As ex-husbands go, he isn't so bad." The smiled faded. She touched Rachel's cheek.

"She'll be fine," Jack said. "As soon as the bruise inside is healed enough, she'll wake up. It'll be a straight shot home after that."

Faye nodded. For a minute she didn't say anything. Then she pressed a hand to her chest, swallowed, and took a deep breath. After a second one, she said, "Do you know that last Monday night was the first book-group meeting that Rachel ever missed? In five years. That's something."

"It meant that much to her?"

"To her, to all of us."

He gave her the chair nearest Rachel and pulled up a second one. He was done retreating to the window when her friends came by. They were as much a source of information as Katherine was.

He bit into his sandwich, chewed thoughtfully, and swallowed. "Why?"

"Why does it mean so much?" Faye considered it for a minute. "Because we're good friends. We're all different. We have our own lives and don't always see each other between meetings, but we've grown close. Something happens when you're discussing a book and you touch on personal issues. You open up. I probably know these women better than some I see every day. I think it's the fact that our lives are so separate that gives us the freedom to speak."

"Instant-rapport kind of thing?"

"Not instant. It took a while for some of us to feel comfortable with the confessions that others made in the course of discussions. It took that long to . . . bond." She smiled. "Trite word, I know, but that's what we did. We learned to trust. We're not unique. There are a dozen other book groups in town."

"All because of Oprah?"

Faye chuckled. "Ours started *years* before hers. Some of those dozen other book groups have been going twice as long as ours. I've heard of groups that are into their second generation. And ours aren't fan clubs. We aren't afraid to discuss the downside of books." She frowned. "There's a need."

"For downside discussions?"

"For support." Reflective, she took a bite of her sandwich. When she finished chewing, she set it back in its wrapper. "Sixty-somethings like me know what it means to live in a community. When I was a child, I had grandparents in the apartment upstairs, two aunts and their families across the street, a second set of grandparents down the block. My mother had a built-in support group.

Then one by one our parents bought houses and moved to the suburbs, and we went to college and married and lived wherever our husbands took us, and suddenly the support network was gone. So we pushed the kids' carriages through the neighborhood and made friends with other mothers doing the same, and we were fine. Then the kids grew up and we went back to work, and there was no one. Now most young women work. Who's their support group?"

Jack pictured Rachel back in San Francisco. "Their husbands and kids?"

Faye smiled sadly. "Not good enough. Men don't know what women feel, and kids are kids. Women need other women." Smiling more brightly, she touched Rachel's arm and asked her if she remembered *Plain and Simple*. "It's a little book by a woman who leaves the city to spend time with the Amish," she told Jack. "There she finds groups of women who live, work, and play in close proximity to each other. They talk all day, help each other with chores, back each other up. It's the kind of support system the rest of us used to have, but lost."

Jack had designed a language center for a college in Lancaster. Since that was in the heart of Amish country, he knew something about the sect. "Would *you* want to live like an Amish woman does?"

"Not on your life," Faye declared. "I like my luxuries. But there are times when I'm lonely, when my husband is playing golf and I wish there were a clothesline in my backyard and other women in neighboring backyards wanting to talk while we hang out the wash. We all have driers now."

"But backyards are for gossip. Book groups are for intellectual discussion."

"They can't be for both?" she asked, eyes smiling. "Intellectual discussion can be personal. There are times when we discuss the book, and times when we discuss ourselves. Some books have so much meat in them that we don't get to ourselves at all. Others are only good as facilitators."

Jack smiled. *Facilitators*. He had never heard the term used quite that way before, but he supposed it fit.

"The thing is," Faye went on, "that we never know until we get there which way it'll be. The promise of the intellectual is what some of us need. Take me. I'm programmed to be home with my husband at night. I'd never have the courage to leave him alone if it was just to gab with girls. Same with Jan. She has four very young children. Granted they have a nanny—Jan teaches golf at one of the clubs—but the nanny's gone by six. Jan's husband wouldn't dream of baby-sitting the kids without Jan if she didn't have a good reason to be gone."

"What if one of the kids is sick?"

"One of the kids is always sick." She smiled. "Obviously, there are emergencies." She touched Rachel again. "We won't kick Rachel out of the group because she missed last Monday night." She was suddenly sober, suddenly dismayed.

Jack knew what she felt. At times he could take part in normal conversation as though nothing was wrong. Then he looked at Rachel and his insides bottomed out. With the bruise on her face healing, there was more paleness to her. Her freckles stood out, waiting for the rest of her to return to life.

He couldn't conceive of it not happening. But it had been a week. So maybe she had blinked earlier that morning. Since then, *nada*.

"Book group is a commitment," Faye went on, sounding determined to distract them both. "That was a ground rule. We only have seven members. If half of them don't show up, it's not the same."

"It's still strange to me," he said. "Rachel was always such a nonjoiner."

"In the city. It's different in the city. There are people everywhere. There's noise everywhere. There's *action* everywhere. Not so in Big Sur. The canyon is a great isolator. The same thing that Rachel loves about the place is its worst drawback. An artist needs to be alone, but not all the time. I'd guess that Rachel feels more of a need to join a group now than she did in the city."

"Who picks the books?"

"Whoever hosts the meeting."

"Has Rachel hosted?"

"Everyone has. That's another given."

"Isn't it out of the way for you all to drive to Big Sur?"

"No more than it's out of the way for her to drive to us." She let out a breath, suddenly sober again, and Jack knew where her mind went.

"The accident could have happened anywhere," he reasoned, recalling what the state trooper had said at the scene. "She could have been heading to Carmel for a completely different reason, and it could have been a lot worse. Once she wakes up, she'll be fine." When Faye remained grim, he said, "Tell me what books Rachel chose."

As he had hoped, she brightened. He liked it when she smiled. It made reality easier to take.

She was looking at Rachel, mischievously now. "This woman is a romantic at heart. One year, she had us do *A Farewell to Arms*. Another year, she had us do *Tess of the D'Urbervilles*. Both made her cry."

Jack tried to remember if he had ever seen Rachel cry over a book. "Once the girls were born, she didn't read as much. Magazines, yes. But the girls were little then, and active. If she wasn't doing things with them, she was painting. Five minutes of reading in bed at night, and she was out like a light."

"The city exhausted her," Charlie Avalon said from the door. She wore another tank top, a short skirt, and high platform shoes. Today, instead of feathers or beads, a shimmer of silver fell from her left ear. The streak in her hair was as pink as before, but she seemed subdued. Her eyes were on Rachel. Standing there at the door, she looked nearly as young and vulnerable as Hope.

Jack rose. When Charlie didn't enter, Faye went to her. For a minute, they hugged—an unlikely couple on the surface, not so unlikely what with all Faye had said. When Faye returned to the bed, Charlie was with her. She refused the offer of a chair, though, refused the offer of a sandwich, just stood with her hands on the bed rail and her eyes on Rachel.

"I used to live in San Francisco," she said. "We talk about it sometimes."

"Did you hate it as much as she did?" Jack asked.

"More. She was the one defending the place. Restaurants. Funky clothing boutiques. I knew San Francisco was where her marriage went wrong, but she never said much that was negative. Not until *Now You See Her.* It's about a woman who turns forty and suddenly starts to disappear."

"Disappear?"

"Really. Rachel said she felt like that in San Francisco. There were too many artists, too many people, too many noises, too many things going every which way at once, so that she couldn't clear her head and paint. She didn't have an anchor. Vital parts of herself were just floating every which way, up and away."

"Charlie. That's a little dramatic," Faye scolded, and told Jack, "The book is about a woman whose identity comes only through other people—you know, Jack's wife, Samantha's mother, Charlie's friend."

"But Rachel had her own identity," Jack argued. "She was an artist."

"Struggling," Charlie insisted. "She couldn't be self-supporting. Not in San Francisco. She had to rely on you for her basic needs."

"I was her husband. That was my job. What was the problem?"

Charlie looked at Faye, who patted the air with a warning hand. But Charlie Avalon wasn't being warned. Defiant, she said, "She hated the way her mother thought money was the be-all and end-all of life. She feared you were getting to be the same way."

Jack drew back. "When did I throw money around?"

"You bought her a rock."

It was a minute before he realized what she meant. Then he hung his head and rubbed the back of his neck. When he looked up again, he said, "It wasn't a rock. It was a three-carat diamond ring."

"That's a rock."

He blew out a breath. His stomach was starting to knot. "I had a buddy of hers—a totally artsy guy—set it in a shield of platinum and gold. It was unusual. I thought she'd love it."

"She said it was a consolation prize to make up for the traveling you did."

Jack was hurt. "I was trying to tell her that I thought

she was worth the cost of the damned ring and more. I was trying to tell her that since I hadn't had the money for a diamond ring when we got engaged, she deserved a *special* one. I was *trying* to tell her I *loved* her."

There was silence. Pushing the remnants of his sandwich aside, Jack left his chair and braced his elbows on the rail by Rachel's head. She hadn't said she hated the ring. She just hadn't worn it the way he had hoped she would. She should have told him. He could have said what he felt.

He studied her face, looking for answers, looking for *movement*. He took her chin, rubbed it lightly with the pad of his thumb, ran the backs of his fingers along her jaw. Finally he straightened.

"Apparently," Faye said in soft apology, "a ring wasn't what she needed."

"What was?" he asked.

She thought for a minute. With a sad smile, she hitched her chin toward where he stood so close to Rachel. "Maybe this?"

SAMANTHA loaded her backpack with books to bring home, then checked herself out in the mirror inside her locker door. She ran a comb through her hair. She wiped a finger under her eye to get rid of runaway liner and studied something on her forehead. If it grew into a zit just in time for the prom, she would *die*. When she had looked enough and prayed enough, she straightened and tossed her hair back. She mashed her lips together to make them red. Finally, when Lydia didn't show up, she took her baseball jacket from its hook. She was closing her locker when Pam Ardley turned the corner.

"Hey, Samantha!" she called, breaking into a trot. "Wait up!" She was all smiley white teeth and sleek black hair. Cocaptain of the cheerleading squad, she was probably the most popular girl in the class. Samantha wasn't going anywhere, not when Pam Ardley called.

Pam slowed to a walk, then stopped and leaned a shoulder against the locker's edge. "Teague says you asked him to the prom. I think that's awesome. He's hot. We're having a party at Jake Drumble's. Maybe you two want to come?"

Samantha couldn't *believe* it. Jake Drumble played football, basketball, and baseball. If Pam was the most popular girl, he was the most popular boy. And gorgeous? Drop dead.

"I'd like that," she said without raising her voice. She didn't want to seem overeager. Cool was better. Suave was best.

"What can you bring?" Pam asked.

Samantha scooped her hair to the side. "What do you need?" Something told her that salsa and chips weren't on the wish list. Not for a party at Jake's. This was big stuff. Unbelievable.

"Whatever you have at home—vodka, gin. You don't have an ID, do you?"

An ID. No, she didn't have an ID.

Pam waved a hand. "Not to worry. Bring whatever."

"I may have a problem," Samantha warned, but boldly. If she sounded weak, she would give herself away. "My mom's been in a coma for a week, so my dad's with us. It's a nightmare. He drives us here and back. He watches us like a hawk. If he gets even the slightest idea that I'm smuggling out vodka—" Like there was a drop of vodka in the house. There was *nothing* in the house.

Pam waved a hand. "Don't do it. We'll manage without." She stood back and grinned. "I'm glad you're coming, Samantha. I never understood what you were doing with Lydia and the others. They're very young."

"Tell me about it."

Pam started bouncing from one toe to the other of crisp white platform sneakers. "No need. You know. Saturday night at six for something before the prom. See you then." She jogged off.

HOPE had turned the corner unaware and stopped short, watching from the other end of the hall. She didn't move again until Pam was gone. "Sam?"

Samantha whirled around. She put a hand to her chest. "You scared me."

"What did she want?"

She was suddenly nonchalant. "Not much." She closed her locker and slung the backpack on a shoulder. "She's a friend." She started down the hall.

Hope fell into step beside her. "Since when?"

"What do you mean, 'since when?' We've been in the same class for *years.*"

"Does Lydia like her?"

"Lydia," Samantha spoke clearly, "is not in this equation."

"Why? Did you guys have a fight?"

"We didn't have to. Lydia and I have been heading in different directions all year. Those guys are young." She swung through the door and started down the stairs.

Hope hurried to keep up. "They're your age."

"In years. That's all. They have no idea how to have fun."

"But you're going with them to the prom, aren't you?"

"I haven't decided," Samantha said as she pushed open the outside door and hit the steps.

Hope followed her, squinting against the sun. "Mallory Jones said you were going with Teague Runyan. I don't think Mom would like that."

Samantha stopped short, came up close, and said with lethal quiet, "Mom's in a coma, and if you say one word to Dad, you're dead." Scooping her hair back, she set off again.

Hope watched her go. Lydia, Brendan, and Shelly were watching, too, but from an even greater distance than Hope.

Halfway to the curb, Samantha turned and yelled, "Are you *coming?*"

Hope ran forward, because Jack was there and she didn't want him waiting, but during the entire drive to the hospital, she tried to decide what to do. Samantha would never forgive her if she told Jack—and it seemed like his mind was somewhere else anyway. If Rachel was still in a coma, the only one left was Katherine. But Katherine wasn't at the hospital when they got there, and when she finally came, it was late, and then Jack said he needed to talk with her and took her out in the hall.

So, while Samantha stared at her forehead in the bathroom mirror, Hope tacked a drawing she had made of her mother up on the bulletin board, then sat beside Rachel and told her that Angela Downing's mother was running Friday's picnic, but Jack was bringing drinks. Whispering, she read Rachel a poem she had written about Guinevere's death. She pulled a jar from her backpack and opened it under Rachel's nose.

"What's *that?*" Samantha asked.

"Paste. Remember all the signs we used to make? Thanksgiving, Christmas, end of the school year, start of the school year." Construction paper cutouts pasted on poster board. "She likes the smell."

Samantha snorted and turned away, but Hope didn't care. She couldn't do much if Sam decided to make a mess of her life with Teague Runyan. But if that happened, she wanted Rachel awake to help clean things up.

JACK stood in the hall with his back to the wall and his hands in his pockets. He didn't know whether to be embarrassed, angry, or hurt. "I was so proud of myself, asking questions and learning little things about Rachel, and then Charlie hits me with the business about trying to buy her off with a ring. Do you know about that?"

Katherine was unruffled. "I didn't know Charlie had said it. But I have seen the ring."

"What did Rachel do? Present it as display number eighteen, proof of Jack's materialism? Did the two of you sit back and laugh? If she thought it was so gaudy, why didn't she sell it and give the money to the International Save the Walrus Foundation or something?"

Katherine looked amused. "For the record, I thought the ring was beautiful. For the record, so did Rachel."

"Charlie said—"

"Charlie is young. Charlie is poor. Charlie is the product of every possible kind of abuse. She is wonderfully loyal to the women in the group and lends a different insight to conversations, but what she told you may have been tinged by her own feelings, not the least of which is envy. Charlie would give her right arm to be married to someone who could support her while she worked. She gave you her own take on the ring. It may not have been a fair representation of what Rachel said."

"What *did* Rachel say?" When Katherine shot him a beseeching look, he said, "I gave her that ring because I loved her. I can't believe she took it any other way."

"You gave it to her at a time when she wanted you, not a ring. She worries, Jack. She sees you buying lavish gifts for the girls."

"On birthdays. For Christmas. And what *should* I do? If they want CD players—or Patagonia jackets—or leather backpacks, and I have the money, why *not?* It's not like I see them all the time. It's not like there's much *else* I can do for them."

"Do you really believe that? What about more time with them? That was what Rachel wanted most. That was what she missed. She didn't want the money. She had it once. It didn't help."

"Ah." Jack pushed a hand through his hair. "We've been down *this* road before, Rachel and I. She had it and spurned it. Me, I grew up poor. Dirt poor. Money means something, after that."

"But it's not *about* money," Katherine said, suddenly impassioned. "You could have made *billions,* and Rachel wouldn't have cared, if you had been there emotionally. But you were so obsessed with work, you lost sight of what mattered. Your days were exhausting. Come night-time, you had less and less left over for Rachel and the girls. I see it, too. You walk in every day with briefcase, laptop, and phone. Hey"—she held up a hand—"I'm not complaining. I think it's great that you're here. I think that if you'd been half as portable with work when you were married, you'd still be married. But are you enjoying it? Doesn't look to me like you are. You look hassled. So some of that's worry about Rachel, but I see you on the phone. I hear you. You're not having fun. How much is enough?"

Jack stared at her silently for a time, then dropped his eyes. "I don't know," he finally said.

But he thought about it when he returned to the room, and thought about it back at the house. He thought about it when he woke up in the middle of the night and found Hope with tear streaks on her cheeks, wrapped in her quilt on the far side of Rachel's bed, sound asleep. He thought about it when he woke up and Hope was gone.

Sitting on the edge of the bed rubbing a stiff shoulder, he still didn't know. He opened the window. The morning chill felt good on his skin. He stretched, flexed that stiff shoulder a time or two, put his hands on the windowsill and his face to the air, and wondered about a place that didn't need screens.

It was a good place. It was a different place. There was no cover price here, no charge for admission. All he had to do was walk, breathe, listen, and look, and the beauty was there.

Just then, *that* was enough.

He pulled his head in and closed the window. Picking up the phone, he called his would-be client in Boca and said that Sung and McGill was withdrawing from the project. Life was too short to be held ransom by a bunch of two-bit politicians, he said. No, he didn't want to take one last crack at it; he had already compromised too much. Yes, he knew he wouldn't be paid if he quit. But he wouldn't be paid, anyway, when perfectly good designs ran into last-minute code interpretations. So he was cutting his losses. Thanks a lot. Bye-bye.

When he hung up the phone, his shoulder felt better, and no wonder. The load had been lightened a little. David would be upset. But that was a passing thought. The one that lingered was that he couldn't wait to tell Rachel.

chapter thirteen

COLOR AND CUT normally opened at nine, but Katherine believed that loyalty stemmed from accommodating the client; hence she was often at the shop far earlier. She had a seven-thirty this Wednesday morning, a young woman who worked a ten-hour stint as concierge at a resort in the valley. Even if Katherine hadn't been fond of her—which she was—she knew that Tracey LaMarr was a showcase for her work. Besides, Tracey was fun to do. She gave Katherine the freedom to try new things and had the kind of thick chestnut hair and pretty features to wear it all well.

Today they had agreed on a partial face frame. Katherine was carefully layering Tracey's hair, using foil and three shades ranging from light brown to ash to create a subtle glow around Tracey's face. There wasn't much talk. Early morning appointments rarely jabbered, and Tracey didn't need therapy. She was refreshingly content with her young marriage and her work. So this was a gentle wake-up time for them both. The sounds of a New Age harp drifted through the shop, along with the scent of freshly brewed coffee. Tracey, a tea drinker like Katherine, was nursing a fragrant lemongrass herb tea when, almost dreamily, she said, "Mmm. There's a nice one."

Katherine followed her line of sight out the front window. The shop was on a street that was a block off Carmel's main drag. This early in the day there was little by way of either vehicular or pedestrian traffic, which meant what Tracey saw stood right out. It was a runner, a man. He was gone before Katherine could do more than admire his shorts and his stride.

"I'm envious," she said, resuming her work. She slipped the tail of her comb under another layer, deftly catching alternate strands. "Certain people have the build to do that." She took a square of foil. "It's a physiological thing. Have you ever run?" She knew that Tracey was into aerobics; they often compared classes and instructors. But running was something else.

"Not me," Tracey said. "If I have to exercise, I'd rather enjoy what I'm doing. Running is torture."

Katherine used a brush to slather the separated hair onto foil with one of the three colors in nearby bowls. "Not so torturous, if your body is made for it. Watch a marathon, and you'll see it. Those runners are *lean*. They're not even heavily muscled, though you know they're in perfect condition." She set the brush aside and folded the foil in half.

"Which comes first," Tracey asked, "the chicken, or the egg? Are they lean because they run? Or do they run because they're lean?"

Katherine started again with the tail of the comb. "Both. I think there's a genetic factor. I tried running two years ago. I was about to turn forty and decided that running a ten k would be a great birthday gift for myself.

That's only six-something miles. Piece of cake." She reached for the foil.

"No?"

"No." A second brush, second color. "After two miles, wicked shin splints. I rested and tried again. Same thing. I backed up to a half mile and slowly added. No go. I had every test in the book done. The only thing they could find was that I was pronating. I changed sneakers. I got orthotics. I did special stretches and longer warm-ups." She folded the foil. "It bought me a mile. So I could do *three* before the pain."

"What did you do for your birthday?"

"A friend threw a party. It was a ball. A little caviar and champagne, a little cake with sugary icing. My shins felt great." She took up the comb. "So that's my running story."

"There he is again."

Katherine's first thought was that it couldn't be the same man, but the stride had the same length and litheness, and those running shorts were the same—navy and of normal length. She noticed things like that. She hated running shorts that showed groin. She also hated ones that were so long and loose that they could hide diapers underneath.

"Sharp guy," she remarked.

"He's looking here," Tracey said.

Katherine noticed that, at the same time that she noticed his hair. It was a brown-gray shade, sweaty and spiked. She had seen that hair before.

She returned to the rhythm of her work—separate hair, insert foil, brush on color, fold foil; separate hair, insert foil, brush on color, fold foil. She had wanted to do this to Rachel's hair, to add a subtle variation in color.

Rachel had been on the verge of giving in when the accident happened.

She missed Rachel. Rachel thought the way she did. Katherine didn't know what she would do if Rachel didn't wake up.

Enya was chanting something soulfully Celtic. Katherine let it take her to another time, another place, and it worked for a bit. Then two things happened. First, she finished with foil and color and turned on a three-headed ultraviolet lamp to speed the processing. Second, she looked out the window again.

"That's his third time around," Tracey said. "Do you know him?"

Katherine sighed. "I do." With a reassuring hand on her client's shoulder, she leaned around the lamps. "You'll need fifteen minutes here. Can I get you anything—more tea, *biscotti?*"

"I'm fine," Tracey said, opening the latest *Vogue.* "Go."

Katherine stripped off her thin rubber gloves—surgical gloves, irony of ironies—and pushed the color cart aside. She checked the appointment book, giving Steve Bauer a chance to leave. But he remained across the street, feet firmly planted in front of the curb, hands on his hips, sweat on his T-shirt, which was navy as well. Though it galled her to admit it, he looked gloriously male.

She went outside.

"I thought it was you," he said, breathing faster than normal.

Katherine worked too many early mornings to know that he didn't normally run down this street. She made no effort to hide her cynicism. "Were you just . . . trying out a new street today?"

Bless him, he didn't even blush. Rather, he took a steadier breath, drew himself up, and smiled. "Actually, the Internet had two numbers, work and home. I called work and got the name of the shop, decided to run by and take a look. I wouldn't have expected you here so early."

"I wouldn't have expected you here so *late*. Don't you have rounds or something to do?"

His eyes sparkled. In broad daylight, they were a striking blue. "Yesterday was my long day," he said, "rounds at dawn, teaching in the city, private patients between surgeries." A trickle of sweat began to roll down his cheek. "I was in the OR until nine last night. I figured I'd sleep in today." He wiped the sweat from his cheek with a shoulder. "So. That's your shop?"

"Uh-huh."

"Looks chic."

"It has to be, in a town like this, or I'd be out of business in no time flat."

"Have you had it long?"

"Five years."

"Ah. Steady clientele?"

She thought about that and conceded, "Steady enough with locals. Tourists fill in the gaps."

"How do tourists know you're here? Do you advertise?"

"I give referral discounts to the hotels."

He smiled. "Clever." He gestured toward an Italian restaurant halfway down the block. "Ever eaten there?"

Katherine was grateful when he looked that way. Always a sucker for blue eyes, she was relieved to be released. "I have. It's great."

Too soon his eyes caught hers again. "I've never tried it. Want to go with me?"

"Mmm, I don't think so."

"Any special reason? Husband, fiancé, significant other?"

She thought about lying, but that wasn't her style. "No. I'm just . . . not interested right now."

Those blue eyes clouded. "Is it me?"

Oh, it was. She liked the way he looked, liked the way he dressed, liked the way he ran. He didn't evade questions. When she thought he was handing her a line, it turned out to be a legitimate one, and even aside from that, there was something intangible going on. She didn't understand what it was. She didn't *know* why a woman fell hard for a particular man. Chemistry, more than *logic?*

Oh, yes, it was him. But she wasn't ready to take another chance. Not yet. Not when she was finally starting to feel good about herself.

It had taken a long time—*another* thing they hadn't warned her about. She was forty-two and finally believing that she wasn't soon going to die. The shop helped. It spoke of a future. The way people looked at her helped, too. They saw not only the healthy woman she was but the attractive woman she wanted to be.

Still, she wasn't ready to take her blouse off for anyone yet, much less a man—which was no doubt jumping the gun. Steve Bauer had asked her out to dinner. He hadn't asked her to bed.

But it was coming. She saw it in those blue eyes. Worse, she felt it in the tiny place in her belly that hadn't been revved up since her surgery. Oh, it was revved up now. She could do it with this man. The question was whether things would go dead if he had a problem with her breasts.

Those eyes were still clouded. He seemed concerned, on the verge of hurt, and Katherine wasn't one to hurt. "No," she said. "It's not you. It's me."

"Why you?"

"Bad experiences." With a regretful smile, she started walking backward toward the shop. "Maybe someday we'll have dinner. Not yet."

His eyes dropped to her mouth, and for a split second, she felt caressed. "I'd settle for lunch," he said with such endearing directness that her smile grew coy.

"Tell you what. Get my friend out of her coma and I might go for that."

"I'm not God."

She shrugged. Turning, she walked with deliberate reserve the rest of the way back to her shop.

JACK reached the hospital before nine. Cindy was bathing Rachel. The only change that had occurred was the arrival of a new, larger-than-ever flower arrangement from Victoria.

"Hi, Rachel," he said, but she showed no sign of hearing. "No more movement?" he asked Cindy.

She shook her head.

From his briefcase, he took a handful of CDs that the girls had pulled from Rachel's collection. Flipping through them, he said, "We have another Garth, we have Clint Black, we have Collin Raye, Shania Twain, and Wynonna. Okay, angel, what'll it be?" When Rachel didn't answer, he said, "Hope said I'd like Collin, so let's do it." He put the CD on low.

While Cindy finished up with Rachel, he disposed of

the flower arrangements that were dead and went to the shop downstairs for replacements. In response to his request for something vivid, the florist pulled out an orange hibiscus and a deep pink kalanchoe. "They'll bloom for months," the man said, and just that quickly, Jack decided on roses and tulips. The roses were yellow, the tulips pink. They would last a week, no more. He wanted Rachel to be home by then.

Cindy had dressed Rachel in a nightshirt that was bright pink with orange and blue splashes—sent by the owner of a Big Sur crafts shop, along with a card that was tacked on the bulletin board beside Hope's drawings and other cards—and was trying to tuck stray strands of Rachel's hair into the loose topknot that Samantha had created with Hope's scrunchy the afternoon before.

"Leave it," he said to the nurse. "It's pretty, curling against her cheek."

Moments later, alone with Rachel, he touched that curl. It was soft, silky. There was life there yet.

Taking one of the roses, he moved it under her nose. "Bright yellow," he said and, studying the rose, pushed himself to see it as Rachel would. "Sunshine. Barely open but wanting to, just the tips starting to curl outward, like delicate paper." He tipped the rose to his own nose. "And fragrant. Smells like sunshine, too. Makes me think beach roses in Nantucket. Remember those? Good vacation." He returned the rose to Rachel's nose, then exchanged it for a tulip. "This one is soft pink. Baby pink. Smooth. Tall and graceful. A dancer. An elegant spring dancer."

He teased the tip of her nose with the tulip. Then he told her about going out to the car that morning and seeing deer in the woods. A doe and two fawns—*blacktails,* he could have sworn he heard her say, though his own memory may have dredged it up. And he told her about Boca.

"See, it isn't just the money," he said, because if it was he would never have blown off a job. Then he leaned closer, so that no one else would hear, and confessed, "Maybe it was, for a while. But it wasn't conscious materialism. It was wanting to be a success. If I got lost in it, I'm sorry. But success has always been a thing for me, more than for you. Back home, I was shit growing up. I still feel that way sometimes. You, you've always been a success. Hell, just growing the girls for nine months and giving birth was a coup."

Oh, he had been proud, and not only of his daughters. Rachel had been the most beautiful, most serene mom during her brief-as-brief-could-be stays in the maternity ward. He remembered lying just this close when she was back home and nursing, watching her doze off with a baby at her breast. She hadn't changed—same gracefully arched brows, same short nose, same freckles. He felt the same familiarity, the same closeness, that had made their best years so good. Even at the end, some things had worked. Like the girls tumbling with him in the yard, while Rachel captured it all on film. Even at the end there were smiles.

But okay, he hadn't been there emotionally for her. She hadn't pointed it out. He had felt her increasing silence. She had felt his increasing distance.

"It's like you get started in one direction and pick up speed, and you may forget where you're going and why, but the momentum takes you there anyway. Only, you find out when you arrive that it isn't where you want to be." He wasn't sure if he was talking about work or about the divorce. Since the divorce was a done deed, he focused on work.

"The problem," he said, pulling shop drawings from his briefcase, "is that I can cancel on a project like Boca because nothing's been signed yet, but there are too many others where the commitment's been made." He unfolded the drawings. They were the designs for Napa—heat and air ductwork, lighting, kitchen fixtures—submitted by the various subcontractors and overnighted to him in Big Sur. They needed study and approval. It was the least he could do after postponing another set of meetings.

He told Rachel about the project, then talked his way through the shop drawings, wondering if what he said meant anything to her. She used to look over his shoulder sometimes when he was working with drawings like these. He had talked her through the plans then.

At least, he thought he had. Maybe he hadn't. Maybe she had been running in and out, busy with the girls. She would have been bored with these. Hell, *he* was bored with these. They had more to do with supervision than design, and design was his love.

He had barely refolded the drawings and put them away when Ben Wolfe arrived. He carried an arrangement of yellow roses, saw the ones Jack had bought, and said a surprisingly gracious, "Great minds think alike." He set his vase on the nightstand. "Today's my birthday. We were going to celebrate."

"Happy birthday," Jack said, but he didn't leave this time. He stood right there with Rachel while Ben made awkward conversation with her. He seemed like a very nice, very decent, very attentive and accommodating man. Jack had the wildest impulse to introduce him to Jill.

When Ben broached the subject of Rachel's show, Jack said that he would be framing her pictures himself. After all, she had all the materials at the house, and he had framed pictures before, or so he reasoned. But he wasn't thinking about framing when Ben left. He was thinking about painting. He had put it off, put it off, thinking that Rachel would wake up and tell him not to do it, but the show was ten days off and she was still asleep, and he didn't *know* whether this six-years-older Rachel would resent his touching her work. Samantha thought she would. Katherine might have an opinion.

Katherine would *definitely* have an opinion. But he had told her to butt out.

He could apologize. That felt like the right thing to do. He wanted to think that she was his friend now, too. He would do it.

UNFORTUNATELY when Katherine came to visit, she wasn't alone. Dinah and Jan were with her. Dinah looked as successful as ever with her smart red suit, gold brooch, and beeper. Jan was no-nonsense and functional, a woman with muscled calves, sun-dried skin, and sheer polish on her nails. Katherine's own nails were burgundy today.

The three looked worried approaching the bed. With forced lightness, they talked to Rachel in turns. One held her hand, another brushed her hair, the third asked Jack what the doctors were saying.

Thinking to learn more about Rachel from them, as he had from Charlie and Faye, he asked about book group. It was a mistake. Suddenly, though he was standing right there, he faded. Their voices grew quiet, more intimate.

They became four close friends—Dinah, Katherine, Jan, and Rachel—four close *female* friends, reminiscing about things they had shared.

"Why did I join?" Dinah asked in response to Jack's question, but oblivious to him now. "Because I love to read. I always have."

"You were the most avid of us," Katherine said. "We rarely chose a book where you hadn't read another by the same author."

"I was so intimidated," Jan confessed. "I felt like the dummy because my life was either hitting golf balls or changing diapers. I came so close to calling and canceling out of that first meeting. Changed clothes three times beforehand."

"You didn't."

"I did. But I needed to talk about that book. Remember it?"

"*Beloved.*"

"I was sure I'd missed most of the meaning."

"Haunting book."

"Strong."

"Scary." It was Jan, again, speaking softly. "But not as scary as *The Fifth Child.*"

"You were pregnant again."

"Waiting for amnio results."

"I read the book and began imagining that this new child would arrive and mess up the family I already had."

"That was your confession book." This from Katherine with a nod.

Dinah chuckled. "Boy, did you let go."

"I was embarrassed."

"But it gave the rest of us permission to do the same," Katherine said. "I did it with *A Prayer for Owen Meany,* which I adored, but which had nothing to do with me directly." She frowned. "So why that book?"

"It was the timing," Dinah suggested. "Byron had just let you down. You needed to vent."

"I vented all right." She touched Rachel's hair. "What did it for Rachel?"

"*Moon Tiger.*"

"*Woman on the Edge of Time.*"

But Katherine was shaking her head. "*Exit the Rainmaker.*"

"Oh my God." Jan laughed. "About the college president who just disappeared one day. I haven't thought of that one in *ages.*"

"What a great discussion."

Katherine nodded. "We asked each other where *we* would go if we were to walk out of our lives and disappear like he did. Remember what Rachel said?" Jack listened as Katherine's voice grew softer, lyrical. "She described a little town in Maine, not much more than a handful of stores backed up to the shore of a lake. There were huge pine forests, long dirt roads leading to cabins in the woods, and skies so clear you could see the northern lights. She said she would live in one of those cabins and know everyone in town. She thought it would be the simplest, most beautiful life."

Dinah snorted. "Not *my* cup of tea. Remember what *I* said? *I'd* get lost in *Gstaad.*"

She may have said more, but Jack didn't hear. He had gone to the window and was looking blindly out over a cluster of Monterey cypress, realizing that the birds he had found on one of those canvases waiting to be finished in Rachel's studio were loons. He hadn't identified them immediately because his mind was on the West

Coast, not the East. Mention of the northern lights had shifted his sights, because he had seen those lights, that sky. The loons were from Maine. They had been floating on the glassy surface of the lake at dusk on every one of the seven nights he and Rachel had spent in the small cabin in the pines that had been their honeymoon suite.

HE BEGAN painting at eight. He worked until three in the morning, layering Rachel's canvas with that lake and its small center island, its border of trees, and an early evening sky shot with a whisper of green and pink. Where the mirror of the lake called for reflections, he made them lighter than real life would have them, and it worked. When he finally set down his palette and brushes, straightened cramped legs one at a time, and stepped back from the easel, his eye was drawn more strongly than ever to Rachel's loons.

It was another hour before he capped the oils and half again as much before he crawled into Rachel's bed. He woke up after three hours of sleep, opened the window, and inhaled the lifting fog. He was tired, but pleasantly so. He had worked hard and done well. He hadn't felt as satisfied in a long, long while.

He showered, shaved, and dressed. When he arrived in the kitchen, Samantha was standing at the counter drinking coffee. She looked like something from a magazine, all tight top and jeans, silky straight hair, and eyes lined in blue.

"You look so grown-up it scares me," he said, meaning every word. The defiance he saw kept him from telling her to get rid of the eyeliner. "Is that all you're having for breakfast?" he asked instead.

"Breakfast is my least favorite meal."

"Since when?"

A look of annoyance came and went. Even her defiance was down. "Daddy? Can we talk about the prom?"

"Is your sister up?"

"Up and gone."

"Gone where?" he asked, fearing.

Samantha didn't have to do more than look in the direction of Duncan's, and suddenly Jack made for the door. He knew that Hope would show up in time to leave, but she had gone to Duncan's one time too many. A niggling in the back of his mind said that he wanted to see more of where she went.

He had lost one child, perhaps because of his own inertia. He couldn't let it happen again. If he didn't go after Hope, and she was ever hurt in any way, Rachel would never forgive him. More, he would never forgive himself.

chapter fourteen

JACK WAS A MAN with a mission as he strode up the hill. He felt little of the early morning chill, saw little of the sun that was just rising high enough to crest the hills in the east, and if the fragrance of the air had any power at all, it served only to keep him from outright panic. During the precious minutes it took him to reach Duncan Bligh's cabin, his imagination worked double-time. He conjured all kinds of ugly images, all kinds of perverse abuse. Quickening his step, he swore at himself repeatedly for not acting sooner.

The cabin was a log box that might have fit neatly into a corner of the adjacent pen. The barn behind it was larger and newer. Sheep clustered between pen and barn, staring at him as he neared.

He crossed the porch and pounded on the door. Hands on his hips, he clenched his jaw and waited. When Duncan opened up, he said angrily, "I don't know what in hell's been going on here, but I want my daughter, and I want her now."

Looking unperturbed—which bothered Jack all the

more—Duncan *ssh-sh*ed him with a finger and glanced into the interior of the cabin. Wondering what all he *hadn't* imagined, Jack barged past him. He hadn't taken more than a handful of steps when he stopped short.

The first thing he saw was a large hearth with a healthy fire radiating warmth. The second was Hope's blond hair, but it was down low, resting against something. That something was the third thing he saw. It was a minute before he identified a small figure in a wheelchair.

"About time you met Faith," Duncan muttered, walking past Jack. He bent low over the figure in the chair and murmured something Jack couldn't hear. Impatiently, he waved Jack forward. "Say hello to my wife."

The woman in the wheelchair looked back at Jack. Her hair was white, her face creased, her spectacles round and small. Her smile was as warm as the fire.

"Hello," she said, more mouthing than sound. Her hand lay on Hope's head, which lay against the crocheted afghan covering her legs. "She's sleeping," she whispered, but she needn't have reassured Jack. One look at the woman and her sweet smile, and his fears were gone. *Duncan's faith.* He couldn't count the number of times he had heard that phrase uttered in the same breath as *solace* and *peace.* The woman and her smile said it all. *Duncan's Faith.*

Jack took a deep, wry breath. *Duncan's Faith.* He was right for swearing at himself. He should have acted sooner. What an imbecile he was.

Releasing the breath with a self-deprecating shake of the head, he extended a hand. "Jack McGill," he said. Her hand was frail in his, but there was a dignity to it. "I'm pleased to meet you."

Faith nodded. "Hope didn't tell you she was coming?"

"No." He glanced at Duncan, who was regarding his wife with such tenderness that Jack was all the more humbled. *Duncan's Faith.* Why hadn't he known?

He hadn't known because he was thickheaded, because he was driven by jealousy where his family was concerned, because he jumped to conclusions at the drop of a hat. And maybe because the girls had hoodwinked him. So there was that.

Duncan walked off. Jack hunkered down in front of the fire so that Faith wouldn't have to look up.

"It's been hard on her," she said, her voice so soft and lyrical that it wouldn't waken Hope. "I don't think she's sleeping nights very well. How is Rachel?"

Jack hadn't called the hospital that morning. He knew that he would have been notified if anything had changed during the night. "She's the same. Do you know, I had no idea you existed? The girls talked about 'Faith' like it was a religion. I'm afraid I've been rude not coming to thank you before this."

"Thank me for what?"

The words came easily. Faith Bligh radiated goodness. Jack felt no threat here, no risk in baring his feelings. "For being kind to the girls. For taking care of Guinevere." He sputtered out a laugh in self-reproach. "I couldn't quite understand why the cat would be better off up here if Duncan was out in the fields all day." At that moment, Duncan was washing dishes in the kitchen that lined the far living room wall. "Now it makes sense."

"He comes back to check on me every few hours." She smiled again. "Not that I'm going anywhere."

"Do you go outside?"

"Oh, yes. I can wheel myself out to the porch. There's

a beautiful view of the valley. But I need Duncan for much beyond that."

Jack was remembering something—something Hope had said on the very first morning after Rachel's accident. He had been trying to assure her that broken legs healed. She had been convinced that it wasn't always the case.

He was frowning, trying to decide whether he could ask and, if so, how to do it, when Faith said, "Some people think I'm crazy living up here, but I've always loved these hills. If I have to be confined, this is a beautiful place to be. Duncan and I used to vacation here before the accident."

"How long ago was that?"

"The accident? Twelve years. A ski lift collapsed. My legs were broken in so many places that walking would have been an ordeal even if my spine hadn't been injured, which it was."

"I'm sorry."

"Don't be. Three died that day. I could have been one of those, and then I would have missed out on the life we've found here." Her eyes sparkled. "My Duncan used to drive a truck. I never saw him. Now I do."

Hope moved her head. She rubbed her eyes against the afghan, turned them toward the fire, opened them slowly, and saw Jack. "Daddy," she breathed, and quickly sat up.

"I was worried," he said, but gently. There was no other way to speak in this home.

"Mom always knows I'm here."

"Well," he said, pushing himself up, "maybe I'll know now, too." He held out a hand. "You have school. Samantha's waiting."

"She had breakfast with us," Faith said with a fond look at Hope.

"I'm sorry for that. We've imposed enough."

"Imposed? Oh, no. Hope is no imposition. She's a joy. This is the least I can do, after all Rachel has done." She reached for Hope's free hand. "Give your mother a kiss for me, will you?"

"OKAY," HE told the girls as he hustled them to the car. "The joke's up. Tell me about your mom and the Blighs."

"They're good friends," Samantha said. "Can we talk about my prom?"

"Not yet," Jack answered, because he was feeling a little foolish knowing so little. "How did they get to be good friends?" he asked, backing out of the drive.

Hope said, "Mom was exploring right after we moved here. She stumbled across their cabin and Faith was on the porch."

"About my prom—"

"Not yet," Jack said, shifting to drive down the hill. "You owe me. Both of you. No one told me Faith was a person."

"No one told you she wasn't."

"You guys let me think your mother was *dating* Duncan."

"We *never* said that."

Hope said, "The thing about Duncan and Faith is that it never seems right talking about them. Mom helps them out, doing marketing and stuff. She always said that Faith was like a favorite aunt. She has coffee up there a lot. They sit and talk. With Faith you don't even *have* to talk and it feels good."

One meeting with the woman, and Jack knew what

Hope meant. Faith radiated understanding, acceptance, calm.

Samantha's voice was a jarring intrusion. "Dad. We need to talk about my prom. There's been a change in plans."

He would have liked to hear more about Faith, because even picturing her brought calm, but Samantha had an agenda of her own, and he was learning that car time was good time. Oh yes, he was a captive audience here, but so was she. She couldn't stomp off when she didn't like what he said.

He turned north onto Highway 1. "What's the change?"

"First of all, I'm not going with Brendan. I'm going with Teague."

Jack felt something by his arm closest to the door. Hope was crowded against the window there. "Teague?" he asked Samantha.

"Teague Runyan. He's a great guy."

"Why the switch?"

"Brendan and I aren't getting along. It doesn't make any sense for us to be stuck with each other when he wanted to be with Jana and I wanted to be with Teague. I mean, everyone's with everyone anyway, so it's no big thing except for going and coming."

Jack followed that—in a way. "Are you still leaving from Lydia's house?"

"No. That's the second change. Teague's picking me up here."

Hope shifted. Jack felt the movement against his arm, decided that he really did need a bigger car, and shot Samantha a look. "How old is this Teague?"

"Seventeen. He's a good driver, and he has a truck. It's, like, indestructible."

In Jack's day, guys wouldn't be caught dead picking up their girls in a truck, if they had another option. So maybe this Teague didn't. Or maybe it was just that times had changed. Trucks were in. And Jack did like the sound of *indestructible*. What he didn't like was the sound of *seventeen*. Seventeen was a dangerous age. "Okay. So I'll meet him when he comes?"

"Uh-huh," Samantha said a little too brightly.

"What else?"

"Else?"

"Is that it for changed plans? You're still doing the limo thing from Lydia's house and back?"

"The party's at Jake Drumble's."

"I've never heard that name either," Jack said a little less easily. Katherine had warned him that things weren't always as they seemed. Just now with Hope, they had proved to be better. He had a feeling it wouldn't be that way with Samantha. "Who is Jake Drumble, where does he live, and what happened to Lydia's party?"

"Oh God, here we go," Samantha cried, "I knew you'd have trouble with this. You are the most . . . *anal* person I know."

"I just *asked*."

"Like it's the Inquisition," she said with indignation. "It's no—big—thing. As far as you're concerned, the only difference is that Teague will pick me up Saturday and drop me back Sunday."

"Yeah, well, that leaves a whole lot of hours unaccounted for," he said. He felt Hope again. Deliberate? "So. The party's at Jake's. Before and after?"

"I think so. It's not definite about after."

"But you're going back to Lydia's to sleep."

263

"*No,*" She was suddenly impatient. "I'm not *going* with Lydia."

"Not at all?"

"That's the *point*. Like, this is a whole different group. Lydia'll be with Brendan and Jana and Adam and Shelly, and I'll be with Teague and Pam and Jake and Heather."

He was beginning to see the picture. "So Lydia's party is still on, only you're not going. But she's your best friend."

"So?"

He slid her a glance. "So, that doesn't sound right."

Samantha blew out a breath. She folded her arms and stared out the windshield, and Jack was tempted to let it go. The silence was welcome, with his mind so full of other things. But one of those things was Katherine's concern about teenaged girls and proms; another was a little something that was starting to feel like a finger poking his arm where Samantha couldn't see.

"Talk to me, Sam," he said lightly.

"What do you want me to say? Lydia just isn't . . ."

"Isn't . . . sophisticated?"

"No, she isn't, and if I'm with her, I can't be with other kids who are."

"Because those others won't like you if you're with Lydia?"

"They *won't*."

Jack thought about that as he drove. Hope wasn't poking him anymore. She didn't need to. He knew on his own that more than a little something wasn't right. "What about loyalty?" he finally asked. "Lydia's been your best friend for six years. It shouldn't just end in a day."

There was a pause, then a sharp "Your marriage did."

Jack was blindsided for the space of a breath. He

264

rebounded with a firm "No, it didn't. It was months leading up to the end, and it was painful. It wasn't something
either of us wanted."

"Then why did it happen?"

"Because we'd reached an impasse, but it was
between your mother and me and no one else. There
weren't any third parties. We weren't choosing between
one group or another."

"Just one *lifestyle* or another," Samantha said.

"Okay. I can buy that. But it's a far cry from being
best friends with Lydia one day and deciding she isn't
good enough for you the next. So she isn't sophisticated.
What does that mean? She doesn't use eye makeup? Her
T-shirts aren't tight enough? You seemed happy enough
with her last weekend. Was that an act?"

"No." She made a disgruntled sound. "You don't
understand."

"I'm trying to. But it doesn't feel right."

"This is a *prom*," she said, enunciating each word.
"It's one night."

"Sounds to me like it's more than that. Sounds to me
like a *lifestyle* decision," he said, using her word.
"You're choosing between groups of friends. That has
long-range implications. So Lydia isn't as sophisticated
as—what's her name?"

"Pam. And it's *all* those kids who aren't as cool."

"But they're nice kids. They come from nice families.
I haven't seen Pam at the hospital visiting your mother. I
haven't seen Teague there, or any of the others you mentioned."

"That's because they're new friends. They don't know
Mom yet. And why do you assume they're not nice? Just
because they're different doesn't mean they aren't as

good or even better." Her voice turned pleading. "You don't understand. I am *so* excited about going to the prom with these kids. It'll be awesome," she said with feeling, and because Jack did want her to be happy, he settled into the silence of the drive.

But he had a bad taste in his mouth. After meeting Lydia's mom, he had grown complacent about the prom. What did he know about Pam whoever, *or* about Teague Runyan? Hell, he didn't even like the kid's name, which was sick. But he was Samantha's father. And he was a man. He knew what men did. He knew what *young* men did. Seventeen-year-olds were loose cannons.

They were approaching the tree-lined stretch of Carmel Highlands when he said, "I worry about safety. Are Jake's parents chaperoning this party?"

"As far as I know." She took a quick breath. "Don't you dare call. You'll *humiliate* me."

Well, he didn't want to do that. He wanted to treat Samantha like a mature young woman. "Still," he said because the whole thing with Lydia was sitting wrong in his gut, "there's something to be said for loyalty."

"Oh?" Samantha asked. "Is that why you're racing back to the city to have lunch with Jill today? You dumped Mom because she wasn't sophisticated enough."

"Excuse me?"

Samantha barreled on, clearly driven by that agenda of hers. "She didn't want to party all the time, so you dumped her for Jill. Is that any different from what I'm doing?"

"*Totally.* First of all, I didn't *dump* your mother. If anything, she dumped me. Second, I didn't start dating Jill until a long time after your mother and I split."

"You've been dating her two years. Is it serious? Have you given her a ring or anything?"

"No. We're just friends."

"Don't you think *she*'s thinking about loyalty?"

"Samantha," he said with a sigh, "this isn't your business."

"It *is*. I want to know why loyalty has to matter to me, but not to you."

"Loyalty matters to me. Why do you think I'm here? Why do you think I've spent the better part of the past week and a half at your mother's bedside?"

"Why have you?" Samantha asked. "Has it occurred to you that she might not want you there?"

"Yes. It has. But that doesn't change the way I feel. Sitting with your mother feels like the right thing to do. So I ask *you* what feels right—going to the prom with friends you know and trust, or blowing them off to be with a whole other group?"

"This is hopeless," she grumbled and said for what had to have been the third time, "You *don't* understand." This time she turned her head away.

"No," he sighed, feeling defeated. "I guess I don't."

JILL lived in a modest house in Seacliff, which was in northwest San Francisco, overlooking the Pacific. When Jack arrived, at one, he felt a sense of dread. Jill was perfect. Her blond hair was adorably layered, her makeup pleasantly light, her skirt and blouse artsy, her scent spicy—though the scent might well have come from the kitchen. She had decided against the risotto that she would have cooked Monday and, instead, had made a warm Oriental salad with fresh tuna, spaghetti-thin wonton crisps, a dressing that was light and contained herbs Jack had never heard of, and warm, home-baked olive bread.

The granite kitchen island was set with rattan mats, linen napkins, and fresh flowers. One look, one smell, and Jack sensed the effort she had made to make things special. The kiss she gave him tasted of relief, which made him feel worse.

They sat side by side on tall stools, thighs touching, arms occasionally entwined. Jill asked first about Rachel and listened in concern while he tried to verbalize the jolt he still felt each morning walking into that hospital room and seeing her lying inert. He told of helping the nurse bathe her and work her limbs to keep them pliant. He told of talking to Rachel about the girls and the past in the hope of eliciting a response.

Then Jill asked him about work. Fresh from two hours at the office, he talked about that for a while. David had been upset over Boca, but they had worked it through. More worrisome to Jack was his partner's lukewarm response to his latest Montana design, which he described to Jill to her nodding approval. He told her about sending Brynna to Buffalo, elevating Alex to a project manager for Napa and San Jose, and alerting the others that he needed backup for Austin. He told her that he had just learned about a new project that might be interesting.

He asked Jill about the final take from the benefit the week before, and listened while she outlined plans for the next year's benefit, proposed several days before. He asked about her tennis lessons and asked how her diabetic mother was doing.

When they stopped talking, Jill slipped her arms around his waist. She rested her head on his shoulder, then raised her face. They kissed once, and again. She slipped off her stool, came between his legs, and wrapped her arms around his neck. Her breasts settled against his chest. As she kissed him again, she undulated ever so slowly.

Jack tried to get into it. He told himself that it might work after all, that Jill was an incredible woman, that he would be a fool to let her go. He tried to feel, but nothing came, so he tried to fantasize. But Rachel's was the only face he could see, and his body wasn't falling for the switch. It knew the difference between the women. He had spent more than a few hours of late painfully aroused in Rachel's bed. The only pain he felt now was the knowledge that he couldn't keep doing this and, because of that, he was about to hurt Jill.

Her mouth was doing its very best against his throat when he took her arms and gently disengaged. He put his forehead to hers. "This isn't working," he said quietly. "I . . . can't."

She drew back frightened, studied his face. "Is it Rachel?"

"It's everything."

"But is it her?"

He wasn't sure. Early on, Katherine had asked him why he was still at her bedside. Samantha had asked him the same thing that morning.

"Do you love her?" Jill asked.

"I don't know. I don't know. My life just seems to be turning on end."

"You need space. That's okay. I'll wait. You can take your time. I'm not going anywhere."

He felt a stab of annoyance. It was a minute before he realized that the annoyance wasn't *at* her, but *for* her. She was too good. He could take advantage of her offer in no time.

Clasping her hands together in his, he said, "I can't do this anymore, Jill. It isn't fair to you."

Her voice went high, urgent. "Am I complaining?"

"No. That's the problem. You don't complain. You don't demand. You don't give me ultimatums."

"I don't have to. You know what I want."

"I do, and you've been patient, waiting, wanting it to happen, but it isn't going to."

"How do you *know?* Your life is turning on end; you just said so. Why not wait? Why call it off now?"

"Because," he said with greater feeling, "it's not going to happen. It's not, Jill."

"But—"

"Shh." He pressed a finger to her lips, stroked the blond hair that was so much like Rachel's but not. He spoke in a half whisper, urgent now himself. "Listen to me. Please. I love you, Jill, I do, but as a person, a friend. It won't ever end in marriage, which is what you want, what you *should* have."

Her eyes were large, teary. "Why . . . won't it? What's . . . missing?"

"Nothing. Nothing in you. It's me. I'm just . . . I'm just . . ."

"Still in love with Rachel?"

He released a breath. "Maybe. I honestly don't know. But I don't feel free now. My marriage is still there. Unfinished business."

"Rachel ended it. She left you. You always told me that."

"It helped keep me angry, but there are reasons why she left, things I didn't know about until now. I have to talk with her, Jill. I won't know where I'm going until I do."

Bewildered, Jill asked, "Was it *that* good with her?"

That good and better, he would have said if he hadn't cared so much, but he was hurting Jill enough without. "It was different. Unique in its way. Rachel and I have a history, Jill. We go way back."

"What if she doesn't wake up?"

"Then I'll have the girls. And regrets." He sighed, running his hands up and down her arms. "Don't add to the regrets, Jill. I could keep this going between us and just take what I want. But I'm trying to do the right thing. Help me? Please?"

"IT'S DONE," he told Rachel barely two hours later. Jill had cried at the end. They had agreed to talk from time to time. He was feeling empty, alone. But he had done the right thing. "She was a perfectly lovely woman, but Christ, you have a hold on me. You always did. I was dating someone when we met. Remember? I broke up with her, too."

Only, then, Jack had been madly in love with Rachel. Now, they weren't married anymore. But he remembered clear as day the tingling he had felt deep inside whenever she talked, touched him, even *looked* at him. He remembered the anticipation of seeing her and the pleasure when he did. It had been that way through the birth of the kids. Even after they'd started to want different kinds of everyday lives, there were times when a word, a look, or a touch could start the tingling.

"Were things so bad at the end?" he asked, studying her face. It was healing by the day. Her color was improving. He wanted to think that was propitious.

He curled and uncurled the fingers of her right hand,

271

then did the same with the left. "Maybe we jumped the gun. Gave up too soon. Let it happen without enough of a fight. We had good stuff going." He concentrated on her ring finger, so slim and bare. "Didn't we?" He searched her face for a blink or a twitch.

"I keep thinking about that baby. Feeling that loss. Thinking maybe that would've done it, made us yell and scream and get it all out. Six years. What we could have had and done in six years." He felt a wave of weariness. "Talk to me," he whispered plaintively. "*Tell* me."

Katherine turned into the room. He took a tired breath, sighed, straightened. "How goes it?"

"Not bad. And here?"

Jack shrugged. He followed her gaze to the tray table that was covered with papers.

"Are you getting much done?" she asked without spite.

"Nah. I spread stuff out and pretend, but it's hard to concentrate. What I'm working on feels stale. I was in the office this morning and got a call about a new project. If I hadn't been right there, I wouldn't ever have known. My partner would have said thanks, but no thanks."

"Why?"

"The job is to build a private home. Granted, there are four acres to work with and the client wants more an estate than a home, but it's smaller than most of our recent jobs. David thinks it's a step back for us."

"What do you think?"

"I think," he said, flexing his spine side to side, "that it'd be a fun job to do. It's in Hillsborough. Local. The zoning's all done. The client knows my work. He wants me to use what I've done in the past as a springboard. I.e., he wants something new and imaginative."

Katherine nodded her approval. Jack wanted to think Rachel approved, too.

He sat back and smiled. "So, how's the good doctor?"

For a minute he saw the old, defensive Katherine. Then his smile registered, and she softened. "Sent me flowers yesterday afternoon," she said.

"That's impressive."

She gave a one-shouldered shrug. "Byron sent me flowers, too. The good doctor is as much in the dark about you-know-what as Byron was then."

"You don't think Bauer is used to medical quirks?"

"Quirks? That's rich. And I'm sure he is. But that's a problem in itself. If he deals with medical . . . quirks all day long, why ever would he want to face them at night?"

"The flip side of that argument is that he's become so inured to them, he wouldn't notice."

"He'd notice."

"Are they that bad?" Jack asked, frankly curious. From the outside, nothing was wrong. Absolutely nothing.

"Well, they aren't," Katherine conceded. "They just . . . take a little getting used to. There are scars."

"Few people make it to forty without those."

"It's the idea of the whole thing."

"That may be more in your mind than anyone else's."

"Possibly." She paused. "Why are you pushing this?"

"Pushing what?"

"The good doctor and me. Why do I need a man?"

Jack sat back. "There's an interesting question. From what I've gathered, you and Rachel are two peas in a pod, very much alike, yes? Strong, independent women?"

Katherine considered that. "I'd say so."

"Okay. Early on, I said that Rachel never really needed

me. You said I was wrong. If you tell me how she needed me, there might be a message for you." When she didn't immediately respond, he said, "I assume you two talked about it."

"Not in as many words. Strong, independent women like us don't use the word *need.* We use the word *want,* like we have the power to choose." But she grew reflective as she focused on Rachel. "She sometimes talks about things she misses."

"Like?"

"Help with the girls. Raising kids is hard. The bigger they get, the bigger the issues. Rachel misses having you there to talk things through with."

"She always had answers."

"Maybe when the girls were little. She had to. You weren't around, and little kids need immediate response. Big kids, big problems require more thought. That's the discussion she misses."

You weren't around. Well, he was, but not enough. He had missed some important times for the girls. And for Rachel? Okay. He should have been there more. He certainly should have known about that baby. He should have cut that trip short and come home. If he was haunted by the loss of that child now, he could imagine what Rachel had felt at the time.

She should have told him. He should have been there.

But if he had been there for her all along, she *might* have told him.

Accepting his share of the blame, he sighed. "What else did she miss?"

"I don't know," Katherine said, seeming embarrassed. She pushed her fingers through her hair from underneath, then shook her head. "I know what *I* miss. I miss someone to be with after work. Someone to share wine with. Someone to share silence. Sharing. I guess that's it. I'd venture to say that Rachel misses that."

"Sounds to me she found some of it with Faith Bligh. Sharing the silence over coffee."

"Not the same. There's something about lying in bed late at night or very, very early in the morning, talking, silent, whatever."

Memory had Jack right back there, lying with Rachel. They were special times, which had started coming fewer and farther between. Then they had ended. "When you work and have kids, you're exhausted."

But it was a stock excuse. Katherine's arched brow said as much.

You make time for what you want, Rachel had said once. And she had tried. He recalled a time when he was due back from a trip in the evening. She hired a baby-sitter and made reservations at Postrio weeks in advance, then picked him up at the airport and drove him there. He proceeded to tell her that he had eaten at the place six times in the last month and couldn't bear to do it again.

He had missed the point, which wasn't form but substance. He realized that now, with no pride at all.

"I miss taking vacations with Rachel," he offered.

He was rewarded when Katherine said, "She misses being pampered once in a while."

"Strong, independent women need pampering?"

"We're human, too."

"Any man can suffice for that."

She shook her head. "Only certain ones. It's an . . . intangible something. A man can be in a room with fifty women and fall for only one. A woman can be in a room with fifty men and fall for only one. Why? I don't know the answer. Do you?"

Jack didn't. But he hadn't fallen in love with Jill the way logic said he should. "Does Rachel have that . . . whatever with Ben?"

Katherine laughed. "Not quite."

He was immensely pleased. "Really?"

"What do *you* think?"

"Well, the guy doesn't turn *me* on," he said, then asked a cautious "She hasn't found it with anyone else?"

Katherine slowly shook her head. Softly she said, "It's a very special quality. When it works, it works. Rachel had it with you. She still thinks about that. She thinks about it a lot."

SO DID JACK, most notably Katherine's use of the present tense. He might have taken it more lightly if it had come from anyone else. But Katherine said what she meant.

He could ask her for specifics, could prod and dig. But did he want to risk her saying that Rachel was simply analyzing and understanding the past, rather than feeling it in the present?

No.

Because the fact was that he *did* feel things now. He felt things every time he touched her, whether applying skin cream or exercising her limbs. He felt things looking at her mouth, or at those freckles that promised such spirit. He felt things walking down the hospital corridor and turning in at her room. Anticipation. Purpose. Rightness.

Fine to say that he was here out of guilt, or for the girls, or for old times' sake, but the truth was that he still felt a connection with Rachel. Unfinished business, he had told Jill. He wondered if it was more than that. One of the things he had loved most about Rachel when they first met was believing that she brought out the best in him. He wondered if she still could.

SO HE SAT with her following his talk with Katherine, and though he didn't deliberately think about work, his mind wandered there on its own. Looking at Rachel, holding her hand, he began to talk out the Montana project, and suddenly he saw a design possibility. No, it wasn't the one he had originally wanted, or any one of his subsequent revisions, but yes, it would work.

Fearful that he might lose it once he left Rachel, he pulled up a pad and quickly sketched out his thoughts, then booted up his laptop and drew it there. He saved what he drew and took longer studying it, but way deep down in his fast-beating heart he knew it was finally, finally right.

His agonizing was over. The client would be pleased. The resort would be built in this design. Done deal.

RIDING THE TIDE of that sense of accomplishment, he painted in Rachel's studio again that night. He was up until four in the morning this time, but the satisfaction was worth it. He woke up to have breakfast with the girls and drive them down the road to the bus stop, to call the hospital for an update on Rachel, and to fax the new design from his laptop to the office. Ignoring E-mail from

277

David, he went back to bed and slept until ten. Even then, he took the time to drink a leisurely cup of coffee, sitting on the fallen log in Rachel's woods, watching the foraging of half a dozen wild turkeys, big brown things the likes of which he couldn't imagine cooking and carving.

He didn't bother to shave. Rachel never minded stubble. He stopped at the market for a dozen two-liter bottles of assorted sodas and, feeling another bit of accomplishment, dropped them at school just in time for Hope's class picnic. Then he went on to Monterey.

He had known that Rachel was still comatose. What he hadn't known was that she had new guests.

chapter fifteen

JACK WAS ALWAYS amazed when he saw Victoria Keats. She looked younger each time—and it wasn't generosity toward his ex-mother-in-law that made him think that. It was fact. She was six years older now than when he had seen her last, but she didn't look a minute of it. Her eyes were bright and wide, her skin smooth. He figured she was on her third face-lift. She was always on the run, hence well toned, and not only had impeccable taste in clothes but refused to believe that trendiness had either age or business limits. She wore a chic wrap dress in a jersey print, produced by a designer whose styles were making a dramatic comeback. The print was heavy in brown, black, and beige. She wore sheer brown stockings and stylish brown heels. Her hair was a tasteful platinum, drawn back into a knot at the nape of her neck. Her face had a mois-turized glow; her lipstick was a flattering coral.

She was extraordinary looking, particularly in comparison to the plain woman standing at the foot of Rachel's bed.

"Mom!" Jack said to the plain woman, feeling the

same tug at his heart that he felt each time he saw her. "I didn't expect you here!"

"Of course, you didn't," scolded Victoria Keats. "You didn't call her, because you wanted to spare her the worry, but Rachel is, after all, her daughter-in-law and the mother of her grandchildren. Eunice was so upset when I told her about the accident that she insisted on meeting me here."

Jack was about to ask how his mother, who rarely left Oregon, had managed to get to Monterey on her own, when Victoria said, "Well, Rachel doesn't look as bad as I thought she would. That's a nasty scrape on her face, but it looks to be healing well, and the doctor tells me her leg will be just fine. It looks like she's sleeping." She patted Rachel's arm. "Well, you go right ahead and sleep, darling, that's the best thing for you. The doctor assures me it's only a matter of days before you'll be awake and then you'll have to face this man." The look she turned on Jack might have been a scowl if her face had worked properly. The smooth stretch of her skin watered down dismay into puzzlement. "You look like something the cat dragged in. You know, they did tell me that comas can be psychological."

They had told Jack that, too. Everything about Rachel suggested that she was healing well. Since they didn't know why she wasn't waking up, they were looking for excuses. Personally, he couldn't believe she wanted this.

"She may be terrified of facing you," Victoria said. "Is that how successful architects dress these days? It must be a West Coast thing, because they would never walk around New York looking like that. In New York they're a dapper group, which they *have* to be; it's part of the statement they make, knowing about fashion and style, *and* good grooming. But then, in New York, *everyone* has higher standards. When was the last time you shaved?"

"Yesterday morning."

"Your father shaved every day," Eunice reminded him.

"It looks like longer than that," Victoria decided, giving him a slow head-to-toe, "but we won't put you on the spot. After all, you do have a lot on your hands. Rachel, they tell me he's been here every day. Now isn't that something? He's living with the girls in Big Sur, and after all that hullaballoo about preferring to live in the city, aside from the stubble he doesn't look bad. Well, he could use a pair of tailored slacks; those jeans have seen better days, as have the loafers—are those Cole-Haans? No, they wouldn't be. You need Cole-Haans—the leather is exquisite—but that would be for the city, and if you're living in the country now, I suppose what you have on is all right. Oh my"— she lifted Rachel's hand—"look at your nails. Someone did a *beautiful* French manicure. It makes your nails look longer and more elegant. *How* many years did I tell you that you ought to let them grow?"

"She paints," Jack said. He had rounded the bed, greeting his mother with a shoulder touch along the way—a grand show of affection, by his family's standards. Taking root opposite Victoria, he put a protective hand against Rachel's neck. "Long nails get in the way."

"I don't see why they should," Victoria argued, "not if she uses a brush. Of course, that manicure calls for something classic and white, certainly something more elegant than flannel," she said in distaste. "And lime green? Oh my. Lime green is not terribly classy. Subtle is the way to go, subtle and rich. But where is the lingerie I *sent?*"

"In Big Sur . . ."

"I sent it *here*."

"I know, but—"

"Ah! Didn't I read once that silk and electronic devices like monitors don't work well together?" She hit her beautifully smooth forehead—but gently. "I should have remembered! I could as easily have sent cotton. We could have shopped in the city," she told Eunice, then told Jack, "I rented a car at the airport, fetched Eunice at the train, and here we are, but I should have thought to stop. Honestly, I assumed that she had everything she needed."

"She does."

"Do you know how *rude* drivers are around here? I have never been honked at so much. And *trucks?* All *over* the place, getting larger and longer by the day. You take your hands in your life trying to pass one of *those* on the highway. I thought about hiring a driver, but I wanted this to be a break from business. You know"—she was pensive, looking at Eunice—"we *should* have stopped in the city. There's a marvelous restaurant at the Huntington, although we probably aren't dressed right—"

Victoria was, Jack thought. Eunice was not. She wore a plain white blouse, a just-below-the-knee skirt, and serviceable tie shoes. What with her home-cut gray hair and a tightness in her face that had nothing to do with plastic surgery, she looked every one of her seventy-something years. His heart ached for her. She would have stood out at the Huntington like a donkey at Ascot.

"—and we did want to get down here as soon as possible," Victoria was saying. "Maybe another time. I hear Diane loves the place."

"Diane?" Jack asked.

"Your *senator,*" Victoria said.

Eunice confirmed his ignorance with a dismayed "Jack."

Victoria waved it aside. "Naturally, the city was *covered* with fog, so it was probably just as well we didn't stop. We'll have another chance. I have to say, Jack, I kept expecting you to move Rachel to the city. I was *not* terribly impressed with the way I was treated when I called here on the phone. Fine to say that the important thing is the quality of the medical care, but the term *bedside manner* is a broad one, and it comes right down from management, at least, that's what I say to *my* management team. So I was expecting the worst, and then I met Kara in person, but what a lovely young woman!" She confided, "And what *gorgeous* pearl earrings. *There's* a woman who knows how to make a statement. As it happens, I know her parents. They're a side branch of the Philadelphia Bateses, who have a summer place in Newport. A *fine* family."

"Aren't Kara's parents younger than you?" Jack said.

"Jack!" cried Eunice, but Victoria was undaunted.

"Not by much," she assured him. "She's the youngest of four, she told me. A lovely girl. And where are yours? I'd like to see my granddaughters. I don't come this way often, and I can't stay long. It's quite pathetic, with my own daughter in a coma, but the board of directors is holding its quarterly meeting in New York on Monday. I have to fly back tomorrow. I know you said not to come at all, Jack, but I had to, even for this little time. Where *are* those girls?"

"School," Jack said. Single words had less of a chance of being cut off.

"Well, how do they get here from there? They are coming, aren't they? I would think that the *very* best thing for Rachel is to have her daughters here. Of course, they're probably the ones responsible for that music." She winced. "What awful stuff. I turned it right off. There has to be something more appropriate."

"Appropriate?"

"If she's listening to music, it might as well be something worthwhile. Rachel used to love symphonies. Did you know that she wanted to be a concert pianist?"

A concert pianist? Jack thought not. Victoria had wanted it. Not Rachel. Victoria had given them a piano as a wedding gift, and they had toted it from Tucson to San Francisco because one didn't sell a Steinway, especially if it was a gift from a parent—not until you were divorced, which Rachel had promptly done. Before then, in her inimitably irreverent way, she had used it as a table for photographs, the girls' projects, and wine and hors d'oeuvres. The bench was perpetually open and filled with green plants.

Concert pianist? To Jack's recollection, Rachel had never actually sat down and played the damned thing.

No. That was wrong. She had played it one night, near the end of their marriage. He had come home from work and had more work to do. The girls were asleep. Startled by the bits of sound coming from the living room, he had gone down and found her there. The plants were on the floor, the piano bench an actual seat for once. Her left elbow was on top of the piano, left palm on her forehead, right hand on the keys. She was picking out a slow, soft, sad tune that might indeed have been an echo of Beethoven.

He had leaned against the archway, struck by the pensive picture she made. For the longest time, she didn't know he was there, and he watched, just watched, wishing he had the time and skill to paint her that way. Then she looked up and brightened. "Done with work?"

"No. But I heard you playing. You're very good."

"I am not. That was the extent of my expertise. Three painful years of lessons, and I can't coordinate the right hand with the left, so one-handed single notes are the best you get."

"It's strange, seeing you there. What made you play?"

She studied the keys, pensive again, sad. "I don't know. I don't feel like doing anything else. I feel . . . aimless." Her eyes found his.

"I'll give you some of *my* aim," he said, slapping the woodwork as he straightened. "I wish I had less. There's at least two more hours of work up there." As he started off, he called back, thinking about an important meeting he had the next morning, "Is my pin-striped suit back from the cleaners?"

He had cut her off. Only now, looking back, did Jack realize that. He had cut her off for the sake of his own agenda, had done just what her mother always did.

And Victoria was rattling on. ". . . never seemed to be time for lessons and practice, and then she was too old. I had the most *delightful* lunch *à la Rive Gauche*"—pronounced the French way—"with a flautist. What was her name? . . . *Geneviève,* I believe. She was talking about what it took to play at that level and the touring that was involved . . ."

Jack moved his hand against Rachel's jaw. He hadn't given the piano playing incident a second thought. He wondered how many similar memories were hidden— wondered if they would be as condemning. He had cut Rachel off because he couldn't deal with her problem. Selfish of him. Blind of him. *Just* like Victoria, who was managing the conversation even here. And Eunice? Eunice was her usual, caustic self. She didn't say much but had a consistently negative way of saying it. Jack had visited briefly at Christmas, *briefly* being the operative word. An hour or two in the same house with his mother, his sister and brothers, and their families, and he was desperate to leave. The whole lot of them were negative. Their major delight in life was in finding fault and placing blame. He knew it was a cover-up for insecurity, but it got old fast.

Still, he kept trying, hoping it would be different, angry when it wasn't. Visiting there had been easier when Rachel was with him. Her physical presence reminded him that his life was different.

"Positively *grueling*," Victoria was saying, "and that was even *before* the recording dates. That's such a large part of it now, you know; it's become as commercial as anything *we* do, but you can almost understand it, what with the cost of sending an entire symphony orchestra on the road."

"It's greed," scoffed Eunice. "The food chain."

"Well, it's a shame. This young woman had taken two days off and looked as though she needed another two *weeks*. Are you hungry, Eunice? I haven't had a *thing* since breakfast, which was in Los Angeles ages ago."

"Los Angeles?" Jack asked.

"Well, I flew Nice to Paris to London. Would you believe that Los Angeles was the closest I could get to here from London on such short notice, unless I wanted to go through Miami, which I did not, thank you; I don't speak Spanish. So I spent the night at the Beverly Hills Hilton. I always like staying there. It isn't the Pierre, but it's close. I went down for an early breakfast, and who should be sitting two tables over but Paul. Now *there* is a stunning man. And decent? I remember what he said once when he was asked whether it was difficult being faithful to Joanne. 'Why go out for hamburger when I can have steak at home?' he said, or words to that effect." She pressed her chest. "Isn't that heartwarming? Not that I need steak for lunch, but is there anywhere nearby where Eunice and I can get a decent lunch—salad, quiche, whatever? Hospital cafeterias are pathetic. I don't mind driving, either. There must be something worthwhile in the center of town."

Jack gave her a name and directions, and the two of them left. The silence was heavenly.

Putting his elbows on the bed rail, he let his eyes roam Rachel's face, touching on all the old familiar spots, divining the same solace he always had in the past with her when visiting family. He could take Victoria. After a while, he just tuned her out. He didn't have to talk; she did it all. She didn't want to hear, wouldn't listen to anyone but herself.

Eunice was harder for him. She was his mother. For a time in his life, she had bathed him, clothed him, fed him. He remembered precious few times when she had smiled, or hugged him, or praised him. He was the only one of his siblings who had broken out and made good. Eunice had never been interested in hearing the details of his career, and he hadn't offered them. He continued to send her money, which she chose not to spend. The only way he had known that she was pleased with his marriage was the satisfaction with which she agreed to the festivities, and the fact that she blamed him for the divorce.

In Eunice, he saw a woman he had often wished wasn't his mother—and though he kept expecting God to strike him dead for thinking it, the thought still came.

It might have been nice to have felt loved, might have been nice to have a mother who showed feelings and shared her thoughts.

Rachel did those things. He had fallen in love with her, in part, because when they were together, they were the antithesis of their parents.

At least, he had always thought it. Suddenly he wondered.

IN A STROKE of luck, Katherine arrived soon after the mothers returned. Jack immediately enlisted her to stay while he went for the girls.

"I can't leave her alone with those two," he whispered at the door. "Let her know you're there. She needs someone sane at her side."

Having met Victoria before, Katherine stayed.

DRIVING from the hospital to the school, he savored the silence. The return trip was louder. Between Hope telling him that the drinks were *the* best part of the picnic after the ooey-gooey peanut butter brownies that one of the mothers had made, and Samantha telling him that she had aced a biology test, gotten an A-minus on an English paper, and had the *neatest* lunch with Pam and Heather, there wasn't time to tell them about the grandmothers until they were at the hospital.

They grew quiet then. They flanked Jack in the elevator, watching the lights above the door, and walked beside him down the hall. They offered their cheeks to

coast road

their grandmothers for the kind of mutant kisses that
came, in Victoria's case, from not wanting her skin dis-
turbed, and in Eunice's, from being awkward with physical gestures. They weathered Victoria's seamless chatter
and Eunice's evaluative scrutiny from positions close to
Jack and were visibly relieved when, with profuse apolo-
gies and another round of those barely-there kisses, the
two women left.

Jack felt so many things in the aftermath of their
visit that he couldn't begin to sort them out, except for
one. Just because his mother would choke on a compliment didn't mean he had to. Looking from one daughter to the other, he said, "Y'know, I'm really proud of
you guys."

"Why?" Samantha asked.

"For being kind. And respectful. They aren't easy
women, either of them, but they are your grandmothers."

"I hope I look the way Gram Victoria looks when I'm
her age."

Hope, who was using the electric controls to raise
Rachel's head, asked, "Why does she talk so much?"

Nervousness? Jack thought. *Selfishness? Control?*
"It's just her way."

"Thank God Mom doesn't do that," Samantha said.
"I'd lose my mind."

Hope adjusted the pillows to support Rachel's head.
"If Mom was like that, I wouldn't ever talk. I'd just get
tired of trying."

"That's pretty much what your mom did," Jack said,
watching Hope pull a fistful of something from her pocket. "She was a quiet lady when I met her. What have you
got there?"

289

"Unshelled peanuts." She put several in Rachel's hand and very carefully folded her fingers around them. "There was a whole bag of them at the picnic. Mom loves peanuts." She started cracking one.

Samantha screwed up her face. "You'll get crumbs all over the sheets." To Jack, she said, "So if Mom was quiet because her mother wouldn't shut up, did you talk a lot because yours didn't?"

Jack thought back. "No. No one talked much in my house."

"Why not?"

"My parents didn't want it. They didn't think we had anything to offer."

"They told you that?"

"Not as politely. But that was the gist of it."

"Wow. Amazing that you and Mom talked at all!"

IT *WAS* AMAZING, Jack realized. Driving back on the coast road that night, he thought about what he had felt meeting Rachel in that laundromat in Tucson, nearly eighteen years before. She had opened him up with a combination of quiet, sweetness, curiosity, and chemistry, and she had opened up herself. They told each other things they hadn't told anyone else, and because that felt so good, it became self-perpetuating. They shared feelings and fears. It was quality communication, interspersed with silences that were made special by that exchange of honest thought.

At some point they had stopped talking. He tried to look back and figure out when—it was surely before the piano incident—but then he reached the River Inn, where he had promised to take the girls to dinner, and by the time they got home, he wanted to paint, and then he was lost.

THE NIGHT'S subject was quail. Rachel had painted a covey roosting low in a sycamore tree. Her work was detailed and exact—the male with his larger, curved plume and blue-gray feathers, the female with her reduced features and scaled belly. Using acrylics and a palette knife, she had re-created the exact texture of the feathers. Even before Jack studied the photographs affixed to the back of the canvas, he knew that the background had to be the duller tans and browns of winter, against which the birds would be simultaneously camouflaged and crisp. He hadn't been in the Santa Lucias during that cool, rainy season, and wondered if he could do it justice. Then he realized that the justice had been done in Rachel's rendition of the quails. He was like a male dancer in the ballet, boosting the prima ballerina into the air, supporting her in her landing.

Several years ago, that might have bothered him. But he had a name in his own right. Supporting Rachel this way, being background, felt good.

He worked with care, but it flowed. He used brushes exclusively, wanting nothing as crisp as the palette knife would carve, but there were wide brushes and narrow brushes. He used umbers, ochers, siennas, and grays, mixing and matching until he had the right feel for a background that would highlight the quails.

By the time he was done, the adrenaline was flowing fast and hard. Tired as he was, it was a while before he fell asleep.

HOPE was the first one awake on Saturday morning. She stood for a time watching her sister sleep, then stood for a time watching Jack sleep. Slipping a fleece jacket over her nightshirt and her boots on her feet, she let herself out of the house, picked a handful of newly blue lupine from the roadside, and ran through the forest to Guinevere's grave. She brushed the dirt with her hand until it looked artful, and carefully arranged the flowers in a way she hoped Guinevere would like. Then, sitting on her heels, she wrapped her arms around her knees and rocked slowly, back and forth, back and forth, until worrisome images of her grandmothers faded and worrisome images of Samantha faded. Closing her eyes, she focused on Rachel and Jack and the safety she had felt when she was little.

She wanted that again.

SAMANTHA had planned to sleep her usual Saturday-morning late, but she woke up when Hope left her room and couldn't fall back to sleep. Her head was a battle-field of emotions. The prom came first; she was totally excited. But she was angry at Jack for making her feel guilty about Lydia, and *furious* at the grandmothers for giving her an empty kind of feeling. That empty feeling made her worry more about Rachel.

She missed her. They disagreed on lots of things, but at least Rachel cared. Samantha wasn't sure Jack did, and she knew the grandmothers didn't. There was always Katherine. But Katherine wasn't family.

Samantha wished she were twenty-one. If she were, she wouldn't be worrying about a prom. She wouldn't be worrying about whether or not to wear a bra, whether or not to wear nylons, whether or not to wear the three-inch heels Heather had lent her. If she were twenty-one, she wouldn't be worrying about a zit on her forehead. Or about what to drink. Or about what to do when Teague kissed her.

Rachel would have told her what to do. But Rachel wasn't there, only Jack, and that annoyed her.

JACK set off early with Hope. Samantha had pleaded exhaustion and stayed home, and a part of him wished he could, too. That part was tired of the drive to Monterey, tired of sterile corridors, hushed silences, smells of sickness. That part felt the monotony of visiting a comatose Rachel.

But not visiting her would be worse. Besides, the day's visit would be short. He had promised Samantha to be back by noon with food.

They stopped at Eliza's for hot coffee and brought it along, moving the cup under Rachel's nose in the hope that the smell would reach her. They put on a T-shirt that Eliza had sent; it had Rachel's name spelled in large, hand-painted letters. While Hope used a tiny scissors to cut exquisitely detailed snowflakes from white paper she had brought, they talked about the weather, about the grandmothers, about Samantha's prom.

Then Hope hung the snowflakes from the IV pole and whispered, "Tell her about the quails."

Jack hesitated. He hadn't told Rachel about doing *any*

painting. Hope loved what he had done, but Samantha refused even to look. If he viewed his daughters as the two sides of his wife—Hope the commonsense Rachel, Samantha the emotional one—he feared that on this issue, Rachel might side with Samantha.

Suddenly it struck him that that might be good. If there were psychological reasons for her continuing coma, angering her might shock her out of it. If she didn't want him finishing her paintings—didn't want it bad enough— she would wake up and tell him.

So he told her about the loons he had done Wednesday night, the deer he had done Thursday night, and the quails he had done Friday night. He gained momentum talking about the colors he had used and the effects he had sought, got caught up in excitement and satisfaction. His face was no more than a foot from Rachel's the whole time, but he saw no movement.

They left when Faye arrived, and stopped again at Eliza's, this time for a big bag of sandwiches, and yes, Jack was impatient standing in line. He took a deep breath, told himself that he wasn't in a rush to get any-where, smiled at Hope, and wasn't as frayed as he thought he would be when they reached the front of the line. He was actually in the middle of paying when he had a thought. "Pecan rolls for Duncan and Faith?"

Hope's surprised smile was all the answer he needed. He bought a dozen.

JACK had initially thought he might do schematic drawings for the Hillsborough job, and there was more of Rachel's work to do, but he barely lasted in the studio for twenty minutes. For one thing, there was another fax from David, the follow-up to a phone message, neither of which he wanted to answer. For another, it didn't seem right closeting himself there and leaving the girls alone.

Samantha had gone back to her room after lunch, so it was just Hope, curling beside him on the living room sofa with a book. Her presence was a lulling warmth. He sprawled lower, put his head back, and slept for an hour. When he woke up, he stretched, then had a distinct urge to move.

"Is Samantha still in her room?" he asked, sitting up.

"Yes."

"On the phone?"

"No. She's making herself beautiful."

It was said with enough sarcasm that he chided, "You'll be doing it, too, before long. Want to go for a walk?"

She nodded and closed her book.

Jack knocked on Samantha's closed door. "Sam? Come for a walk with us?"

"I just washed my hair," she called out.

"You could still come."

"Take Hope. I'll stay here."

Jack stood at her door for another minute. As difficult as she was at times, he really did want her along. There was something about the three of them being together that seemed more important after the grandmothers' visit. He wanted family, damn it, he did. He *liked* being with his daughters. They filled up the emptiness of childhood memories, made his life more *full*.

There was also something about Samantha's prom being that night. It was a milestone. He wanted to do something to mark it, wanted to somehow make up for Rachel missing it.

"Are you sure?" he called a final time.

"*Positive,*" she yelled.

Fearing he would make things worse if he pushed, he let it go.

HE HAD BROUGHT his hiking boots from the city the Thursday before. He hadn't worn them since the divorce, but they felt good on his feet. He put water and snacks in a backpack, slipped it on, and left with Hope.

She had temporarily traded her lucky boots for hiking boots of her own, and a good thing it was. The winding trek she led him on, between spreading redwood trunks, aspens, and fir, was arduous. At times they climbed, at others they walked straight. Where the sun broke through the overhead boughs, it touched them, but the air remained cool, particularly as they approached the stream. Jack felt the anticipation of it, heard the crescendoing rush of water. When it came into sight, he discovered it was as much waterfall as stream, spewing over a rocky bed in tiered cascades.

They stopped and knelt by its side, saying nothing, just watching the bubbling play and listening to the flow.

When they stood, Hope said, "It's loudest this time of year. By fall, it's only a trickle." She led him across a rough-planked bridge and on through a fragrant eucalyptus grove to open meadow, and the temperature jumped. "See Duncan's sheep?" she asked.

They grazed in random clusters in the sun. It was a bucolic bouquet of color, with the deep green of live oaks in the distance blanching to the newer green of the spring grass, interspersed with patches of red poppy and yellow iris and the sheep, with their gray-white coats and their brown eyes and muzzles, paying them scant heed as they crossed the top of the meadow.

They continued on through oak and madrone on no path Jack could see, but Hope seemed to know where to go, and she went at a clip. By the time the land tipped and chaparral took over, a path emerged. It was even warmer here. As they walked, Jack pulled off his sweatshirt and tied it around his waist. They moved higher, into a stand of pines, and beyond those, the world suddenly gaped open.

They came on it so quickly that he wasn't prepared. "Wow!"

Hope slanted him a knowing smile. "Isn't it neat?"

"I'll say." They were higher than he had thought, looking into the belly of the canyon over the tops of pines and firs. Just as spectacular was the succession of ridges beyond. Those more distant, near the ocean, were dusted with fog.

Jack had taken his daughters to Muir Woods more than once, and those woods were beautiful. But this was something else. Rachel knew what breathtaking meant.

They sat on the ground looking out, legs crossed, drinking bottled water and munching granola. "Do you come here often with your mom?" he asked.

She chomped on a nut. "Uh-huh. We both love it. You look out and the world just keeps going."

Jack looked out, and the world *did* just keep going. The ocean did that. But there was also the sense of endless fingers of granite, patchy with pine, cedar, or fir, stretching for miles down the coast.

Muir Woods didn't have that. You could close your eyes and pretend, but it wasn't the same. The city was too close. Here, it was easier to breathe, in every sense of the word.

He glanced at Hope, about to say that, then stopped. She, too, was looking out, but her brows were drawn. "What's wrong?"

Her eyes flew to his, then returned to the view. It was a minute before, quietly, she said, "Do you think Mom will ever come here again?"

His insides shifted. It wasn't the knotting he used to feel; that was better. This was something higher, something more closely tied to his heart. "I want to think so."

"But you don't know."

"None of us do."

"What if she dies?"

"She's not about to do that."

"What if she stays in a coma for years?"

Ten days before, he would have denied the possibility. *Five* days before, he would have denied it. But the doctors had taken Rachel out of Intensive Care and settled her into a regular room. She was nearing the end of her second comatose week. Everything else seemed to be healing but her head. Her GCS score hadn't budged.

Still, in a coma for *years?* They were just words. He couldn't grasp their meaning.

Hope picked raisins from the granola and put them one by one into her mouth. She took a drink of water and gazed out over the trees, frowning again. "Daddy?"

"Hmm?"

"Remember the other morning when you were telling Sam about loyalty?"

"Um-hmm."

"I feel bad for Lydia. But I can't say anything to Sam."

"Why not?"

"Because she's my sister. I owe the same loyalty to her that she owes to Lydia. So I have to support what she's doing. Don't I?"

"Not if you think what she's doing is wrong."

Hope swiveled on her bottom and faced him. Her eyes were large and expectant. "I do."

He wasn't sure what she wanted. "Maybe you should tell her."

"She'll kill me. You're going to meet her date tonight, aren't you?"

"That's the plan."

"What if you don't like him? Will you tell her not to go?"

He heard an urgency. "Do you *not* like the guy?"

"Would you make her stay home?"

"From her prom? I don't know, Hope. That might be going too far."

Her eyes teared up. "I have a bad feeling, like I did before Guinevere died."

Jack picked a strand of blond hair from her sweaty cheek. "Oh, sweetie."

"Don't *you?*"

The truth was that he hadn't thought much about Samantha's date, largely because there wasn't a hell of a lot he could do about it. He had made his best argument on Lydia's behalf, but he couldn't force Samantha to be with people she didn't want to be with. He knew. He had been there. His parents had said one thing; that was incentive enough to do the other.

Yes, it scared him where Samantha was concerned. And yes, he had *lots* of bad feelings, but they were more worry than omen, and had to do as much with Rachel and with Sung and McGill as with Samantha.

He caught Hope's hand. It was small, not yet womanly, but with promise. "At some point," he said, thinking it out as he spoke, "a parent has to trust that upbringing will guide a child when he isn't around. You've both been close to your mother. She raised you well. She may not be here to send Samantha off to the prom, but I want to think that Samantha will know what her mother expects."

Hope stared at him. "She knows. That doesn't mean she'll do."

Which was exactly what Jack thought seconds earlier. "Do you know something I don't?"

She said a quick "no."

"What's she planning?"

Both shoulders came up. "I don't know."

"Are you sure?"

She nodded vigorously.

He didn't believe her, but he couldn't force the issue. There was that thing about loyalty, *thank you, Jack.* If he wanted to know what Samantha was planning, he was going to have to ask Samantha.

chapter sixteen

THE SMARTEST THING Samantha did was to start getting ready very early. She ended up taking two showers when her hair didn't blow right the first time. Her deodorant took forever to dry; she botched her eyeliner and had to start all over with that; and though she had decided that sheer black stockings looked more sophisticated than none, she still hadn't made up her mind on the bra issue when it was time to put on the dress.

She owned two black bras. Each had straps. If she reached a certain way, which she was bound to do when she danced with Teague, who was at *least* six-two, the straps showed.

She rummaged through Rachel's drawers for a strapless bra. The only things of interest she found were her father's boxer shorts and some framed photographs. She didn't know why her mother kept them. Rachel *hated* Jack. He might talk a blue streak about loyalty, but talk was all it was. They were divorced. That said it all.

She shoved the drawers closed and turned to leave.

"Everything all right?" Jack asked from the door. He

looked sweaty and relaxed, like he'd had a good time in the woods with his favorite daughter.

Everything is not all right, she wanted to cry. *My mother is in a coma, my father is a jerk, and I don't have a strapless bra.* "Just fine," she ground out and brushed past him.

"Doesn't sound it," he said, following her down the hall.

She whirled on him. "I'm nervous. All right? This is a big night. Just leave me alone."

He held up a hand and backed off—and even *that* angered her. She wanted to argue. She wanted to scream and shout and let off the steam that was building inside. A part of her even wanted to cry, but she'd be damned if she would do that in front of him. Hope cried. Samantha didn't.

Beside, she didn't have time to do her eyes *again.*

BY SIX, Jack was freshly showered and in the kitchen, spooning chip dip into a bowl. Having spent most of the hike back through the woods thinking that Rachel's coma couldn't possibly be psychological since she wouldn't have missed Samantha's prom for the world, and wondering what she would have done for a send-off, he had mixed up her favorite dip recipe, while Hope arranged crackers on a dish around the bowl. They had barely put it in the living room when the doorbell rang.

"*Oh God,*" Samantha wailed from her room. "*Talk to him. I'm not ready.*"

Jack opened the door to a young man who was just his height, but dark-haired, dark-eyed, dark-jawed. He was wearing a tux . . . barely. Where a pleated shirt should have been was a white T-shirt; where a cummerbund should have been was a wide leather belt; and the scuffed black shoes sticking out from his pants looked to Jack to be boots.

O-kay, Jack thought. *Times have changed. Go with the flow.* He extended a hand. "I'm Samantha's dad."

The returning handshake was firm, perhaps cocky, even defiant. "Teague Runyan."

Jack drew him into the house with the kind of firm hand that said he had no choice in the matter. "Samantha says you live here in Big Sur?"

"Up the street a little," he said, tossing his head in a direction that could have been north or south. "How's Samantha's mom?"

"She's the same. Thank you for asking. Does she know your folks?"

"She may. They run the gas station right outside the center."

Jack nodded. He knew of two gas stations there. Both gouged.

Hope approached with the dip and crackers, staring smilelessly at Teague.

"Hey, Hope," Teague said. "Did you make this?" He topped a cracker with dip and popped it whole into his mouth. "Mm. Good."

Jack waited until he had swallowed. "So, what's the plan?"

"Plan?" Teague asked, brushing cracker salt off his hands.

"For tonight."

"I don't know. It's Samantha's prom. She made the arrangements."

"When can I expect her back?"

Teague looked mystified.

"When do your folks expect you back?"

"Sometime tomorrow."

"Tomorrow, as in the wee hours of the morning?"

He thought about that. "Nah."

"Later tomorrow morning?"

"Maybe. Maybe afternoon. It depends how late we sleep."

That wasn't what Jack wanted to hear. "Where will this sleeping be?"

Teague shrugged. "It's Samantha's prom."

"Hi, Teague," Samantha said. She stood at the edge of the living room, looking gorgeous enough to take Jack's breath. He was suddenly terrified.

"Hey," said Teague by way of greeting. "Ready to go?"

There was no *You look great,* no *Here's a corsage,* no *Have some of this dip, it's great; thanks, Hope.* Jack didn't like those boots, or that wide leather belt. There was something on the T-shirt that was too faded to make out. No matter. He didn't like the T-shirt, either.

He crossed to Samantha, pointing her back into the hall, and kept going until he was in her bedroom, glancing behind only to make sure she followed.

Oh, she did that, but she wasn't happy. "I have to go," she hissed.

"You look beautiful," he said, taking her off guard. He could have sworn he saw a look of disbelief on her face, before she grew cautious.

"I do?"

"I wish your mother could see." He had an idea. "Wait. I'll get a camera . . ."

She grabbed his arm. "No, Daddy, *please.* He's *waiting.*"

He should have had the camera ready, should have thought ahead. "You really do look spectacular," he said and felt another kick of terror. She was growing up too fast. "Can we talk about curfews?"

She looked at him like he had horns. *"Curfews?* This is an all-nighter. You *knew* that."

"I knew you were sleeping at Lydia's, but that's changed. So tell me the plans. I want to know where you'll be."

"The prom is at school."

"That's not the part that worries me." He rummaged through the refuse on her desk for a pen and tore a scrap of paper from the nearest notebook. "There are parties before and after. I need phone numbers."

"You do *not,*" she cried. "You *can't* check up on me. If you call, I'll *die.*"

"What if your mother wakes up?"

That got her. She stood with her eyes wide and her mouth half open.

He compromised. "Give me names, then. Just names." He could always call directory assistance. "The party before is at Jake's—is it Jake Drummer?"

"Drumble."

"Where's the party after?"

"Pam's, I think, but I'm not sure. It depends on who leaves the prom when, whether we want something to eat, and what we feel like after that, so I don't know."

Jack wouldn't run *his* business that way. "Would your mother be satisfied with that answer?"

"Yes. She trusts me."

"So do I. It's the other kids I don't trust." He had another idea. "Take my cell phone."

Again, that where-are-*you*-from look. "Why?"

"So we can be in touch."

She looked horrified. "Kids don't take cell phones to proms. Besides, where would I *put* it? This dress does *not* have pockets."

"A purse?"

She held up a thin thing on even thinner straps.

He sighed. "Okay. No phone. What's Pam's last name?"

She gave it grudgingly. He had barely begun scribbling it down when she started out of the room. "Wait," he said, because he was uneasy still.

She turned back with an impatient *"What?"*

"Call me if there's a problem."

"Are you expecting one?"

"No." He approached her. "I just wanted to say it. I won't tell you when to be home. I'll trust you know what you're doing. But I'd like a call by ten tomorrow morning, please."

"Ten? *Dad.*"

"Samantha, you're only fifteen. All I'm asking for is a phone call."

"Fine," she said and disappeared into the hall.

He followed her back to the living room, arriving just as she swept Teague to the door.

"Bye," she said with a wave to no one in particular, and before Jack could say that they needed something solid in their stomachs and why didn't they have crackers and dip, before he could open his mouth to warn Teague that if anything went wrong there would be hell to pay, they were gone.

JAKE DRUMBLE'S house was a zoo. Samantha had never seen so many kids in such a small place in her life, and they weren't all from her school. She would have recognized faces. The boys were huge, with the kinds of big necks and wide shoulders that went with playing football. The girls were perky and bright and talking in tight little clumps.

"Do you know these people?" Teague asked, snapping up two beers from the bar and putting one in her hand.

"I think they're football buddies of Jake's," she said and, for a split second, feeling alone and lost, would have given anything for the sight of Lydia or Shelly.

"Talk about slabs," Teague said under his breath.

She forced a laugh. "Hey. There's Pam. Pam!" She led Teague through the crowd, stopping now and again when she felt resistance against her hand to look back and find him talking to one girl or another. She couldn't blame those girls. He was the coolest guy in the place. She hooked an elbow through his when they reached Pam, so that no one would doubt that he was Sam's for the night.

They talked and laughed with Pam and Jake, then moved on to talk and laugh with Heather and Drew. They munched on nachos and drank beer, ate popcorn and drank beer. Teague was the perfect date, always knowing when she needed a refill, always knowing where to find it.

"How're you doing?" he said with a grin as he backed her into a corner.

She was feeling light-headed and free. "I'm doing fine. This is a great party."

Putting his hands on either side of the wall, he gave

her the weight of his body. His mouth was inches from hers. "I could do with fewer people. You're sweet." He erased those inches with a kiss that was so soft and gentle that all of her earlier worries seemed absurd. His mouth moved, showing hers what to do, and was gone before she wanted it to be.

"Nice?" he asked.

She grinned. "Mmmm."

"More?"

"Um-hm."

It was a deeper kiss this time, more mobile and open. Samantha had read about breathlessness. She had read about feeling a fire inside, but she hadn't experienced either in response to a kiss until then.

Rachel would not be pleased. She believed in restraint, in saving it for someone special, but who was to say Teague wasn't? There was such a thing as instant attraction, not to mention love at first sight. And was Rachel a virgin when she married Jack? Samantha thought not. So who were *either* of them to criticize her? Besides, if Rachel was so worried, she would have woken up from the damn coma. She would have *been* there to give orders and warnings, instead of leaving it to Jack. She would have demanded a detailed itinerary as a condition for leaving the house, would have phoned some of the other parents, and Samantha would have been docked for sure. If her mother were well, she wouldn't be here right now.

That thought made her head buzz in a grating way. To still it, she poured herself into Teague's kiss, not a very hard thing to do, for at that minute he took her hands, put them behind him, and pressed his hips to hers, and oh, what she felt! When she caught her breath, his tongue entered her mouth. Startled then, she would have pulled back if there had been anywhere to go, but the wall was behind her, his hands were framing her face, and he was saying into her mouth, "Don't stop. It's cool. Take my tongue." And he was right, it was cool, unbelievably grown-up and sexy, the feel of that tongue sliding in and out against hers, and his body, anchoring hers when it started to tremble. "Ride the feeling," he whispered, and she did. Her mouth fell open a little, then a little more, then even more, and suddenly her tongue caught the wave.

Breathing hard, he made a guttural sound and put his forehead to hers. "Whooh. We gotta go somewhere."

Samantha was barely beginning to understand what he meant when the room began to empty. "The prom," she managed to say.

"No. Somewhere alone."

"The prom," she insisted. She wasn't missing her first prom for the world. She wanted people to see her with Teague Runyan. They were a great-looking couple. Lydia would *die* when she saw how cool they looked, not to mention the fact that super kissers had to be super dancers. Samantha wasn't doing anything else until she danced with Teague.

She did, actually. She shared another beer with him in the truck, driving between Jake's house and school. They finished it parked in a dark corner of the lot, away from the others. This time when he gave her an open-mouthed kiss, right at the start, she knew just what to do. She was feeling smart and strong. The only thing she was thinking about was having a good time. Life was too short to be uptight about drinking. Look at her mother, a good little do-bee who followed every rule in the book and was now lying in a coma because someone she didn't know had hit her car.

Teague came over her in the cab of the truck, holding her head while he kissed her, then dropping a hand to her breast. Samantha had ended up wearing no bra, so she felt every inch of his fingers. Startled, she cried out into his mouth, but he soothed her with words she barely heard, and his kneading felt good, so good.

"Fuck the prom," he whispered.

"No, no," she said and pulled away. He was moving too fast, scaring her a little. She wanted to know what she was doing, wanted to be in control. "I want to go." She took his hand and dragged him from the truck. Seconds later, he had her pinned against its side.

"You're a tease, Samantha."

"No. I *want* to go to the prom."

"Can we do this after?" he asked, pushing both breasts up, lowering his head to kiss the swell he had created above her dress.

It felt a little rougher now, not as good. She wanted to tell him that, but the words didn't come, and all she could think to do was to slither out from under him and say, "This is my *prom*." If she was relieved that he came along without a fight, she forgot it the next minute. This *was* her prom. She was with the coolest guy in the world, and she turned him on. It didn't get much better than that.

But it did. The school gym was transformed by dark red lights into something pretty neat, and with everyone she knew in the world watching, Teague was an *awesome* dancer. He didn't move much, just kind of throbbed in time to the music with his eyes on her the whole time. She felt the same tingling inside as when he kissed her, so that when the slow dancing came, body to body, it was a relief.

She put her head on his shoulder and moved with him, feeling tired now, more mellow. When he said he needed air, she didn't argue. They walked outside, back to the truck. He popped open a couple of beers and chugged his fast, helped her with hers, and opened a third. He kissed her, touched her. She pulled him back into the school.

JACK and Hope stood in Rachel's studio, surrounded by wood moldings that would soon be frames.

"Are you sure you know how to do this?" Hope asked.

"You bet," Jack said. "I've done it before." But not in years, and never for a show. "Those lengths of wood"— he pointed their way—"have to be cut to size with that"—his finger shifted—"miter saw. Then you predrill nail holes, apply wood glue, hammer in nails, clamp in that"—he pointed toward a heavy metal contraption— "miter vise. Piece of cake."

"But . . . but what about putting the picture in it?"

"Not tonight. The frame has to dry in the vise. Then it fits on the canvas, and we pack it in with nails."

Hope grinned. "Piece of cake."

"You bet." If it didn't come out well, he could dump the framing on Ben. "I was thinking you'd help. It isn't hard. Want to?"

Hope's eyes told it all, even before she said an excited "Yes."

"Which picture first?" he asked.

After giving careful consideration to the canvases that were lined up and ready, Hope pointed to the loons. "That's my favorite."

Jack didn't know if she had chosen it to please him, but

he wasn't about to argue. The loons were his favorite, too. When he projected himself into the scene, he felt closer to Rachel, which was something he very much wanted to feel on this night. He had thought that taking a break from the hospital would be good, but he missed being there. He had called. Rachel was the same. Still, he felt unnerved.

No doubt some of that had to do with Samantha. He didn't think he had handled her well, but hell, he was groping blind. Maybe Rachel would have known what to do and say. Then again, maybe not. In any case, he would have liked her input. They used to discuss things— Rachel had rightly told that to Katherine. Now Jack was feeling the loss firsthand. Deciding whether to punish the temper tantrum of a four-year-old with a spank or time alone in the bedroom was a far cry from deciding whether to insist on a curfew, forbid drinking, or lay down the law about sex—and Teague Runyan was into sex. Jack didn't doubt it for a minute. The guy was too good looking, too physically developed, too cocksure of himself not to be experienced.

Jack should have insisted Samantha take the phone.

Whether she would have used it was another matter entirely.

His stomach was knotting for the first time in days. Taking a deep breath to relax it, he scooped up a bunch of the moldings and the miter saw. "Okay," he told Hope as he carried them to the worktable, "let's see what we can do."

SAMANTHA and Teague left the prom shortly after ten and followed Pam and Jake to Ian McWain's house. The music was canned here, but there was pizza, beer, and a punch that was incredibly sweet and good. Samantha was starting to recognize more faces, so she didn't feel so alone when Teague wandered off. But he wasn't gone long. He was never gone long. He always returned, eyes bright at the sight of her, arms catching her up and swinging her around.

She was relieved. He seemed to be having a good time, which must have said something for his feelings for her. If he didn't like her, he would be bored. He would be aching to leave. He would be standing against a wall with a scowl on his face.

But he was treating her like she was gold, grinning nonstop, bringing her drinks, dancing body to body regardless of how fast the beat, and he wasn't the only one warming to the night. Minute by minute, the kids grew looser and louder, the music faster, the dancing wilder than it had been at school. When the dining room table was cleared of pizza boxes, bottles, and cans, and became a dance floor, there was hysterical laughter all around. Laughter turned to applause when one couple jumped up and began necking. The applause was joined by raucous calls when a girl removed the top of her dress as she boogeyed.

Teague was holding Samantha from behind now, doing that same throbbing thing to the beat of the music with his body flush to hers. He had his arms wrapped around her and was alternately nibbling on her ear and moving his hands along the undersides of her breasts, teasing, teasing, she knew, and it felt good.

"Look at her," he whispered, leaving his mouth open, and Samantha couldn't seem to focus anywhere else. The girl on the table was laughing and singing with her arms over her head now, her bare breasts bobbing to the beat of the dance. Samantha might have been embarrassed, if that part of her hadn't been muted. She was high, feeling part of the crowd, part of the fun, part of Teague Runyan even, so that when he maneuvered her back, swiped a pair of fresh long-necks with one hand, and led her outside, she wasn't alarmed. She could hear the beat even from here. Teague felt it, too. They danced in the dark, body to body in a way she would never have thought to do, never have *dared* to do before, but it was nice, drinking beer as they danced, so nice, exciting, even dangerous. She was dizzy with laughter and dance. She felt sexy and adult. When Teague took her hand and, laughing, ran toward his truck, she went right along.

Pulling her close on the bench, with an arm around her and his beer dangling between her breasts, he started driving.

"Where to?" she asked, wondering how he could see, since her world was still spinning, but he was older, larger, protective.

"Somewhere quiet," he said. "You're too special to share."

There was nothing she could say to that, so she smiled, closed her eyes, and buried her face in the rough spot under his jaw where his beard was a darkening shadow, and even that was erotic. None of the other boys she knew had to shave more than once or twice a week. Teague's stubble was a manly thing.

They hadn't driven far when he pulled the truck off the road. Killing engine and lights, he took a long drink, put the bottle on the floor of the cab, and turned to her. He didn't say anything, just caught her face and held it while he kissed her. She tasted beer first, then his tongue, and it was firmer now, but welcome. Her body was a mass of tingles, confusing almost, so that the only thing it knew was that it needed something more.

He held her face until she was into the kiss, then he lowered both hands to her breasts. He kneaded them and found her nipples, tugging until she felt it all the way to her belly. She arched her back, wildly dizzy but feeling good, especially when something changed. It was a full minute of bliss before she realized that her breasts were bare, scooped right out of that stretchy dress. She looked down at them in amazement, until his head blocked the view, and then while his thumb rolled one nipple, his lips caught the other, and suddenly the sensation was too great. She made a sound of protest, feeling dizzy and high and confused.

"Ride with it," he whispered and, shifting, lowered her to the seat.

"Teague, I don't—this isn't—"

"Sure it is," he said in that grown-up, sexy way he had. He was moving against her now, making a place between her thighs and slipping a hand there. She tried to close her legs, but he rubbed her, and it felt so good that for a minute she let him, let him, even moved against him until the dizziness prevailed.

"We—have to—stop," she whispered, trying to think straight when a part of her wanted him to keep on, but more of her was frightened. His teeth were rougher on her nipple now, and she didn't know how, but his hand was suddenly inside her nylons, touching things he shouldn't be touching.

"No," she said, trying to slip out from under him the way she had at the truck earlier, but she was on her back with her legs wide, and his weight pinned her this time.

barbara delinsky

His hips were moving rhythmically, allowing only enough room for his hand, which rubbed and opened.

"I'll do it with my finger first," he said, breathing hard, and she started to squirm. It wasn't fun anymore. She pushed at his shoulders for leverage, but his finger followed. He was hurting her.

She tried to scramble back. "Let me *go!*"

"I'll get you ready—"

"I feel sick," she cried, and it was true. Through the nausea and the dizziness, she found his hair and pulled.

"What the—"

Kick him in the groin, her mother had always said, and Samantha did it. It didn't matter that she couldn't do it very hard, but it moved him enough for her to wriggle free, tug at the truck door, and fall out.

"What the hell'd you do *that* for?" Teague yelled through the open door.

But she'd had enough of music and dancing and beer, and more than enough of Teague Runyan. Tugging her clothing back into place, she ran. She stumbled when her heels caught in the grass, caught herself, and barreled on. She ran through a small wooded stretch, ran until she couldn't breathe, then stopped and was violently ill in someone's pitch black backyard. Holding her stomach, she backed up to the dark house, slid down to the ground, turned sideways against the wood, and drew her knees close. When more threatened to erupt from her stomach, she swallowed it down. She took shallow breaths, listening hard in between. She couldn't hear Teague, couldn't see Teague, but there was a noise in her head and her eyes wouldn't stay in one place long enough for her mind to figure out what she saw.

She lost the battle with her stomach and threw up

316

again. As soon as she was done, she pushed up and away from the house. When she searched the street from behind a tree and saw no sign of the truck, she ran in what she hoped was the opposite direction. She turned a corner and sat on the edge of the road to regain strength in her legs, then forced herself up and ran until she rounded another corner. She retched again and sank to the ground, praying that no one would see her. She was in a residential area. She had no idea which one. Her head was starting to hurt. If she'd been able to dig a hole, she would have climbed in and pulled the dirt in over her. She felt sick and embarrassed and scared.

She started off again, clutching her shoes to her chest and walking in her stocking feet, trying to recognize the names on street signs and failing. She turned one corner just as a pickup approached, and ducked behind a shrub, but it wasn't Teague's truck. She walked on, feeling sick in deeper ways now. She turned another corner and another pickup passed. She didn't duck away this time, just kept walking as though she knew exactly where she was headed, all the time wondering where she *was* headed and what she was going to do. When the same truck passed a third time, more slowly, she was uneasy.

"Hey, baby," said a voice that sounded older and more dangerous than Teague's, and suddenly she'd had enough of being alone. Terrified, she turned in at the nearest walk and fumbled in her purse as though for the house keys. When the truck drove off, she stole away.

She ran the length of several blocks through people's backyards, and emerged desperate to find a phone. She felt sick enough to vomit again, and wanted to lie down, just lie down and sleep while her mother kept watch, only her mother was in the hospital in a coma, and she couldn't call Lydia, after what she'd done, and *she didn't have a phone!*

She listened, trying to separate out traffic sounds from the other ones in her head. She walked another block and listened again, then headed in the direction she thought would be right. Her head hurt, her breasts hurt, her stomach hurt, her feet hurt. Looking behind her when she thought she heard another truck, she missed a break in the sidewalk and fell on her wrist, and that hurt, too.

She imagined what might happen if those men found her, or if Teague did. She imagined wandering around all night, freezing in the night air, making it to morning and not knowing what to do then.

More frightened by the minute, wanting only to be home, she began to cry softly. She was nearly frantic by the time she reached the end of another block and recognized the name on the street sign. *Thank God thank God thank God,* she murmured and started running again. It wasn't more than five minutes before she found her phone. She lifted the receiver, dialed the number, and waited for her father to answer.

chapter seventeen

JACK WAS PAINTING when the phone rang, and felt an instant jolt. He didn't have to look at the clock to know that something was wrong. He had sent Hope to bed at midnight, more than an hour before. Either Rachel was in trouble or Sam was.

Dropping palette and brush, he grabbed up the phone. "Hello?"

There was a pause, then a broken "Daddy? Come pick me up."

He swallowed hard. Not Rachel. Relief. Fear. "Where are you? What happened?"

"I don't feel good."

"Too much to drink?" It was the least of the evils.

"I feel *sick*. Can you come?"

He was already wiping his hands. "Right now. Tell me where you are." When she gave him a set of cross streets, he asked for the house address.

"It's a pay phone," she cried. "Can you come *soon?*"

He could do the drive in thirty-five minutes if he

pushed it, but a pay phone? "Are you alone?" Where in the hell was her date? And *what had he done?*

"Hurry, Daddy."

"Samantha, do I need to call an ambulance? Or the police? Is there trouble—"

"*I just want to come home!*"

"Okay, sweetheart, okay—I'm on my way—just stay there—don't *move*—and if anyone stops, call the cops, okay?"

She said a shaky "Okay."

He had a thought. "Give me five minutes, then call me in the car." He wasn't sure what all had happened, but he didn't want to hang up and imagine her alone and sick for the length of his drive. Better to talk her through the time. That way, if she passed out or ran into another kind of trouble, he could call an ambulance himself.

"I don't know the number," she wailed.

He told her and made her repeat it. "Five minutes, okay?"

"Okay."

He hung up the phone to find a wide-awake Hope inches behind him. "Can I come?"

He didn't answer, just took her hand and, snatching up his wallet in the kitchen, ran with her out to the car.

FIVE MINUTES passed, then ten, and the car phone didn't ring. He gripped the wheel and pushed the car as fast as he could through a shifting fog, praying she would still be there when he arrived.

"Okay," he said to Hope. "What do you know that I don't?"

"Nothing."

"Loyalty changes sometimes, you know. Showing loyalty to your sister right now means helping get her home safe and sound."

"She knew I didn't like what she was doing, so she didn't tell me. You were the one who was supposed to ask where she was going."

"I did and it didn't get me very far." So he was trying to blame Hope, but that wasn't fair. Hope was right. It was his job, and he had bungled it.

At least Samantha had had the sense to call.

IT WAS AFTER two in the morning when he reached Carmel. The streets were deserted. He found the intersection Samantha had named, spotted the phone booth, pulled up fast, and saw nothing. He left the car, looking in every direction, thinking she might have been standing, waiting, somewhere else, when he heard her call.

"Daddy?" For all her maturity and bravado, she was a wisp of a girl, huddled on the floor of the phone booth, her tear-streaked face looking green in the night light. "I messed up the number," she cried; "couldn't remember. It wouldn't go through. I tried *everything*."

He knelt, lifted her up and into his arms. Hope ran beside him and helped him fit her into the front seat and strap her in, then ran around the car and snaked behind the driver's seat into the back. He slipped off his jacket and covered Samantha up, because she was trembling, bare armed and bare shouldered in the nippy night air. Then he put a hand on the top of her head.

"Do we need a hospital?" he asked softly. He hadn't

321

seen bruises or blood, but he wasn't looking at the places that scared him most.

She shook her head. "I just drank too much."

"Where's your date?"

She began to cry. "He wanted—to do things—I didn't."

Jack's heart ached. "Good girl," he said, softly still. Leaning over, he pressed a kiss to the crown of her head, then turned the car for home.

HE DROVE to Big Sur slowly and sensibly, despite the hour. The car seemed a safe place between wherever it was that Samantha had been and whatever Jack was going to have to face when they got home. For most of the drive, Samantha huddled under his jacket and slept, and it seemed a natural thing to do with the fog rolling in. He touched her head every few minutes. He told her to tell him if she felt sick and wanted to stop. But her eyes remained closed and her breathing even. She didn't look drunk. She wasn't convulsing, and the way she stirred every so often suggested sleep, not unconsciousness. He could tell that she had thrown up, and assumed she had lost whatever hadn't already made it into her bloodstream. He guessed that whatever manner of sick she was had to do with heart as well as body.

He wanted to do things I didn't, she had said, and it haunted Jack, ate at his stomach, what those things might be. But he didn't ask. He remembered being grilled by his father when he was Samantha's age—worse, remembered his *sister* being grilled by his father, guilty until proven innocent. Jack wouldn't do that to Samantha.

So, was the alternative silence? Jack had been taught

silence by a father who needed to place blame and a mother who loathed dissension. Rachel had been taught it by a mother who knew everything about everything. When Jack met Rachel, they had been like souls freed from confinement, talking at length and with substance. Then time passed and old habits returned. Yes, that was what had happened. He saw. He understood. But silence wasn't the answer in dealing with Samantha. They couldn't sweep what had happened under the rug. There had to be talk.

WHEN THEY got home, he carried her to her room. While she showered, he stared out at the forest through the living room glass, wondering whether she was washing evidence away. She claimed she didn't need a hospital. If he insisted, he would be saying he didn't believe her, didn't trust her. It was a no-win situation.

The water went off. He gave her enough time to get into bed, then went to her room to make sure she was all right. He didn't turn on the light. After a minute, he adjusted to the dark and made his way to her bed. The window was hand-high open. The smell of moist earth, leaves, and bark drifted in. It was a cool, familiar comfort.

Samantha had the quilt up to her chin. If she had been sleeping he would have left, but her eyes were open and wet. He hunkered down by her face.

"What I need to know most," he said gently, "is whether he . . . touched you in ways he shouldn't have." He wasn't sure how else to ask. The truth was that he didn't know for sure whether Samantha had been a virgin to begin with.

She didn't answer at first. So he said, "If it was rape—"

"No."

"Date rape."

"*No.*"

He waited for her to say more. When she didn't, he said, "Talk to me, Sam. I'm worried. I'm scared. You're upset. I want to help." After another minute, he said, "If your mother was here, she'd be doing what I am. She'd be sitting right here talking to you. It's not prying. It's not accusing or finding fault. It's trying to make sure that you don't need medical care, or that we don't need legal help. But I have to tell you," he added with a small laugh, "I'll strangle the guy if he raped you."

"He didn't," she whispered.

"But you ended up alone in a phone booth in the middle of town." He tried to tease her into talking. "Want to tell me what happened—I mean, as much as you think my sensitive ears can take?"

She closed her eyes. One tear, then another slid out of the downward corners. He felt the pain of each. When she covered her face with a hand and broke into long, deep sobs, he felt that, too—felt it in helplessness, inadequacy, and fear.

He wished Rachel was there. *He* didn't know how to talk to a fifteen-year-old girl. This was *woman* stuff.

But Rachel wasn't there and might not be for a while. He didn't like that thought, but it was a reality he had to face. Besides, Samantha wasn't telling him to leave. That seemed significant.

Sitting back on his heels, he continued to stroke her head until her crying slowed. Then he blew out a breath. "I wouldn't want to be your age for all the tea in China."

She sniffled. "Why not?"

"It's in between nowhere." How well he remembered.

"You aren't a child anymore, so you can't just play and be cute and play dumb when things go wrong. Your body is doing weird things. You feel grown-up, but you're not that either. You can't drive a car, or make the kind of money you want to spend, and you can't do what you want when you want it, even though that's just what you want to do. You're expected to do a lot of grown-up stuff because you need the experience, only you don't *have* the experience, so half the time you don't know what in the hell you're doing. No. I'd like to be twenty-seven again. But fifteen? Not on your life."

"What was so great about twenty-seven?"

He thought about that. "Your mom."

Samantha started to cry again.

He moved his hand on her head.

"I *need* her."

"I know. But she isn't here, so we're going to try to work this through together the way she would. Want to tell me about tonight? Or do you want to sleep?" He kept expecting to be tired himself, but he was all keyed up.

She grunted. "I slept in the car. I'm not sleepy now."

He thought about putting a light on. But there was something about the foggy dark, something so dense as to be a buffer. "Tell me, then. I want to hear."

"That's because you love knowing"—her voice caught—"what a *loser* I am."

Fiercely, he said, "You aren't a loser. If you were, you'd still be at some party with kids making fools of themselves, drinking and laughing at nothing and dancing on tables and taking off their clothes—"

Her eyes went wide. "How did *you* know?"

"I've been there, sweetie. Your music may be different from what mine was, and God knows there are more beer labels to choose from these days, but human nature hasn't changed much."

"Did you know Teague would have beer in his car?"

"No. I didn't want to know that. It doesn't surprise me, though."

"You didn't like him."

"How *could* I? He didn't even tell you how pretty you looked. And you looked pretty, Sam—prettier, I'd bet, than most everyone at that prom. So. Did he just leave you at the phone booth, or what?"

"I ran there. He was somewhere . . . blocks away. He probably went back to the party."

"Nice guy," Jack muttered, but couldn't leave it at that. "If he was cool, he'd have followed you and driven you home. If he was *really* cool, he'd have kept his hands to himself in the first place. You're a minor. We're talking statutory rape."

"It didn't *get* that far. Besides, it wasn't all his fault. I let him, a little."

Jack had figured that. He took Samantha's hand and kissed it. It smelled of soap, good and clean and healthy. Quietly, he said, "Letting him, a little, is okay as long as you trust the guy and there isn't booze involved. I'm guessing there was more than beer."

"Punch."

"Spiked with vodka." When she didn't deny it, he said, "That was what made you sick. The rule of thumb is that if you have vodka first, the beer's okay. Beer first, and vodka will make you sick. Mind you, I'm not saying drinking's all right. It isn't. Drinking makes people do dumb things. It makes them do *tragic* things." His voice rose. "I didn't smell anything on Teague when he got here. When did he start drinking? Was he drinking in the truck? At the end there, was he *drunk?*"

In that split second, Jack heard his father's voice. In the next second, he regained control of himself. "Don't answer," he said softly. "It's over and done. And maybe I shouldn't be telling you how to drink and how not to drink. Maybe that's giving the wrong message. Only, kids *do* drink sometimes, and if I want you safe, you need to know. Knowledge is the key. It's right up there with experience." He paused. "See, the downside of being a grown-up is that you're held accountable for your actions. Okay, so you weren't raped. You could have been killed if Teague crashed the truck. You could have died of alcohol poisoning, or an overdose of something that someone slipped into that punch. Someone *else* could have died. That's the kind of thing you carry with you all your life. I don't want that for you, Samantha. I really don't. A big part of growing up is learning when to be cautious. It's realizing that there are consequences to everything you do."

She was quiet for so long that he wondered if she had fallen asleep, and part of him felt that was fine. He liked the note he had ended on. For a father muddling his way through, he wasn't doing so bad.

He should have known better.

In the same quiet, very grown-up voice he had used, Samantha asked, "How does all that fit in with the divorce? Are you accountable for your actions in a marriage, too?"

It was a minute before he said, "Yes."

"Then you accept the blame for that?"

"No. It takes two to make a marriage, and two to break it." Which was what Hope said Rachel had said, and quite an admission on his part. Two weeks before, he would have blamed the breakup of the marriage on Rachel. She was the one who had walked out.

Only, her leaving San Francisco was a symptom, not a cause. He could concede that now. The cause of the breakup went deeper. Rachel may have been abandoned in the broadest sense. He may have put his work first.

"But how could you guys just let it go?" Samantha asked, and there were tears in her voice again.

"We didn't."

"You *did,*" she cried with a vehemence that reminded him of something. Katherine had said that she was obsessed with the divorce. Katherine might be right. "You didn't argue about it, you just split," she charged. "What was *your* side of the story?"

He wasn't sure he should say, not without Rachel there. But Samantha sounded like she needed an answer. "I felt," he began, considering it, "that your mother didn't want me. That we had grown apart, maybe needed different things. I was tied to the city because of work, and that was the last place your mother wanted to be."

"Then it was about *place?*"

Two weeks ago he might have said that, might have boiled down the cause of the break to a word or two. But it was more complex. He saw that now. "Place was only a symptom of other things."

"But you loved her."

"Yes."

"Do you still?"

He thought about the hand-around-the-heart feeling he experienced walking into that hospital room every day. "Probably."

"So why didn't you *fight* to keep her? Wasn't it worth it? Weren't *we* worth it?"

The question stunned him. "Yes. *Yes.*"

"I kept thinking about that when I was waiting for you to come get me. I kept thinking you were right. We weren't worth it. Me, especially me."

"Are you *crazy?*"

"See?" she cried. "You'd *never* say that to Hope."

"No, I'd say other things to Hope, because Hope and you are different people. Different. Not better or worse."

"She's *lovable* and I'm not."

"But I do love you."

"I'm *not* lovable. I say too much."

"That's one of the things that *makes* you lovable. I always know where I stand. That's a real plus in a relationship. Honesty. Trust. Ease. Well, sometimes we don't have ease, you and me, but that's because you're your age and I'm mine, and you let me *know* when I'm being . . . being . . ."

"Old."

He sighed. "I guess. So, see, we can talk about that, too."

She turned onto her back and stared at the ceiling. "I couldn't talk to Teague. Not the way I wanted to. I was afraid he'd think I was a *kid.*"

"Teague's crud," Jack said. "You can do better, Sam."

"I thought he *was* better. Shows how much *I* know."

"You knew enough to get the hell away from the guy when things started to get out of control. Didn't you?" When she didn't instantly answer, he felt another moment's doubt. "The truth, Sam. Didn't you? Or," he pushed himself to say, "do we need to talk about the facts of life?"

She shot him a glance. "Mom already has, but I didn't do it with Teague. He wanted to. That was when I left."

"See? You learned. That's what growing up is about. What went wrong with Brendan and Lydia?"

Unexpectedly, Samantha started crying again. When she tried to turn onto her side away from him, he rolled her right back.

"Talk it out, sweetheart."

Between sobs, she said, "I blew them off, so now I don't have them—and I won't have Pam and Heather, because Teague must have gone back there and told them what happened. I'm not going to be able to show my face in school again, not *ever*. I am such a *fuckup*."

"No. No, you're not."

But she wouldn't be assuaged. "I messed up, just like I messed up with Mom. If it hadn't been for me, she wouldn't have had the accident."

"How do you figure that?"

"We had a fight that afternoon."

"What happened in the afternoon has nothing to do—"

"It does, because she was thinking about the fight and brought her book to the studio, and if she hadn't had to get it there later, she would have left the house earlier."

"Don't do that, Sam," he warned. "If you do, I have to."

"Have to what?"

"Blame me. Do you think it hasn't occurred to me that if I'd been around more for your mother in San Francisco, she wouldn't have moved down here in the first place? If she hadn't moved down here, she wouldn't be in that hospital. But it doesn't do any good to think that way. It's done. Over. Not your fault or my fault, but the fault of the woman who was driving the other car."

"She's dead, isn't she?"

He figured that if Samantha was old enough to drink

beer and vodka and do God knew what with a boy she'd never dated before, she was old enough to know the truth. "Yes. She's dead. So we have to let it go, Sam. We can't blame her, and we can't blame us. We have to do what we can to help your mother wake up. And we have to carry on and move forward here. I think you should call Lydia later."

"I *can't*. She's not going to want to talk to me! I was *horrible* to her!"

"You could apologize."

"That wouldn't work."

"Why not?"

"Because."

"That's not a real answer, Samantha. Try again."

"She won't want me back."

"Do you want her back?"

"*Yes*. She's my *friend*."

"More so than Pam?"

Samantha thought about that. "Yes. I feel safer with Lydia."

"Tell her that." When she didn't speak, he said, "That's your strength, expressing yourself. It's a precious thing, Sam. Not everyone has what it takes inside to do it. I know it's hard, but the important things in life are. You have to put yourself out there and risk the possibility that she's feeling so hurt that she won't want any *part* of you, but I don't think that'll happen. Lydia strikes me as a forgiving person."

Samantha started to cry again.

"What's wrong now?" he asked, because he thought they had it all worked out.

"I miss Mom."

Feeling a wrenching inside, he smoothed the hair

back from her face. "Me, too," he said and realized that he did, very much.

HE CONTINUED to stroke her hair until she quieted. Then he heard something new and went to the window. It sounded like rain. Only it wasn't raining.

Samantha came up beside him, wrapped in her quilt. "It's fog feet."

Fog feet. That had to be a Rachel expression.

"It's like," she said, "when the fog is so thick that it makes noise moving through the forest."

He looked at her. "Want to go outside? Nah. You feel lousy."

"I'll go," she said.

So they went outside, Jack in his paint-spattered sweat suit, Samantha in her nightgown and quilt. They were both barefooted—crazy, Jack knew, but somehow feeling the earth beneath their feet was important. They didn't go far, just to a level spot where the tree trunks rose and narrowed and stretched toward branches that spawned needles, and the sky.

They didn't move, didn't speak. They felt the moisture on their faces, a gentle curative, and listened to the steady, soothing sound of fog feet, and it occurred to Jack that this was a gift, standing here with his daughter, after the night that had been. He tried to think of when he had last felt as content, and realized it had been in these same woods. Then he had been with Hope. Now Samantha.

"I used to stand like this with Mom," she whispered so softly that he might have missed it if he hadn't been so close. She didn't say anything else. She didn't have to, because Rachel was suddenly with them, so strong a presence that Jack actually looked behind him, half expecting her to take form from the fog.

Did he still love her? There was no *probably* about it. And saying that he missed her told only half the story. The truth—realized, admitted only now, with the fog so thick that only the largest things in life were visible— was that he had been missing her for months.

HE WOKE UP Sunday morning, feeling her in bed with him, memory was so strong. Her hand moved on his chest, side to side through a matting of hair, and down his belly. The soft, sexy voice in his ear said that she loved it when he was this hard, so hard that he shook. He smelled the warm woman of her, kissed the wet woman in her, and came in a climax so cruel that for long minutes after, he lay with an arm over his eyes, breathing hard, swearing again and again.

His heartbeat had barely begun to steady when the peal of the phone sent it through the roof. Sunday morning at eight, with Samantha and Hope safe in bed?

"Jack? It's Kara. Rachel's thrown a clot."

chapter eighteen

" 'THROWN A CLOT.' What does that mean?" Samantha asked. They were in the car, speeding back to Monterey. She looked pale, almost green. Jack suspected that had as much to do with it being the morning after as with Rachel's condition. He had given her aspirin before they left. She was holding her head still against the headrest.

Hope had her lucky boots back on and was leaning forward between their seats, waiting for his answer.

He tried to repeat the gist of what Kara had told him. "On rare occasions, a broken bone—in Mom's case, her leg—creates a clot, a wad that enters the bloodstream and moves through the veins. Sometimes it gets stuck in the head or the heart. Sometimes it gets stuck in the lungs. That's where your mom's got stuck."

"How do they know?"

"They did a scan."

"Before that, how did they know something was wrong?"

"The monitors she's been connected to showed changes in the oxygen level in her blood. The problem was discovered as soon as it happened." He had asked that right off. If there had been a delay because she had been moved from Intensive Care to a regular room, he would have screamed.

"But what *is* the problem?" Samantha persisted. "Like, could she die from this?"

Bite your tongue. Words from his past. And wrong, here, because Samantha was only asking what Hope was surely wondering. Not addressing it would frighten them more.

"She could, Sam," he said, "but she won't, because we've got Bauer and Bates with her right now. The problem is that a clot can cut the flow of blood. In your mother's case, that's the last thing they want. Her brain is healing. It needs all the oxygen it can get, and since blood carries oxygen, they don't want anything slowing the flow." There was also a little problem with pneumonia, if a lung infection developed. That could kill her. But he wasn't mentioning it now.

"So do they operate and cut it out?"

According to Kara, operating posed more of a risk to Rachel's system than they cared to take. "They're treating it medically, with something they call a clot buster. It's heavy-duty stuff that will break up the clot."

"Right away?"

Hadn't he asked it himself, with the very same fear? "They hope so."

"What if it doesn't?"

"Don't look for trouble, Sam."

"But—"

"Sam." He took her hand. "Let's work together here. It doesn't do any good to think the worst. I don't know much more than you do. But we're due for a break, aren't we?" When she didn't answer, he gave her hand a jiggle. "Aren't we?"

"Yes," she whispered and closed her eyes.

He held her hand for a while. It comforted him, as did the weight of Hope's cheek on his shoulder.

KARA had forgotten to tell Jack three small things.

First, Rachel was back in ICU. They discovered that when they arrived at her room, found it empty, and in a panic ran down the hall.

Second, her lips and the area surrounding them were blue, which would have been frightening enough without the third thing. That was the gasping sound she made.

"What's happened," Kara explained as Jack and the girls watched Rachel in horror, "is that because there's a block, the blood can't participate in ventilation. Blood carrying oxygen can't get to her lungs to exchange with blood carrying carbon dioxide. The gasping you hear is her attempt to get more oxygen to her lungs. She sounds a lot worse than she is."

That was putting it mildly. To Jack's ears, Rachel sounded on the verge of death. He was appalled. "How long until the medicine starts working?"

"We're hoping to see results within a few hours."

THE FIRST HOUR crept. Rachel's gasping breaths counted the seconds.

Jack didn't know what to do. He was frightened and unsure, as terrified by the grating sounds Rachel made as he was by the tinge of her skin. For a time, he simply stood with an arm around each of the girls, but they were all tired. Eventually, they sat down on the bed, the girls on one side, Jack on the other. He tried to think of things to say, but it seemed important, so important, to listen to those gasping sounds, to hear the slightest change, to imagine that there were words in there somewhere.

"She sounds *awful*," Samantha whispered at one point.

Jack nodded. He held Rachel's hand, occasionally touched her face or her neck, and thought it ironic that when the scrapes on the side of her face were nearly healed, she should be turning blue. His stomach was tight, his insides chilled. Prayers came to him from a long-ago childhood of enforced practice. His memory fragmented them and they emerged watered down, but he thought them anyway. *Dear God, help her . . . give her strength . . . let her heal . . . serve you again . . .*

THE SECOND HOUR began, and the gasping went on undiminished.

"Hang in there," Jack murmured. "You can lick this, Rachel. Breathe long and slow, long and slow." He made a dry sound.

"What?" Samantha asked.

"We've done this before, your mom and me. When you were born. I coached her. 'Hang in there, Rachel. You can do it. Breathe long and slow.' Then out you came."

"Yelling and screaming?"

"No." He paused, smiled. "Actually, yes. You were vocal from birth. Very vocal. You let us know when you wanted something, all right."

"What about me?" Hope asked.

"Less vocal." His smile was for Rachel now. The memories were sweet. "In some ways, that was harder. You didn't tell us as much, so we had to guess. You guys were different even then. Your mom claimed you were different in the womb."

"How could she tell?" Hope asked.

"The way you moved. Sam was more active even then."

"But I slid out easier."

"Second deliveries are like that. She had to work harder with Sam." He heard that breathing again, as loud as ever. His smile faded. "Long and slow. Hang in there, angel. You're doing good, you're doing good."

KATHERINE arrived looking pale, upset, and totally different from any other way Jack had seen her. Her face was washed clean, curls a dozen shades of beige caught up in a ponytail. She wore a lightweight warm-up suit and sneakers. Only her fingernails were done, but even then, lighter. They were pink.

Jack took comfort in her presence. Even pale and upset, she conveyed competence. She knew what to say, what to ask. If there was something he wasn't doing for Rachel that should be done, she would tell him. She was his friend now, too. They were allies in the same war.

When he sent the girls to the cafeteria for drinks, she said, "Thanks for calling. I was working out. I got your message as soon as I got back." She made a general gesture toward her hair and face, apologetic, Jack thought. "Just took time to shower."

"You look great," he said. When she gave him a skeptical look, he added, "I'm serious. All natural. Very Rachel. Thanks for coming." He touched Rachel's lips. They were parted, air grating in and out. "I didn't expect this. The girls are pretty shaken. *I'm* pretty shaken."

"The medicine will work," Katherine said firmly.

"I've been praying. It's the first time in years. I don't want to lose her, Katherine. Do you think she wants to hear that?"

Katherine looked at him and sighed. "You're not a bad-looking guy. Need a haircut. Need a shave. But you clean up good. So, yeah. She'd want to hear it. What woman wouldn't?"

"I think you're missing my point," Jack said, but the girls returned then, and when Katherine took her tea with thanks and suggested that Jack take the girls back to the cafeteria for breakfast, he figured he'd leave well enough alone.

"HI THERE."

Katherine was leaning over the bed rail, letting Rachel know she was rooting for her, when Steve Bauer walked in. She had known he would appear, had felt it in her gut well before she decided to forgo makeup and mousse. She figured it was time to give him a preview of the less glamorous side of the woman she was.

"What's happening here?" she asked, straightening.

"Clot. Drip. Wait."

"Ahh. Thanks."

He approached the bed, studied Rachel, then the monitor. He adjusted the solution dripping from the IV bag, then leaned in and said in a voice loud and authoritative enough to be heard over her breathing, "Rachel? I'm speeding up the drip. You won't feel the change, but it should help."

Katherine sensed his worry. "Should she have already responded?"

He checked the wall clock. "No. But she can use more."

"How does something like this affect the coma? Can it snap her out of it?"

"It can. It may not." He turned his blue eyes on her, along with a small smile. "How are you?"

"Nervous."

"I'm flattered."

"Nervous about *Rachel*," she said, focusing again on her friend. There was no pretending she was asleep, not with the noise she made with every breath.

"I'm envious. How far back do you two go?"

"Six years." But she had never had a friend like Rachel. "I feel like I've known her forever, we're that much alike."

"You look more alike now than usual."

"Ashen skin? Blue lips?"

"Unadorned. You look pretty."

Jack had said the same thing, but it felt different coming from Steve. She squeezed Rachel's hand. "He's hitting on me again."

"No. Just saying I'm in for the long haul." Before she could begin to analyze *that,* he said, "So you and Rachel are alike. Tell me how."

Katherine could do that. "She's an only child. So am I. She grew up in the city. So did I. She hated it. So did I."

"Why?"

"In Rachel's case, she felt pressured to conform to a way of life she didn't like."

340

"In yours?"

"I felt lost. I like bumping into people I know."

"Like Rick Meltzer?"

Rick was the anesthesiologist who had called out her name. She should have known Steve would notice. "Like Rick," she admitted, since denying it would only make him curious. "I also like privacy. Drive half an hour from here, and you're in the middle of nowhere. For someone like Rachel, that's important. She's artistic. We have that in common, too."

"Then it isn't just—" He made a speedy snipping motion.

"No. It isn't just." She held his gaze. "There's an art to coloring and styling hair. Even in that, Rachel and I are alike."

"How?"

"We're both adherents of realism. We spend our professional lives trying to bring out the best and most beautiful of what nature has to offer." She looked at Rachel again, suddenly resentful of what she saw. "I don't think she'd like these blue lips."

"We don't either, but they're telling us what's going on inside."

"Can she do herself harm, gasping like this?"

"No. She needs the air."

"When will the medication kick in?"

"Hard to tell. Another two or three hours. Maybe more." He was holding Rachel's shoulder. "I've seen her work. I stopped in at P. Emmet's."

Katherine was surprised. She had thought detachment was a medical school basic. "Aren't you risking emotional involvement doing that?"

"Yes. The more you know, the harder it is when

patients fail, or when you have to recommend one of two lousy alternatives. The flip side is that when patients respond and recover, there's greater satisfaction. The brute fact is that medicine is becoming a service profession. The customer wants his doctor to be involved. Isn't that why Jack brought in these pictures? Or why Rachel is wearing a T-shirt with her name in big bright letters? It's why I'm asking you these questions."

"And here I thought you had an ulterior motive," Katherine said, knowing that he did. He wanted to learn about her, so he was asking about Rachel.

Those blue eyes said she was right. "Does she like to travel?" he asked.

Katherine sighed. He was incorrigible. Something about his persistence was nice, though. If he wanted her bad enough . . . "Yes. She travels for work. She'd like to travel more for fun, but money's tight. Paying for three. You know."

"I do. Does she like movies?"

"Good ones." She arched a brow. "There aren't any around, so don't even suggest it."

"I wasn't about to. You'd feel guilty going to a movie with Rachel struggling in here, but you have to eat, and I can't go far from the hospital. I was thinking something quick and easy, like smoked salmon on the Wharf."

Katherine couldn't help but grin. "With the tourists?"

"It's quick. It's easy. It's public. Tell you what. I'll be in and out of here for another few hours. If you're hungry at two, meet me out front. My car is the dark green CJ-7." He briefly turned away to check the speed of the drip, looked back at the monitor for another minute, then, with an endearingly vulnerable glance at Katherine, left the room.

WHEN JACK returned with the girls, he was discouraged to find that nothing had changed. Rachel's coloring was as poor as before, her breathing as labored.

"Bauer was just here," Katherine said. "He didn't seem overly concerned."

But Jack was. He kissed Rachel's hand and pressed his mouth to the scar there. It was a fine line, growing finer by the day, but her hand was thinner. All of her was thinner. She was fading away right before his eyes. It struck him that this was his punishment. He had let Rachel walk out of his life. Had let her. Samantha was right. He hadn't fought.

He had been preoccupied and too proud. He had let the silence win.

"Goddammit," he muttered, cursing both that silence and the gut-wrenching noise Rachel was making, and suddenly his eyes filled with tears. He squeezed them shut, swallowed, and pressed Rachel's hand to his brow.

"Hey, guys," Katherine said to Samantha and Hope, "let's take a walk. Your parents need some private time."

Jack didn't look, but he knew when they were gone. He felt the special connection with Rachel that used to reduce the rest of the world to fringe. Memory, or reality? He wasn't sure. But it was strong, and a good sign maybe, if she was still putting out vibes.

Taking a steadying breath, he lowered her hand from his eyes. "I don't know if you can hear me, Rachel, but there are things I need to say. There are things *we* need to say. If you wanted to get my attention, you couldn't have done it better. It's been an . . . enlightening few weeks."

He whispered his thumb over her eyelids, feeling tissue-thin, soft skin that was surprisingly warm. "I want to talk about what happened. We never did that. We just kind of split up and went separate ways. Stopped talking over the piano." He was haunted by his memory of her picking out sad tunes that night, when she had given him an opening and he had walked away. "We fell back into who we were before we met, but that wasn't us. It was me. It was you. It wasn't us. Together we were something different, something better than we'd been. When did we lose that?"

Through the ruckus of gasps, he imagined her voice, thoughtful and warm as it was in the best of times, but there were no words, no answers, no insight.

Suddenly angry, he whispered, "Don't you leave me in the lurch, Rachel Keats. Keats—God, I hate that. With all due respect to fuckin' women's rights, I hate it. You should be Rachel McGill. Or I'll be Jack Keats. But we should be the same." He took a shuddering breath and said, fiercely, "We had a pretty damn nice marriage, Rachel. I want it back. Don't you die on me now."

He watched her face closely, hoping for a reaction. "Did you hear what I said?" he fairly yelled. "I want it back!"

She didn't move, didn't blink, just took one gasping breath after another.

Frightened, he pulled up a chair and sat back.

chapter nineteen

JACK WAS IN the same chair an hour later. Samantha had squeezed in beside him and was sleeping under his arm. Hope was dozing, curled on her side against Rachel's hip. Noon had come and gone. Rachel was still blue, still gasping.

Samantha stirred. She looked at him groggily, then less groggily at Rachel. "No better?" she asked.

"Not yet. How's your head?"

"Okay." She settled back against him in a way that spoke of how far they had come. If the chair was crowded, he didn't care. He wouldn't have moved for the world.

"I keep thinking about Lydia," she said softly. "I should tell her about Mom."

With only a minor stretch, he pulled the cell phone from his pocket, turned it on, and held it out.

It was a minute before she took it. "What if she hangs up when she hears my voice?"

"She won't hang up." If she did, he would never forgive her. Samantha was headed in the right direction. He didn't want her derailed. "She's not that kind of person. Isn't that the lesson here?"

Samantha fingered the phone for a long time. "Maybe I should wait." He thought of the things he wanted to say to Rachel, things he should have said before, things he might never, ever have a chance to say. "Do it now, Sam. That's a lesson we *all* have to learn. If you know something's right, don't let it go."

SAMANTHA wanted privacy. Calling Lydia to grovel was hard enough. Doing it in public would be worse. So she walked to the end of the corridor and wedged herself in a lonely corner, and even then she hesitated. If Lydia refused to talk, she didn't know what she'd do. But Rachel had given her a perfect excuse. The blood clot was something to tell Lydia. Lydia adored Rachel. *All* of Samantha's friends adored Rachel. They thought she was the nicest, most interesting, most *fun* of the moms. Of course, they didn't have to live with her.

Feeling guilty to have thought that, she pressed in Lydia's number. When Lydia's mother answered, Samantha's throat closed. In that instant, she would have given *anything* to hear her own mother's voice.

She cleared her throat. "Hi, Mrs. Russell. Is Lydia up?"

"Samantha! We missed you last night. I thought for sure you'd stop over. Did you have fun?"

Samantha's eyes teared up. She debated lying, but she was too tired, too nervous, too needy. "No. It wasn't . . . what I thought. Is everyone still there?"

"Shelly just left. I think Lydia's in the shower. Hold on. I'll check."

Samantha turned in against the wall and waited.

"Yes, she's in the shower," Mrs. Russell said a little too brightly. "Is there a message?"

No *Hold on, she's getting out,* no *She'll call you right back*—either of which Lydia would have done the week before. "Um, it's kind of important. My mom is worse."

There was a gasp, then the kind of worried "Oh dear" that Samantha would never have heard from Pam, Heather, or Teague, let alone any of their mothers. "Hold on, Samantha." She was an ally now. "Let me get her out."

Samantha pressed her head to the wall. It seemed forever until Lydia's voice came through. It, too, was worried, but there was a distance to it. "What happened to your mom?"

Acting as though nothing had ever come between them, Samantha told her about the clot and ended with, "She's making an awful sound. It's very scary."

There was a silence on the other end, then a wary "Do you want me to come?"

Groveling sucked. If Samantha was willing to forgive and forget, she didn't know why Lydia couldn't. "Not if you don't want to."

"I want to if you want me to be there. Do you?"

"Yes."

"Okay."

The line went dead before Samantha could say another word. The coward in her was relieved to be let off the hook. But the hook was still there, so she felt dread. She also felt humbled. Lydia hadn't sounded young or stupid. She had taken the phone when she had every right not to. It remained to be seen how she would be in person, but maybe Jack was right. Maybe there was a lesson here.

She jumped when the phone in her hand rang. Thinking that Lydia wanted to say more, even reconcile there and then, she pressed *send* and was about to speak when a loud male voice beat her to it.

"It's about time you turned on the fuckin' phone, Jack. I've been leaving messages at every number you have, and you don't call me back? We're partners in this business, pal. You gotta carry some of the weight. I know Rachel's sick and you have a lot on the brain, but so do I. The natives are getting restless in Montana. They hired an architect, they want some plans, and I don't think they're gonna like those new ones you faxed. What's going on with you? Are we talking midlife crisis here? I'm getting the distinct impression you don't care about work anymore. Tell me this is a temporary thing." He paused, waited. "Jack?"

"This is Samantha," she said, standing taller. "If you want to speak with my father, you'll have to hold on." Dropping the phone to her side, she walked with deliberate leisure back to Rachel's room.

JACK saw her coming. He took heart from her composure, until she handed him the phone and said, "It's David. He is . . . *fuckin'* mad."

He stared at her for the time it took to rake his upper lip with his teeth. Then he took the phone and stepped into the hall. "How're you doin', Dave?"

"I'd be doing better if I thought you just weren't *getting* my messages. Why haven't you called?"

"Rachel's in the middle of a crisis."

"What kind of crisis?"

"She's having trouble breathing. She can't get enough oxygen."

"Where are the fuckin' doctors?"

"Right here, but they're doing all they can. We're waiting. That's all we can do."

"Jesus." He gave a long, loud sigh. "How long this time, Jack? When are you coming back on board?"

"I don't know."

"Not good enough. I'm trying to run a business. We need you here, Jack."

"I can't *be* there. Not now."

"When?"

"I'll let you know," Jack ground out and turned off the phone.

When Samantha raised a fist and said, "Yesssss," he smiled. It was a single fine moment in the middle of a mess.

KATHERINE had no intention of going to the Wharf for lunch. It felt wrong, with Rachel so sick. She wanted to be at the hospital, rooting, supporting, fighting for her right by her side.

But Jack and the girls were doing that, Jack surprisingly well. And they were family. Besides, she was hungry. She'd had nothing but tea all day.

There was still the matter of how she looked. The sweat suit was fine, but the hair? The skin? She prided herself on being a walking ad for her shop. She wouldn't win many customers looking like this.

But this was Fisherman's Wharf, the major tourist attraction in Monterey. She wouldn't look any different from the average visitor. She might not gain customers, but she sure wouldn't lose them. And she *was* hungry. By promising to be back in an hour with lunch for Jack and the girls, she made it a practical mission and easier to justify.

She went down to the front door, assuming that a CJ-7 was a snappy sports car. The dark green car that waited, though, was an old-fashioned Jeep, with a roll bar on top, neither roof nor windows, and what looked like tin for doors.

"Wow," she said, fastening her seat belt first thing—second thing being grateful that her hair wasn't loose. "Quite a car."

He grinned. "Thanks." He worked the stick shift, stepped on the gas, and the car headed out. "It's an eighty-six. I had to look for two years. Then I found it in La Jolla. *CJ* means *civilian Jeep*. Know any Jeep history?"

"Uh, no. Beauty school doesn't go that far."

He laughed. "Neither does med school. Jeeps go back to World War Two—1941—when the army needed a reconnaissance vehicle that would go anywhere. Lore has it that the name *Jeep* is a derivation of *GP*—general purpose. The first CJs hit the road as early as forty-six. So there's your trivia for the day."

She had to admit there was a classic feel to the thing. The dashboard was metal—dark green to match the outside of the car—with chrome circling the dials. He touched that chrome once or twice. She couldn't begrudge him the affection.

He took his time driving—enjoying the fresh air, she imagined, because she surely was. The May sun was relaxingly warm, the ocean air a far cry from the hospital's sterility.

Despite his promise to make it quick, he parked a distance away. Katherine didn't fault him on it, nor did she rush the pace as they walked to the Wharf. She figured she owed herself the leisure after two weeks of shuttling between work and the hospital. She figured Steve deserved it, too. Without the lab coat, he looked totally casual—sport shirt rolled up his forearms, old jeans, sneakers. She could have sworn he was taking the same reinvigorating breaths she was.

Tourists were milling in groups at the head of the Wharf. They joined one group that circled a tiny monkey who was stuffing his pockets with the quarters children offered, but Katherine could only watch so long. "I always feel bad for that poor little thing," she murmured when they broke away and set off.

They passed storefront after storefront as they ambled down the pier. Had she been there alone, Katherine would have simply picked out a grill, ordered food, eaten, and left. But the ambling was pleasant, and the Wharf wasn't long. They reached its end just as a bench opened up. Steve parked her there and left, returning several minutes later with cups of clam chowder, grilled-salmon sandwiches, and iced tea.

Katherine rather liked being waited on. She had spent so much of her adult life doing for herself that it was a treat. She ate every last bit of her portion, not in the least embarrassed, since Steve ate every last bit of his, and with the very same grinning gusto. Passing the bench on to another pair of eaters, they stood a bit longer watching a seal in the water. When they spotted a group of kayakers on the bay, he told her that he was a canoeist. She told him she had never learned to swim. He told her it was easy. She said that was nice. He told her she didn't know what she was missing. She said she'd take his word for it. They smiled at each other, no offense taken either way.

Walking back up the pier, she bought sandwiches and chowder for the McGills. Steve guided her to the car.

He didn't immediately start it, but turned to her and sat back. "Thanks. I needed that."

Feeling safe enough, she smiled back. "So did I. Thank you."

He looked out the windshield, pensive. Then he looked at her. "There. That didn't hurt, did it?"

She laughed. "No, Doctor."

"I'm serious." She could see that he was. There was no humor in his eyes, just concern and that same vulnerability. "I know it's hard to do things like play tourist on the Wharf when people you know are in Intensive Care," he said, "but I *live* with people I know being in Intensive Care. Part of me wants to be back at that hospital watching Rachel. That part would be at the hospital twenty hours a day. So I make a concerted effort to leave. That thing about emotional involvement? I have to balance it somehow. Walking the Wharf helps. Canoeing helps. Gardening helps."

"Gardening? Oh dear. I have a brown thumb."

"I said that once, too. Funny, how resilient nature is. I do my best, and it may not be everything a plant needs, but it's more than the thing would get without." He stretched his fingers, palms to the steering wheel. "I kind of look at medicine the same way. Take Rachel. Thirty years ago, without drugs like mannitol and streptokinase, she would have died. Yes, I want her awake. I want her awake *now*. I do the best I can. It may not be everything she needs, but she'd be worse off without." His eyes found hers and held for a silent minute. Then, quietly, he said, "I'm a good guy, Katherine. You can trust me."

She knew he was talking beyond Rachel, and the air grew charged. She tore her eyes away, focused on her lap, then on a brick building adjacent to the parking lot.

"I've been divorced for ten years," he said. "I've had it with dating."

She chewed on her cheek.

"So if I come on faster than you want," he continued, "it's because I don't see the point in beating around the bush when someone appeals to me. Few women have. You do."

She put her elbow on the door and pressed her knuckles to her forehead.

"Say the word, and I'll get lost," he said.

She wanted to say the word, wanted to say *any* word, but none came.

"Either tell me to get lost," he said without a bit of smugness, "or give me a kiss."

"That's not a fair choice."

"Ask Rachel about fair. Look, I know the timing of this stinks, but I'm fifty-three. I'm too old to play games. Do you want me to get lost?"

She thought about that. There was something about him, something beyond those blue eyes and that fit body, that appealed to her, too. "No."

"Then kiss me."

She eyed him from under her fist. "Why?"

"I want to see if it works."

"What a male thing to say."

"And because I said it, you're totally turned off."

"I should be." But she wasn't, because it went two ways. If his kiss left her cold, she wouldn't have to worry

353

about the rest. They could be friends without the threat
of anything more.

"Okay," she said and looked at her watch. "One
minute. Then we have to leave." She leaned over and put
her lips to his, moved them a little, backed off. "Am I
doing a solo here?"

Smiling, he shook his head. He slid one hand around
her neck and moved gentle fingers into her hair, slid the
other around her shoulder in a gentle message that rose
to her jaw before she could begin to fear it would head
south. His hands framed her face. His eyes touched her
lips. He took his time, moved closer, tipped his head,
took more time. His mouth was an inch from hers
when, with a less than steady breath, he drew back,
faced front, cleared his throat, and turned the key in the
ignition.

Katherine stared in disbelief. "What are you doing?"

"Minute's up."

She knew that, but her insides were humming. She
would have been flexible on the time. "I thought you
didn't play games."

Shifting in his seat, he headed out of the parking lot.
"I don't. It works. Wasn't that the point of the exercise?"

"Works for *who?*" she cried. "Is that *your* idea of a
kiss?"

"Oh, no." His laugh was quintessentially male. "But it
works, Katherine. Tell me you didn't feel it."

She jabbed a finger at her lips. "I didn't feel a damn
thing."

He shot her one look, then, when she didn't relent,
shot her another. Seconds after that, he pulled over to the
curb, took her into his arms, and without once giving her

cause to tense up by going anywhere near her breasts, gave her a kiss that spelled trouble.

SAMANTHA stood beside Rachel's bed watching the door. Her head was throbbing again, her stomach was twisting. Her wrist ached and her feet hurt. Going to school in the morning was unthinkable. She didn't care if finals were coming up. She would make them up in the summer, when no one else was around. By fall, people would forget.

It was thirty minutes since she had called Lydia. Jack had his elbows on the bed rail. He was staring at Rachel. Hope was looking around the room, sitting cross-legged with her butt against Rachel's cast. Barely five minutes passed without either Kara or a nurse stopping in. Samantha wished Cindy was there, but she wasn't on duty until tomorrow morning.

Hope straightened her legs and slid off the bed. Her boots hit the floor with a thunk. "I'm getting stuff from the other room. This room could be *anyone's.*" She strode into the hall.

"She shouldn't do that," Samantha warned. "The point is getting Mom back there as soon as the medicine works."

Jack had straightened. He was flexing his neck, dipping his head from side to side. "That is the point. But then there's Murphy's Law. It says that as soon as we move everything here, she'll be ready to move back. Hold the fort," he said and left.

Rachel's breathing was louder than ever in the silence that remained.

Samantha went to the door and looked down the hall just as Jack turned into Rachel's regular room. In the other direction, several nurses were clustered, heads together. Lydia was nowhere in sight.

Back at the bed, she curled her fingers over the rail. Just thinking about the fiasco of the prom, she felt lost and sick and scared. The best part, the *best* part, was getting home. She didn't know how many of the other dads would have been as supportive as hers had been. So it was possibly a fluke. So maybe he wouldn't have come for her if he'd been working his head off in the city. So maybe if Rachel woke up he would be gone again.

But, boy, it had been nice listening to fog feet with him. It reminded her of times before the divorce.

The blue tint around Rachel's mouth brought back another memory. "Omigod, Mom, remember Halloween? We always had *the* best costumes. Hershey's Kisses and Crayola boxes and bunches of grapes. And makeup out of food coloring and flour? Blue lips? *Purple* lips?"

"Sam?"

She whirled around. Not knowing what to say, she turned right back to Rachel. When she sensed Lydia beside her, and still there weren't any words, she dared a look. Lydia's eyes were on Rachel, reflecting the same horror Samantha had felt seeing her mother like this for the first time.

"Can't they *do* something?"

Samantha waved at the IV pole. "It's up there. We have to wait for it to work."

"Oh." She wrapped her arms around her middle. "Does she know about last night?"

"You mean, did my telling her cause this?" It wasn't

the vote of confidence Samantha needed. "No, Lydia. I haven't told her. She did this all on her own."

"You don't have to get angry. She'd be upset about last night, and you know it."

Samantha looked at her then. "What do you know about last night?"

"You want me to say? In front of your Mom?"

"Yeah, I want you to say." Rachel would have to know sometime. Better when she couldn't speak.

Lydia kept her eyes on Rachel. "You went to Ian's but left there with Teague and got so sloshed you passed out, so he drove you home. At least, that's what Teague said when he got back to the party. He ended up with Marissa Fowler, who was supposed to be with Mark Cahill. Mark's Amanda's cousin. He picked her up at my house this morning."

"And told *everyone* that story?" Nightmare!

"Told Amanda and Shelly and me. Is it true?"

"No, it is not true. I didn't get sloshed or pass out, and Teague did not drive me home. He came on so strong that I could nail him for rape, hands down—only it never got past the attempted stage. I ran away before it did. Me sloshed? Try Teague. And stoned. My father came and got me."

Lydia's eyes were wide. "You had to *call* him?"

"I wanted to call you, but I didn't think you'd care."

Lydia looked suddenly close to tears, and totally like the sweet person Samantha loved. "You're stupid, you know that?" she cried.

Samantha was about to say she was right, when Hope walked in loaded down with cards, signs, and pictures. Jack followed with vases of flowers, which he set on the windowsill. Hope sank to the floor and opened her arms.

Samantha said to Lydia, "We're counting on Murphy's Law. Want to help?"

JACK was buoyed when sweet, unsophisticated, loyal Lydia stayed. He couldn't help but think that if Samantha could go through life with friends like this one, she would survive and flourish. She certainly had a role model in her mother. Rachel had Faye and Charlie, Dinah, Jan, and Eliza. She had bridge friends, and friends at the girls' school. She had Ben. And she had Katherine—who returned with an incredibly good lunch.

Steve Bauer arrived minutes later. He checked Rachel's chart, the monitor, and the IV drip. He lifted her lids and studied her pupils. He called her name, then leaned closer and called it again. He left the room to order another lung scan. Within minutes, the necessary equipment was wheeled in. Jack sent the three girls out to walk around in the sun. He and Katherine waited in the hall.

He stuck his hands in his pockets and blew out a frustrated breath.

"She'll make it," Katherine insisted. "There are too many people working too hard to make her live."

"The point isn't just to make her live. It's to make her wake up and be well." He thought about Faith Bligh. "She could wake up not whole. You asked me once what I'd do then. I think I'd be destroyed."

"Would you leave?"

"No." It was a sober admission. "No. I couldn't." When Katherine said nothing, he met her gaze. It was open and warm. "What?" he asked, vaguely embarrassed.

"Man has risen to the occasion," she declared. The words were no sooner out of her mouth than her eyes flew toward Rachel's room. "Oh, man," she murmured, folding her arms on her chest.

Jack followed her gaze. All he could see was Steve Bauer, alternately watching the technicians and looking out into the hall at them. And there was Katherine, with windblown air and warm apricot cheeks.

"Did I miss something?" he asked.

She bowed her head and made a strangled sound. "Don't ask. This is *so* not the right time."

He disagreed. If that strangled sound she had made was related to a laugh, the time was right. "I could use a lift. Make me smile."

She was sober when she raised her head. "He's a great kisser. What should I do?"

Jack did smile. He liked the doctor. The smile faded when he realized what she meant. "Ah. The old breast thing."

She settled against the wall and looked into the room again. She kept her arms folded and her voice low. "He didn't try to touch them, but he will. Men always do. It's only a matter of time."

Jack tried to imagine what he would want if he were Bauer. He thought about Rachel. All too well he remembered arriving at the hospital that morning, unprepared for what he would find. "I think you should tell him. If it were dark, would he know?"

"By feel? Yes. Silicone was the best, but it's been banned. Mine are saline. There's a difference."

"Then tell him. You'll be too nervous to enjoy it, if you don't."

She made another of those strangled sounds. "Yeah,

well, I'd have thought that, too, before he kissed me. I didn't have time to think of much, it was that good. I mean, he did *everything* right."

"It's chemistry."

"It was chemistry with Byron. Funny how body mutilation can kill a good thing." She pressed her lips together and met his gaze.

"And you don't want it killed," Jack said, "so there's more at stake this time."

She nodded.

Jack tried to think of all the women he had dated. The ones before Rachel hadn't been anything special. The ones after had been nice enough, but Jill was the first he had viewed as a friend. For a while he had thought she might be it. But she wasn't Rachel. Poor Jill wasn't Katherine, either.

Hard to believe, but he liked Katherine a lot. Totally aside from all that she gave Rachel and the girls, she did things for him, too. Like now. Confiding in him. Telling him things he guessed she would normally tell only another woman. She made him feel like his opinion mattered, which was quite a compliment from a woman as strong as Katherine.

"There's an analogy here," he said, reaching out to tuck in a windblown piece of hair, then leaving it because it looked so nicely undone. "Samantha was sure Lydia wouldn't want any part of her. I told her it was a test. If Lydia didn't, then she wasn't the friend Samantha thought, so the loss wasn't as great. The same goes for you. Any man who loses it because of what you've been through isn't worth your while."

"Easy to say. You're not the one baring all."

He understood that. It had to be hard for Katherine to

open herself to the kind of rejection she had already experienced twice. "But breasts are only a small part of a woman, and pretty fickle things, when you get down to it. They swell, they shrink, they sag. Intelligence is more constant. So is warmth, and humor. So is loyalty. Truthfully? If Steve was younger, I'd warn you off. Breasts mean more to young guys. They're a symbol. I'd be lying if I denied it. But Steve's not a kid. He's been around the block. Look at him in there with Rachel. He doesn't have to be here. It's Sunday. Give a guy like that the choice between a bimbo with natural knockers and an intelligent, warm, funny, loyal, beautiful woman with rebuilt ones—come on, Katherine, no contest. Hell, I'd go after you myself if I weren't still in love with my wife."

JACK'S wife remained unresponsive to the clot buster. The scan showed no noticeable improvement in the passage of air through her lungs, and on the outside, to the eyes and ears of the people who loved her, the symptoms didn't ease. The doctor said it would take longer. He wouldn't say how *much* longer.

Sitting with her that afternoon, Jack thought about love, but he couldn't relate to it in the abstract, only in specifics. Eighteen years ago, love had meant spending every free minute with Rachel. Seventeen years ago, it meant making monthly payments on a small diamond ring. Sixteen years ago, it meant marrying her; fifteen years ago, having a child.

Men like action, Katherine had said during one of their earliest discussions. He had made it into a semantic argument, but the truth was that he did like action. Having admitted that he loved Rachel, he wanted to *do* something. Talking to her, moving her arms, applying Vaseline to her lips or scented lotion to her legs was only part of that.

He wanted to believe she would wake up, and wanted things to be right when she did. He had gotten Hope through her picnic and Samantha through her prom. Okay, so he had canceled doctor and dentist appointments, but they could be done later. Right now, he needed to paint. He needed to frame. He needed to buy a car.

chapter twenty

THE CAR JACK BOUGHT was technically a truck. It was a large, loaded, four-wheel-drive vehicle with power, luxury, and class, and if Charlie Avalon wanted to accuse him of flaunting his money, he didn't care. He wanted the best for Rachel and the girls. He didn't know why in the hell he had busted his butt to make money or what in the hell he was saving it for, if not this.

And he could afford it. How well, he discovered in Rachel's studio that night. He hadn't planned on scrutinizing his finances, had hooked his laptop to the modem for the sole purpose of transferring money from one account to another for the car. Then he set about framing more of Rachel's pieces. The girls were helping. Hope had done it once, and Samantha was a quick study. In no time, he had Samantha predrilling holes and Hope applying wood glue. He was the one using the miter saw to cut the molding to size, then hammering the nails in once the wood was glued, but neither job was taxing. His mind wandered. Transferring money had put a bug in his ear. So, when it was time for a break, he went back to the laptop and accessed other of his bank records. After another round of leveling and bracketing corners, he accessed his investment accounts.

He hadn't deliberately saved money in the years since his divorce. He simply hadn't spent much. He also discovered, several links later, that San Francisco real estate was at a healthy high, which meant that the value of his house had appreciated considerably.

He was, it seemed, fairly well off. For a guy who had started with nothing—with *less* than nothing when school loans were factored into the equation—he had done well.

That thought gave him the same kind of good feeling that Katherine's confiding in him had.

When Hope put her head down on the worktable, he sent her to bed. Samantha worked a while longer. He knew she had to be exhausted, given what she had been through the night before, but he suspected she was feeling some of what he was. As important as visiting with Rachel was, after a while it was discouraging. Working here, there was progress.

She didn't say anything about the paintings themselves. Given the strength of her initial objections, he guessed that was asking too much. He chose to let her prolonged attentiveness to the framing speak for itself. By the time she finally went off to her room, six paintings were one step away from being done and ready to hang.

Alone, Jack went to work on a wolf. It was a beautiful thing, lying low in a carpet of khaki green summer grass, with the top of its head and body outlined, white fur backlit by the sun. Rachel had gone to the Arctic the summer before, with the girls this time. Studying the photographs she had taken, he wished he had been along. He found prints of wolves in packs, hunting, and at play. There was a primal power to them, foiled by surroundings that looked quiet and serene, in those things much like Big Sur. He felt Rachel's appreciation in these prints, in her field sketches, in the wolf she had brought to life with her brush. Jack's challenge was to render that appreciation in an understated backdrop.

She had used mixed media for this one—india ink for the detail of eye and muzzle, acrylic for the fur, watercolor for experimental patches of distant grass. The choice was just right. She had that vision. He was awed enough to hesitate, wondering if he was foolish to touch the canvas, if he could do it justice or would only ruin it.

Then he pictured Rachel, blue around the lips and gasping for air. Wanting, wanting to do it for her, he dug deep inside and began.

Warming up with a large brush on the distant grasses, he used a light watercolor wash of gray, ocher, umber, and green. He gave it depth with charcoal and sap green, gave it warmth with sepias. Layering acrylic over watercolor edges, he moved inward. He kept the grasses neutral in color, but textured. Though Rachel hadn't put flowers on her canvas, they were on her field sketches. Several photographs depicted them well, cotton flowers, like the wolf, caught from behind by the sun.

Did she want them added?

It was his decision to make, but no decision, really. He saw harmony between animal and plant life in a barren land. The flowers were a must.

He stayed with acrylics to re-create the small cotton buds. When they didn't capture the halo effect he wanted, he switched to a white pencil with a dulled tip, blending the lines with his finger, then a tissue, then a cotton swab. Nearly there, he put a scrap of paper toweling around the end of the swab and polished the buds. Satisfied at last, he stepped back.

IT WAS NEARLY five in the morning when he cleaned up. He slept for two hours and awoke exhausted. Samantha said she was too tired for school. Hope said she wanted to be with Rachel. He called the hospital, praying that Rachel had improved, but she hadn't.

He pushed his hands through his hair. "I'll be running around talking with the doctors. Your mother would want you in school, and it would do my mind good to know you're there. I'll pick you up right after. You can see her then."

Samantha argued as they drove, but he held firm. He needed time alone with the doctors to express fears that he didn't want the girls to hear.

When he pulled up at the school, Samantha didn't budge. Where a mutinous pout would have been days before, now there was sheer apprehension.

He tried to understand what she was feeling. "Lydia had no problem with this."

"There's all the other kids. And Pam and Heather. And *Teague.*"

"Teague," he said, monitoring his language with care, "is not worth your spit. As for Pam and Heather, they're not much better if they side with him. Life is about making choices, Sam. You can go in there and try to salvage something with Pam and Heather. Or you can stick with

Lydia." When she didn't speak, he said, "It's hard. I know."

"It's *mortifying*."

"Yes." He sighed. "But the sooner it's done, the sooner it's done, if you get my drift." He put his elbows on the steering wheel and watched a line of reluctant teenagers stumble from a bus. He looked back at Samantha. If she wore makeup, it was light and more in keeping with the natural curl that, for a change, she'd left in her hair. "I was wrong the other night."

"You? Wrong?"

"When I told you how gorgeous you looked all dressed up. You did look gorgeous, but you look even better now. More beautiful. More you."

She flipped down the visor and moved her head in the mirror. "I look dorky."

"Beautiful. Anyone says different, they're jealous."

She scooped her hair back. Without the sleek swing, the effect was more feminine.

"Here goes nothing," she mumbled, flipping up the visor. She opened the door and had barely stepped out when Lydia came toward her. The door closed with a solid new-car thud.

One down, Jack thought, and looked back at Hope. She seemed a great distance behind him, belted safely in, but too far away. When he motioned her forward, she unbuckled herself, shimmied into the passenger's seat, and sat.

"What, sweetie?"

So softly that it was nearly a whisper, she said, "I have a funny feeling."

"Funny feeling?"

"I want to be with Mom. Like I was with Guinevere."

Jack's heart buckled. He reached over and pulled her into a hug over the center console. "Your mother isn't dying," he said into her hair. "We won't let her die."

"I said that about Guinevere."

"Guinevere had a tumor."

"Is a tumor any different from a blood clot?"

"God, yes," he said, wondering how long she'd been agonizing over that. "A blood clot isn't poisonous in itself. It just gets in the way until we break it up. A tumor has bad stuff in it. It grows and spreads and does sick things to the places it touches." It was a simplification, possibly inaccurate, but hell, he was doing his best. "They can just give her a megadose of that medicine to bust up the clot, then we'll fight harder than ever to wake her up."

"How?" came her small voice.

"I don't know. I don't know, but we'll think of a way."

THEY couldn't give Rachel a megadose of medicine. They hadn't even continued the drip through the night. "It's a question of weighing the risks against the benefits," Steve explained. They were in the hall—Jack, Steve and Kara, two residents and a nurse who had worked with Rachel, and Cindy. "Anticoagulants thin the blood and break up the clot, but thinning the blood raises the risk of bleeding elsewhere. We don't want Rachel bleeding."

Jack agreed. But he was frantic. "Why isn't she responding?"

Steve shook his head. When none of the others offered an explanation, he said, "We'll start another dose of the same drip, and then just watch her closely."

JACK did that himself. Lowering the bed rail, he sat on the bed and exercised Rachel's hands and arms. He told her that the medicine was working in places they couldn't see, and that it was only a matter of time before her breathing quieted and her coloring improved. He went so far as to say that once those things happened, she would wake up.

"Sounds like a course in the power of positive thinking," David Sung said from the door. He wasn't a tall man, but he wore his suits well. Today's was a light gray plaid. His hair, eyes, and shoes were dark, shiny, and straight.

He entered the room with those dark eyes on Rachel and put the heels of his hands on the bed rail across from Jack. "I thought I'd come see for myself what's happening here, maybe give you a little support." He swore softly. "I can see why you're scared. I hadn't realized it was this bad."

Jack was just edgy enough to lash out. "Did you think I was joking? Made it all up, just looking for an excuse to get out of work for a couple of weeks?"

David held up his hands. "Hey, this isn't my fault."

Wasn't it? If David hadn't pushed, the business wouldn't have grown as fast, Jack wouldn't have been sucked in and blinded, Rachel wouldn't have left him and moved to Big Sur and been hit by a car on the coast road.

But no. Too easy to shift blame. Jack could have stopped the treadmill at any time. He could have stepped off.

David pushed his hands into his pants pockets. It was

a sure sign of deliberate restraint. "Let's start over. Is she showing any improvement?"

Jack blew out a breath. "Nah. Not yet."

"How're the girls doing with this?"

"Hangin' in there."

In the silence that followed, Jack didn't look at his partner. He didn't want to talk business, but business was all they shared. Once, he had thought it might be different. But David had never had a family. He had divorced one wife after another. Even after Jack, too, was divorced, they didn't mesh on a personal level the way they had when they were back on the bottom rung.

David cleared his throat. "Listen, Jack, I don't mean to be the heavy . . . " He tore his eyes from Rachel and glanced back at the hall. "Uh, can we—can we talk out there? It doesn't seem right talking work in here."

"It's okay. It's good for Rachel to hear voices. Say what you want."

It was a minute before David did. His voice was subdued, but the words came fast. "You're right. This is a family emergency. It's tough. I'm sorry I didn't see that sooner"—he took a breath—"but the truth is, I'm worried. Something's going on here that I don't get."

Jack threaded his fingers through Rachel's. They looked bare. He wondered what she had done with her wedding ring.

"We had no business losing Boca," David said. "We can't afford things like that, any more than we can afford to take on the kind of house designing we did ten years ago. The word over lunch at Moose's is that we're passé. So rather than doing client development, I'm doing damage control. This isn't where I want to be at this point in my life."

"Me, neither," Jack said. Odd, given Rachel's condition, but only now was his middle starting to knot.

"So okay, we lost Boca. It was more trouble than it was worth. Okay, we lost associates. We can hire others. But on principle alone we can't do Hillsborough. It's too small, too minor. We need Montana, which is still up in the air but which is ours if you can get up there to argue the last design in person, and"—he grew expectant—"we need Atlantic City."

"What's in Atlantic City?"

"A new hotel," he said with barely banked glee. "Big gloss, big press, big bucks."

Jack didn't share his excitement. He wasn't even curious to know more. He didn't like the feel of that knot in his middle, didn't like the buzz that business talk put in his head.

And David went on, still gleeful, still dense. "I've been courting these guys for weeks. They've seen enough of your work to think that they might get something a little different from what the others would do. They want us out there, both of us. We're talking high-rise, Jack."

High-rise? He was talking a casino. A fuckin' casino.

Jack raised Rachel's arm, angled it slowly across her chest. This movement was personal, even intimate. So was Hope's painting of Guinevere, taped to the wall, and the single small braid that Samantha had made on one side of the mass of Rachel's waves. What David described was so far removed from any of this as to be otherworldly.

"Well?" David said, both hands out now, inviting response. "Come on. Did I do good, or did I do good?" He rubbed his hands together. "This could do it, Jack. It's

a biggie, one step beyond Montana. No one'll be laughing at Moose's if we get this nailed down. It'll mean
doing some significant hiring, but we can handle it.
Would-be draftsmen are picking up their degrees as we
speak. They're looking for jobs. The timing couldn't be
better. Okay, it'll mean travel for you and me, but, hey,
you can't—"

Jack's warning look stopped him short.

David dropped his hands. He stared at Jack over the
bed for several long, silent minutes. When Jack made no
attempt to either look away or soften, David sighed.

"I think," he said with deliberate care, "that we've
come to a crossroads. There's this new deal on the table.
It's the moment of truth. I have to know if you're in, or
out."

In or out. In or out. In or out. An ultimatum?

David's eyes remained steady. "The harsh reality is
this. Ideally, Rachel gets better, and you return to your
own life. I want that, Jack. I want it like nothing else.
But harsh reality says there's another side. There's the
chance that Rachel *won't* get better, and you have to
shift things around to accommodate the girls, but sooner
or later you'll have to work, Jack." He was suddenly
pleading. "We've known each other, what, fifteen years?
Thirteen of those we've been partners, working hard for
the same thing, and we're right there, right there, pal.
We're on the verge of grabbin' that big brass ring we've
been running so hard after. Don't blow it now, Jack.
Don't lose sight of what matters. We're too close." His
words hung in the air. Finally, he let out a breath and
straightened.

Jack tore his eyes away and returned them to Rachel.
He counted the breaths she hauled in and pushed out,

indeed a harsh reality. No, he couldn't blame David for her physical condition. But the man stood for everything that had gone wrong between Rachel and him.

"Are you in?" David asked.

Was he? Did he want that big brass ring? Did he want to design that casino and keep running until the next big gold ring came into sight? Was there satisfaction in it? Or challenge? Or *fun?* Did he want the same thing for this firm now that David did?

The choice wasn't cut-and-dried. Building his own firm had been his goal for as long as he could remember. He had given it his heart and soul for years.

Don't lose sight of what matters, David had said. That was the clincher.

Jack raised his eyes and slowly shook his head. He was tired of evading David, tired of erasing messages, crumbling faxes, deleting E-mail, and feeling guilty about it. He was tired of doing projects he didn't like. He was tired of traveling. He was tired of the kind of tension that knotted his middle. "It's not working for me anymore. I want out."

David looked startled. "Out? Out of the *firm?*"

"Wasn't that what you asked?"

"Yeah, but I didn't expect you'd chuck it. This is your firm as much as it's mine."

"Actually," Jack said with a sigh, "it hasn't been that for a while. Isn't that what's been wrong between you and me? It's more yours than mine. I've been pulling back for a while."

David continued to look stunned. Jack couldn't remember when he had ever seen his partner that way. David's confidence had been a mainstay of the partnership. Jack was sorry to undermine it now, but if David

Sung was nothing else, he was a hustler. He would survive.

"Regardless of what happens with Rachel," Jack said, "I want to downsize. I want to represent people; you want to represent conglomerates. I want Hillsborough. You want Atlantic City. It's time we split."

"Just like *that?*"

Jack rubbed his forehead. His thoughts were fragmented, but they were all headed in one direction. "Not just like *that*. There were good years. And there are details. People to reassure. Tina, some of the others. Assets to split." *Still,* David was stunned. "Why are you surprised? You're here now. You *see.*" Loudly, rhythmically, Rachel breathed in, breathed out, breathed in, breathed out. "This is not a vacation. It's my *life.*"

Perplexed now, David asked, "Was it a choice, then? Me, or your marriage?"

"Christ, no." Jack pushed his hands through his hair. "It's been me all along. Me, biting off more than I wanted to chew. Me, learning the *hard* way that I'd bitten off more than I wanted to chew. I just want out, David. I'm tired."

David looked appalled. "Do you *know* what you're giving up?"

Jack actually laughed. "No. I'm too tired to give it much thought. All I know is I'm out."

"*Fuckin' A.*"

Jack was tired of that, too. It had been funny once. Not anymore.

Suddenly it seemed that David needed to recoup the emotional advantage he had lost. More sharply, he said, "She left you once. So now you're out of work. Does she need that?"

"Hey," Jack warned. "We did well together for too long to become enemies now. Let's just quit while we're ahead."

"Are you gonna open your own fuckin' firm, or what?"

Jack's voice rose. "I don't *fuckin'* know."

David stared at him for the longest time, then turned on his heel. The last Jack saw of him he was shaking his head and picking up the pace of those shiny black shoes. Only when he was completely gone from sight did the enormity of what Jack had done hit him, and then he was as stunned as David had been. Stunned, but relieved. Relieved. Incredibly relieved. Though he hadn't planned it this way, another of those weights had been lifted. He was suddenly breathing easier.

Then it struck him that he wasn't the only one who was. He looked at Rachel, swallowed, listened. The noise was easing, it definitely was. Holding his breath that he wasn't imagining it, he rang for the nurse.

SAMANTHA was fine as long as she was with Lydia. Lydia was the charm that instantly put her back in good standing with Shelly and Brendan, which said something for how badly Samantha had underestimated Lydia's strength. Come second period, though, she was on her own, heading for American history with Pam.

She took her seat without looking around and focused on the teacher, which was fine, until the teacher began to drone. Her pen slowed and her mind wandered. She imagined that every other bored person in the room was staring at her back, and kept her eyes on the teacher and a confident mask on her face, all the while remembering how foreign she had felt at that party and how scared she'd been with Teague. She didn't look back, not even when she thought she heard the rustle of note passing behind her.

An eternity later, the bell rang. She closed her notebook, pushed her things together, and slid out from behind the desk. She had no sooner reached the hall than Pam fell into step beside her and said, "I don't care what the others say, I still think you're okay. So you couldn't handle Teague. I had a feeling he'd be a little much for you."

"A little much?" Samantha asked, feeling something but not sure what it was.

"Well, I mean, he's more than you're used to, isn't he? Like, he's totally cool. Is *Bar-rendan* totally cool?"

Annoyance. That was what Samantha felt. She had seen Pam drinking, dancing, laughing her head off over a half-naked dancer. Pam had seen her leave the party with Teague. Had she tried to stop them? "No, Brendan isn't—"

"See?" Pam cut in. "I *knew* you'd agree. So I forgive you. If you want to sit with us at lunch, we'll let you. By the way, is that natural curl? What, did you sleep too late to blow it out?" She was walking at an angle to look, bouncing on the balls of her feet. "I know *the* best stylist in the center. He'll get that straight."

"I don't want it straight," Samantha said. *More beautiful. More you.* It was something her mother would have said, too.

Pam made a face. "You like it *curly?*"

Samantha stopped walking. "Actually, I do."

Pam stopped, too. "It's very . . . Lydia."

Life is about making choices. "Thanks," Samantha said

with a pleased smile. "Hey, I have Spanish. I have to run."

Pam tossed her shiny black, stick-straight hair over a shoulder. "So, are you meeting us for lunch, or not?" she asked. "Because if you're not, that's it. I mean, forget it. I'm through sticking my neck out. If you want to be with Lydia, *be* with Lydia."

Samantha took a last good look at the most popular girl in the class. She moved closer, focused in. "Is that eye makeup? No, it's a blackhead, right there on the side of your nose. *Gar-rowsss.* Do you have a skin doctor? Like, I never needed it, but there's one I've heard *great* things about." She glanced at the clock. "Omigod. I'm late. See you around."

HOPE tried to concentrate, but she had that *feeling.* Something was happening; only, when she tried to decide whether it was something good or bad, she couldn't. Her head was too full of things that had to do with her mother and her father—whether her mother would wake up, whether they'd get back together, what would happen if they did, what would happen if they *didn't,* whether Rachel would *die* first—and Hope still missed Guinevere, still woke up mornings aching to hold her.

The class ended. She filed out with the others, but when they turned right, she turned left. She ducked into the bathroom and closed herself in a stall, but stayed only long enough for the bathroom to empty. Then she went out and walked down the hall like she had every reason to be headed for the door. *If you hold your chin up and act like you know what you're doing, people will think that you do,* Rachel always said. She had been talking about going to things like birthday parties, because Hope *knew* that everyone would be staring when she got there, unless she pretended that they were all just waiting for her to arrive because she was the best part of the group. At least, that's what Rachel said.

Hope held her chin up and pretended there was a note filed in the principal's office saying that her mother was waiting outside to take her to the dentist. She fingered her jaw as she went down the steps, frowned toward the curb where the parents usually waited, even looked off down the street. She checked her watch. Apparently her mother was late. She figured she'd walk down a little way to intercept her. That wasn't against the rules. She wasn't in elementary school anymore.

Off she went. She walked with confidence until she reached the corner, then turned it and ran until she came to a spot where she could catch a bus. No one else was waiting, which meant that either the bus had just come or there was no bus at all. It didn't run during the winter. She couldn't remember whether it started up again in April, or May.

For a long time, she stood there with her backpack on her back, thinking that she was wearing her lucky boots and that it was about time they did something. She shifted from one foot to the other. She sat down on the curb. She stood again and hopped from foot to foot like a runner waiting for a traffic light to change. Something was happening. She knew it was.

She shrugged out of the backpack and was scrounging around inside to see if she had enough money for a taxi when her boots delivered and the bus came down the road.

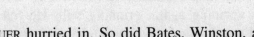

BAUER hurried in. So did Bates, Winston, and everyone else on the floor who had been involved with Rachel's care. The monitor showed improved oxygenation; the gasping was softer; and while her lips weren't the soft pink that Jack loved, they were definitely less blue.

There were high fives all around. Rachel might still be comatose, but everything in medicine was relative.

Long after they were gone, Jack was still grinning, breathing one loud, relieved sigh after another against Rachel's hand. Then, because he needed to hug her and it had been too long, he slid his arms under, carefully drew her up, and fitted her upper body to his. She felt thin and limp; his memory fleshed her out and gave her shape. She smelled hospital white; his own hands supplied threads of paint thinner; his imagination supplied lilies. He closed his eyes on unwanted tears and gave several more immense sighs.

He didn't know how long he held her. There was no rush, no rush at all. When he opened his eyes, Katherine was smiling.

Very gently, he settled Rachel into the pillows. He could have sworn her lips were more pink than they had been when he had picked her up, and guessed that it was from holding her, perhaps from nearness or the change of position. In any case, it was a gratifying sight.

"Steve called and told me the news," Katherine said. "He was nearly as excited as I was." She came to the bed. "This is a good sign. A good sign."

Jack thought so, too. As far as the doctors were concerned, the medicine had finally kicked in. As far as Jack was concerned, Rachel had been listening in on his conversation with David and had reacted with a show of support. He was grinning again, grinning still. He felt so tired, so good, so *shocked*. "Katherine, I just deep-sixed my job."

"You what?"

He told her about David's visit. "We'll be dissolving the firm."

"Wow," she said, then, "Good for you. You'd outgrown it. Besides, you have a name. You can work on your own, whenever, wherever."

"Yeah, well, I want to work out of Big Sur, but that's Rachel's turf. For all I know, she wants no part of me."

"Is that what you think?"

"I don't *know* what to think, since she isn't talking. You're her best friend. You've heard her side. Do you think she'd consider giving it another try?"

Katherine held up her hands. "Not my place to say."

"You know her. Give me a hint."

Cautious, she said, "A try, as in living together? Remarrying?"

"Remarrying," Jack said, since it was a day of shockers. He felt a twisting inside when Katherine looked troubled. "Come on. Say it. I'm a big boy."

"It's not that. It's this. One crisis is over, but the other goes on. You want her back based on memories of how it was during the best of times. But what if it isn't ever like that again? What if she wakes up and can't walk or talk?"

"We've been through this before."

"What if there's permanent brain damage, so that she can't think the way she used to? What if she can't understand what it takes to paint? Or to cook a meal, or drive a car, or bathe?"

"Why are you obsessed with this?"

"Because it's part of what it means to love Rachel."

"But why are you *pessimistic?*"

"I'm *not,*" she cried, then composed herself and said a quieter "I'm not, but I could be. I could assume that next month or next year I'll find that they didn't get it all and my cancer has spread. For a year or two after my diagnosis, I panicked every time I felt a pain. Then I decided that hope was a better way to go. I choose to believe that I'll live to grow old. But there are no guarantees. If I become involved with someone, he has to know that."

Ahhh. Jack understood. She was asking him what she would have to ask Steve Bauer. Jack could argue that Rachel's situation was more traumatic. If Katherine woke up one day with a recurrence of cancer, there would be treatment and remission and, still, the possibility of some good time. If Rachel woke up mentally diminished, there would be nothing.

No. That was wrong. There would be something. But it would be different.

He guessed that was what Duncan had experienced with Faith. Life after the accident was different. Duncan changed jobs. He learned to do things around the house. He gave up much of what was social in their lives, all because he loved Faith.

If that old, leathery clod of a mountain man could do it, Jack certainly could.

One thing was for sure. If Rachel woke up disabled, he didn't trust that anyone else could take care of her the way he would.

He said a quiet "You didn't answer my question. Do I have a chance? Is the feeling there? Or gone?"

Katherine looked past him at something and brightened, then frowned almost as quickly.

Jack turned to find Hope at the door. Her hair was a mess of blond waves. She was breathless and sweaty. Wide eyes were on Rachel.

He started toward her, but she ran past to the bed. "I *knew* it!" she cried, breaking into an excited smile. "I *knew* something was happening, only I didn't know which way it would go." She hugged Jack, jumping up and down, then gave Rachel a big, smiling, smacking kiss on the cheek. When she straightened, she breathed out a satisfied sigh and looked triumphantly from Jack to Katherine and back.

Jack felt as though he ought to scold her, but he couldn't figure out what for. It was Katherine who finally cleared her throat and said, "Uh, Jack, maybe you should call the school before they call the cops, and tell them she's with you?"

KATHERINE had to return to work, Jack had to call his lawyer, and Hope had to put several more braids in Rachel's hair. By the time she announced she was hungry, Jack was starved. He took her to lunch in downtown Monterey and returned to the hospital in time to open more gifts from Victoria—cotton nightgowns, perfume and powder, and no less than a dozen CDs, all symphonies. They had moved Rachel back to a regular room, where Jack promptly fell asleep with his head on the bed near her hand. When he woke up, it was time to get Samantha. He talked with his lawyer again while the girls were busy with Rachel, then he told Rachel about dissolving the firm. He drove the girls back to Big Sur, cooked dinner, and went to the studio.

Samantha worked with him for a while before heading off to make calls. Jack was relieved enough that she was back to normal to let her go. Hope continued to work by his side until he finally sent her to bed. They had framed another six pictures that night. Twelve were done in all. They couldn't do much more until Jack finished painting.

He chose a canvas depicting a great egret spreading its wings for takeoff. His task was to fill in the murky dusk of the Florida Everglades against which the white bird was poised. He had barely taken up palette and brush when Hope returned. She wore a T-shirt that reached her knees and nothing on her legs and feet.

"Everything okay?" he asked.

She nodded. Her hands were linked behind her. She looked like she just wanted to hang around. So Jack started talking about the canvas. He told her why he mixed certain colors and showed her the effect of different brushes.

She watched what he did, nodded, said the kind of distracted "Uh-huh" that suggested her mind wasn't on it. After a few minutes she began wandering around the studio. He watched her make one leisurely turn, then another. Each time, she stopped at the desk backed against the wall.

"Hope?"

She shot him a smile that was a little too bright, shrugged, and moved on. But she was back in the same spot three minutes later.

He set down his things and went to the desk. His laptop was there, closed. Several shop drawings lay under it, but they wouldn't interest her. They didn't interest *him*. He had only planned to study them later as a concession to his lawyer, who suggested that he complete as much of the firm's work as he could until a dissolution agreement was signed.

"What's going on in that pretty head of yours?" he asked.

She spoke quickly, barely opening her mouth. "There's other stuff here. I'm not supposed to know."

"What stuff?"

"Sketches."

"Where?"

She made an offhand gesture toward the desk. "Behind."

From where Jack stood, he saw nothing. Only when he leaned over to where the desk hit the wall did he see the edge of something wedged behind. Dragging the desk forward, he removed a slim portfolio. He set it down with care, remembering the last time he had opened a surprise portfolio. Then he had learned about a child he had lost.

With some trepidation, he opened this one—and was suddenly back in life drawing class, sitting with Rachel, drawing nudes. She had used charcoal on thick ivory rag. The view was a rear one—hips, torso, shoulders, head. Without a face it might have been anonymous. But that was his shape, his hair, his scar at the back of the elbow, all drawn with such feeling that the sorrow of things lost rushed through him.

He paused. The scar was from a runaway piece of scaffolding. It was six months old. Rachel had seen it and commented on it once when he had come for the girls.

Wishing that she was right there right then, he turned from one sheet to the next to the next. Some had been done with charcoal, others with watercolor. Some had features as distinct as his profile, others were as faceless as the first. But her voice spoke, answering his question in each and every one.

Is the feeling there? Or gone? Katherine hadn't answered because Hope arrived. Hope must have heard.

She had given him a gift, but by the time he turned to thank her, she had gone.

chapter twenty-one

JACK SHOULD HAVE been used to being woken by the phone, but he jumped as high as ever when it rang Tuesday morning at dawn.

He reached it on the first grab. "Yes?"

"Mr. McGill?" The voice was authoritative. "This is Janice Pierce. I'm one of the residents—"

"What happened?" he cut in, sitting up.

"Rachel is starting to move."

He was utterly still for a second. Then he dared breathe, but barely. "She's waking up?"

"Not exactly. She's moving her fingers and toes."

"Moving them how?"

"Wiggling. It's spontaneous. Not in response to commands. We call it 'lightening,' as in limbs that have been dead weight becoming lighter. Typically, it starts from the outside and moves in. It definitely boosts her GCS score."

"Which means?"

"She may be starting to wake up."

"May be," he repeated, wanting to hope, but Rachel

had moved before. He had seen her blink, flinch, whatever.

"It doesn't always lead to full awakening," she said. "This could be as good as it gets. But it's more than we've had so far. We thought you'd want to know."

THE GIRLS had heard the phone and were beside him even before he hung up. He told them what Janice had said. Within five minutes, they were dressed and in the car.

The air outside was moist. Fog floated in pale gray bands through the woods and over the narrow road. Sitting higher in the new car than he had in the old, Jack should have been able to see more, but anything too distant was a blur.

As he turned onto the highway and picked up speed, he struggled not to get carried away. He had read enough to know that comatose responses were unreliable. The movement might end before they reached the hospital, having been nothing more than the last little spasms in limbs that would never move again. Or this kind of movement could go on forever, never spreading beyond fingers and toes.

Still, his hopes edged up along with the sun behind the fog.

WHEN THEY arrived, Rachel was propped on her left side. There was no sign of movement. Pillows held her in place. She lay as still as ever.

Fearful, Jack eased lank blond hair back from a face

that was growing thinner by the day. "Hi, Rachel. Hi, angel. They told us you're moving. Can we see?"

"Hi, Mommy." Hope crowded in beside him. "It's me. We didn't even have breakfast; we just came here first."

"*Move,* Mom," ordered Samantha.

"She won't move if you tell her like that."

"Come on, Rachel," Jack coaxed. "Sun's coming up. It's gonna be a nice one. *That's* poetic, don't you think?"

"*There,*" Samantha cried, pointing at the sheet. "Her foot."

Jack moved the sheet away. When there was nothing, he tickled her sole.

Hope said a worried "That *always* makes her laugh."

"How can she not feel it?" Samantha asked.

"She's still comatose," Kara said as she joined them. "The movement isn't conscious. It usually comes in waves, brief periods of activity alternating with periods of rest."

"Ah!" Jack cried, victorious. "Her ankle jerked!"

"I saw it!"

"Me, too!"

Energized, he straightened. "What do we do now?" he asked the power-pearl lady. "How do we get her to do more?"

"Keep doing what you've been doing. Something's working."

KATHERINE was coming out of the shower when the phone rang. The mirror was covered with steam, but she wrapped herself in a bath sheet before she passed.

"She's starting to move," Jack said without preamble

and went on to describe what he'd seen. "It could be nothing or the proverbial last gasp, but I don't want to let anything go that might help. I thought I'd call her friends and get them in here. Bombard her with stimulation. Can you give me numbers?"

Katherine's first instinct was to make the calls herself. Then she took a slow, understanding breath and went for her address book.

Five minutes later, she returned to the bathroom. The mirror was clearing from the bottom up. She loosened her towel, figuring that this would be easy as pie with her face obscured. She could be more objective that way, less emotional. Rachel was moving right along. She should, too.

But . . . not yet. Opening the medicine chest wide so that the mirror faced the wall, she quickly slathered her body with cream and put on a bra and a blouse. Covered up, she relaxed. She reached for panty hose and let excitement about Rachel erase every negative thought.

JACK called the numbers Katherine gave him, plus others he found in the phone book. He called Faith Bligh. He called Victoria, then remembered a message that she had left for him. She was in either Chicago or Detroit, he couldn't remember which. He settled for leaving a message on her machine in New York.

When Cindy came to bathe Rachel, he drove the girls to school. Then he turned around and drove back to Big Sur. Having lined up successive visits by Dinah, Charlie, and the bridge player, Bev, he knew that Rachel would have stimulation until he returned. Between now and then, he had something urgent to do.

The sun was making short shrift of the fog, unveiling a day as full of color as any Jack had seen. The farmland flanking the road just south of Carmel was green with lettuce and artichoke; the hills beyond were wild mustard yellow. Granite outcroppings on the shore side of the road were a richer gray, almost slate under an emerging blue sky. Beyond rock, the ocean was kelp-green, then aqua descending into a deep, dark charcoal blue. The sky was endless and new.

Turning off the highway at Rachel's road, he felt the glow of familiarity. Oak, sycamore, redwood, even scrub chaparral—all substantial, all thriving. He climbed from the car that was really a truck and stretched, smiled, filled his lungs with air so clear that his body tingled. Inside, the phone began to ring. Hopeful, terrified, he rushed to get it. "Mr. McGill?"

"Yes." He didn't recognize the voice, but the hospital had dozens of doctors.

"My name is Myron Elliott. I'm a developer. I want to talk business."

Jack felt an instant letdown. "What business?"

"I heard about your break with David Sung. I wanted to approach you before others do. My company specializes in building resorts. We like the designs you did in Montana. If you're wondering how we saw those, the answer is a spy, but I won't dwell on that, because I understand that your time is short. We talked with David a month ago, but the price he quoted was, well, ridiculous. I was hoping you'd be more flexible."

Totally aside from the fact that Jack didn't want to be thinking business, he was mildly put off. "Why would I be?"

"You may be joining another firm or going solo, but

in either case, you need to establish your name quickly. We're not as big as the group doing Montana, but we're getting there. We won't overpay, but we'll pay. We'll also offer you more than one project. That would take a load off your mind, wouldn't it?"

It certainly would, if assuring a steady income was his major concern. It was definitely a concern. But major? "Uh, look, I'm not sure I can think about this right now. I'm in the middle of a family emergency. If you give me your number, I'll get back to you." He wrote down the number on the flap of an envelope on the counter.

"We'd like to move ahead on this immediately," the man said. "When will I hear from you?"

Jack pressed thumb and forefinger to his brow. "Today's Tuesday. Give me a week?"

"Can you make it sooner? I need to know if we're in the ballpark. If we are, we'll hold off on seeking other bids until we see something from you."

Jack felt a gnawing in his stomach. The man was right. He needed work. A group that promised more than one job would give him instant security. But a resort? "Friday. I'll call you Friday."

"Good. Great. Talk with you then."

Jack hung up feeling uncomfortable. He didn't want to be thinking about this now. But at some point he had to. According to his lawyer, David was claiming, as his, every prospective client that hadn't yet been signed. Jack could take him to court. Those clients had been developed on Sung and McGill time. They should be split half-and-half.

Did Jack have the stomach for a court case? No. Did Jack *want* those clients? No. He wanted a smaller, more humane practice. That was all.

Tearing off the phone number, he stuffed it in his pocket and went to work. He moved in and out of the house like a man possessed, carrying framed canvas after framed canvas to the car that was, *thankfully,* a truck. When twelve were carefully stacked around foam buffers, he closed the hatch and drove right back to Carmel and P. Emmet's.

Ben was waiting. They quickly carried the pieces inside and stood them against a wall not far from the three paintings already there. Ben's excitement was obvi- ous. He hadn't expected there would be so many new ones. What kept Jack waiting nervously were the man's thoughts about what he saw.

Ben moved in, hunkered down before one, moved on to the next, moved back.

When Jack couldn't bear the suspense, he said, "Well? What do you think?"

"I think she's brilliant," Ben said. "She captured everything I wanted her to. These have the same feeling as the bobcat pups. She listened, she heard, she did." He darted Jack a glance. "Nice job with the frames."

Feeling validated and exuberant, Jack grinned. "Thanks."

WHEN KATHERINE got a midmorning cancellation, she had her receptionist move the two appointments following it to the afternoon, and headed for the hospital.

Cindy was with Rachel, slow-talking as she exercised her limbs. Katherine stood silently, watching in vain for movement. But Cindy was smiling. "Watch." She took a pen from her pocket and pressed it against Rachel's thumbnail. She pressed harder. Rachel pulled her thumb away.

Katherine's heart raced. "Do it again," she said. The movement had been so small, she wanted to make sure it was real.

Cindy pressed with the pen, and there it was, a tiny recoil.

Katherine clapped her hands together, put them to her mouth, and beamed. She was enough of a realist to know they had a long way to go. Reponse to pain was bottom-line basic, but it was a step beyond the random move-ment begun earlier that morning, far and away the best thing they had seen in two whole weeks.

JACK was at the hospital by noon, staking out a bedside spot. By two he regretted making so many calls. Rachel had a steady stream of visitors, but he wanted to be alone with her. When he imagined her opening her eyes, he wanted to be the first thing she saw. Wanted to be the *only* thing she saw. Wanted her to know that he had been there more than anyone else.

It was juvenile. But he was getting nervous. Charcoal sketches might suggest she still loved him; same with framed pictures stashed in a drawer. But the fact remained that she had chosen to leave him. He under-stood now why she had. It was his job to show her that things had changed.

So he sat beside her and talked with the friends who came. He kept track of her movements, looking for the little more that suggested she was coming further out of the coma. She continued to do small things with fingers and toes, occasionally twitching an ankle, elbow, or knee, but there wasn't anything new until that evening. He was helping the night nurse turn her when she moaned. When they repeated the motion, she repeated the moan. Then she settled into silence.

They were small sounds, but his heart soared. He called the girls, who were back in Big Sur after dinner with Katherine. He called Katherine, who had returned to Carmel. He kissed Rachel's pale cheek and told her that she was wonderful, that she was strong, that she could do it, and he waited.

The expectancy was so strong and his adrenaline flowing so fast that he didn't think he would feel tired. But nights on end of moonlighting in Rachel's studio and catching precious few hours of sleep took its toll. He was dead asleep in his chair by the bed when the night nurse came to turn Rachel again.

There was no moan this time. Nor was there motion. Jack would have been discouraged if the nurse hadn't been able to evoke the thumbnail response. It was still there, that recoil.

"Go home," she urged. "We'll call if there's any change. Once she wakes up, she'll need you even more. You should be rested for that."

Jack wasn't so sure about the needing-him-even-more part, but he liked the way it sounded, and the girls were alone. He drove home.

HE FELL into bed at eleven and slept straight until Hope shook his shoulder. His eyelids were heavy. With an effort, he raised one.

"We're taking the bus," she whispered.

He came awake fast then, startled to see that it was light, and late. "No, I'll get ready," he said, pushing himself up, but his head was nearly as heavy as his eyes.

"Sleep longer," Samantha said from the door. "I called the hospital. She's doing the same stuff, but she isn't awake. They promised they'd call when she is."

Jack wanted to get up anyway, but he made the mistake of putting his head down for one last minute after the girls left. He was asleep in seconds.

He slept for another three hours. When he woke up, he called the hospital. Rachel hadn't come any further, but she hadn't regressed. They were pleased.

Jack tried to be pleased, too, but he kept thinking about the possibility that she would be stuck at that point for the rest of her life. He meant what he'd told Katherine. He would take care of her. He would set her up in the canyon she loved and care for her much as Duncan cared for Faith, but, Lord, he didn't want it to come to that. He wanted Rachel with him, in every sense of the word.

Sipping hot coffee, he stood in his boxers at the wall of windows overlooking the forest. It was another beautiful day. The fog had burned off, leaving the earth beneath the redwoods a rich mahogany broken by patches of deep sorrel green. Higher up, where the boughs hung, the needles were a lighter green. Pretty. Peaceful.

He turned around. Same with the house. Pretty. Peaceful. The floors were of natural wood, the sofa was red-and-maroon plaid. The church bench was green, with lilac flowers on fat cushions. The planters that flanked the bench were a deep purple with orange splashes, and brimming with chaotically leggy plants.

Pretty? Peaceful? But the house *was*. It was fun and

full of life, very much the irreverent Rachel he had met so long ago. If the customary brush to use on a subject was a number five filbert bristle, she would use a number five bristle round just to see what she could do. In some cases she ended up with the filbert after all; in others she ended up with something wonderfully unique. That was the Rachel he felt in this house. It was the Rachel he had married.

With that thought, he set off for the bedroom. He searched the dresser and the night table, searched the closet and the bathroom. He searched the kitchen cabinets that he didn't regularly use. He searched the storage pantry. He stood in the living room with his hands on his hips and wondered where she would have put it.

If she had kept it.

She might not have.

He went to the studio and stood, again, with his hands on his hips. He had been working here. He knew what was where. He had explored. But she had hidden pictures of a baby that had died. She had hidden charcoal sketches. Granted, Hope knew about this latter.

On a hunch, he strode back through the house to Hope's room. Everything here was sweet. What better spot for a ceramic angel—and there it was on the dresser, a fat little postmodern cherub with wings, keeping watch over a crystal cut box filled with trinkets, a tiny ceramic cat that may or may not have resembled Guinevere, a comb and brush, a smattering of scrunchies, and a pile of acorns.

If Rachel had wanted something cherished, she couldn't have chosen a better guardian than Hope.

He picked up the angel, turned it over, and slipped two small latches hidden under the wings. He lifted off a back panel, pulled out a velvet bag, and emptied its contents in his hand. There were the pearl earrings Rachel had worn at their wedding, given to her the night before by her father, who had died two months later. There was a National Honor Society key. There was a watch with Minnie Mouse on the face. And the ring.

It wasn't the big flashy ring. He suspected that was in a safety deposit box along with numerous lavish pieces of jewelry given her by Victoria over the years. The ring in his hand was simple and gold. It was the only one that mattered.

JACK was heading for the car, bent on getting that ring on Rachel's finger, when Duncan Bligh came striding down the hill, bellowing, "Saw your truck on my way up from the lower pasture, figured you hadn't left." He stomped to a halt. "My wife wants to see Rachel. I thought I'd drive her up after work. Any problem with that?"

"Uh, no. None." When Jack got his bearings, he was touched. He knew that Faith didn't get out often. "Rachel would really like it. I mean, she's not awake yet, but it could help."

With a single nod, the older man turned to leave.

"Wait," Jack said on impulse and waved an arm back. "I'm heading there now. Since I have the truck, I could put the chair in the back. Show me what to do, and I'll get her in and out."

Duncan's expression was unfathomable. "She doesn't go far without me."

"It means she'd be able to spend longer with Rachel."

Duncan looked up toward his cabin. "I suppose."

After another minute, he started climbing. "Get the truck."

JACK had selfish reasons for wanting Faith in his car. He envisioned forty-five minutes of conversation that would naturally turn on Rachel. There were gaps in his knowledge of her early years in Big Sur. If anyone could fill them in, it was Faith.

And the conversation was easy. Faith was chatty, sitting in her long flowered dress that hid pencil-thin, useless legs. What she chatted about, though, was Big Sur. She talked about the early cattle ranchers and those who traded sea otter pelts. She told of lime smelting and smuggling, of arduously long trips from Monterey by stagecoach. She gave a blow-by-blow of the building of the highway and had something to say about each bridge they passed.

"Tourism has been a mainstay in these parts since the turn of the century," she said, "but tourists rarely understand what living here means. It's an isolated life, and we like it that way. We keep our private roads unpaved and our lives simple. There's little privately owned land, and even less chance for development. Electricity is a recent thing in some canyons. We all lose it regularly during storms. We have no fast-food chains, no banks, no supermarkets." Daylight flashed off her spectacles. "It's a quiet life. We socialize among ourselves from time to time, but people who decide to live here are usually self-sufficient sorts. Artists, yes. Writers. Ranchers, like us. Retirees. People who work at the resorts. Free spirits. Have you walked the beach?" she asked and went on to tell of solstice celebrations, whale sightings, and riptides.

Jack listened to every word, hooked not only by what she said but by the lyrical way she said it. It wasn't until they reached the hospital that he realized he had been warned.

JACK and Rachel were divorced. The hospital personnel knew it. Rachel's friends knew it. Faith Bligh knew it.

So Jack felt a little awkward about the wedding ring. Technically, he had no right putting it on her hand. But he wanted it there. He wanted to think it might help. He wanted her to see it when she woke up.

He thought he did it brilliantly. After parking Faith on Rachel's right side, he went immediately to her left side. He took her hand while he kissed her cheek, then straightened. Holding her hand close to his chest, he worked her fingers through a round of exercises. Slipping the ring on was part of the motion. No matter that it was looser than it had ever been. It was on.

Faith saw it instantly. The eyes behind those small, round glasses flew there—stricken eyes, because she was grappling with seeing Rachel this way. Seconds later, still stricken, she looked back at Rachel's face.

Jack sighed. "Well, hell, I'm trying everything. There's part of me that says if she doesn't want the ring there, she'll open her eyes and tell me so."

"She used to wear it sometimes," Faith said. Her eyes searched Rachel's face. He imagined she was looking for permission to speak.

"At the beginning?" he asked.

"Every year. On the Fourth of July."

Independence Day. Their wedding anniversary. *"Why?"*

"She said there were good things to remember, but it wasn't easy. She always breathed a sigh of relief when that day was done. I kept telling her to put it behind her. If I spent my days thinking about all I could do if my legs worked, I'd be a sour woman. Rachel, bless her, never turned sour. She learned to live with those memories."

"Did you know about the baby?"

Faith tugged a shawl close on her shoulders. "She told me."

"She should have told *me.*"

Faith thought about that. Her creased face was gentle with its little white cap. There was no accusation when she spoke, only resignation. "She said she was also pregnant on your wedding day, and that she wouldn't use that hook again to make you feel guilty or get you back."

He was startled. "We didn't marry because she was pregnant." He pushed his hands into his hair and laughed. "God, that's funny. Victoria had that monstrosity of a wedding planned long before we knew about Sam. I was locked into the marriage by *that*, not by any baby. Victoria didn't care that Rachel was pregnant. It didn't show. No one knew. But if I'd decided I'd had it with that pomp and circumstance, Victoria would have had the shotgun out fast. No, I wanted that baby. Rachel and I both did. Why in the devil would she think I was forced?"

Faith's brow furrowed. "Have you ever had a disagreement with someone? Hung up the phone and walked away and started thinking about the disagreement? Made assumptions and generalizations about the person, and built them up, built them up until they took

400

on the reality of your anger or hurt? Then you saw the person again, and it was suddenly forgotten, just a petty disagreement that carried none of the weight you gave it?" She smiled that warm, sad smile. "Emotions can be potent. They shade things in ways that may have nothing to do with reality. Rachel was feeling the loss of that child. She was upset. She was hurt that you hadn't wanted to come home from your trip even without knowing she was pregnant. It confirmed what she had been fearing for months, that you didn't care. She thought using the pregnancy to manipulate you was the oldest, lowest trick in the book."

That did sound like Rachel. She was principled. Sad here, but true. She should have told him. But he should have come home even without knowing. He should have let her know how much she meant to him, but he had stopped doing that. He had shut down. The trip to Toronto was only the last in a growing case for emotional neglect. He was guilty, and now six years had been lost.

He ran the pad of his thumb over the scrapes that were nearly healed. Her freckles were ready and waiting, as were her lips, her ears, her hair. Her broken leg still needed time in its cast, but her hands could paint.

Where are you, Rachel?

As though in answer to the question, she moved her eyes.

chapter twenty-two

JACK LEANED CLOSER. "Rachel?" Her eyeballs were moving behind their lids. "Rachel?" She could have been dreaming. "Rachel, wake up! Come on, honey. I know you hear me. Open those eyes. *Open* those eyes."

The movement continued for a minute, then stopped. He waited. Nothing.

He grabbed her shoulders, finding them so thin and frail that he held gently, but he held. "Don't go back to sleep, Rachel. *Please* don't. It's time to *wake up!*" But she was doing it again, using the round bristle brush because someone told her to use the bristle filbert. "Okay." He removed his hands and straightened. "You want to sleep, sleep. It's your choice. Me, I'd like to talk with the people who've been so kind as to come here. I'd also like to wake up in time for a showing at P. Emmet's. I wouldn't want to work so long and hard to build a career to the point of being invited by a gallery like that, only to *sleep* through the whole damn thing!"

He crossed his arms and stood back, frustrated enough to be angry. "She's doing this deliberately," he told Faith. "It's a control thing. She's getting back at me for years when she thought I was controlling her, but it's *her* fault for not speaking up. She never talked about control. What did she say? *I don't like San Francisco. I don't want to live in San Francisco. I don't want to be alone in San Francisco.* So what did she do? She left *me* alone there. Gave me a taste of my own medicine. Well, I learned. Isn't that enough?"

Faith simply smiled her sweet, sad smile.

RACHEL didn't move her eyes again, but by the time Jack brought the girls, her lids were ajar. Not much. Just enough to see a tiny rim of white. Just enough to spark the fear that she might open her eyes and spend the rest of her life staring at nothingness. The doctors couldn't get a pupil dilation, but they called this progress. Jack called it torment. He was frantic with impatience.

"That looks totally gross, Mom," Samantha said. "You always tell me to do things well or not at all. Eyelids like that aren't doing it well."

Hope was ducking down, trying to look under those lids and see something that might see her. She had barely straightened when she saw the wedding band. Her eyes flew to Jack. He was wondering whether she thought he had searched her room and would be angry, when she said, "Where did you find this? Did she send it to you? I always wondered where it was."

"She kept it," Jack said. Unsure, he looked from Hope to Samantha and back. "I thought it might help. Anyone have a problem with this?"

NO ONE did. The girls were as restless as he was as the hours passed, and as reluctant to leave Rachel. Ben stopped by. Jan stopped by. Steve and Kara came in and prodded and tested and talked. Nellie stopped by. Charlie stopped by. Cindy turned Rachel, who moaned, then settled back into place with those same barely open eyes. Duncan picked up Faith. Steve came again. Katherine brought in McDonald's for dinner. They waved fries under Rachel's nose.

By nine, Jack and the girls were the only ones left. Hope was pale and yawning, Samantha's mood was sour, Jack was beat.

Still, they waited. They took turns talking to Rachel, saying the same things over and over again, badgering her, begging her, half expecting her to open her eyes if for no other reason than to shut them up.

By ten, they were ready to leave. They drove home in silence. Halfway there, it started to rain. Jack turned off the highway at the bank of mailboxes, downshifted, and felt an odd power climbing into the canyon. He pulled in at the house. They climbed out and stood in the rain.

"I'm taking a walk," he said, suddenly needing action. Walking in the rain at night was something Rachel would do. "Anyone coming?"

"Me."

"Me."

The only thing they did before leaving was to check the answering machine. There were messages for Samantha from Lydia, Shelly, and Brendan. There were messages for Jack from his lawyer and the potential Hillsborough client. Victoria had called from Detroit, ecstatic to hear the news and promising another call. There was no message from the hospital.

Taking raincoats, Jack's cell phone, and the large flashlights that Rachel kept on hand for the outages that Faith had said were frequent in winter, they pulled up their hoods and set off. In open meadow, the rain would have been harder, but the trees gentled the drops. Their pit-pat was a steady whisper. The air was cool and smelled of damp earth and wood.

Hope led the way to the spot where Guinevere was buried. After several minutes there, they moved on with Samantha in the lead, but she turned back and halted the others before they had gone far.

"I'll take you to my place, but it is mine. You can't come here again. Wait. Close your eyes. I'll lead you."

"Nuh-uh," Jack said. "I'm not walking with my eyes closed. If you want to share, you share. Come on, Sam. It's too dark to see a hell of a lot. I wouldn't recognize anything in daylight."

"Hope would."

"No, I won't," Hope promised. "I *swear.*"

Short of shining a light in her face, Jack couldn't see Samantha's expression. But she turned and began walking again. Less than five minutes later, over a course so circuitous that Jack was as lost as he was sure Samantha intended, they arrived at her place. It was another redwood grove, this one with wide trunks that spread and hollowed and straddled uneven ground.

Samantha escaped from the rain into one. Hope slipped into another close by. Jack took shelter in the largest, to the right of the others, in easy view. He skimmed his light at each, saw small bits of color from their slickers, and turned off his light.

The night was thick and black. There was no moon, no fog, just a dense forest under a high, dense cover of clouds. The steady pit-pat of rain was the only real sound. The laughter beside him was pure fantasy, as was Rachel snuggling close. He heard, he felt, he craved.

He settled back, praying that nothing live was behind him, then nearly died when, after a quick scurrying sound, something hit his side.

He twisted away. "Jesus Christ!"

"It's *me*," Hope whispered. "Shhh. I don't want her to know I'm here. She'll think I'm a wimp. But yours is *better* than mine."

Jack laughed. "Damn it, Hope, you just took ten years off my life." But he had an arm around her and was holding her close. When another scurrying sound came, they both yelled.

"What is *wrong* with you people?" Samantha cried, crowding in. "I mean, like, who do you think is out here? *Jason?* Pu-leeze."

Jack was laughing again. He pictured the three of them filling a single redwood trunk, a jumble of arms, legs, and bodies not very different from the jumble on the hill in the photograph that lay facedown in Rachel's drawer, and he was suddenly light-headed. Oh yeah, exhaustion did that, but there was more to it. Crammed in a pitch black hole with his daughters, with more than a few clods of mud and the smell of wet wood and raincoats, he had recaptured something he had thought forever lost.

It was one heartrending thought. Another was that Rachel knew the three of them were there.

She couldn't, of course, unless she was dead and watching from above, but he refused, absolutely refused, to buy into that. No. She was still in a coma, and even if the phone in his pocket rang to say she had woken up, she couldn't possibly know where they were. He was fantasizing again. But boy, was the feeling real.

IT STAYED real. Rachel was with them when they traipsed back through the woods to the house and shook themselves off. She took a shower with Jack, put on a robe that matched his, helped him make hot chocolate for the girls. She took her turn kissing them good night and followed him into the bedroom.

He shook off the fantasy when he climbed into bed, but it returned in a flash. He sat up and stared into the dark. He thought about how tired he was. He looked at his watch.

It was twelve-thirty. He had a sudden urge to drive back to the hospital.

He called there instead and was told that Rachel hadn't woken.

He lay down again and slept for two hours. He called the hospital, lay down again, slept for three hours this time. He called the hospital. He lay down. He got up and opened the window. The rain continued, peaceful and clean, restorative. And he felt it, felt Rachel.

When he turned away from the window, Hope was at the door. She didn't say anything, just hung on the knob and looked at him.

"Are you sensing things?" he asked.

She nodded.

"Me, too." He ran his hands through his hair. So maybe they were both going mad, wanting something so much that it became real in their minds. The only thing he knew for sure was that he wouldn't be able to fall back to sleep. "Wanna take a drive?"

HOPE was belted sideways into the backseat. Samantha was in front, with an elbow against the door and a fist to her chin. Her eyes were closed. Jack kept both hands on the wheel and an even foot on the gas.

The rain had slowed to a drizzle. It was nearly thirty minutes past sunrise on a gray day. Traffic was light. No one spoke.

Jack pulled into what they had come to think of as their normal place in the parking lot, then backed out and picked another spot. The old one hadn't worked. This one might. He looked at the girls, daring them to ask. Neither did.

As they left the car and entered the hospital, he tried to stay calm, but he didn't have the patience to wait for the elevator. He found the stairs and took them two at a time, while the girls trotted close behind. They swung onto Rachel's floor, strode quickly down the hall, and turned into her room—and so help him, despite all cautionary thoughts, he expected to see Rachel propped higher, with her eyes open and alert, and a smile in the works.

He stopped just inside the room. Samantha was on his left, Hope on his right. Rachel was on her back, her eyes that same little bit open that they had been the night before.

"Mom?" Hope called.

Samantha wailed a soft "No change!"

Jack swallowed. His body drained of energy and felt like rubber. Disappointment lay thick in his throat.

He approached the bed. Sitting by Rachel's hip, he put an arm on either side of her and gave her the lightest, softest kiss on the mouth.

"What *happened,* Daddy?" Hope asked.

"I don't know, honey. I guess we got ourselves wound up with wanting."

"This is getting old," Samantha complained.

He let out a breath, then spoke with angry force. "You're toying with us, Rachel. That is not fair. It is not *nice.*" He pushed off from the bed and went to the window, but seconds later he was back at the bed, arms straddling Rachel again.

This time he stared. He looked at her long and hard, willing her to open those barely open eyes. Her lips were pink, her freckles mauve, her hair gold. The rest of her was paler than pale, and thin.

He continued to stare. Something was going on in there. Her eyes were darting around. He saw a pinch between her brows at the very same spot where the worry line was on his own face. It happened a second time, a tiny frown.

He poured himself into it this time, digging deep, cursing her for punishing them with this unbearable waiting game, willing her finally, finally, finally awake. He heard one of the girls call, but he didn't respond. Everything he had was focused on Rachel.

Another frown came. Her eyes began moving more slowly. He caught his breath when she did. Again one of the girls spoke. Again he ignored it.

Come on, Rachel, come on, come on, Rachel.

Her lids fluttered. They shut, then pressed together. Slowly they rose.

Jack was afraid to breathe. After initial gasps from

behind him, there was no sound at all. Rachel's eyes stayed on his face, stayed there so long that he half feared she was still comatose. Then her eyes broke from his and moved past to Hope.

"Mommy?" Hope cried.

Her eyes shifted to Samantha, who said a breathless "Omigod."

When those eyes returned to him, they were confused. Slowly she moved her fingers into a loose fist with the thumb inside. Puzzled eyes went to Hope, to Samantha, and back to him. Jack was beginning to think she might have amnesia when she looked at the girls again and smiled. In a voice that was weak but very Rachel, she asked, "What's doing?"

He gave a shout of relief, and suddenly the girls were crowding in, hugging Rachel, talking and laughing at the same time, and though Jack felt the same exuberance they did and wanted to hug her, too, he gave them room. This was the most important thing, after all, Rachel and her girls. She was awake. She was back. With another shout of relief, he left to tell the doctors the news.

KATHERINE was in bed when Jack called. She bolted upright, ecstatic. "Wide awake?" she asked.

"Wide awake!"

"Speaking? Remembering?"

"She's confused about what happened and what day it is, and she's weak, but awake!"

"Oh, Jack, that is *the* best news! Has Steve been by?"

"He's on his way."

"So am I," she said and hurried into the shower. It was

only when she was under the spray and surrounded by steam that she remembered Jack's dilemma. She was rooting for him. She planned to tell Rachel that.

She turned off the shower and stepped out, letting the steam fill the room. With her back to the mirror, she rubbed skin cream all over her body. By then, the mirror was fully fogged. She worked on her hair by feel, using the humidity to enhance the curls.

Wrapping a towel around her, she returned to the bedroom. The clothes she had chosen weren't right. There would be celebrating today, even, perhaps, if she could work appointments around it, a special lunch. In any event, she would see him. So she picked an outfit she loved, soft pants and a two-tiered top, and returned to the bathroom.

Hooking the clothes hanger over the door, she reached for her bra, thought twice, and exchanged it for panty hose. She pulled them up carefully, flexed her ankles, slipped a hand inside along her hip to even the stretch. Then she reached for the bra again.

She held it, turned it. It was black, one of Victoria's Secret's sleekest numbers. She looked wonderful with it on. She looked sexy with it on. Steve would like it.

And with it off? Her plastic surgeon said her breasts looked good. So did Rachel, who was the only other person in the world she had trusted enough to show. She trusted Steve. At least, she thought she did. He knew what he faced. He had surely seen worse. She didn't think he would run from her, screaming and limp.

It was time she showed the same courage.

The mirror was to her right, and clear now. Drawing herself tall with a deep, deep breath, she stepped before it, and for the first time in months and months, took a good long look.

EXCITEMENT spread down the hall. Doctors came and did their tests. Nurses came and helped. Families of other patients, framed in envy, stood outside looking in.

Jack didn't know what to do. He watched it all from beside the bed, from a spot just behind Rachel's head. He was there, but he wasn't. He felt relief and worry, happiness and fear. He was the ex-husband, relegated to silence again.

chapter twenty-three

RACHEL EMERGED from her coma thinking it was just another day of waking up with Jack on her mind, until she found him there in the flesh, inches from her face, looking worried and involved. Her first thought was that something had happened to one of the girls, but she saw them in her periphery, as alive and intense as Jack. So she went on to thinking that she had imagined Big Sur and six years of life without him. When she looked directly at the girls, though, she saw that they were too old, too tall. Jack's hair was less pecan and more beige, his jaw was rougher, his brow more creased. Oh yes, those six years had passed. With Jack? In San Francisco, with Big Sur wishful thinking?

No. Big Sur was too clear in her mind and heart. She couldn't have dreamed the woods, the cabin, the coast any more than she could have dreamed the aloneness. She was definitely divorced. But there was a wedding band on her finger. It was bigger than it had been last time she had put it on, which was as odd as the way her body felt—tired, heavy, weak.

She was clearly in a hospital. How else to explain coarse white sheets and a medicinal smell? So now she was frightened as well as confused. But the people she loved were all there and alive. Jack must have been the one who brought the girls. He wouldn't stay. He never stayed.

Thinking that mothers had to be strong, she mustered a smile for Samantha and Hope. "What's doing?"

Suddenly, like a paused video starting to play, the two of them came to life. Displacing Jack, they began hugging her, laughing, chattering about an accident she didn't remember, a coma she didn't remember, a broken leg, a blood clot, twitching, moaning, gross half-opened eyes.

She didn't remember any of it. She couldn't grasp the fact that she had been lying there for sixteen days— though the doctors and nurses who came in to look and prod confirmed it. It did explain her weakness and the thinness of her fingers. She had lost weight. Sixteen days without solid food would do that. Other than soreness from intravenous needles, though, she felt no pain. Apparently she had slept through that.

The girls jabbered on about Jack staying at Big Sur, Jack driving them to school, Jack being at the hospital every single day. Jack didn't say anything. He had backed off to the side somewhere. She closed her eyes. Too much too soon. He had come through as a father. She was grateful for that.

She rested a bit. Life was hazy. Sixteen days were a long time to have missed. There were things she was supposed to have done. One by one, those thoughts began to congeal.

When she opened her eyes to ask, Samantha and Hope were sitting on the bed on either side of her, looking at her with wide, frightened eyes. She guessed a sixteen-day coma would do that, too. "I'm here," she said, smiling, when their features abruptly relaxed. But she was still feeling confused. She asked what day of the week it was and what time. She asked why the girls weren't in school.

"We've waited too long for this," Samantha told her. "Dad said we could skip."

Rachel wondered what else he had said they could do. Sunday fathers had a way of indulging. Jack usually did it with money. He would have other means, if he was seeing the girls every day. It sounded like he had scored points. The two of them were pushing his virtues awfully hard, which was especially not like Samantha.

A sweet nurse—*Cindy,* the girls informed her; *she's been helping Dad take care of you; she's wonderful*—cranked up her head a little, then a little more. She was dizzy, but it passed, and the girls began again. Samantha listed off all of the people who had come to visit. Hope told her about the flowers and the cards, the lingerie and the perfume. Samantha told her about Faye's brisket and Eliza's pecan rolls. Hope told her about Katherine's crush on the doctor.

When Samantha told her about the prom, Rachel was heartsick. When Hope told her about Guinevere, Rachel cried.

Jack went off somewhere, which was fine. This was the life she was used to now, just the girls and her. But as soon as he disappeared, the girls started talking about him again.

"He drove down in the middle of the night right after the accident."

"He loves the woods. He takes *us* for walks."

415

"He dug around for the recipe and made your favorite dip for my louse of a prom date, Teague."

"He even made a *coffin* for Guinevere."

"He bought you a new car, Mom. You'll *love* it."

"He framed your pictures, so the show's going on."

"He hasn't worked in two weeks. I think he's changed."

Rachel smiled and nodded, then dozed off, which was a wonderful way of escaping what she didn't want to hear. When she woke up, the girls were staring at her again, frozen, scared.

"Come *on*, you guys," she said, with a laugh this time. "You can't panic every time I fall asleep."

"But you don't know how *awful* it was," Samantha cried, and the two of them proceeded to tell her again, until she couldn't help but get their drift.

"Tell me about the show," she said. "You said that your father framed my pictures?"

"Framed them and delivered them," Hope said.

Samantha added, "Ben's setting things up. We haven't seen much of him lately. Dad's the one who's been here most."

Before Rachel could ask about the less-than-subtle lobbying, Katherine arrived—dear Katherine, who would have kept an eye on the girls even if Jack hadn't shown up—suave Katherine, who actually blushed when the doctor who had earlier introduced himself as Steve returned to the room. The crush Hope had mentioned? *Katherine?* Rachel was overwhelmed. But that wasn't the first thing she asked when she and Katherine finally got a minute alone.

She wiggled her ring finger. "What's with this?"

"Did you ask him?"

"No. Katherine, did *you* call him after the accident?"

"I did," she said, looking defiant. "I figured you'd want him here."

"*Want* him here? He shut down on me. You *know* it still hurts."

"You still love him. That's why it hurts. That's why I called."

"It hurts to *see* him."

"You don't think he feels that, too? You think he's been here for sixteen days for his health?"

"He's here for the girls."

"And you."

"He feels obligated."

"He cares."

"Caring isn't love, and even if it was, you can love someone and still shut them out." Worn out, Rachel closed her eyes and said a muddled "We've been through this, Katherine. You know how I feel."

"So take the ring off," Katherine said.

Rachel didn't, because she was too tired, and a fresh round of medical people were there when she woke up, which would have meant making a public thing of it. Besides, she figured the ring might be a charm. She had been wearing it when she had come out of the coma. She figured she would wear it until she got home.

LEAVING RACHEL'S room, Katherine saw Steve from a distance and, stopping where she was, watched him talk with a nurse, lean down to study a computer, straighten, turn, and smile when a colleague approached. She found such pleasure in watching.

Why him? Because he was skilled, smart, kind, and sensitive? Because he was the right age for her? Because he was the right height, the right weight, the right everything, physically?

When he looked down the hall and saw her, he grinned, said something to his colleague, and started toward her with that lean-limbed walk. He was grinning broadly when he arrived.

"You owe me lunch," he said.

She grinned back. How not to? His pleasure was infectious. She felt its warmth at the same time that she felt a contradictory chill, deep inside, in a spot she couldn't place. "I know."

He gave her a once-over that raised both the warmth and the chill. "You look great." He glanced at his watch, then said in a coaxing way, "I can buy a couple of free hours this afternoon. Can you?"

Katherine made a show of looking at her own watch. That chilly spot inside was growing worse. She grimaced. "I don't know. Thursdays are packed."

"Forget *hours,* plural. Try one hour. Any chance?"

She winced. "I'm already starting off late, being here now. How about Monday?"

His face went through changes—disappointment to doubt to caution—which was another thing about him that worked for her. She could see what he felt. He was definitely suspicious when he said, "Isn't that restaurant closed on Mondays?"

"Only off-season. It's open now."

"Then it's a date?"

"Uh-huh," she said, grateful for the reprieve. "The shop's closed Mondays. I'm free."

"I'll make reservations, say at one o'clock?"

She nodded vigorously.

He smiled again. His lids lowered a hair, gaze dropped to her lips. He mouthed the kind of tiny kiss that no one could see but her, and set off back down the hall leaving her hotter than ever—but only from her knees up. As she headed for the elevator, she located the chill. It was lower.

She had cold feet.

BY THURSDAY afternoon, word had spread that Rachel was awake. By evening, friends were coming by to see for themselves.

Jack had felt awkward enough when just the girls and Katherine were talking with Rachel. It was worse now. He had come to respect her friends and they him, but hearing them sing his praises felt like . . . charity. Rachel didn't do more than glance at him every once in a while, and then, without giving a clue as to what she felt.

So he idled in the hall on the phone, calling his lawyer at home, calling Tina Cianni at home. He intercepted a man delivering a huge bouquet of balloons from Victoria—*incredible! appropriate!*—and with Hope's gleeful help, tied them to Rachel's IV pole. Superfluous once again, he ambled to the door, then leaned against the wall just beyond it. When Steve returned for a last evening look, he caught him before he entered the room.

"What happens now? Is she out of the coma free and clear?" He shared the same fear the girls did every time Rachel closed her eyes. "I read a newspaper story once about a guy who came out of a coma and was talking with his family, as lucid as Rachel. He lapsed back into a coma the next day and later died.''

Steve said, "As I recall, that fellow had been comatose for several years. Rachel's case is more logical. Her head was injured. It took sixteen days for it to heal enough for her to regain consciousness. We'll do scans in the morning, but I don't expect to see anything wrong. She'll be on meds for a while to minimize chance of the swelling returning, maybe a lightweight anticoagulant for six months to make sure there isn't another clotting problem, but that's it."

"When can she go home?" It would be a moment of truth. He had been sleeping in Rachel's bed.

"The IV will come out later," Steve explained. "We'll start her on a liquid diet and move on to soft solids when she's up to it. We'll monitor her oxygenation level for another day, get her out of bed in the morning. We want her eating and walking. Once that's done and she's regained full bladder tone, she's yours."

Jack wished it was as easy as that. "Best guess, how many days till she's out?"

"Three. She should be home by Sunday."

THE GIRLS slept soundly that night. Jack knew, because he looked in on them every few hours. Their ordeal was ending. They were excited enough about Rachel's awakening not to be worried about Jack's future role in their lives, but he sure was. He was worried sick. Sleep came only in short stretches, broken by restlessness and fear. He called the hospital several times during the night. Rachel remained out of her coma. Between hours of healthy sleep, she was drinking juice and eating pudding.

Friday morning, he went to the hospital alone. Her IV pole was gone. Her hair was damp and waving gently, her face was shiny clean. The tray table held a plate with dried egg streaks and toast crumbs, and an empty cup of coffee. She was reading the newspaper, looking as thin and small as Hope in a huge magenta T-shirt. The wedding band was still on her finger, but she looked startled to see him.

"How are you feeling?" he asked, standing just inside the door. Despite all that had been, coming closer seemed an intrusion on her turf. If she wanted him there, she had to let him know.

"Better," she said. "Where are the girls?"

"School. They've missed too much of it. They'll be here this afternoon."

She nodded.

"So," he said, "they got you up for a shower?"

She smiled and nodded. "Uh-huh. They wrapped the cast in plastic. It was a little bulky, plaster and crutches. They're giving me a waterproof one later."

"That's good." He slipped his hands in the pockets of his jeans and looked around. "Do you need anything? Candy? Magazines?"

"No, thanks. I'm fine. When are you going back to the city?"

"I don't know. Not for a while. You'll need some help."

"The girls can help. School will be out in a few weeks."

"Well, between now and then. Unless you'd rather have someone else. If you'd rather have a nurse, I'll hire one."

"That might be best if you have to get back to the city."

A deep dark hole was eating his insides. He had just *said* that he didn't have to go, hadn't he? Hadn't anything the girls said registered with her?

"Perfect timing," said Steve Bauer as he slipped past Jack and went to the bed. "I want you taking another walk down the hall. Jack can take you."

"I'm still tired from the last one."

"You ate. Good. We'll get more in here in a little while. Fatten you up a little. The more you walk, the stronger you'll be and the faster the plumbing will start up again. As soon as that happens, you can go home." He held out a hand.

She sighed, took it, and pushed herself to a seated position. When she was steady there, he handed her a furry red slipper. She fitted it to her foot—bending stiffly, Jack thought. Steve gave her a single crutch, helped her up, then gave her the other. When both crutches were in place, she stood for a minute with her head down.

"Okay?" Steve asked quietly. Jack envied him the intimacy.

She nodded and took several uneven steps.

"Hand hurt?" Steve asked.

"A little, but it's okay," she said. Her voice was as shaky as the rest of her looked.

"Is she up for this?" Jack asked. He imagined her falling and hurting herself more.

But Steve kept an arm around her back, preventing that. "She can't go home until she is." When they reached Jack, he said, "Your turn."

THEY walked slowly and haltingly down the corridor.

"Okay?" Jack asked; then after several more steps, "Hanging in there?" When they reached the end, he said, "You're doing great," and when they were halfway back, "Nearly there."

She gave him single-word answers, clearly concentrating on keeping her balance. By the time they were back in the room, she had broken into a sweat. He helped her into bed and asked if she needed anything. She shook her head and closed her eyes.

Jack was devastated.

"HOW'S MOM?" Hope asked as soon as she climbed into the car. She was still wearing her cowboy boots, which told Jack she wasn't yet completely relaxed.

"She's great," he said and pushed open the door for Samantha, who promptly repeated the question. "She's been up and hobbling around. Had a sandwich for lunch."

"Did you get it for her?" Hope asked.

"Eliza dropped it off before I could." With a glance in the rearview mirror, he pulled away from the curb.

"But you've been with her all day," Samantha said.

"Yup."

"So did you guys talk?"

He shot her a curious glance. "About?"

"Stuff, Daddy," Hope said, leaning in between the seats. "You know. Your living with us and all."

He had figured they were getting at that. It followed, after all of the good things they had told Rachel the day before. "Is your seat belt fastened, Hope?"

"Well, did you?" Samantha asked.

Jack darted glances in the rearview mirror until he heard the click that said Hope was belted in.

"*Dad.*"

"No, Samantha. We didn't talk about that. Your mother's just been through an ordeal." He had been telling himself that all day. "She's concentrating on getting up and eating. Her first priority is getting home."

"What happens then?"

"What do you mean?"

"Are you staying?"

"That depends."

"On what?"

He drove silently, until she repeated the question. He caught Hope's eyes in the rearview mirror. She was waiting for his answer, too.

"On things that your mother and I decide to do," he finally said. "But there's a whole lot of other *stuff* we need to think about before we think about that, so I'd appreciate it if the two of you backed off. Okay?"

"SO DAD's been here all day?" Samantha asked.

They hadn't been there five minutes. Jack was at the window looking out, listening to the girls tell Rachel about school. He hung his head when he heard the question, pursed his lips, waited.

"He has," Rachel said. "It's tricky getting used to crutches. He walked me up and down a few times. He brought me a hot fudge sundae."

"With mocha almond ice cream?" Hope asked in obvious delight.

"Uh-huh. It was good. I'm still sleeping a lot. Funny,

you'd think after sixteen days I wouldn't be tired."

"I think Dad should stay with us," Samantha said. "You know, like, after you get home?"

Jack put a hand to the back of his neck.

"We'll talk about that later," Rachel said.

"When later? You may be home in two days. He's really a good guy, Mom."

"I never said he wasn't."

"Maybe you need to hear his side of the story."

"Samantha," Jack warned, turning to face them.

Hope said, "He did *everything* while you were sick. I mean, he came right down from the city that first day and shopped and cooked and drove us around. He even drove Faith to see you. Did you know he did that?"

"No," Rachel said without looking at Jack. "I'm grateful to him."

"He left the *firm* for you!" Samantha cried.

Jack said, "No, I didn't, Sam."

Blond hair flying, she looked at him fast. "You *did!*"

"I left it for me. For me, Sam. It wasn't working for me anymore, so I gave it up. Don't lay that on your mother, too. It's not like I'm out of work. My phone's been ringing. I can get clients now that I couldn't get before. New doors are open now." He stopped. He didn't know why he had said all that. It wasn't what he wanted to tell Rachel.

"Fine," Samantha said, staring at him with his very own defiant eyes. "But if you go back to San Francisco, I'm going, too."

"Samantha!" Rachel cried, sounding totally displeased, even hurt.

"I can live both places, can't I? And, anyway, it's summer. I can get a job there."

Jack said, "You're not doing that."

"I will!"

"No, you won't, because your mother's going to need your help, and besides, I won't be in San Francisco. I'm moving here. I like it here. I'll buy my own place if I have to." The timing was all wrong to say that. The idea was half-baked. It would never work if Rachel was against it. He resented his daughter forcing the issue. This wasn't Samantha's business. It wasn't Hope's business. It was between Rachel and him. That was all. Rachel and him.

The fact that Katherine was suddenly standing in the door didn't help. Annoyed, he stalked past her, right out of the room, then realized it was another wrong thing to do. He should have told Katherine to take his daughters away. They had given Rachel a rundown on what the last few weeks had been like for them. He needed to tell her what it had been like for him.

But he couldn't turn around and go back. Forget talking. Rachel was barely looking at him. He might have started seeing things differently in the last few weeks, but she sure hadn't.

Disgusted, he went down the hall to the bank of telephones. It was Friday. He had told Myron Elliott that he would call. There was no point in delaying. Regardless of where he lived, Jack didn't want the job.

"WHY DIDN'T you *say* something?" Samantha asked.

"He *loves* you, Mommy," Hope said.

Katherine had approached the bed. "Can I talk to your mom, guys?"

"Someone better," Samantha remarked and, with a

look of disgust at Rachel, grabbed Hope's arm and hauled her out of the room.

Rachel watched them go. "That was a quick honeymoon."

"Why *didn't* you?" Katherine asked.

Rachel's eyes flew to her face. She didn't understand the edge in Katherine's voice. "Why didn't I what?"

"Say something to Jack."

"About what?"

"His leaving the firm. His moving here."

Rachel tried to replay the conversation without opening herself to hurt. "Did he ask my opinion?"

"Do you need a formal invitation? Come on, Rachel. The guy hasn't left your side. Help him out a little here."

"Help him with *what?*" Rachel cried. "Maybe I don't want him moving here. Fine, the girls are attached to him, but maybe I don't want to have to see him all the time. Big Sur is mine. Why does he think he can just barge right in?"

"He loves you, Rachel."

Rachel closed her eyes and turned away.

"Tell him you love him back," Katherine said.

Rachel's heart was aching. It was a veteran at that, where Jack McGill was concerned. "I don't know if I can," she said. She had precious little energy when her heart ached. It had been aching so long.

"What are you afraid of?"

"Depending on him and being abandoned again."

"You'd rather live the rest of your life without?"

Rachel opened her eyes and looked at Katherine hard. She could understand that her daughters would have conflicting loyalties, but her best friend should be on *her*

427

side. "He hasn't said he loves me either, y'know, and don't say he's shown it, because it's not the same. If he loves me, let him say it. Let him go out on a limb and take a risk that I'll say no. Wouldn't *you* do that, if you wanted something bad enough?"

Katherine looked at her a minute longer, then headed for the door. Rachel wanted to ask where she was going, but didn't have the strength.

KATHERINE kept her head down and scowled as she walked. She was angry at Rachel for being stubborn, angry at Steve for being persistent, angry at herself for being afraid to take the kind of risk she just told her best friend to take. She was angry at Jack. And then, there he was at the bank of phones.

JACK had made his call and didn't know what to do next. His life was in a limbo—professionally, personally. The phone booth seemed as good a way station as any.

"What are you doing?" Katherine asked, looking and sounding again like the woman who had thought him lower than low several weeks before.

He was feeling raw. He didn't need prodding from her. Pushing away from the booth, he held up a hand and set off for the elevator. "Not now, Katherine."

"If not now, when?" she asked, keeping up with his stride easily. "You told me you loved her and wanted back into the marriage. Why don't you tell *her?*"

He put a hand over his ear. "Not now, Katherine?"

"Then *when?* What's with you and silence? What's this whole thing been about? Haven't you lost enough time? Jesus, Jack, haven't you learned *any*thing?"

He stopped short and put his face in hers. "Have you?"

That got her fast. She swallowed, blinked, pulled back. She frowned in the direction of the nurses' station, then lowered her eyes.

"Yeah," she said, suddenly humble, "I want to think I have. I took a good look at myself, and you were right. What I have isn't so bad." Flattening a hand on her chest, she seemed to be speaking more to herself than to him. "Am I pleased with these? No. But I can live with them. I can live with them."

She dropped her hand, straightened her spine, raised her eyes to his, and said with determination, "I'm gonna give it a shot, risk that ole rejection, because maybe there's something that's worth it." She smiled, becoming the friend he wanted, needed. "So what's with you? Can't you just do it, too?"

She made it sound easy. He started walking again. "You're talking apples and oranges."

"I'm talking trust," she said, beside him still.

"Christ, Katherine, where's *hers?* She knows I'm done with the firm. She knows I'm done with San Francisco. She *knows* I've been here taking care of her." He stopped at the elevator and faced her. "She hasn't said a goddamned word about *any* of it."

Katherine stared at him, stared deep. He felt genuine caring—from her, from him—when she put a hand on his arm. "Three weeks ago, I'd have said you were a guy through and through. Guys don't think, they don't analyze, they don't understand. They just *do*—whatever, whenever, however. But you can be more than a guy,

Jack." She squeezed his arm. "Why isn't she talking?" She tapped her head. "Think."

She looked at him a minute longer, took a deep breath that he could have sworn reverberated with courage, did an about-face, and started back down the hall.

BY THE TIME she reached the nurses' station, Katherine was starting to tremble. She consciously laced her fingers and kept them low when she asked if Steve was around. There was some confusion and consulting of one another behind the desk. Katherine was starting to wonder if her bravado would hold over for another day when he emerged from a door far down the hall. He spotted her. His blue eyes smiled and closed in fast. The shaking inside her went deeper.

He was still smiling when he reached her. His hands were in his pockets, pushing back the lapels of his lab coat. He raised his brows. "Can you take a break?" Katherine whispered.

He spoke briefly with the nurse at the desk, walked Katherine to the elevator, pushed the buttons both outside and inside. The ride was short, and they were alone. He leaned against one wall, she leaned against the other. She spent the entire time running through all the things she had seen and learned that suggested he was worthy of trust, but it was thinking about Jack and Rachel that kept her on track. If she expected them to risk something of themselves, she had to be willing to do it herself.

The elevator took them to the lowest level. Steve stuck a finger toward outside, then a thumb toward a long corridor. "Is this about Rachel?" he asked. When she shook her head, he followed the thumb. Holding her hand, he led her down the corridor, around a corner, and into a room that was small and dark. He leaned against the door to shut it, at the same time pushing his fingers deep into her hair. "This is so gorgeous," he whispered, using the leverage to bring her in for a kiss. His mouth was as willful as it had been on Sunday, but no stick shift stood between them now. They were in full body contact. A deep breath caused an undulation. Katherine didn't know whose breath it was, but the shaking in her belly grew worse.

It was a while before he dragged his mouth away. When he wrapped his arms around her, her head had nowhere to go but his shoulder. She smelled the starch of his lab coat, and something male beneath it.

Her chest was flush to his. She wondered if he felt anything strange.

"Where are we?" she asked. Beyond the sound of their own heavy breathing, she heard the hum of a machine in the wall.

"Broom closet," he murmured into her hair. "I've always wanted to do it in a broom closet. If a doctor is worth his salt, he's done it in a broom closet, right?"

"On TV," she chided, but the darkness helped. "We have to talk, Steve. *I* have to talk. You need to know certain things about me before this relationship goes any further."

He made a humming sound, leaned down a little, and lifted her closer. He felt like a man in ecstasy.

"The thing is," she began, wanting to give in and melt, but fearing disaster, "there are never guarantees in any relationship, because no one knows what the future holds. I mean, look at Rachel, perfectly healthy one day and comatose another through no single fault of her own. We think we'll be here next week, but we don't know for sure. I mean, *you* could be running down the street and be hit by a car, and *zap,* you're gone, just like that—God forbid, I *don't* want that to happen . . . Steve, I have breast cancer."

There should have been an abrupt silence with her announcement. But life hadn't stopped. There were heartbeats, ongoing breaths, and the hum of that machine in the wall.

He drew her closer. His voice was deep and sure. "Wrong tense. You *had* breast cancer. It's gone."

She caught her breath. "Excuse me?"

"Past tense. You're cured."

She drew her head back, unable to see him but needing the distance. "You *know?*"

"You looked familiar when I saw you after Rachel's accident, and you kept bumping into hospital personnel who knew you, too. I put two and two together and checked our database."

"So much for my privacy!" she cried and would have pushed him away if he hadn't had his hands locked at the small of her back. "That's a breach of ethics, Steve."

"Probably, but I was desperate. You were special, and you didn't want any part of me. I had to know why."

She had *agonized* over this. "Why didn't you *tell* me you knew?"

"I couldn't. It had to be this way. I had to know you cared enough about me to share it."

"Well, I do," she complained. She swallowed, feeling close to tears. "It's been a long time since I cared enough." Her breasts were flush as ever against his chest. "Last time I did, he dumped me as soon as he learned."

"Does it feel like I will?"

Not only was he still holding her, but he was hard. She wanted to believe, oh, she did. "Maybe it's a perversion," she muttered.

"No. It's just not as big a thing as you think, Katherine. We all have something."

"What do *you* have?"

"Me, personally, now? Nothing. But my dad died at forty-two of prostate cancer, and his dad died at forty-eight of lung cancer, so there's part of me that feels like I'm living on borrowed time, which is maybe why I want that time to be good. I bought the CJ-7 when I turned fifty. I always wanted a car like that. I figured that if I wasn't already dead, a topless car wouldn't kill me, and—want to know something?—I love that car. It's probably the cheapest one I've ever owned, but I've never enjoyed driving another as much. It's just plain fun. You fit in it well."

"I had reconstruction," she blurted out, because he seemed too cheery to have gotten the whole picture. "Have you ever made love to a woman with reconstructed breasts?"

"No, but they don't feel so bad right now. There's more to you than your breasts," he said, just as Jack had. "I can appreciate that. I've seen enough in my line of work to know about putting the emphasis on the right syl-*la*-ble."

Priorities. Rachel was going to love him. "My husband couldn't hack it. He couldn't look, couldn't touch. He couldn't get an erection."

"I don't have that problem."

No. He didn't. At least, not right then. "Talking's different from doing."

433

He cupped her face in the dark. "Want to try now? I'll do it now."

She had to laugh. She half-believed that he would.

"I have a feeling your breasts bother you more than they'll bother me," he said with such gentleness that her hackles couldn't rise.

It struck her that he might be right.

"We can work with it," he said. "If my touching them turns you off, I'll wait. I could kiss you all night and get pleasure enough from that." He cleared a thick throat and said through a smile, "Well, almost. There's"—he swallowed—"a kind of pressure down low, but I can wait, I can wait." He took a deep, shaky breath. "There's pleasure to be had from an erection alone. Enjoyment of the process." He ducked his head and caught her lips in a kiss that started innocently enough but quickly escalated.

Katherine didn't know how he managed to do it. He had her as into the thing as he was, using her tongue and teeth with an enthusiasm she shouldn't have been able to feel, given the circumstances, but he did taste divine.

Her breasts would have loved him. She was dreadfully sorry they weren't there.

But *she* was there. She was alive and well, and she had found a caring man who claimed to be willing to live with saline. Granted, the proof of the pudding was in the eating. But she had never gotten this far before. Maybe, just maybe, things were looking up.

chapter twenty-four

JACK WAS MORE than a guy. He thought, he analyzed, he understood. He was waiting for Rachel to talk. Rachel was waiting for him to talk. Whoever talked first took the greater risk.

The thing was that if he didn't take any risk, he was sure as hell going to end up with the kind of life he had just had. That life was gray, foggy, muzzy, damp. It was flat.

Rachel's life had depth. It had color and warmth. She could afford to wait for him to speak. She had less to lose if they never did.

So it was up to him.

That was what his brain said. His heart said that he couldn't bare all with the girls there, and when the girls weren't there, Katherine was, or Charlie, or Faye, and then the girls were back.

Evening came. He drove them home. The coast road was bathed in the amber of a setting sun that gilded wildflowers, granite boulders, layer after layer of greening hills. There was a poignance to its beauty, a soft whisper from the surf. *Tell her, ask her, beg her,* it said, repeating its message with the rush of the waves.

At the bank of mailboxes, he turned off the highway and started up the hill. If the message hadn't already been ingrained in him, the canyon would have done it. There wasn't a sound from the woods when he climbed from the car, just that nagging whisper all around. *Tell her, ask her, beg her.*

"Uh . . ." He stopped on the front porch. Samantha and Hope were already inside. "Hey . . . uh."

Hope came back to the door. "What's wrong?"

He pushed his hands into his hair, feeling a sudden dire need. "Where'd Sam go? *Sam?*"

Samantha came up behind Hope.

"Listen, can you two look out for yourselves for a while?"

"We're not babies," Samantha said, but kindly. "Where are you going?"

He was already heading back to the car. "I, uh, need to talk with your mom."

The drive back to Carmel wasn't as easy. The sun set. The road grew darker. He turned on his headlights, but they didn't show him what he needed to do. It wasn't until he passed the Highlands and saw the lights of Carmel across the bay that he had a clue.

RACHEL hovered on the brink of tears. With each hour that passed, the reality of the accident, the coma, and the blood clot sank in deeper. She had never been one to dwell on her own mortality, but it was hard not to now. She was vulnerable. She was human. She thought about Katherine and about Faith. Just picturing them gave her strength.

So there was that, and the girls, and her work, and Jack. And Jack. And more Jack. She was trying to process all she had been told about him, trying to figure out what was what and where it went. She liked putting things in piles. She didn't care if there was a mess within a pile, as long as there was a semblance of order, pile to pile.

Since the divorce, she had kept Jack in a pile of his own. It wasn't a neat pile. Dozens of thoughts and emotions were stacked randomly and high. For the most part, she managed to keep them separate from the rest of her life. The occasional spillover was quickly contained. That was how she survived.

Now, though, Jack was scattered everywhere. He touched the girls. He touched Katherine. He touched friends in Carmel, touched the house in Big Sur, touched Duncan and Faith. He touched her work.

She wanted to sort and separate, but her heart kept messing things up. She couldn't unwind Jack from those other people and things.

Then he appeared at the door to her room and her heart moved right up to her throat. She swallowed, but it didn't budge.

"Hi," he said. After several seconds on the threshold, he came inside. "I dropped the girls back home." He put his hands on his hips and looked around the room. Then his eyes returned to hers.

Say something, she told herself, but her throat was closed and her eyes moist. *Say something,* she cried, directing the plea to him.

"I thought maybe—" he began and cleared his throat. "I know it's late—well, there's—" He took a breath and asked straight out, "Do you want to take a ride?"

She hadn't expected that. The tears hung on her lids. Something more than her throat squeezed her heart. Standing there, all six two of him—with his sport shirt rolled to the elbow, faded jeans, his weathering hair, and unsureness—he looked so *dear.*

"You haven't been out of this place in two and a half weeks," he went on. "I have the new car downstairs. I won't keep you out long—unless you're nervous being in a car, after the accident."

"I don't remember the accident."

"If you're too tired—"

"I'm not," she said. She pushed herself up, carefully easing her casted leg over the side. Her nightgown fell to her ankles. She reached for her crutches.

"If I carry you, you won't wear yourself out," he said with such gentleness that the tears returned. She brushed them away with the heels of her hands and nodded. It wouldn't be the first time that he had carried her, but it would be the first time since well before the divorce. It would be the first time in six long years that their bodies had been so close.

"I've been doing this for seventeen days," he corrected as he slipped his arms under her. He lifted her with the same exquisite gentleness that had been in his voice.

She held herself stiffly at first.

"Not comfortable?" he asked as he headed for the door.

"Awkward." She wanted to wrap her arms around his neck, bury her face against his throat, and hang on, but she was frightened. Giving in to a want could mean trouble if the want was taken away again. "Is this allowed?"

He strode to the nurses' station and said to two nurses and a resident, "I'm taking my wife for a ride. We'll be gone an hour. Is there any reason we shouldn't?"

The nurses looked at each other, then at the resident, who was nonplussed. "It isn't normally done."

"That's not a good reason," Jack said. "Medically, any problem?"

He reached for the phone. "I'll check with Dr. Bauer."

Jack took that as permission and set off down the hall.

I'm not your wife, Rachel thought, but didn't say it. She didn't want to argue over words, not when being carried felt so nice. She settled in a little and thought about seeing the car. She thought about smelling fresh air, rather than hospital sterility. She thought about feeling alive.

The night was warm and clear. It no sooner enveloped her when her eyes filled with tears again. She took a deep breath, then gasped when she saw where Jack was headed. A tall halogen light lit the car well. "It's red!" she cried. "The girls didn't tell me it was red! I haven't had a red car since–"

"Since the VW. I thought it was time." He freed a hand enough to open the door and carefully settled her inside. He adjusted the seat to make more room for her cast and fastened the seat belt before she could do it herself.

"Why?" Rachel asked when he slid behind the wheel.

He started the car. "Why what?"

"Why did you think it was time?"

He left the parking lot and drove several blocks before he said, "Because you loved that car. I shouldn't have sold it the way I did."

Rachel was startled by the admission so long after the fact, but there was too much to see and do to dwell on it. She rolled down her window and put her face to the

439

warm breeze that blew in as he drove. Her lungs came alive, hungry for more. "Where are we going?"

"P. Emmet's."

The show! Exciting! Her paintings were like her children, now all dressed up in their new frames and on display. She had seen Samantha and Hope. She wanted to see her work. But, "At *this* hour?"

"It's Friday night. They're open late."

"It's nearly ten."

"No, it's not," Jack said. But it was. He looked at the clock and swore. "Well, we're going anyway. I want you to see the paintings."

"We won't be able to get in."

"We'll get in."

She didn't argue, didn't have the strength. Jack was determined. It was all in his hands.

Laying her head against the headrest, she said, "I haven't thanked you for doing the framing. I'm grateful."

"You had everything there. The girls helped."

She rolled her head to look at him. Six years hadn't changed his profile. His hair remained thick and too long in the back. His nose was straight, his mouth strong, his chin and neck firm. She had always thought him beautiful. That hadn't changed.

"Thank you for staying with them," she said.

He nodded, but didn't speak.

When tears pricked her lids, she looked forward again. They used to talk, used to go on and on about whatever they wanted, or keep utterly still, but there was an ease. She felt no ease now, only a dull ache inside. It hurt to be with Jack like this, locked out as surely as she had been at the end. It hurt. She had warned Katherine.

"There's no point in this," she said, feeling tired and

weak. Her paintings could wait. What she wanted most in that instant was to bury her head in a pillow and cry.

"We're almost there."

"Jack, they're *closed.*"

He didn't answer, simply drove on through the back streets of Carmel and pulled up in front of the gallery. The place looked dark and deserted. Swearing, he left the car and peered in the front window. Using his hands as blinders, he tried to see more. He knocked on the glass, went to the door and knocked harder.

"Custodian," he called to Rachel. He knocked again, studied the door, jabbed his thumb on the bell. He cupped his hands on the glass and peered inside again. He hit the bell several more times.

Rachel was picturing a person wearing headphones to blunt the noise of a vacuum when Jack turned to her and raised a victorious fist. Seconds later, a man was on the inside of the door, waving a hand no, shaking his head.

Jack spoke loudly. "My wife is the artist whose show is about to open. She's been in the hospital in a coma. I stole her out to show her this. Two minutes. That's all we'll need."

The man opened his hands in a helpless gesture.

Jack held up a finger, telling him to wait. In two long steps, he was at the car, lifting Rachel out, carrying her to the door.

"See her cast?" he yelled through the glass. "This is legitimate, bud."

"Show him ID," Rachel tried, because, having come this far, being this close, she wanted in.

Her arms were around his neck. He looked at her, so close, so tender. "My name, not yours," he said with regret. She watched the little line come and go between

441

his eyes. Gently lowering her to her good foot, he anchored her to his side while he removed his watch and held it up. "It's a Tag. Want it? It's yours."

"Jack!"

"I don't need it," Jack said as the man opened the door.

Rachel saw that he was an older man. His head had a constant shake. "I don't want your watch," he mumbled, barely opening his mouth. "I want my job. Place is closed. No one's s'posed to be here but me."

"This is the artist."

"Could be a thief."

"Does she look like a thief? Her name's Rachel Keats. Look." He thumbed the window. "See this notice. Rachel Keats." To Rachel, he said, "Was Ben putting your picture on a flyer?" Before she could say she didn't think so, he told the man, "Go inside and look for a flyer. Check out the picture. It's her face."

The man scratched his nose. His head continued to wag. "I don't know."

Jack lifted Rachel again, shouldered the door open, and entered the gallery. Rachel felt a little naughty, but excited, very excited.

"Mr. Wolfe won't like this," came a complaint from behind, but Jack went right on through to the room where shows were hung, the room where Rachel had previously only dreamed of seeing her things.

It was dark, almost eerily silent. She held her breath there in his arms, catching it when he suddenly turned and went back to the wall. She held on tighter when he angled himself to snag the lights with an elbow. When they came on, he carried her to the center of the room and carefully lowered her. Standing behind, he slipped his arms around her waist and put his chin on her head. The familiarity of the pose alone would have made her cry, except that she was distracted—and not by the voice from behind that said, again, "Mr. Wolfe won't like this." She barely breathed. Her eye ran around the room, not knowing where to settle, wanting to see everything at once. She felt surrounded, overwhelmed. These were her babies, but more in content, more in style, more in *numbers*. When tears blurred her vision, she pushed both hands against her eyes to stem them. Leaving her hands over her mouth, she began with the bobcats. That canvas was her favorite. She had already seen it framed and hung, likewise the two that flanked it, but then came the butterflies . . . and the rattlesnake. And the gray whale. And the sheep. And her Arctic wolf, her lone Arctic wolf, with the sun making a full-length halo of its white fur.

She gasped. She hadn't finished the Arctic wolf. "Omigod." She hadn't finished the quail . . . or the deer . . . or the great egret, either. *"Omigod."* The loons. The loons, sitting on that mirrored surface of a lake at dusk, with the island in the center and the sky lit by the aurora borealis. Jack had done this. No one else could have. He had done it for her so beautifully, *so beautifully.* He might as well have put her on a pedestal and draped that plain stone pillar with variations of the softest, richest, most exquisite velvet.

There was no stopping her tears this time. They came hard and fast along with huge, wrenching sobs. She was touched and lonely and needy and wanting and afraid, so afraid that those paintings were as good as it got.

When Jack turned her into his chest, she coiled her arms around his neck and clung. "Don't cry, angel," he begged, "please don't cry. I only want you to be happy."

She wanted to say that what he had done was so beautiful that she was more happy than she would ever, ever be again. She wanted to say that she missed the days when they painted together and that she wanted to do it again. She wanted to say she loved him, only she couldn't stop crying.

She had never cried like this. She had never cared like this.

She felt his arms around her, felt movement, and the next thing she knew they were sitting on the floor. He cradled her close, absorbing the spasms of her weeping with a soft rocking.

Then he began to speak. His head was bowed over hers, his arms protective, his voice beseeching but loud enough to carry over her sobs. "It wouldn't have occurred to me if I hadn't come in here and seen the bobcats. Ben was raving about them, saying that the canvas was his all-time favorite, and I remembered how we'd done it together. He didn't know that, so he wouldn't know if I did it again, and I was torn, Rachel, totally torn. You got this show all on your own, not because of the bobcats but because of the whole body of your work. That was you, your skill, your talent, your perseverance. I wouldn't have done a thing if you'd shown signs of waking up, but you didn't. The longer it went on, the more we realized how long it *could* go on, and then I started thinking that if you didn't wake up, there wouldn't be another show. I wanted you to have at least one, Rachel. I figured you'd worked too hard and too long not to."

He held her head to his chest. Her sobs had slowed to hiccuping murmurs. She was hanging on every word.

"I was feeling helpless there in the hospital," he said. "I talked to you and helped move you, but you weren't waking up. I'd get back to Big Sur at night wanting to do something useful. I couldn't stand the sight of my own work, and the materials were all in your studio, waiting, so I decided to try one, just one." She felt the swell of his chest when he drew in air and a warm reverence when he blew it out against her hair. "It was incredible. I haven't painted like that in years. I haven't been lost in anything like that in years. I felt more alive, more talented, more purposeful.

"So I've been dreaming," he said. "Know what of?"

She shook her head under his hand, against his chest, all too aware of her own dreams and wanting, wanting so badly.

"Of us doing more of this. I don't want a name role in it. You keep the name. I'll still design, but smaller things again, houses for people who can smile at me and love what I've done. I had that in the beginning, but it's been gone for so long that I barely remember it. What you barely remember, you don't miss until something happens to jog your memory. That's what sitting at your bedside did, Rachel, jogged my memory. I remembered things about my work and things about us, things that maybe I didn't want to remember because they were so good, and they were gone."

Rachel knew what he meant. She *knew* what he meant.

"I don't regret going into architecture. I grew up needing money, and architecture gave me that, but I have enough of it now. I've had enough of it for years. Never saw *that,* boy. You always talked about priorities and mine were messed up, but sitting at your bedside fixed that, too. So I want to design houses and paint your backgrounds. I want to live in Big Sur and be with the girls, and I want us to talk, Rachel. We let old habits take over,

445

but if we broke them once, we can do it again. I want us to talk. I want us to be married."

Rachel started crying again, but it was a gentler weeping this time, from the heart, not the gut. Twisting, she drew herself up against him. Her tears wet his neck, but she held on tightly, held on until she needed a kiss.

His mouth moved on hers, reinforcing everything he had said, taking her to places she hadn't been in too many long years. She felt his hunger and tasted his need, weak with it all, when he finally broke the kiss and framed her face with his hands. "I never stopped loving you," he whispered. "Never did."

She could see it in his eyes. But the light had been there once before and died. "You shut me out," she accused in a nasal voice.

"I was stupid. I was proud. I didn't know what mattered." He threw back an accusation. "You walked away."

"I was hurting. I had to distance myself from the source of the pain."

"I didn't know you were pregnant when you called me that time. I should have come. I'm sorry you lost the baby. It would have been something."

"Yes." She had mourned that child. It would have been . . . something. "Did you really leave the firm?"

"I did. What do you think?"

"I think it's good. David brought out the worst in you."

"He may have. Do you mind that I finished your pictures?"

"I love that you finished my pictures. What's with Jill?"

"Over. I knew there was no future. What's with Ben?"

"Nothing. Nothing. Nothing."

"I like your friends."

"They like you. What'll you do with your house?"

"Sell it. We could buy something bigger, but I like the place you have."

"Really? Are you sure? You're not just saying that?"

"Really. I'm sure. I'm not just saying that."

"Will you like it in five years?" she asked, knowing he knew what she meant. It was there in his eyes, with his love.

"I've been alone. Five years, ten years, twenty years living with you in that house is so much more than what I was facing before . . ." His voice broke. His eyes were moist.

Rachel touched his lips. *I love you,* she mouthed and said it again in a kiss. When it was done, he gave a huge sigh of the relief she felt and hugged her with arms that shook.

From somewhere off to the side came an edgy "Mr. Wolfe won't like this."

No, Rachel figured, he wouldn't. She also figured he had known all along that something was missing in her life. She suspected that in his own kind way he would be pleased to know she had found it again.

Barbara Delinsky recently took time from working on her next book to talk to us. Here are the highlights of that conversation.

Q: How did the writing of *Flirting with Pete* differ from the creation of your earlier novels?
A: It differed in several ways. First, the plot actually came to me nearly ten years ago. Prior to then, I had always written about functional characters, but I wanted to do something different—I wanted to explore the games the human mind plays when pushed to emotional extremes. Jenny Clyde evolved, neither smart nor successful nor physically adept, and her mind did indeed play games when pushed to extremes. The writing was an unbelievable experience for me. By the end of the book, I felt I had created my strongest work.

But it was a novella, and therein lay the second difference between *Flirting with Pete* and my earlier work. I knew that I would have to expand upon it to satisfy the expectations of my publisher and my readers—particularly given its ending, which was very, *very* different from anything I had written. I knew I would have to alter that too, but I wasn't ready. So I put *Flirting with Pete* aside and wrote a handful of other books. But Jenny remained with me, patiently awaiting her turn. When the time was right, she gave me a nudge. It was one of those visceral things.

Q: If *Flirting with Pete* is about Jenny Clyde, where did Casey Ellis come from?
A: Casey came from my need to keep Jenny's story intact. Casey gave me a context in which to view Jenny. She pro-

vided an environment more typical of my books, and while her story doesn't exactly parallel Jenny's, there are strong analogies. Both women are haunted by their fathers and irrevocably affected by the relationship between their parents.

Q: Are you a gardener?
A: Aha. You're wondering about Casey's town house and that gorgeous garden hidden behind brick walls. Truth be told, I have a brown thumb. But I do love looking at flowers, and I know how to do research. I have to confess that there were times when I was overwhelmed trying to remember which flowers and shrubs grow in sun and which in shade, which bloom in spring and which in summer or fall. I made elaborate charts. I think I got it right.

Q: Casey is a social worker, and you are schooled in psychology. Was this a case of writing about what you know?
A: No. I never did therapy, as Casey does. But I do love people. I've always been attuned to feelings and motivations. Plus, I have a daughter-in-law who is a therapist. She tutored me in the art. I learned a lot.

Q: You must like that—learning. You have written too many books to always write about what you know, which raises a whole other issue. What's this we hear about lobster trivia?
A: (Smile.) Well, it isn't exactly trivia, since much of it is serious stuff to do with the daily life of a lobsterman. It all has to do with my next book, *The Summer I Dared*.

Q: Which is about lobstering?

A: That's the backdrop—lobstering off the coast of Maine. The story is about three people who survive a horrific boating accident that claims the life of nine others. Julia Bechtel is a wife and mother from New York, Noah Prine is a lobsterman, and Kim Collela is a young woman with a secret. The lives of the three are deeply entwined in the aftermath of the accident.

Q: Which did you pick first—lobstering or the plot?

A: The plot. It's the issue of random tragedy, such as the deaths of September 11, 2001. How to explain those? How to deal with being in the wrong place at the wrong time? Conversely, how to deal with walking away unscathed from something like that? The tragedy that opens *The Summer I Dared* has nothing to do with terrorism, but the questions are the same. I warrant a guess that most of us looked at our lives differently after September 11. Likewise, Julia, Noah, and Kim are irrevocably changed by the accident they survive. Each faces the dilemma of how to reconcile these changes with the lives they've known.

Q: Is the accident the focal point of the story?

A: No. It's simply the catalyst. Honestly, I don't think I could dwell on a tragedy like that through nine months of writing a book. What happens to the characters after the accident—how they deal and adjust and grow—is far more interesting to me.

Q: Can you give an example of this growth?

A: Not without giving away too much of the story. I will say that my main female voice is that of Julia, who has been the obedient daughter, wife, and mother. Following the accident, she wonders if obedience is enough, and whether she owes it to those who died to learn to be proactive.

Q: Why Maine?
A: I like to rotate my settings among the six New England states, and I hadn't done Maine since writing *For My Daughters* in 1994. Not only was it time for Maine in that sense, but I'd been *pining* for Maine. I spent all my summers there as a child. My mother's family came from Portland; I visited my grandfather there many times. He owned a barrel business on the waterfront. It was housed in a cavernous stone building, and produced wooden barrels with metal stays and rims. In recent years, the waterfront of Portland has been transformed into a charming area called the Old Port. I imagine that embedded somewhere among the restaurants and businesses there is an old cornerstone with the name *Finn & Sons* on it.

Q: Getting back to lobster trivia, though, it goes beyond the book, doesn't it?
A: Yes. I had done tons of research on lobstering in preparation for writing *The Summer I Dared,* far more than I ever used in the book, and it seemed a shame to simply file all that way—particularly since I hadn't found such a collection of little bits of information in one place anywhere else! So I gathered it all, put it into a cohesive form, and had it printed. It's not for sale. At this point I'm simply sending it to the people who've been involved in the publication of *The Summer I Dared.* This version will never be for sale, unless it's in exchange for

donations to breast cancer research. That can be done through my website.

Q: And if some of your readers hate lobster? What then?
A: I invite them to vent. My web address is www.barbaradelinsky.com, and in addition to all sorts of news and offers and book summaries and reviews, there's the Post Office, through which notes to me can be sent. I can also be reached the conventional way, through P.O. Box 812894, Wellesley, MA 02482-0026. I receive all notes, and answer as many as possible.

Scribner
Proudly Presents

THE SUMMER I DARED

Barbara Delinsky

Now available in hardcover

Turn the page for a preview of
***The Summer I Dared*. . . .**

Prologue

The *Amelia Celeste* was born a lobsterboat. An elegant lady, she ran a proud thirty-eight feet of mahogany and oak, from the graceful upward sweep of her bow, down her foredeck to the wheelhouse and, on a straight and simple plane, back to her stern. True to the axiom that Maine lobstermen treat their boats with the same care as their wives, the *Amelia Celeste* had been doted on by Matthew Crane in much the same way he had pampered the flesh-and-blood Amelia Celeste, to whom he had been married for forty years and on whose grave every Friday he continued to lay a dozen long-stem roses, even twelve long years after her death.

Matthew had the means. His grandfather had made a fortune logging, not only the vast forests of northern Maine but the islands in its Gulf that bore trees rather than granite. He had built the family home on one of those evergreen islands, aptly named Big Sawyer. Two generations later, Crane descendants were equally represented among the fishermen and the artists who comprised the core of the island's year-round residents.

Matthew was a fisherman, and for all his family money, remained a simple man at heart. His true delight, from the age of sixteen on, had been heading out at dawn to haul lobster traps from the fertile waters of Penobscot Bay. A purist, he continued to use wooden traps even when the rest of the local fleet had switched to ones made of wire mesh. Likewise, he would have died before trading in his wood-hulled boat for a newer fiberglass one that would be lighter and faster. Matthew didn't need speed. He lived by the belief that life was about the "doing," not the "done." As for gaining a few miles to the gallon with a lighter boat, he felt that in a business where no two days were alike, where the seas could change in a matter of minutes and abruptly unbalance two men hauling loaded traps up over the starboard rail, the stability of the *Amelia Celeste* was worth gold. And then there was the noise. Wood was a natural insulater. Cruising in the *Amelia Celeste* was quiet as no fiberglass craft could be, and quiet meant you could hear the gulls, the cormorants, the wind and the waves. Those things brought him calm.

Reliability, stability, and calm—good reasons why, when Matthew turned sixty-five and his arthritis worsened enough to make his hands useless in the trade, he fitted the vessel with a new engine and tanks, rebuilt the pilothouse with permanent sides to keep out the wind, polished the mahogany to an even higher sheen, installed a defogger on the center window and seating for passengers in the stern, and relaunched the *Amelia Celeste* as a ferry.

During the first few years of this incarnation, Matthew skippered her himself. He made three daily runs to the mainland—once early each morning, once around noon, and once at the end of the day. He didn't carry cars; the ferry run by the State of Maine did that. Nor did he publish a schedule, because if an islander had a special need, Matthew would adjust his schedule to meet it. He charged a nominal fee, and was lax about collecting it. This wasn't a job; it was a hobby. He simply wanted to be on the boat he loved, in the bay he loved, and if he made life easier for the local folk, particularly when the winter months imposed a craze-inducing isolation, so much the better.

On that Tuesday evening in early June, however, when the idyll went tragically awry, Matthew—to his deep regret—was not at the helm of the *Amelia Celeste*. She was being piloted by Greg Hornsby, a far younger cousin of his who had spent all of his own forty years on the water and was as skilled a fisherman as Matthew. No, there was no shortage of experience or skill. Nor was there a shortage of electronics. As a lobsterboat, the *Amelia Celeste* had been equipped with multiband radios, fish finders, and radar. As a passenger-toting vessel, she had the latest in GPS navigational systems along with the rest, but none of it would help that day.

Riding low in the water as lobsterboats did, the *Amelia Celeste* left Big Sawyer at six in the evening carrying the photographer, art director, models, and gear from a photo shoot done earlier on the town docks. The sun had come out for the shoot, along with a crowd of locals wanting to watch, but the water remained cold, as Atlantic waters did in June, and, by late afternoon, the approach of a warm front brought in fog.

This was no problem. Fog was a frequent visitor to the region. The lobsterman who let fog keep him ashore was the lobsterman who couldn't pay his bills.

Between the instruments at hand and Greg Hornsby's familiarity with the route, the *Amelia Celeste* deftly skirted lobster buoys clustered in the shallows leading to inlets at nearby Little Sawyer, West Rock, and Hull Islands. After taking on a single passenger at each pier, she settled into the channel at an easy twenty-two knots, aimed at the mainland some six miles away.

Fifteen minutes later, the *Amelia Celeste* docked at Rockland and her passengers disembarked with their gear. Eight others were waiting to board, dressed not in the black of that city crew, but in the flannel shirts and hooded sweatshirts, jeans, and work boots that any sane islander knew to wear until summer truly arrived. These eight all lived on Big Sawyer, which meant that Greg would have a nonstop trip home, and that pleased him immensely. Tuesday was ribs night at the Grill, and Greg loved ribs. On ribs night, the wife and kids were on their own. His buddies were saving a booth; he'd be joining them there as soon as he put the *Amelia Celeste* to bed.

He took two bags and a large box from Jeannie Walsh and stowed them under a bench while she stepped over the gunwale. Her husband, Evan, handed over several more bags and their one-year-old daughter, before climbing aboard himself. Jeannie and Evan were sculptors; their bags held clay, glazes, and tools, and the box a new wheel, all purchased in Portland that day.

Grady Bartz and Dar Hutter, both in their late twenties, boarded with the ease of men bred on the water. Grady worked as dockman for Foss Fish and Lobster, the island's buyer and dealer, and was returning from a day off, looking only slightly cleaner than usual. Dar clerked at the tackle and gear store; once in the boat, he reached back to haul in a crate filled with stock, set it by the wheelhouse wall, and moved down to the stern for a seat.

It was a wise move, because Todd Slokum was the next to board. Thin and pale, Todd was the antithesis of a seafaring man. Even after three years on the island, he still turned green on the ferry to and from. Local gossip had never quite gotten a handle on why he had come to Big Sawyer in the first place. The best anyone could say was that Zoe Ballard was a saint to employ him.

Now he stumbled over the gunwale, hit the deck on rubbery legs, and tripped toward the nearest bench as he darted awkward glances at the others already there.

Hutchinson Prine was only a tad more steady. A life-long lobsterman, his aversion to talk hid a wealth of knowledge. Nearing seventy, he still fished every day, though as sternman now, with his son at the helm. Hutch wasn't well. He had been in Portland seeing doctors. The scowl on his face said he didn't like what they had told him.

"How's it goin'?" Greg asked, and got no answer. He reached for Hutch's elbow, but the older man batted his hand away and boarded the *Amelia Celeste* on his own. His son Noah followed him aboard. Though Noah was taller, and even smarter and better looking than his father, he was just as silent. His face, at that moment, was equally stony. But he did reach to untie the lines.

The *Amelia Celeste* was seconds shy of pulling away from the dock when a pleading cry came from the shore. "Wait! Please, wait!" A slender woman ran down the dock, struggling under the bulk of heavy bags that bounced against her body. "Don't leave!" she cried beseechingly. "I'm coming! Please wait!"

She wasn't a local. Her jeans were very dark, her blouse very white, her blazer stylishly quilted. The sandals she wore wedged her higher than any islander in her right mind would be wedged, and as if that weren't odd enough for the setting, fingernails and toenails were painted pale pink. Her hair was a dozen shades of blond, fine and straight, blowing gently as she ran. She was simply made-up, strikingly attractive, and married, to judge from the ring on her left hand. The large leather pouch that hung from her shoulder was of an ilk far softer than that worked by local artisans; same with a bulging backpack.

Big Sawyer often saw women like her, but not in early June, and rarely were they alone.

"I have to get out to Big Sawyer," she begged, breathing hard, addressing Noah first, before realizing her error and turning to Greg. "I had my car reserved on the five o'clock ferry, but obviously I missed that. They said I could park back there at the end of the pier for a day or two. Can you take me to the island?"

"That depends on whether you have a place to stay," Greg said, because he knew it was what everyone on board was wondering. "We don't have resorts. Don't even have a B&B."

"Zoe Ballard's my aunt. She's expecting me."

The words were magical. Noah took her bags and tossed them into the pilothouse. She passed him the backpack, then climbed aboard on her own, but when Evan Walsh rose to give her a seat, she shook her head, and, holding the rail that Matthew had installed when he had turned the *Amelia Celeste* into a ferry, worked her way along the narrow path to the bow.

Noah released the stern line and pushed against the piling of the pier. He said something short to his father, but if there was an answer, Greg didn't catch it. As he edged up the throttle, Noah stalked past the wheelhouse. Stationing himself on the far side of the bow from Zoe

Ballard's niece, he folded his arms and stared into the fog.

Quiet and graceful for a boat that was broad in the stern, the *Amelia Celeste* slipped through the harbor at headway speed. Although two hours remained yet of daylight, the thick fog had drained the world of color. Only the occasional shadow of a boat at its mooring altered the pale gray, as did the clink of a hook the silence, but these were quickly absorbed by the mist. Once past the granite breakwater, the waves picked up and the radar came on, little green dots marking the spot where a boat, rock, or channel marker would be. Painted buoys bobbed under the fog, signalling traps on the ocean floor. The *Amelia Celeste* gave these as wide a berth as possible, throttling up to speed only when she was safely in the channel.

The chop was fair to middlin', not overly taxing to the boat, even riding low as she was. In turn, she elicited little noise beyond the soft thrum of her engine, the steady rush of water as the point of the bow cut through the waves, and an occasional exchange of words in the stern. Nothing echoed. The fog had a muting effect, swallowing resonance with an open throat.

Far to starboard, a hum simmered in the thick soup before growing into the growl of a motor. In no time, it had grown louder and more commanding, belying the soundproofing of the fog, just as its owner meant it to do. That owner was Artie Jones, and he called his boat *The Beast*. Infamous in an area dominated by the boats of working fishermen, it was a long, sleek racer of the alpha-male type, whose aerodynamic purple body shot over the surface of the water driven by twin engines putting out a whopping 1100 horses. It was capable of going seventy-five without effort, and from the rising thunder of those twin Mercs, it was approaching that now.

Noah shot Greg a *What the hell?* look.

Bewildered, Greg shrugged. The fog yielded no sign of another boat in the area, but his radar screen painted a different picture. It showed *The Beast* tracing a large arc, having sped from starboard to a point astern of them now, crossing through the last of the wake left by the *Amelia Celeste* and heading off to the north. The rumble of the racer's engines faded into the fog.

One hand on a bronze spoke of the wheel and one on the throttle, Greg kept the *Amelia Celeste* aimed at the island. Dreaming of ribs, he forgot about Artie Jones until the sound of *The Beast* rose again. No mistaking the deep chain saw growl that came from the monster engines in the tail. The racer was headed back their way. Radar confirmed it.

He picked up the handset of the VHF, which was pre-set to the channel the local boaters used. "What the hell are you doing, Artie?" he called, more in annoyance than anything else, because he didn't care how macho it was, no man in his right mind would be playing chicken this way in the fog.

Artie didn't answer. The roar of those twin engines increased.

Greg sounded his horn, though he knew it didn't have a chance of being heard above the noise. His eyes went back and forth, from the radar screen, which pinpointed the racer, to the GPS screen, which pinpointed the *Amelia Celeste*. It occurred to him that if he didn't do something, the two boats would collide. For the life of him, though, he didn't know what to do. Artie wasn't behaving rationally. The radar screen showed him cutting through prime fishing grounds, plowing past buoys at a speed that was sure to be destroying the potwarp tied to hundreds of traps. If he was aiming at the *Amelia Celeste,* playing some kind of perverted game, he had the speed to follow wherever she turned.

"Artie, what the *hell*—throttle down and get out of the way!" he shouted, uncaring that he might alarm his passengers, because what with the way they were all staring wide-eyed into the fog in the direction of the oncoming howl, they were already highly alarmed.

He sounded the horn again and again, to no avail.

What to do, with the island barely a mile away, the responsibility of nine people in his hands, and Artie Jones a loose canon in his muscle boat, capable of calling on all those horses, shooting off like a bullet with his bow in the air, propelled who knew where in the fog at a speed faster than the *Amelia Celeste* could ever hope to move?

Studying the radar screen for a final few seconds, Greg tried to guess where *The Beast* would go based on where it had been and what it could do. Then he made a judgment call. Unable to outrun the powerful boat, he yanked back on his own throttle to let *The Beast* pass.

It would have worked, had *The Beast* continued along its established arc. What Greg couldn't possibly have known, though, much less plugged into the equation, was that Artie had been hugging the wheel of his beloved machine at the moment his heart stopped, and was slumped against it, unconscious during much of the last arc—but that at the same moment the *Amelia Celeste* made her defensive move, his lifeless body began to slide sideways, pulling the wheel along with it.

* * *

Matthew Crane knew what had happened the instant he heard the explosion. He had been in his usual spot on the deck of the Harbor Grill, nursing a whiskey while he waited for the *Amelia Celeste* to emerge from the fog and glide to the pier. His ear was trained to catch the drone of her engine, distant as it was at the mile point, and he hadn't been able to miss *The Beast*. He had plotted its course in his mind's eye, had foreseen bisecting paths and felt the same sense of dread he had known when his flesh-and-blood Amelia Celeste had been admitted to the hospital that final time. The horrific boom had barely died when he was hurrying down the steps and across the beach. Scrambling onto the dock, he ran waving and shouting toward the handful of men who had just returned from hauling traps, and who were themselves staring into the fog in alarm.

Those men set off within minutes, reaching the scene quickly enough to fish the first two survivors from the water before they were overcome by smoke from the fire or cold from the sea. The third survivor was picked up by another boat. None of the three suffered more than minor bruises, a true miracle given the fate of the rest.